江汉大学研究生教材建设项目、江汉大学外国语学院教材资助项目

英国小说批评教程

刘晓燕 曾 莉 主编

中国·武汉

内 容 提 要

本书共23章,每章包含两个部分:第一部分是小说家的背景介绍;第二部分是有关小说家或者小说作品的批评文章介绍。书中涉及关于23位英国著名小说家的批评文章,跨越整个英国文学史的多个历史时期。这些批评文章从不同的批评视角,运用不同的批评理论,采用不同的批评方法,对小说家及其作品的背景、文本、结构和主题等进行分析,具有一定的代表性。本教材重点在于英国小说批评文章的写作思路和批评方法,可供本科生和研究生学习使用。

图书在版编目(CIP)数据

英国小说批评教程/刘晓燕,曾莉主编. —武汉:华中科技大学出版社,2022.10
ISBN 978-7-5680-8754-4

Ⅰ.①英… Ⅱ.①刘… ②曾… Ⅲ.①小说评论-英国-教材 Ⅳ.①I561.074

中国版本图书馆CIP数据核字(2022)第180293号

英国小说批评教程　　　　　　　　　　　　　　　　　　刘晓燕　曾　莉　主编
Yingguo Xiaoshuo Piping Jiaocheng

策划编辑:刘　平
责任编辑:江旭玉
封面设计:原色设计
责任监印:周治超
出版发行:华中科技大学出版社(中国·武汉)　　　电话:(027)81321913
　　　　　武汉市东湖新技术开发区华工科技园　　　邮编:430223
录　　排:华中科技大学出版社美编室
印　　刷:武汉开心印印刷有限公司
开　　本:787mm×1092mm　1/16
印　　张:19.75
字　　数:380千字
版　　次:2022年10月第1版第1次印刷
定　　价:58.00元

本书若有印装质量问题,请向出版社营销中心调换
全国免费服务热线:400-6679-118　竭诚为您服务
版权所有　侵权必究

Contents

Chapter 1   Daniel Defoe /1

Chapter 2   Jonathan Swift /17

Chapter 3   Henry Fielding /28

Chapter 4   Jane Austen /42

Chapter 5   Charles Dickens /58

Chapter 6   William Makepeace Thackeray /74

Chapter 7   Emily Bronte /83

Chapter 8   Thomas Hardy /91

Chapter 9   D. H. Lawrence /105

Chapter 10   James Joyce /121

Chapter 11   Virginia Woolf /137

Chapter 12   Martin Amis /172

Chapter 13   George Orwell /179

Chapter 14   William Golding /204

Chapter 15   Doris Lessing /212

Chapter 16   Iris Murdoch /226

Chapter 17   John Fowles /243

Chapter 18	Anthony Burgess	/250
Chapter 19	Ian McEwan	/256
Chapter 20	Julian Barnes	/270
Chapter 21	V. S. Naipaul	/278
Chapter 22	Salman Rushdie	/289
Chapter 23	Kazuo Ishiguro	/296

Chapter 1

Daniel Defoe

Daniel Defoe(1660-1731)

As a London-born son of a butcher, Daniel Defoe spent his early life as a traveling hosiery merchant and as the owner of a brick and tile factory. His first book-length work, *An Essay upon Projects* (1697), revealed an energetic and original mind, an inquiring, visionary intelligence that soon turned to political writing such as the enormously popular poem *The True-Born Englishman* (1701), and the satirical pamphlet *The Shortest Way with the Dissenters* (1702), for which he was briefly imprisoned and made to stand in the pillory. Financial difficulties led to several bankruptcies, and Defoe became a prolific professional author and secret political operative for successive Tory and Whig governments. From 1704 to 1713, he single-handedly produced *The Review*, a thrice-weekly political periodical, along with innumerable pamphlets and book-length works on politics, history, morality, and commerce. He is best known for the series of narratives he produced after the spectacular success of *Robinson Crusoe*(1719)—*Moll Flanders*(1722), *A Journal of the Plague Year*(1722), and *Roxana*(1724).[①]

---

① Richetti J, Bender J, David D, et al. The Columbia History of the British Novel. New York: Columbia University Press, 1994.

Critical Perspectives

1. Biographical Study

Anna Faktorovich, in "Fictional Biographical Scholarship: False Attributions to Daniel Defoe", reviews the intersection between truth and falsehood among novelists and biographers. The author considers that the scourge of falsehood in biographies and attributions continues to mix propaganda and intuitive beliefs with slim evidentiary evidence to support fictitious claims. Computational linguistic proof of Daniel Defoe's de-attributions frames the theory behind this controversy. [1]

2. Marxist Criticism

Peter DeGabriele, in "Colonel Jack's Pocket: Subjectivity, Money, and Metaphor", argues that a literary criticism is presented of the book *Colonel Jack* by Daniel Defoe. Jack identifies his self or subjectivity with a generalizable proverb at exactly the same time as he finds the boundaries of his self or subjectivity expanded by money. It relates figuration to money and property means, focusing closely on how Defoe's exploration of the trope of metaphor works as an intervention into Locke's theory of money and its relation to his natural history of property. [2]

---

[1] Faktorovich A. "Fictional Biographical Scholarship: False Attributions to Daniel Defoe". Pennsylvania Literary Journal, 2020, 12(1):7-24.

[2] DeGabriele P. "Colonel Jack's Pocket: Subjectivity, Money, and Metaphor". The Eighteenth Century: Theory & Interpretation, 2020, 61(2): 245-261.

3. Canonization Study

Sandro Jung, in "Book Illustration and the Transnational Mediation of *Robinson Crusoe* in 1720", presents a literary criticism for the book *Robinson Crusoe* by Daniel Defoe. It mentions that printed images, especially book illustrations, do not have the status they deserve in scholarly accounts of the transmission of knowledge. It also talks about writing of the transnational publishing history.①

Maximillian E. Novak, in "Defoe's Role in the *Weekly Journal*: Gesture and Rhetoric, Archive and Canon, and the Uses of Literary History in Attribution", intends to restore Defoe's contributions to a single journal not included in the list of his works. But in the process, it clarifies some of the problems created by P. N. Furbank and W. R. Owens's apparent sole reliance upon external evidence in their *A Critical Bibliography of Daniel Defoe* and explains at least one of the reasons why some of his major works of fiction were mostly ignored until the beginning of the twentieth century. "Indeed, if we believe that Defoe was a writer of little significance in his time and paltry artistic interest in ours, it may seem as if this is an exercise in historical and literary trivia. This article, however, treats a body of journalism that was ascribed to Defoe by William Lee in 1869, a body of journalism that involved Defoe's contributions to the *Weekly Journal* published by Nathaniel Mist from 1715-28. In so doing, it will consider some more general aspects of the Defoe canon to explain why these essays were important in 1869 and why they remain significant for us today, as well some of the reasons why a number of the essays appear likely to be by Defoe."②

---

① Jung S. "Book Illustration and the Transnational Mediation of *Robinson Crusoe* in 1720". Philological Quarterly, 2020, 99(2):171-201.

② Novak M E. "Defoe's Role in the *Weekly Journal*: Gesture and Rhetoric, Archive and Canon, and the Uses of Literary History in Attribution". Studies in Philology, 2016, 113(3):694-711.

Melvin Maddocks, in "The Ungarnished Plate of Daniel Defoe", presents literary criticism which focuses on the contributions of Daniel Defoe. Nobody would presume to put Defoe in a class with Leo Nikolayevich Tolstoy, or even Charles Dickens, who happened to despise him. Defoe was not a great novelist, as Maximillian E. Novak is all too aware. Defoe is a plotter of then-and-after-that-then who hooks a reader into dying to know what comes next. Without really satisfying logic, Defoe, an oddly devout man, presumes it may be God's will to put us in danger in order to save us in the long run, either here or hereafter. There is no doubt that Defoe was as self-contradictory as Novak insists. In his ambition for power as well as wealth, he attached himself to the coattails of the powerful, using his talents as a scribbler to produce pamphlets of bad propaganda contrary to his own convictions. As idealists of the family, Tolstoy and Defoe shared a failure to practice what they preach. Tolstoy's *Family Happiness* is a work of genius far beyond Defoe's reach, while Defoe too believed in family happiness. [1]

4. Thematic Study

James Robert Wood, in "*Robinson Crusoe* and the Earthy Ground", argues that the Crusoe trilogy works to bring the character Robinson Crusoe close to the earth, even to the point of merging him with a vital earthiness. In doing so, Daniel Defoe draws on the Genesis account of humanity's origin in the earth and destiny to return to it. He also follows early modern scientists in departing from Aristotel's understanding of the earth as an inert element, instead viewing it as a dynamic substance comprised of heterogeneous parts. *The Life and Strange Surprising Adventures of Robinson Crusoe* (1719) envisages the earth as an agent that mediates

---

[1] Maddocks M. "The Ungarnished Plate of Daniel Defoe". The Sewanee Review, 2003, 111(4): 615-620.

between the novel's spiritual and material worlds. *The Farther Adventures of Robinson Crusoe*(1719) uses the ambiguities of the terms "China" and "earth" as a means of moving from individual colonial and commercial projects to the planet as a whole. *Serious Reflections of Robinson Crusoe*(1720) attempts to bring the work of spiritual self-examination down to earth through anecdote and metaphor.①

Aparna Gollapudi, in "Criminal Children in the Eighteenth Century and Daniel Defoe's *Colonel Jack*", discusses the correlation between criminal children in the eighteenth century and Daniel Defoe's book *Colonel Jack*. It states that modern scholarship too has been fairly approbatory of the children's criminal underworld Defoe represents, and mentions Defoe's depiction of the child pickpocket. It notes views of critics Peter Jochum Klaus on Defoe's representation of childhood, and cites Defoe's dual construction of criminal children.②

5. New Criticism

Clint Wilson, in "A Table of Prohibited Degrees: The Appetites and Affinities of *Robinson Crusoe*", focuses on novel *Robinson Crusoe* by Daniel Defoe. This novel major encounters with nonhuman and non-Western others that are almost universally coded in the language of consumption. The article mentions retracing Crusoe's own account of conceiving and constructing the object and table as a metonym for both religious and cultural presence. It also mentions ideological encounters invites to reimagine the porous boundary existing between human sovereign and nonhuman other.③

---

① Wood J R. "*Robinson Crusoe* and the Earthy Ground". Eighteenth-Century Fiction, 2020, 32(3):381-406.
② Gollapudi A. "Criminal Children in the Eighteenth Century and Daniel Defoe's *Colonel Jack*". Philological Quarterly, 2017, 96(1): 27-53.
③ Wilson C. "A Table of Prohibited Degrees: The Appetites and Affinities of *Robinson Crusoe*". The Eighteenth Century: Theory & Interpretation, 2019, 60(3):293-310.

6. Ecocriticism

Paul Kelleher, in "A Table in the Wilderness: Desire, Subjectivity, and Animal Husbandry in *Robinson Crusoe*", argues that Daniel Defoe's *Robinson Crusoe* offers a surprising account of how the human subject is imagined and constructed. The author reads Defoe's novel as a deep—often opaque and contradictory—meditation on how human subjectivity is produced through the inter relations between human and non-human animals. The logic and practices of animal husbandry are central to the way Defoe frames the questions of "wildness" "desire" and "mastery". The novel's account of Crusoe's taming of the island's goats is not merely a semi-comic or picturesque touch. Rather, the process of taming a wild goat mirrors the way that Crusoe subjugates Friday, as well as the way that Crusoe masters and shapes his own mind and body. Crusoe's practices of self-mastery resonate with Michel Foucault's final thoughts on the history of sexuality, in which he theorizes the "practices of the self" that bring the "subject of desire" into being historically.[①]

Lucinda Cole, in "Crusoe's Animals, Annotated: Cats, Dogs, and Disease in the Naval Chronicle Edition of *Robinson Crusoe*, 1815", argues that the 1815 edition of Daniel Defoe's *Robinson Crusoe*, edited by the Hydro-grapher of the Naval Chronicle, is intended to promote "a nautical point of view". In this article, the author examines the copious notes to the 1815 edition, focusing on the role of animals in the British maritime enterprise, especially cats and dogs. The notes by James Stanier Clarke illustrate both the ways that Defoe's text was read a century after its publication and the debates that helped to define Britain's maritime enterprise. Dogs aboard ship lead Clarke to a long discussion of the "cosmopolitan"

---

① Kelleher P. "A Table in the Wilderness: Desire, Subjectivity, and Animal Husbandry in *Robinson Crusoe*". Eighteenth-Century Fiction, 2019, 32(1):9-29.

strain of rabies that eventually showed up in the South Sea islands. Clarke rejects textual evidence of zoonotic transmission of the disease, exposing either the limits of his own scientific understanding or the limits of his willingness to acknowledge the role of Europeans and their shipboard animals played in spreading disease.①

Robert Markley, in "Defoe and the Imagined Ecologies of Patagonia", focuses on Daniel Defoe's 1725 novel, *A New Voyage Round the World*, especially perceptions of the global climate in the early 18th century before the beginnings of the science of climatology. It presents how the novel helped to shape early modern understandings of Patagonia and a global climatology based on analogies between the Earth's known and unknown regions. It notes the struggle to explain the relation of weather and climate, in terms of science, experience and narrative.②

7. Space Study

Bethany Williamson, in "Inexhaustible Mines and Post-lapsarian Decay: The End of Improvement in Defoe's *Tour*", argues that while some scholars read Daniel Defoe's *A Tour through the Whole Island of Great Britain* as celebrating human improvement of the natural world, in descriptions of the key improving activity of mining, the narrator records how improvement and depletion go hand in hand. In the process, the narrator raises the question of whether improvement can continue indefinitely. As he toggles between literal description of what he observes in Britain's landscape and metaphorical fantasies of the resources he hopes to find beneath the Earth's surface, the narrator reflects a discourse of natural history shaped by competing narratives of Edenic abundance and post-lapsarian decay.

---

① Cole L. "Crusoe's Animals, Annotated: Cats, Dogs, and Disease in the Naval Chronicle Edition of *Robinson Crusoe*, 1815". Eighteenth-Century Fiction, 2019, 32(1): 55-78.
② Markley R. "Defoe and the Imagined Ecologies of Patagonia". Philological Quarterly, 2014, 93 (3): 295-313.

Read through the lens of this theological dialectic, *Tour* registers a concern about the long-term consequences of improving endeavours as its narrator observes how nature is depleted and made unpredictable by human exploitation. [1]

Jennie Dorn, in "Following Daniel Defoe across England's South-West Coast", argues that the Daniel Defoe Road runs through an area in Stoke Newington in North London where novelist Daniel Defoe lived in two separate houses from 1709 to 1729. Defoe was one of the earliest travel writers, and though he did not mean for his letters and essays to be used as guidebooks, they offer itineraries that a new generation of travellers can still follow. Defoe, as a guide, leads the visitors to the serene and beautiful English countryside of Dorsetshire and Devonshire through the pretty town of Dorchester, where *Emma* was filmed on location a few years ago, into Bridport, where Defoe marvelled at the method used to catch "mackerell". [2]

8. Philosophical Study

Nathan Peterson, in "Above the Power of Human Nature: Defoe, Necessity, and Natural Law", discusses seventeenth- and eighteenth-century British author Daniel Defoe, exploring his beliefs regarding necessity and natural law, and focusing particularly on how self-preservation can be a motivator of behavior in the 1697 work *An Essay upon Projects* and novels including *Moll Flanders* and *Roxana*. Topics include autonomy, self-fashioning, social progress, Defoe's use of dialectic arguments, and the influence of economics on behavior. [3]

---

[1] Williamson B. "Inexhaustible Mines and Post-lapsarian Decay: The End of Improvement in Defoe's *Tour*". Eighteenth-Century Fiction, 2019, 32(1):79-99.

[2] Dorn J. "Following Daniel Defoe across England's South-West Coast". British Heritage, 2004, 25(1):44-51.

[3] Peterson N. "Above the Power of Human Nature: Defoe, Necessity, and Natural Law". The Eighteenth Century: Theory & Interpretation, 2019, 60(1):1-21.

Maximillian Novak, in "Did Defoe Write *The King of Pirates*?", presentes a literary criticism of the book *The King of Pirates* by Daniel Defoe. This paper outlines the characters and explores their symbolic significance. It examines money, potential violence, and sex. It also mentions capture the ships bringing the princess and her retinue to a marriage with the King of Pegu.①

P. N. Furbank and W. R. Owens, in "On the Attribution of Novels to Daniel Defoe", focus on issues concerning the attribution of two novels *Moll Flanders* and *Roxana* to English writer Daniel Defoe. It notes that the attribution is extremely problematic and not paralleled in the case of any other classic English writer. It highlights the book *A Critical Bibliography of Daniel Defoe*, exploring the works of Defoe that are already regarded as novels.②

Lynn Festa, in "Crusoe's Island of Misfit Things", presents literary criticism of the book *Robinson Crusoe* by Daniel Defoe. It explores the relationship between subject and object in the novel, with a particular focus on the relationships between humans and things. Emphasis is given to the role of skins in the novel. Details related to 18th-century debates on the place of description in the arts and sciences are also presented. Other topics include pairs, imagination, and subjectivity.③

Jody Greene, in "*Captain Singleton*: An Epic of Mitsein?", presents literary criticism of the book *Captain Singleton* by Daniel Defoe. It references the book *The Rise of the Novel* by Ian Watt. The author believes that the concept of Mitsein, or being-with in Defoe's novel, is related to the theories of philosopher Jacques Derrida. It is suggested that Defoe and Derrida carefully considered Mitsein as part of their explorations of solitude. Other topics include imperialism, isolation,

---

① Novak M. "Did Defoe Write *The King of Pirates*?". Philological Quarterly, 2017, 96(4):475-488.

② Furbank P N, Owens W R. "On the Attribution of Novels to Daniel Defoe". Philological Quarterly, 2010, 89(2/3): 243-253.

③ Festa L. "Crusoe's Island of Misfit Things". The Eighteenth Century: Theory & Interpretation, 2011, 52(3/4):443-471.

friendship, and the depiction of women in Defoe's novel. ①

9. Historical Study

Peter Walmsley, in "The African Artisan Meets the English Sailor: Technology and the Savage for Defoe", presents a literary analysis of the novel *Captain Singleton*. Focusing on scenes that describe Mozambican artifacts, the story of a rebellion aboard a slave ship, and a meeting with a naked Englishman in Africa, it argues that Defoe depicts savagery as a product of history rather than a result of inherent incapacity. The author goes on to suggest that the novel indicates the technologies that made Great Britain a global power could be lost or forgotten. ②

Andreas K. E. Mueller, in "A 'Body Unfitt': Daniel Defoe in the Pillory and the Resurrection of the Versifying Self", presents literary criticism of several texts by Daniel Defoe, including the books *An Elegy on the Author of the True-Born Englishman* and the poems *A Hymn to the Pillory* and *The Storm*. It focuses on Defoe's authorial self-representation immediately before and after his public humiliation at the hands of the British government. According to the author, Defoe attempted to create an alternative and disembodied authorial persona in response to his persecution. ③

Gabriel Cervantes, in "Episodic or Novelistic? Law in the Atlantic and the Form of Daniel Defoe's *Colonel Jack*", offers literary criticism of the novel *Colonel Jack* by Daniel Defoe. Particular focus is given to ways in which the novel addresses the legal aspects of British legal authority in the Atlantic Ocean during colonial

---

① Greene J. "*Captain Singleton*: An Epic of Mitsein?". The Eighteenth Century: Theory & Interpretation, 2011, 52(3/4):403-421.

② Walmsley P. "The African Artisan Meets the English Sailor: Technology and the Savage for Defoe". The Eighteenth Century: Theory & Interpretation, 2018, 59(3):347-368.

③ Mueller A K E. "A 'Body Unfitt': Daniel Defoe in the Pillory and the Resurrection of the Versifying Self". The Eighteenth Century: Theory & Interpretation, 2013, 54(3):393-407.

times. Its status as a work of historical fiction is explored and the actions of the title character Colonel Jack are examined.①

Morgan Strawn, in "'Zealous for Their Own Way of Worship': Defoe, Monarchy, and Religious Toleration during the War of the Quadruple Alliance", argues that Daniel Defoe divides his historical novel *Memoirs of a Cavalier* (1720) into two parts. The first follows King Gustavus Adolphus of Sweden in the Thirty Years War (1618-1648); the second examines the Bishops' Wars (1639-1640). This diptych portrait of kingship highlights the advantages and limits of the monarch's ability to promote religious toleration, resonating with contemporary political developments. During the War of the Quadruple Alliance (1718-1720), Britain partnered with Catholic countries in order to preserve the Continental balance of power. The representation of Gustavus Adolphus's ecumenical leadership in *Memoirs of a Cavalier* reflects Defoe's newfound appreciation for such interfaith cooperation. While eighteenth-century conflict revealed the benefits of co-operating with Catholic foreigners, it also revealed the dangers of weakening religious establishments at home. When Spain attempted to disrupt the British war effort by sponsoring an uprising of Episcopalian Highlanders, many blamed the disturbance on laws that weakened the Presbyterian Church of Scotland. For British readers in 1720, the re-enactment of the Bishops' Wars was a timely reminder of the dangers that arose when king and kirk quarrelled.②

Ruth Mack, in "Seeing Something That Was Doing in the World: The Form of History in *Colonel Jack*", presents a literary criticism of the book *Colonel Jack* by Daniel Defoe. It examines the relationship between personal consciousness and history in the work, emphasizing the role of form in the book's chronological

---

① Cervantes G. "Episodic or Novelistic? Law in the Atlantic and the Form of Daniel Defoe's *Colonel Jack*". Eighteenth-Century Fiction, 2012, 24(2):247-277.

② Strawn M. "'Zealous for Their Own Way of Worship': Defoe, Monarchy, and Religious Toleration during the War of the Quadruple Alliance". Eighteenth-Century Fiction, 2012, 25(2):327-357.

structuring historical events. The author focuses on the actions and experiences of the character Colonel Jack in light of Defoe's representation of events such as the battle of Preston in 1715 and the War of the League of Augsburg in 1697. [1]

Joseph F. Bartolomeo, in "'New People in a New World'?: Defoe's Ambivalent Narratives of Emigration", argues that a literary criticism of the books *Moll Flanders* and *Colonel Jack* by Daniel Defoe is presented. It discusses the books' themes of emigration, financial security, and social status as portrayed through the transatlantic travels of the characters of Moll and Jack. The author examines the plots of these works in light of English colonialism in the 18th century, the African slave trade, and indentured servitude. [2]

Robert J. Griffin, in "Did Defoe Write *Roxana*? Does It Matter?", discusses arguments concerning the attribution of the novel *Roxana* to English writer Daniel Defoe. It aims to urge critics not to dismiss the later editions of *Roxana* because the contained non-authorial material or as in the case of the Francis Noble and Thomas Lowndes's edition of 1775. Arguments from writers P. N. Furbank and W. R. Owens are discussed. [3]

Ashley Marshall, in "Did Defoe Write *Moll Flanders* and *Roxana*?", explores an issue concerning the authorship of the two novels, *Moll Flanders* and *Roxana*, highlighted in *A Critical Bibliography of Daniel Defoe*, by P. N. Furbank and W. R. Owens. It raises arguments among Defoe scholars wherein they pointed out that *Moll Flanders* and *Roxana* published anonymously and were never publicly linked to Defoe. [4]

---

[1] Mack R. "Seeing Something That Was Doing in the World: The Form of History in *Colonel Jack*". Eighteenth-Century Fiction, 2012, 24(2):227-245.

[2] Bartolomeo J F. "'New People in a New World'?: Defoe's Ambivalent Narratives of Emigration". Eighteenth-Century Fiction, 2011, 23(3): 455-470.

[3] Griffin R J. "Did Defoe Write *Roxana*? Does It Matter?". Philological Quarterly, 2010, 89 (2/3):255-262.

[4] Marshall A. "Did Defoe Write *Moll Flanders* and *Roxana*?". Philological Quarterly, 2010, 89 (2/3): 209-241.

10. Cultural Study

Mihaela Culea, in "Addressing the Age-old Question of Human Perfectibility in Daniel Defoe's *Mere Nature Delineated: Or, a Body Without a Soul*", discusses the concern with the improvement or perfectibility of human nature in eighteenth-century English society and the necessity of its encouragement considering the prevalence of human degeneration at different levels: intellectual, moral, social, political or cultural. After a brief presentation of the philosophical and literary background of the perfectibility debates, this paper looks into Daniel Defoe's literary representation of human improvement and degeneration in his *Mere Nature Delineated: Or, a Body without a Soul*(1726). Defoe's pamphlet had its roots in a real case of human imperfection or degradation, namely in Peter the Wild Boy's story, which gave him the opportunity to criticize his contemporaries' vices and failures. ①

Andrew Jerome Williams, in "'Differ with Charity': Religious Tolerance and Secularization in *The Farther Adventures of Robinson Crusoe*", explores issues of religious conflict and toleration in the relatively neglected sequels to *Robinson Crusoe* (1719). Crusoe's return to his island in *The Farther Adventures of Robinson Crusoe* (1719) and his reflection on his adventures in the *Serious Reflections*(1720) allow Defoe to offer a more nuanced response to religious difference than the one contained in the first novel. Looking at a number of sermons and pamphlets by Anglicans and Dissenters, the author of this paper shows that Defoe responds to a vibrant contemporary' discourse of charity in his depiction of religious tolerance. Defoe surprisingly locates these virtues in the character of a French Catholic priest, using the priest's interactions with Crusoe to exemplify the epistemological humility,

---

① Culea M. "Addressing the Age-old Question of Human Perfectibility in Daniel Defoe's *Mere Nature Delineated: Or, a Body Without a Soul*". Brno Studies in English, 2013, 39(1):199-209.

which forms the core of charitable tolerance as he formulates it in these texts. [1]

Daniel Yu, in "Sociality and Good-Faith Economy in Daniel Defoe's *Robinson Crusoe*", argues that *Robinson Crusoe* by Daniel Defoe is long hailed as the founding myth of "Economic Man", with critics until the mid-twentieth century tending to portray the shipwrecked narrator as the exemplar of utilitarian individualism. The novel's reception among economists from David Ricardo to Karl Marx was largely determined by Jean-Jacques Rousseau's revisionary reading, which excluded large parts of the narrative from consideration. In revisiting the parts that Rousseau thought extraneous, this essay finds that the character Crusoe is an eminently social being who relies on the charity of several generous benefactors. Their relationships are notably amicable, constituted by mutual trust and goodwill. As an intimate society, they share gifts and exchange favours without apparent regard for profit-making. In representing themselves as generous friends, they belie the economic realities that support their accumulation of wealth. [2]

11. Psychological Analysis

James Cruise, in "*A Journal of the Plague Year*: Defoe's Grammatology and the Secrets of Belonging", considers the 1722 novel *A Journal of the Plague Year* by Daniel Defoe. It explores how the book portrays the events of the 1665 plague in London, England. Topics discussed include grammatology, naivete in writing, the importance of place to the novel's sense of realism, modernity, and belonging. [3]

---

[1] Williams A J. "'Differ with Charity': Religious Tolerance and Secularization in *The Farther Adventures of Robinson Crusoe*". Religion & Literature, 2016, 48(1):27-49.

[2] Yu D. "Sociality and Good-Faith Economy in Daniel Defoe's *Robinson Crusoe*". Eighteenth-Century Fiction, 2017, 30(2):153-173.

[3] Cruise J. "*A Journal of the Plague Year*: Defoe's Grammatology and the Secrets of Belonging". The Eighteenth Century: Theory & Interpretation, 2013, 54(4):479-495.

12. Reader-response Criticism

Kate Loveman, in "'A Life of Continu'd Variety': Crime, Readers, and the Structure of Defoe's *Moll Flanders*", argues that *Moll Flanders* is a contribution to debates on the structure of Daniel Defoe's novels, and the design and much of the content of this work can be better understood through identifying common eighteenth-century reading habits and the ways in which authors sought to cater to them. A significant factor in shaping works was the conviction of authors and publishers that their readers wanted "variety" in prose fiction. Efforts to ensure the provision of variety for readers helped shape *Moll Flanders*, notably the treatment of Moll's crimes and the long deferral of her descent into the criminal underworld. This principle of providing variety also meant that certain episodes could unproblematically invite greater attention than the plot strictly required in order to engage a more diverse audience by catering to sociable reading practices and the love of gossip. Considering *Moll Flanders* in this way invites revision of current critical ideas about what constituted a well-designed prose narrative for readers of the early eighteenth century. [①]

[①] Loveman K. "'A Life of Continu'd Variety': Crime, Readers, and the Structure of Defoe's *Moll Flanders*". Eighteenth-Century Fiction, 2013, 26(1):1-32.

Chapter 2

Jonathan Swift

Jonathan Swift(1667-1745)

An Anglo-Irishman by birth, Swift graduated from Trinity College, Dublin, and spent several years in the household of Sir William Temple, a retired English diplomat. After becoming an ordained minister in 1694, Swift vainly sought ecclesiastical preferment and composed during these years a satire in defense of his patron, Temple, *The Battle of the Books* (1697), which he published with his complex satire against corruptions in religion and learning, *A Tale of a Tub* (1704). Swift produced numerous political pamphlets and poems during his long career. He began as a writer for the Whigs but became disenchanted with that party's sympathy for religious dissent from the Church of England and moved to the Tory side. Resident for long periods in London on ecclesiastical business, he became an intimate of Tory writers and politicians such as Pope, Gay, Arbuthnot, Prior, Harley, and Bolingbroke, who formed the famed Scriblerus Club. With the defeat of the Tories after the death of Queen Anne, Swift spent most of his time in Ireland, where he was Dean of St. Patrick's in Dublin and became a fierce advocate of Irish rights against English oppresssion. His greatest work, *Gulliver's Travels* (1726), is a general satire on human nature.[①]

[①] Richetti J, Bender J, David D, et al. The Columbia History of the British Novel. New York: Columbia University Press, 1994.

Critical Perspectives

1. Eco-criticism Study

Alberto Lázaro-Lafuente, in "The Representation of Jonathan Swift's Human and Nonhuman Animals in Spain", argues that *Gulliver's Travels*, by Jonathan Swift, is one of the classics of English literature, and a biting satire of English customs and politics in particular and of human foibles in general. While literary scholars have traditionally agreed that, in Part IV of *Gulliver's Travels*, Swift uses his elegant anthropomorphic horses and his filthy human-like Yahoos to reflect on society and human nature, some recent studies highlight Swift's ecocritical concern with animal issues, focusing on how the behaviour of the noble horses challenges the conventional hierarchies of the anthropocentric view of the world and anticipates values that are prominent in today's society. However, this article shows that what has traditionally challenged and disturbed readers, publishers and critics for many years is the presence of the other race of the animal world, the Yahoos. Analyzing the reception of Gulliver's journey to the land of the Houyhnhnms helps reviewers understand how Swift's early ecocritical ideas disturbed publishers and translators, who often rejected or modified the text, particularly those passages in which the filthy human-like Yahoos show their harsh and scatological behavior. [1]

Roman Bartosch, in "Seven Types of Animality, Or: Lessons from Reading and Teaching Animal Fictions", delves into the diversity of animal stories in human meaning ecology and argues that the "lessons" to be derived from these stories revolve around the meaning and effect of various forms of ambiguity. Following the

---

[1] Lázaro-Lafuente A. "The Representation of Jonathan Swift's Human and Nonhuman Animals in Spain". Estudios Irlandeses, 2020, 15(2):20-30.

route of a selection of mostly Irish canonical texts, from Swift's *Gulliver's Travels* to Seamus Heaney's *Death of a Naturalist*, it formulates seven lessons for reading and teaching animal fictions in a multispecies world. It argues that we must cultivate a sense of "ciferal" reading that does not resolve but thrives productively on the tensions and ambiguities of human-animal relations that literary fiction excels in putting into words. ①

Mohammad Shaaban Ahmad Deyab, in "An Ecocritical Reading of Jonathan Swift's *Gulliver's Travels*", argues that numerous critics have studied Jonathan Swift's use of animals as satirical tools in *Gulliver's Travels*. However, none has devoted sufficient attention to Swift's forerunning ecocritical concern with animal issues in relation to humans. Although the animal theme in *Gulliver's Travels* does involve satirical intentions, this paper aims at showing that it has more profound implications that manifest Swift's forward-looking ideas regarding the relation between humans and their natural environment, as represented in the human-animal relationship. The ethical stand and moral commitment to the natural world represented by animals, and the care for making the themes of a literary work a means to create connections between man and the natural environment around him, are basic ecocritical values that Swift stresses both explicitly and implicitly throughout the novel. ②

Bryan Alkemeyer, in "The Natural History of the Houyhnhnms: Noble Horses in *Gulliver's Travels*", focuses particularly on the novel's dealing with the world of the Houyhnhnms, the intelligent and noble horses who call people Yahoos. Topics include animal-human relationships, logic, rationality, and the philosophy of English author John Locke. ③

---

① Bartosch R. "Seven Types of Animality, Or: Lessons from Reading and Teaching Animal Fictions". Estudios Irlandeses, 2020, 15(2):6-19.

② Deyab M S A. "An Ecocritical Reading of Jonathan Swift's *Gulliver's Travels*". Nature & Culture, 2011, 6(3):285-304.

③ Alkemeyer B. "The Natural History of the Houyhnhnms: Noble Horses in *Gulliver's Travels*". The Eighteenth Century: Theory & Interpretation, 2016, 57(1):23-37.

2. Religious Study

Brian Barbour, in "The Crucifix and the Post: A Note on the Christian Theme in *Gulliver's Travels*", discusses the Christian theme in the book, the loss of faith in the book, the apostasy of Gulliver in the Fourth Voyage, the distinction between Dutch Calvinism and Gulliver's presumptive Anglicanism, and Swift's emphasis on the importance of Gulliver's conversion from Christianity to atheism. [1]

3. Biographical Study

Feargal Whelan, in "'No Nation Wanted It So Much': Beckett, Swift and Psychiatric Confinement in Ireland", argues that Samuel Beckett displays an interest in portraying figures normally regarded as insane within their communities. Taking the representation of three asylums in three separate works, this paper aims to explore a developing and complicated meditation on the subjects of mental health and incarceration by the author. Beckett's recurring reference to Jonathan Swift and the constant presence of sexual anxiety in these narratives allows him to produce a nuanced critique of the development of modes of confinement in the emerging Irish state. [2]

Anthony Daniels, in "A Shared Wretchedness", examines the logic and philosophy of the eighteenth-century authors Jonathan Swift and Samuel Johnson. Particular focus is given to how Swift and Johnson often criticized the times and the world in which they lived. Johnson's attitude towards Swift is explored in

---

[1] Barbour B. "The Crucifix and the Post: A Note on the Christian Theme in *Gulliver's Travels*". Renascence, 2021, 73(3):149-160.

[2] Whelan F. "'No Nation Wanted It So Much': Beckett, Swift and Psychiatric Confinement in Ireland". Estudios Irlandeses, 2019, 14(2):92-103.

Johnson's work *Life of Swift*, which was published in the book *Lives of the English Poets*.①

Stephen D. Powell, in "Cor Laceratum: Corresponding till Death in Swift's *Journal to Stella*", examines how Jonathan Swift chronicled his stay in London, England in the book *Journal to Stella*. Topics include recognition of the book as a source of historical and biographical information during the 18th century; death as a prime topic of Swift's works; and attempt to both hide and convey feelings about the death vigil.②

4. Psychological Study

Kelly Swartz, in "The Maxims of Swift's Psychological Fiction", argues that in Jonathan Swift's *A Tale of a Tub* and *Gulliver's Travels*, maxims—pithy statements of general truth—convey individual confusion rather than collective wisdom. The author illuminates the experimental function of maxims in Swift's fiction by turning to his interest in the philosophy and sententiousness of Francis Bacon. Bacon pioneered a form of aphoristic writing that was designed to help empiricists access nature by avoiding psychological pitfalls. Swift, attuned to psychological pitfalls and skeptical of a person's ability to avoid them, made innovative sententiousness a feature of his two longest fictional satires, works long considered important to the novel's emergence. This essay argues that Swift's maxims create effects of inwardness in his fictions, in large part by operating as satires on empiricist methods. In response to Bacon, Swift uses maxims to figure consciousness as "knowledge broken"—failures of private thought made public to humble readers. This essay studies the early novel by demonstrating the importance

---

① Daniels A. "A Shared Wretchedness". The New Criterion, 2010, 28(9):10-15.
② Powell S D. "Cor Laceratum: Corresponding till Death in Swift's *Journal to Stella*". Modern Language Review, 1999, 94(2):341-354.

of Baconian sententiousness and epistemology to eighteenth century fictional explorations of interiority. ①

5. New-historicism

Julian Fung, in "Early Condensations of *Gulliver's Travels*: Images of Swift as Satirist in the 1720s", argues that Jonathan Swift's *Gulliver's Travels* is allegedly very popular immediately following its publication in 1726. But the high price at which it was sold made the book prohibitively expensive for book-buyers, as evidenced by several cheaper abridgments and condensations of *Gulliver's Travels* that appeared soon after the book's publication. Many readers likely encountered *Gulliver's Travels* through these condensed texts instead of through the full version. These condensations differ substantially from the original, especially in their treatment of the caustically misanthropic voyage to Houyhnhnm Land. The version of Swift that many readers encountered is a gentler, milder satirist than the Swift we are familiar with from the full text. ②

Erin Mackie, in "Swift and Mimetic Sickness", presents literary criticism of the essay *A Modest Proposal* and the books *Gulliver's Travels* and *A Tale of a Tub* by Jonathan Swift. It examines Jonathan Swift's critiques of modernity, with a particular focus on the concept of mimesis as explored in the book *Mimesis and Alterity: A Particular History of the Senses* by theorist Michael Taussig. Topics discussed include authorship, print culture, satire, and illness. ③

---

① Swartz K. "The Maxims of Swift's Psychological Fiction". Eighteenth-Century Fiction, 2017, 30(1):1-23.

② Fung J. "Early Condensations of *Gulliver's Travels*: Images of Swift as Satirist in the 1720s". Studies in Philology, 2017, 114(2): 395-425.

③ Mackie E. "Swift and Mimetic Sickness". The Eighteenth Century: Theory & Interpretation, 2013, 54(3): 359-373.

Ashley Marshall, in "'Fuimus Torys': Swift and Regime Change, 1714-1718", points out that Swift's life in the months and years following Queen Anne's death (August 1714) stresses his melancholic acceptance of the new world of Hanoverian rule. However unhappy he was about Whig ascendancy, he was unequivocally supportive of the Hanoverian accession and resigned to the Tory collapse. The extant evidence, however, suggests that Swift's hopes for the Tory future died quite slowly and that his attitude toward the Hanoverian regime was not as conservative and innocuous as most scholars seem determined to believe. Significantly, in 1714, he transferred his allegiance from the Earl of Oxford to the Viscount Bolingbroke—in other words, from the moderate to the radical, from the man looking to join and temper a Whig ministry to the man wanting to challenge it. Swift's correspondence in this period is frequently partially coded, and many incriminating letters were evidently burned by Swift and his friends, which means that readers will never fully know what Swift thought or wanted in the first years of George Ⅰ's reign. But what is clear is that the dominant view of Swift's politics—"Old Whig" despite his being a Tory in religion—does not satisfactorily encapsulate his multifaceted response to regime change in 1714-1716.①

6. Linguistic Study

Paddy Bullard, in "Swift's Razor", describes the interdependence of several themes such as the symbol of the razor, knife or blade, the ethics of being violent to people with words, modernity's historical nature, and literary refinement's stylistics in the published writings of satirist, essayist and poet Jonathan Swift. Topics covered include satirical surgery and dissection, classical texts about blades and aggressive speech acts, the brutality and precision of Swift's satire, and blade

---

① Marshall A. "'Fuimus Torys': Swift and Regime Change, 1714-1718". Studies in Philology, 2015, 112(3):537-574.

figure in *A Tale of a Tub*. ①

7. Narrative Study

Katie Lanning, in "'Fitted to the Humour of the Age': Alteration and Print in Swift's *A Tale of a Tub*", argues that alteration links seemingly disparate ideas and pieces of the text in Jonathan Swift's *A Tale of a Tub*. In the *Tale*'s allegory, brothers alter their coats through over-embellishment. In the *Tale*'s digressions, the Grub Street narrator alters texts by overvaluing and reading only added commentary and prolegomena. The *Tale*'s material format also demonstrates surface alteration in its constant shifting between forms and in the changes Swift makes to the 1710 edition. Books and bodies alike are altered by layers of new surfaces in the *Tale*. Swift suggests that in both cases these exterior alterations possess the ability to disrupt and distort interiors, producing madness in bodies and misreading in books. Uneasy with the possibility of alterations unbalancing or destabilizing his meaning in an attempt to fit the text "to the humour of the Age", Swift creates a work that possesses the potential to grow with material alteration. Any errors, additions, or changes to his text over time, even if Swift might despise them, validate his strategy. ②

Pat Rogers, in "'How I Want Thee, Humorous Hogart': The Motif of the Absent Artist in Swift, Fielding and Others", presents information on Jonathan Swift. A unique feature—he is still clearly close to the methods employed in the traditional style of advice to a painter— marks Swift's handling of the topos. In contrary, his eighteenth-century posterity generally use the motif without obvious awareness of the advice style. Nobody ever used the motif more effectively than

---

① Bullard P. "Swift's Razor". Modern Philology, 2016, 113(3): 353-372.

② Lanning K. "'Fitted to the Humour of the Age': Alteration and Print in Swift's *A Tale of a Tub*". Eighteenth-Century Fiction, 2014, 26(4): 515-536.

Swift, and his own powerful example underlay the repeated use of the formula for the remainder of the eighteenth century. ①

Jeffrey Meyers, in "Swift and Kafka", provides information about the literary influences of *Gulliver's Travels* on the animal stories of Franz Kafka. Topics include dominant themes in *Gulliver's Travels* and the story of Kafka; similarities between the animal characters in the works of Swift and Kafka; and an overview of the elements of the literary works of the two authors that suggest disgust for the human body. ②

8. Philosophical Study

Erin Mackie, in "Gulliver and the Houyhnhnm Good Life", presents a literary criticism of the book *Gulliver's Travels*, by Jonathan Swift. Particular focus is given to the depiction of the philosophical concept of the good life within the book, including in regard to the main character Lemuel Gulliver's encounters with the fictitious characters—the Houyhnhnms. An overview of Gulliver's attempts to maintain happiness throughout the book is provided. The article references the professor Lauren Berlant to examine the element of fantasy in the book. ③

9. Thematic Study

Chlöe Houston, in "Utopia, Dystopia or Anti-utopia? *Gulliver's Travels* and the Utopian Mode of Discourse", argues that the novel *Gulliver's Travels*, by Jonathan Swift, contains images of and interactions with ideas of utopia and

---

① Rogers P. "'How I Want Thee, Humorous Hogart': The Motif of the Absent Artist in Swift, Fielding and Others". Papers on Language & Literature, 2006, 42(1):25-45.
② Meyers J. "Swift and Kafka". Papers on Language & Literature, 2004, 40(3):329-336.
③ Mackie E. "Gulliver and the Houyhnhnm Good Life". The Eighteenth Century: Theory & Interpretation, 2014, 55(1): 109-115.

dystopia, which reflects its engagement with the utopian mode and qualifies it as simultaneously utopia and dystopian. According to the article, the ideal language schemes and mathematical systems described in *Gulliver's Travels* are reminiscent of the satire on such practices in John Amos Comenius' *The Labyrinth of the World and the Paradise of the Heart*. The article notes that *Gulliver's Travels* can also be seen as utopian in its refusal to concede that the ideal society can exist in the real world. ①

10. Translation Study

Olga V. Borovaia, in "Translation and Westernization: *Gulliver's Travels* in Ladino", focuses on Aleksander Ben Ghiat's translation of Jonathan Swift's *Gulliver's Travels*, a literary document and a valuable resource for the student of Sephardic social and intellectual history. Ben Ghiat was a prolific writer, and he studied in a Jewish religious primary school of the Alliance Israelite Universelle (AIU). The schools were opened during the Ottoman Empire after 1860 by French Jews, whose goal was to bring the Western cultural values, progress, and moral education to their Oriental co-religionists. ②

---

① Houston C. "Utopia, Dystopia or Anti-utopia? *Gulliver's Travels* and the Utopian Mode of Discourse". Utopian Studies, 2007, 18(3): 425-442.

② Borovaia O V. "Translation and Westernization: *Gulliver's Travels* in Ladino". Jewish Social Studies, 2001, 7(2):149-168.

Chapter 3

Henry Fielding

Henry Fielding(1707-1754)

Educated at Eton, Henry Fielding settled in London as a young man and began a difficult but prolific period as a playwright. From 1729 to 1737, he wrote satirical plays, including *The Author's Farce* (1730), *Rape upon Rape* (1730), and his best-known drama, *Tom Thumb* (1730), a wild satire on the bloated tragedies that were all the rage. In 1734 Fielding married Charlotte Cradock, the woman who became the inspiration for the heroine in *Amelia* and for Sophia in *Tom Jones*. He became manager of the New Theatre in 1736, for which he wrote and produced the popular political satires *Pasquin* and *The Historical Register*, the latter earned the censorship of the Walpole government. The Lord Chamberlain's Licensing Act of 1737 brought the effective end of Fielding's theatrical pursuits. Fielding proceeded to read for the bar, but his ill health prevented him from successfully practicing. In 1741, he wrote a parody of Samuel Richardson's *Pamela*, entitled "An Apology for the Life of Mrs. Shamela Andrews". This was followed by three great novels: *The Adventures of Joseph Andrews and His Friend, Mr. Abraham Adams* (1742), *The History of Tom Jones, a Foundling* (1749), and *Amelia* (1751). A great part of his later life was spent as a judge for Westminster, crusading against corruption, public hanging, and organized crime. He died in Lisbon, Portugal, where he had gone for the benefit of his chronically poor health. [1]

---

[1] Richetti J, Bender J, David D, et al. The Columbia History of the British Novel. New York: Columbia University Press, 1994.

Critical Perspectives

1. Narrative Study

Dita Hochmanová, in "The Problem of Ridicule in Henry Fielding's *Joseph Andrews*", argues that starting his career as a provocative dramatist, generally criticized for open political satire and indecency of his plays, Henry Fielding develops into one of the most prominent eighteenth-century novelist and has to work hard to build a reputation which corresponds with the newly developing sensibilities of the reading audiences. The article considers the transition in Fielding's career in the context of changing demands on politeness in society and provides analysis of his first novel, *Joseph Andrews*, which links his technique of the true ridiculous to William Hogarth's fight against sham values and Lord Shaftesbury's idea of freedom of laughter. It also explains how this method helped Fielding create consciously ambiguous characters and make profound moral statements while keeping the possibility to entertain his readers through comedy. [1]

Matthew Risling, in "Ants, Polyps, and Hanover Rats: Henry Fielding and Popular Science", offers a comparison between popular science and experimental science introduced by English author Henry Fielding. A particular focus is given to the book *Familiar Letters* and its themes and characters. Also discussed are suppositions that exaggerate antipathies by Fielding towards science and ignore the context of scientific parodies of Fielding, as well as his parodic treatment for

---

[1] Hochmanová D. "The Problem of Ridicule in Henry Fielding's *Joseph Andrews*". Brno Studies in English, 2019, 45(1):91-104.

satirical attacks.[①]

Kathleen E. Urda, in "Escaping Type: Nonreferential Character and the Narrative Work of Henry Fielding's *Tom Jones*", evaluates the work of author Henry Fielding in *Tom Jones*. Topics include views of literary critic Catherine Gallagher on novel characters in the eighteenth century; requirement of character escape from the categorical in the process of individuation; and views of author Suzanne Keen, on focusing on generic associations including storylines for attracting readers.[②]

Kelly Fleming, in "The Politics of Sophia Western's Muff", reads Henry Fielding's jokes about Sophia's muff in *Tom Jones* in relation to the novel's historical context: the Jacobite Rebellion of 1745. This paper complicates earlier readings by scholars who have argued that the government of Sophia is an allegory for the government of the nation. The author traces how the embedded it-narrative of the muff figures Sophia's marriage contract as an analogy for the social contract, one that considers whether government should be decided by paternal authority or consent of the governed. Sophia's muff foregrounds this analogy and the novel's political allegory because muffs, as references to vaginas, metonymize the body part that determined how monarchies, money, and property were transferred. By attending to the debate about political right around this metonym for sex right, the author examines how Fielding's muff jokes directly engage with the fundamental question posed by the Jacobite Rebellions: which family had a better right to inherit the crown, the Stuarts or the Hanovers?[③]

---

① Risling M. "Ants, Polyps, and Hanover Rats: Henry Fielding and Popular Science". Philological Quarterly, 2016, 95(1): 25-44.

② Urda K E. "Escaping Type: Nonreferential Character and the Narrative Work of Henry Fielding's *Tom Jones*". Philological Quarterly, 2017, 96(2): 219-238.

③ Fleming K. "The Politics of Sophia Western's Muff". Eighteenth-Century Fiction, 2019, 31(4):659-684.

Roger Maioli, in "Empiricism and Henry Fielding's Theory of Fiction", argues that the theory of fiction Henry Fielding developed in *Joseph Andrews* and *Tom Jones* is meant to address an understudied tension between empiricism and the pedagogic ambitions of the eighteenth-century novel. Empiricist philosophers such as John Locke and David Hume dismissed imaginative narratives as possible sources of socio-ethical knowledge, which they insisted should be drawn instead from direct experience or reliable factual reports. The author argues that Fielding's moral epistemology was more fundamentally empirical than scholars usually recognize, and that an important function of his theoretical chapters in *Joseph Andrews* and *Tom Jones* is to show that prose fiction can be sufficiently grounded in the data of experience to meet the epistemic standards of empiricism. Fielding pursues this goal by developing two theses: first, that his characters and events are embodiments of principles derived inductively from observation and experience, and, second, that the conformity between the copies and the originals can be empirically measured by the reader's subjective sense of probability. [①]

Jayne Elizabeth Lewis, in "The Air of *Tom Jones*; Or What Rose from the Novel", presents a literary criticism of the book *Tom Jones* by Henry Fielding. It explores the atmosphere of the novel as related to the experience of reading it. Particular focus is given to the book's reflexivity and historicity. Details related to the book's physical landscape, including air and clouds, are presented. The natural sciences as practiced in the 18th century are also discussed. [②]

Hilary Teynor, in "A Partridge in the Family Tree: Fixity, Mobility, and Community in *Tom Jones*", focuses on the relationship between Benjamin Partridge and Jenny Jones in Henry Fielding's *Tom Jones*. It concentrates on the representation of the structure of the relationship between the master and the

---

① Maioli R. "Empiricism and Henry Fielding's Theory of Fiction". Eighteenth-Century Fiction, 2015, 27(2): 201-228.

② Lewis J E. "The Air of *Tom Jones*; Or What Rose from the Novel". The Eighteenth Century: Theory & Interpretation, 2011, 52(3/4): 303-321.

servant. The main structure discussed is the traditional family and how it has changed from one generation to the next. ①

Jeffrey Plank, in "The Narrative Forms of *Joseph Andrews*", offers criticism on the novel *Joseph Andrews* by Henry Fielding. The author looks at the narrative forms of the novel and information on the interpolated tales of the book. The article also discusses the position of J. Paul Hunter on the book's interpolated tales and the connection between Augustan poetic and prose narrative. ②

Manuel Schonhorn, in "Fielding's Ecphrastic Moment: *Tom Jones* and His Egyptian Majesty", discusses author Henry Fielding's signalling language through an analysis of his contrast of artistic creation versus the political reality of contemporary imperfection in Book 12, Chapter 12 of *Tom Jones*. Topics discussed include description of the episode involving the gypsy kingdom in Book 13, Chapter 10 of *Tom Jones*; use of ecphrases and the ecphrases echoing in Fielding's text; and his vision in Book 12, Chapter 12. ③

Irving N. Rothman, in "Fielding's Comic Prose Epithalamium in *Joseph Andrews*: A Spenserian Imitation", discusses the poet Henry Fielding's use of the comic prose epithalamium in the poem *Joseph Andrews*. Fielding's use of narrative in the poem is commented along with his diction, and the epithalamium tradition is described. Characters featured in the poem are also examined, and the influence of the earlier poet Edmund Spenser is explored. ④

---

① Teynor H. "A Partridge in the Family Tree: Fixity, Mobility, and Community in *Tom Jones*". Eighteenth-Century Fiction, 2005, 17(3): 349-372.

② Plank J. "The Narrative Forms of *Joseph Andrews*". Papers on Language & Literature, 1988, 24(2): 142-158.

③ Schonhorn M. "Fielding's Ecphrastic Moment: *Tom Jones* and His Egyptian Majesty". Studies in Philology, 1981, 78(3):305-323.

④ Rothman I N. "Fielding's Comic Prose Epithalamium in *Joseph Andrews*: A Spenserian Imitation". Modern Language Review, 1998, 93(3):609-628.

2. Gender Study

Sarah Nicolazzo, in "Henry Fielding's *The Female Husband* and the Sexuality of Vagrancy", presents the book *The Female Husband* by Henry Fielding. Emphasis is given to the theme of vagrancy and practices of gendered embodiment in relation to the history of sexuality and vagrancy laws. Other topics include the relationship between desire and crime, religious conversion, and the economic aspects of sexuality.[①]

Nicole M. Wright, in "'Willing Victims'? Disavowed Consent and Formal Deviance in Fielding's *Amelia*", provides a literary criticism on the 1751 English novel *Amelia*, by Henry Fielding. Particular focus is given to the novel's depiction of sexual consent of the main women character Amelia, including in regard to an individual's will, or volition, and women as the victims of crimes.[②]

Paul Kelleher, in "'The Glorious Lust of Doing Good': *Tom Jones* and the Virtues of Sexuality", argues that English novelist Henry Fielding's relation to sentimentalism is not merely a local matter of literary-historical fine-tuning, but directs readers to other, broader or more ambitious, concerns. These concerns include within literary studies, the ongoing critique and revisions on Ian Watt's work on the rise of the novel, and within gender and sexuality studies, the numerous and varied theoretical engagements with the Foucauldian history of sexuality. The author looks at *Tom Jones* to consider Fielding's sentimentalism.[③]

---

① Nicolazzo S. "Henry Fielding's *The Female Husband* and the Sexuality of Vagrancy". The Eighteenth Century: Theory & Interpretation, 2014, 55(4): 335-353.
② Wright N M. "'Willing Victims'? Disavowed Consent and Formal Deviance in Fielding's *Amelia*". The Eighteenth Century: Theory & Interpretation, 2017, 58(4): 469-487.
③ Kelleher P. "'The Glorious Lust of Doing Good': *Tom Jones* and the Virtues of Sexuality". Novel: A Forum on Fiction, 2005, 38(2/3): 165-192.

Deborah Needleman Armintor, in "'Go, Get Your Husband Put into Commission': Fielding's *Tom Thumb* Plays and the Labor of Little Men", discusses Henry Fielding's better-known works of "little man" literature—the popular two-act comedy *Tom Thumb* and the three-act *The Tragedy of Tragedies*, the author's love poem to his future wife. This paper critically explores the prominent comical theme in the two plays of how the thumb-sized protagonist and his beloved fiancée, the statuesque Princess Huncamunca, consummate their impending marriage. Fielding precluded sexual intercourse between a Lilliputin man and the woman he desires, and in *Tom Thumb* Fielding suggests that Tom Thumb's size makes him a superlative sexual partner for the modern English woman. This essay shows how Fielding's *Tom Thumb* plays transform the personal poem's subtle sexual humor into a bawdy social satire on modern courtship in the age of new consumerism. ①

3. Thematic Study

Terence N. Bowers, in "Fielding's Odyssey: The Man of Honor, the New Man, and the Problem of Violence in *Tom Jones*", argues that Henry Fielding's *Tom Jones* deals with the problem of crime. Fielding was keenly aware that violence and its destructive effects pervaded life in eighteenth-century Britain, and that much of this violence originated from conflicts centered on male honor. This essay explores the link between public violence and honor-based notions of masculinity and argues that Fielding addresses the issue in *Tom Jones* by presenting Tom as the exemplar of a new model of masculinity, one not tethered to the code of honor and placed in direct opposition to men of honor. A crucial dimension of Fielding's critique of the culture of honor and his construction of a new paradigm of manhood stems from his

---

① Armintor D N. "'Go, Get Your Husband Put into Commission': Fielding's *Tom Thumb* Plays and the Labor of Little Men". The Eighteenth Century: Theory & Interpretation, 2003, 44(1): 69-85.

decision to cast Tom as a modern Odysseus. While it is well known that Fielding alludes to Homer's epic in *Tom Jones*, why he did so and the effects generated by this intertextual dynamic have not been fully explored. Nor has scholarship on *Tom Jones* fully appreciated that Fielding, in casting his hero as a modern Odysseus, was making use of a venerable idiom in European literary history for rethinking ideals of human character. Comparing Fielding's Odysseus to Homer's reveals how Fielding reimagined one of the most compelling models of manhood in Western civilization, made him less prone to violent impulses, and adapted him to function in a post-honor-based society—a kind of society that would be less violent, and one that Fielding wanted Britain to become.①

4. Biographical Study

Frederick G. Ribble, in "Henry Fielding at the Bar: A Reappraisal", argues that material for an assessment of Fielding's years as a magistrate is comparatively abundant. Almost nothing is known, however, of the earlier part of his career, of his abilities as a practicing lawyer and of the impression he made on his legal colleagues. Considering, though, the prominence given by scholars to the aesthetic functioning of law in Fielding's literary works, it is especially important to get a clearer sense of his forensic competence and reputation. Fielding is generally thought to have had little success at the bar—a result, as some of his enemies insisted, of his legal incompetence. Much circumstantial evidence could be assembled that would seem to refute this hostile charge. A contemporary character of Fielding, which this paper discovers, however, provides a surprising perspective on this question. Although short, it is the only known evaluation of Fielding by one of his legal colleagues and one of the few substantive contemporary accounts of his

---

① Bowers T N. "Fielding's Odyssey: The Man of Honor, the New Man, and the Problem of Violence in *Tom Jones*". Studies in Philology, 2018, 115(4): 803-834.

social interactions with his friends. [1]

Frederick G. Ribble, in "New Light on Henry Fielding from the Malmesbury Papers", focuses on Henry Fielding, first as a playwright and later as a political journalist, novelist, and magistrate. His biographers, however, have been disheartened by the surprising paucity of significant contemporary references to him, and by the meagerness of the documentary record. He lived boisterously and extravagantly, had a wide circle of friends, and enjoyed a reputation as a brilliant conversationalist. Within the last few years, however, an extraordinarily rich archive, the Malmesbury Papers, containing the correspondence of Fielding's best friend James Harris and his extensive circle, has been made fully available to the public. Some of these documents, notably almost all of Harris's correspondence with Henry and with his sister Sarah Fielding, have already been published. [2]

Nancy A. Mace, in "Henry Fielding's Classical Learning", reviews and demonstrates that Henry Fielding read widely in both Latin and Greek literature, but he is unable to read Greek without the help of Latin translations or other aids. Topics include the biographical facts on Eton, Leyden, and the Baker Sale Catalog; mock learning, authority, and classical parodies; classical citations in Fielding's journalism; and allusions to Latin and Greek authors in Fielding's fiction. [3]

5. New Historicism

Andrew Benjamin Bricker, in "Fielding after Mandeville: Virtue, Self-

---

[1] Ribble F G. "Henry Fielding at the Bar: A Reappraisal". Studies in Philology, 2013, 110(4): 903-913.

[2] Ribble F G. "New Light on Henry Fielding from the Malmesbury Papers". Modern Philology, 2005, 103(1):51-94.

[3] Mace N A. "Henry Fielding's Classical Learning". Modern Philology, 1991, 88(3): 243-260.

Interest, and the Foundation of 'Good Nature'", argues that "Literary scholars often take at face value Henry Fielding's most overt rejections of Bernard Mandeville, a writer he associated with egoism and who argued that self-interest is at the core of all virtuous action". Yet Fielding's rejections are not decisive, tending instead towards ad hominem attacks, insubstantial objections, and unexpected accommodations of egoist arguments. Throughout his corpus, Fielding exhibits a creeping Mandevilleanism: egoist thought frequently gets uncredited airing in his works. Fielding's debt to egoism is clearest in his attempts to define "good nature", his highest term of approbation, which appears throughout his writings. Like Mandeville, Fielding understood that self-interest motivates virtuous action. The two writers diverged on whether the social goods of self-motivated action should be recognized, ultimately, as virtuous deeds. For Mandeville, self-interest cancels out the virtue of the act; for Fielding, a mislaid emphasis on motivation fails to account for the disposition of the actor, the consequent good produced, and the socially cohesive nature of mutual empathy. ①

Michael Wood, in "The Facts We Deliver", discusses the theory of fiction elaborated in the works of novelists Henry Fielding and Miguel de Cervantes. These writers suggest that fiction is capable of telling the truth that history cannot tell because of its willingness to make mistakes. But there are doubts about this theory which questions whether any kind of writing can accurately represent the human condition and this makes the novelists as vulnerable as historians. ②

Melanie D. Holm, in "'O Vanity!' Fielding's Other Antisocial Affectation", focuses on Henry Fielding's novel *Joseph Andrews* which depicts that Fielding is worried on how vanity influences his readers and what they may unknowingly do in its service. It notes that Fielding starts his novel with a contemplation on affection,

---

① Bricker A B. "Fielding after Mandeville: Virtue, Self-Interest, and the Foundation of 'Good Nature'". Eighteenth-Century Fiction, 2017, 30(1):65-87.
② Wood M. "The Facts We Deliver". Novel: A Forum on Fiction, 2010, 43(1):184-188.

carefully separating vanity from hypocrisy as two causes of affection. Questions of morality and understanding to Fielding scholarship are discussed. ①

6. Religious Study

Regina M. Janes, in "Henry Fielding Reinvents the Afterlife", presents a literary criticism of the play *A Journey from This World to the Next*. It addresses the play's portrayal of the afterlife and suggests that Fielding's representation of classical views on the afterlife would become accepted in Christianity in the 19th century. The article explores Fielding's interpretation of the perspectives of classical thinkers such as Plato, Lucian, and Ovid and suggests that this interpretation has implications for Christian orthodoxy. ②

7. Canonization Study

Robert D. Hume, in "Fielding at 300: Elusive, Confusing, Misappropriated, or (Perhaps) Obvious?", highlights that Fielding is known as the "father of the English novel" and is included in the principal literary histories in England. The author states that Fielding's works are documented by scholars including Thomas Lockwood, Ronald Paulson, and Claude Rawson. It notes that Fielding's reputation suffers because of changing political allegiances and the idea of decorum. ③

---

① Holm M D. "'O Vanity!' Fielding's Other Antisocial Affectation". Philological Quarterly, 2010, 89(2/3):263-281.

② Janes R M. "Henry Fielding Reinvents the Afterlife". Eighteenth-Century Fiction, 2011, 23(3):495-518.

③ Hume R D. "Fielding at 300: Elusive, Confusing, Misappropriated, or(Perhaps) Obvious?". Modern Philology, 2010, 108(2):224-262.

8. Ethical Study

Roger D. Lund, in "Augustan Burlesque and the Genesis of *Joseph Andrews*", discusses the book *Joseph Andrews*, by Henry Fielding. The author presents the contemporary 18th century criticism the book received. André Michel Ramsay was one of the critics who assessed the book's use of burlesque and morality. Meanwhile, Judith Frank commented on Fielding's dignifying of the comic. Moreover, the author examines the structure of the book. ①

9. Feminism Study

Earla A. Wilputte, in "'Women Buried': Henry Fielding and Feminine Absence", examines author Henry Fielding's reactions to some of the conservative eighteenth-century ideologies concerning women and wives as they were presented in conduct books, didactic fiction, and the covert-baron laws. The author also discusses development of Fielding's feminine absence from the conventional use of the ideal woman motif in his poetry and novels. ②

10. Linguistic Study

Janet Sorensen, in "'As the Vulgar Call It': Henry Fielding and the Language of the Vulgar", discusses the book *A Dictionary of the English Language*

---

① Lund R D. "Augustan Burlesque and the Genesis of *Joseph Andrews*". Studies in Philology, 2006, 103(1):88-119.

② Wilputte E A. "'Women Buried': Henry Fielding and Feminine Absence". Modern Language Review, 2000, 95(2):324-336.

by Samuel Johnson, reflecting his efforts to represent the terms and their many meanings fully. It figures his lexicographic efforts for their significance, extending beyond their endless pursuit. It also describes that throughout Henry Fielding's book on Jonathan Wild, the narrator refers to the language of the vulgar not as low language to represent the strange diversity of English. [1]

---

[1] Sorensen J. "'As the Vulgar Call It': Henry Fielding and the Language of the Vulgar". Philological Quarterly, 2021, 100(3/4):421-442.

Chapter 4

Jane Austen

Jane Austen(1775-1817)

The sixth of seven children, Jane Austen was encouraged to read and write by her father, the Reverend George Austen. Her letters tell us little about her intimate relationships, though she did have several suitors(none of whom she ever married). Instead, she spent her life among her close family, writing her novels at Chawton, Hampshire, in the family parlor. When she was just fourteen, she wrote *Love and Friendship*, followed by *A History of England* at fifteen. A year later saw *A Collection of Letters* and, not long after, *Lesley Castle*. Her major novels were published, though not written, in the following order: *Sense and Sensibility* (1811), *Pride and Prejudice*(1813), *Mansfield Park*(1814), *Emma*(1816), and *Northanger Abbey*(1818). Austen advanced the development of the novel, combining social critique with an elegant, economical style. [1]

---

[1] Richetti J, Bender J, David D, et al. The Columbia History of the British Novel. New York: Columbia University Press, 1994.

Critical Perspectives

1. Biographical Study

Michael D. Sanders, in "'Black and White and Every Wrong Colour': The Medical History of Jane Austen and the Possibility of Systemic Lupus Erythematosus", reviews all of her available letters and extricates relevant medical information which reveal rheumatism, facial skin lesions, fever and marked fluctuation of these symptoms. The severity of these symptoms increased, leading to her death within a year. This range of clinical features fulfils the most recent classification criteria for systemic lupus erythematosus. [1]

Marian Wilson Kimber, in "Miss Austen Plays Pleyel: An Additional Source for the Jane Austen Family Music Collection?", argues that the Jane Austen Family Music Collection consists of twenty-one items, bound volumes and published scores of individual works. This music belonged to the famous novelist, an amateur pianist who practised daily, and three generations of the women in her family. The entire collection, containing nearly six hundred musical works, has been digitised by the University of Southampton, and studied in relation to music in the lives of Austen's characters, and more generally as representative of the gendered nature of music-making in eighteenth-century England. However, a bound set of six *Accompanied Sonatas* by Ignace Pleyel, held by the Rita Benton Music Library at the University of Iowa and labeled "Miss Austen" on its cover, may be a previously unrecognized source for this collection. This article explores the evidence for the possibility that

---

[1] Sanders M D. "'Black and White and Every Wrong Colour': The Medical History of Jane Austen and the Possibility of Systemic Lupus Erythematosus". Lupus, 2021, 30(5):549-553.

Iowa's copy of Pleyel's *Sonatas*, published in London by Broderip and Wilkinson around 1800, was owned by Austen or a member of her family. Fingerings and other markings in this score are similar to those in a 1788 edition of the *Sonatas* found in a volume owned by Austen's sister-in-law, Elizabeth Bridges Austen (cataloged as CHWJA/19/6). Thus, they may have belonged to her or to Austen's musically talented niece, Fanny Knight. Perhaps another small clue about the great novelist's musical life, the volume further confirms the widespread domestic performance of Pleyel's music and suggests the ways in which his compositions were transmitted among female amateur musicians in the Georgian era.①

Nicholas Dames, in "Jane Austen Is Everything", focuses on the life and career of author Jane Austen. Topics discussed include she being featured on a new 10 pound-note by Bank of England, replacing evolutionist Charles Darwin, review of books of Austen by authors E. M. Forster and Virginia Woolf, and Austen's writings focusing on economic dependence on commodities by slave labor in Great Britain's colonies.②

Ruth Knezevich and Devoney Looser, in "Jane Austen's Afterlife, West Indian Madams, and the Literary Porter Family: Two New Letters from Charles Austen", discuss the friendship and collaboration between author Jane Austen and brother Charles Austen of the British Royal Navy. He is cited for contributions to the novel *Mansfield Park* and work in sustaining the literary legacy of his late sister. It takes note of his correspondence with diplomat Robert Ker Porter and his novelist sisters Jane Porter and Anna Maria Porter as well as of their preferences in fiction and allusion to prostitutes as pickles.③

---

① Kimber M W. "Miss Austen Plays Pleyel: An Additional Source for the Jane Austen Family Music Collection?". Fontes Artis Musicae, 2020, 67(1):1-17.

② Dames N. "Jane Austen Is Everything". The Atlantic, 2017, 320(2):92-103.

③ Knezevich R, Looser D. "Jane Auste's Afterlife, West Indian Madams, and the Literary Porter Family: Two New Letters from Charles Austen". Modern Philology, 2015, 112(3):554-568.

2. Psychological Study

Petr Anténe, in "Howard Jacobson's *Live a Little*: The Jewish Jane Austen's 21st Century Novel of Manners", shows that the British Jewish novelist Howard Jacobson calls himself the "Jewish Jane Austen". This paper examines the relevance of this characterization by arguing that Jacobson may be seen as continuing in the tradition of the English novel of manners, as exemplified by Austen. In particular, the plot of Jacobson's sixteenth novel *Live a Little* resembles Austen's *Pride and Prejudice*, as it features a development of a romantic relationship between two characters who first show little interest in each other. However, as Jacobson's couple of protagonists are in their nineties, another text that provides a useful frame of reference is Austen's last novel *Persuasion*, which deals with the themes of aging and the passage of time. In turn, this essay approaches *Live a Little* as a novel of manners reminiscent of Austen, but updated for the early 21st century. [①]

3. Ethical Study

Michelle Albert Vachris and Cecil E. Bohanon, in "Human Nature and Civil Society in Jane Austen", argue that Jane Austen's novels illustrate and extend the classical liberal thought found in Adam Smith's novel *The Theory of Moral Sentiments*. Topics discussed include focus on virtues described by Smith and Austen like self-love and beneficence; information on economic arrangements that recognize the dignity of all and further promote human flourishing; and importance of self-command illustrated by how Elinor Dashwood makes effort to maintain

---

① Anténe P. "Howard Jacobson's *Live a Little*: The Jewish Jane Austen's 21st Century Novel of Manners". Brno Studies in English, 2021, 47(1):129-143.

composure in *Sense and Sensibility*.①

4. Cultural Study

Meenakshi Bharat, in "Going Global: Filmic Appropriation of Jane Austen in India", argues that the dual edged implications of the introduction of English literary studies notwithstanding—the presentation of a fresh cultural perspective and the complete cultural takeover of colony—the pride and fascination of the British with the works of Jane Austen has a deep impact on cultural production in India and its diaspora. Down the years, keeping pace with changing times and backed by technological developments, the Jane Austen-facilitated coming together of the two nations and two cultures, has seen several multilingual, multicultural screen adaptations of the Austen novels for both television and the big screen: *Sense and Sensibility* by Tamil cinema as *Kandukondain Kandukondain*; *Pride and Prejudice* as *Trishna*, a serialized Hindi adaptation for Indian national television, and later, for the big screen by a British Indian in English and Hindi as the internationally acclaimed *Bride and Prejudice/Balle Balle Amritsar to L. A.* and more recently, *Emma* by mainstream Bollywood in Hindi as *Aisha*. The essay broaches an analysis of the nuancing that takes place in the interstices between the word and the visual art forms and of the complexities arising from this interface. The complex agenda of the adaptive engagement underlying this vibrant colloquy between two cultures, between two mediums is interesting enough, but the added dynamic of a hybrid cosmopolitanism that is sometimes gratifying and sometimes problematic, makes the study even more challenging.②

---

① Vachris M A, Bohanon C E. "Human Nature and Civil Society in Jane Austen". The Independent Review, 2020/2021, 25(3):357-368.
② Bharat M. "Going Global: Filmic Appropriation of Jane Austen in India". South Asian Popular Culture, 2020, 18(2):109-121.

Shawn Normandin, in "Jane Austen's *Evelyn* and the 'Impossibility of the Gift'", argues that Jane Austen's *Evelyn* is a remarkably precocious tale that repays philosophical scrutiny. The protagonist's absurd adventures reveal paradoxes about giving that Jacques Derrida would formulate much later. Austen's project of imagining a true gift justifies the tale's lack of closure and realism. Yet the gift is not just one theme among others: since giving is intrinsic to literary language and its production, the tale's concern with giving reflects the challenges faced by Austen as a writer. *Evelyn* provides an oblique commentary on the political, economic, and even ecological interests of the late eighteenth century. [1]

Misty Krueger, in "Handles, Hashtags, and Austen Social Media", focuses on contribution of social media in cultivation of English novelist Jane Austen, as a popular culture icon. Topics discussed include the role of social media in shaping online Austen culture, active engagement of people with the author and other Austen fans, and impact of Austen-inspired social media on community building, sharing ideas and research. [2]

Laura L. Runge, in "Austen and Computation 2.0", focuses on human-scale analyses and computational criticism of English novelist Jane Austen's work. Topics discussed include the role of quantitative approaches such as probabilistic modeling to increase analysis of metrical pattern with speed and consistency, thoughtful engagement between humanism, and computation and role of computational statistics in literary criticism and comparison of a topic across works. [3]

---

[1] Normandin S. "Jane Austen's *Evelyn* and the 'Impossibility of the Gift'". Criticism, 2018, 60(1):27-46.

[2] Krueger M. "Handles, Hashtags, and Austen Social Media". Texas Studies in Literature & Language, 2019, 61(4):378-396.

[3] Runge L L. "Austen and Computation 2.0". Texas Studies in Literature & Language, 2019, 61(4):397-415.

Emma Spooner, in "Touring with Jane Austen", examines Jane Austen's relationship with literary tourism. It argues that Jane Austen tours are more than just a fad that cashes in on Austen-mania, but that they become interactive paratexts which allow glimpses into moments of inspiration which in turn contribute to a new cultural awareness. Literary tourism creates landscapes that can contribute not only to an understanding of a new transnational cultural heritage, but an understanding of self. Literary locations are simultaneously a repository for historical authenticity and a series of imaginative representations of places or things. Today literary tourism may result from readers' desires to connect with the locations of a beloved novel, or find out what Austen was "really like", but for visitors, historical and modern, the tour inspires travellers to imagine themselves within a particular narrative, whether it be a fictional narrative or a narrative of cultural ideology.[①]

Olivia Murphy, in "Jane Austen's 'Excellent Walker': Pride, Prejudice, and Pedestrianism", argues that when Mrs Hurst calls Elizabeth Bennet "an excellent walker", in Jane Austen's *Pride and Prejudice*, the remark is meant to ridicule. For a modern reader, understanding this connotation requires a small exercise in historical imagination. Recent critical studies explore the rise of rambling and the Romantic poets' penchant for lengthy pedestrian excursions, but *Pride and Prejudice* does not feature the sort of lonely wanderings that lead to conversations with leech gatherers and mystical mariners. To appreciate the centrality of walking to the novel, readers must appropriate Miss Bingley's question—"what could she mean by it?". Before we can understand the attitudes towards walking and the responses to walking exhibited by characters in the novel—and the function of walking in the plot—it is necessary to explore the changing place of walking in late eighteenth- and early nineteenth-century society, and the uses of walking in Romantic-era literature. This article examines eighteenth-century accounts of athletic,

---

① Spooner E. "Touring with Jane Austen". Critical Survey, 2014, 26(1):42-58.

touristic, sentimental, and performative pedestrianism, including Austen's attitudes towards her own walks, in order to read walking in the novel. ①

5. Religious Study

Gordon Leah, in "Jane Austen's 'Religious Principle': Reflections on Re-reading Her Novel, *Mansfield Park*", focuses on the novelist Jane Austen's effect on the world of entertainment, film and television, analyzing how a seemingly anodyne woman became a literary juggernaut. It mentions that she shows her skill in allowing Austen's favourite niece Fanny Knight nonetheless to feel satisfaction; and also mentions that Austen's religious principle is a principle suggesting morality, based on judgement and expressed as constancy, purity, inward conviction of what is right and wrong. ②

Whit Stillman, in "Jane Austen: Whither or Whence?", focuses on English novelist Jane Austen's perspective on aspects of romance and marriage reflected in her work. Topics discussed include complete understanding of Austen presupposes, her influence as an author and as a moralist, and her consonant perspective regarding Christianity as the highest perfection of humanity. ③

6. Canonization Study

Michelle Levy and Kandice Sharren, in "Teaching Editions of the Works of Jane Austen: A Survey", focus on a survey which analyzes the comprehensiveness

---

① Murphy O. "Jane Austen's 'Excellent Walker': Pride, Prejudice, and Pedestrianism". Eighteenth-Century Fiction, 2013, 26(1):121-142.

② Leah G. "Jane Austen's 'Religious Principle': Reflections on Re-reading Her Novel, *Mansfield Park*". The Heythrop Journal, 2020, 61(3):459-470.

③ Stillman W. "Jane Austen: Whither or Whence?". Texas Studies in Literature & Language, 2019, 61(4):451-454.

of appropriate editions of Jane Austen's novels for an advanced undergraduate course. Topics discussed include collections of Austen's manuscript writings offered by the publisher Norton, contemporary publications on relevant topics by the publisher Broadview, and cost effectiveness of paperback editions.①

Kathryn Sutherland, in "Inside Jane Austen's Laboratory", discusses about the digital reunification of work of English novelist Jane Austen. Topics discussed include the need to conserve the manuscripts with full transcriptions, provenance records, and detailed descriptions, challenges to recalibrate the manuscripts and making it available to school children, university students and the general public, and need of physical supports for written text.②

7. Narrative Study

Shawn Normandin, in "Symbol, Allegory, and Jane Austen's *Mansfield Park*", argues that Samuel Taylor Coleridge's *The Statesman's Manual* distinguishes between symbol and allegory, and the distinction reveals what is at stake in *Mansfield Park*. Austen alludes to the country house tradition that empowers Edmund Burke's counterrevolutionary rhetoric, but the persistence of allegory in the novel produces anti-Burkean insights. *Mansfield Park* also challenges Paul de Man's famous reading of Coleridge: while Paul de Man's essay *The Rhetoric of Temporality* labors to discriminate between tropes, Austen sometimes blurs tropes and dramatizes the precariousness of a political order dependent on them. Yet Paul de Man's study of Romantic tropes sheds light on the non-realistic aspects of Austen's novel.③

---

① Levy M, Sharren K. "Teaching Editions of the Works of Jane Austen: A Survey". Texas Studies in Literature & Language, 2019, 61(4):443-448.

② Sutherland K. "Inside Jane Austen's Laboratory". Texas Studies in Literature & Language, 2019, 61(4): 438-440.

③ Normandin S. "Symbol, Allegory, and Jane Austen's *Mansfield Park*". Studies in Philology, 2019, 116(3):589-616.

Christopher R. Miller, in "Being and Nothingness in *Mansfield Park*", examines the ambiguous morality of the amateur theatricals, the quiescence of its heroine, the allusions to slavery and war, the specter of patriarchal tyranny, and the harshness of its concluding punishments. The author also mentions about ostensibly successful work of self therapy. An overview of the story is also given. ①

Amit Yahav, in "Leisure Reading and Austen's Case for Differentiated Time", discusses about several studies established by Jane Austen, an English novelist, which distinguishes between fictional writings. Topics discussed include commitment to an absorptive aesthetic of immersion; the eighteenth-century expansion of time-discipline by suggesting the increasing automatization; and command supple alternations between intense absorption in narrative and sharp release. ②

Anne Toner, in "Landscape as Literary Criticism: Jane Austen, Anna Barbauld and the Narratological Application of the Picturesque", argues that in Jane Austen's work there is an affiliation between the experience of landscape and the forms that fictional works can take. This is evident in *Catharine, or the Bower* where an analogy is set up between the reading of a novel and travels through a picturesque landscape, a connection that is returned to in *Pride and Prejudice*. This affiliation can be contextualized first by reference to Austen's comments in her letters about narrative form, and then by reference to contemporary criticism of the novel, in particular that of Anna Barbauld. Barbauld overtly uses landscape for narratological purposes in her introductory essay to *The Correspondence of Samuel Richardson*, alluding to Uvedale Price's *Essay on the Picturesque* to extol Richardson's formal achievements in Clarissa. Austen's views on narrative organization and on landscape design strongly resonate with Barbauld's, and both writers evoke the

---

① Miller C R. "Being and Nothingness in *Mansfield Park*". Modern Philology, 2020, 117(3): 347-369.

② Yahav A. "Leisure Reading and Austen's Case for Differentiated Time". The Eighteenth Century: Theory & Interpretation, 2019, 60(2): 163-183.

picturesque to provide a formalist critique of the novel. ①

Linda Gill, in "Jane Austen's *Northanger Abbey*", offers information on literary works of writer Jane Austen. It is noted that novels of Austen are self-consiously intertextual texts. It is stated that *Northanger Abbey* is the most prominent among her novels, which is full of characters who write their own strategic fictions promoting self-value particularly in the marriage market. ②

8. Feminism Study

Kristine Hansen, in "Replacing Romantic Sentiments with Just Opinions: How Austen's Novels Function like Wollstonecraft's 'Judicious Person'", examines the parallels in the perspectives of English authors Mary Wollstonecraft and Jane Austen about women's nature, education, marriage, and family life. Topics discussed include an analysis of Wollstonecraft's *A Vindication of the Rights of Woman*, evidence for Austen's close familiarity with Wollstonecraft's book, and the difference in the writings of the two authors which lies in their choice of genre and rhetorical strategy. ③

Mary Beth Tegan, in "Training the Picturesque Eye: The Point of Views in Jane Austen's *Persuasion*", presents a literary criticism of the novel *Persuasion* by Jane Austen. Topics include the role of first-person point of view in the book, the relation of the marginalization of women to the notion of spectatorship in the novel's points of view, and the significance of picturesque scenes in the novel. The ideas of artist William Gilpin and art historian Peter de Bolla, as addressed in the book *The*

---

① Toner A. "Landscape as Literary Criticism: Jane Austen, Anna Barbauld and the Narratological Application of the Picturesque". Critical Survey, 2014, 26(1): 3-19.

② Gill L. "Jane Austen's *Northanger Abbey*". Pennsylvania Literary Journal, 2014, 5(3): 36-57.

③ Hansen K. "Replacing Romantic Sentiments with Just Opinions: How Austen's Novels Function like Wollstonecraft's 'Judicious Person'". Women's Studies, 2020, 49(6): 652-685.

Education of the Eye: Painting, Landscape, and Architecture in Eighteenth-Century Britain, are noted. ①

Katie Jones, in "Discrediting Femininity through Patriarchal Control: Catherine Morland's Identity", examines *Northanger Abbey* in the context of Romanticism and presents a feminist literary criticism. Austen's character Catherine Morland exemplifies characteristics of freedom from artificiality or confinement and emphasizes human emotions that connect to values. These ideal Romantic characteristics are paradoxically devalued because they are femininized. The essay explores how characters in the novel and people in modern and contemporary society discredit Catherine's feminine identity despite their expectations of her to retain such an identity, reflecting the oppression of women's femininity. In *Northanger Abbey*, the devaluation of Catherine and her characteristics illustrates the results of patriarchal control over feminine identity, demonstrating that society continuously discredits feminine interests while simultaneously confining women to those interests. This piece argues that *Northanger Abbey* not only comments on Catherine's identity and oppression, but also represents Society's persistent view of femininity. ②

Danielle Spratt, in "Denaturalizing Lady Bountiful: Speaking the Silence of Poverty in Mary Brunton's *Discipline* and Jane Austen's *Emma*", compares and contrasts the 19th-century English novels, *Discipline* by Mary Brunton and *Emma* by Jane Austen. It considers how the heroines, Ellen Percy and Emma Woodhouse respectively, deal with social roles and expectations arising from their upper social classes. It focuses on exploring their attempts to embrace the popular notion of the

---

① Tegan M B. "Training the Picturesque Eye: The Point of Views in Jane Austen's *Persuasion*". The Eighteenth Century: Theory & Interpretation, 2017, 58(1):39-59.

② Jones K. "Discrediting Femininity through Patriarchal Control: Catherine Morland's Identity". LOGOS: A Journal of Undergraduate Research, 2019(12):16-25.

symbolic Lady Bountiful. ①

Christopher Nagle, in "Austen's Present Future Stagings", demonstrates the enduring popularity or contemporary relevance of work of Jane Austen, an English novelist. Topics discussed include prolific expansion of Austen-themed straight play and musical adaptation, engagement of Austen's work with feminist sensibilities and gender politics, and increase in Austen-themed performances. ②

9. New Historicism

Chris Mounsey, in "Henry Crawford as Master Betty: Jane Austen on the 'Disabling' of Shakespeare", argues that Jane Austen's novel *Mansfield Park* with its direct quotes from Shakespeare's *Henry VIII* and its underlying plot reference to *King Lear* may be read as a cri de coeur from Austen at the poor state of the British theatre in the early nineteenth century. At a time when Shakespeare's plays were performed in altered versions to please audiences, when the dialogue was known to many only in fragments, and when children such as Master William Betty were lionized equally by the same audience for playing Hamlet and sentimental roles in the clap-trap comedy *Lovers Vows*, *Mansfield Park* calls for the nation to return to *The Complete Works of William Shakespeare* to rediscover pride in itself, its heroes, and its heroines and to know Fanny Price as the proper subject for a novel. ③

Megan Quinn, in "The Sensation of Language in Jane Austen's *Persuasion*", argues that *Persuasion* represents the culmination of a style in which language is a

---

① Spratt D. "Denaturalizing Lady Bountiful: Speaking the Silence of Poverty in Mary Brunton's *Discipline* and Jane Austen's *Emma*". The Eighteenth Century: Theory & Interpretation, 2015, 56(2): 193-208.

② Nagle C. "Austen's Present Future Stagings". Texas Studies in Literature & Language, 2019, 61(4):472-474.

③ Mounsey C. "Henry Crawford as Master Betty: Jane Austen on the 'Disabling' of Shakespeare". Eighteenth-Century Fiction, 2017, 30(2):265-286.

physical agent, with force that comes from or acts on the body. Embodied language was always part of Austen's aesthetics, appearing in the juvenilia, when the movement of narrative creates the sensation of bodily motion, and in *Emma* through physical word games with children's alphabet blocks. In *Persuasion*, Austen advances the sense of embodied language from her earlier work to language as sensory immersion, particularly through the sensation of words as sounds. With the sense of physical presence and voice that Captain Wentworth's letter imparts, the novel finally reveals a language based on the restoration of the body and its sounds to writing. For Austen, language always gets physical, and her style centres on an emphatic enjoyment of embodied life. [1]

Janine Barchas and Elizabeth Picherit, in "Speculations on Spectacles: Jane Austen's Eyeglasses, Mrs. Bates's Spectacles, and John Saunders in *Emma*", examine the late-in-life health of 19th century novelist Jane Austen and her social milieu based on her novels, her life and her glasses. Topics covered include an analysis of the heroine in Austen's novel *Emma*, details of how Austen met London, England-based ophthalmic surgeon and oculist John Saunders, and the health and economic status of Austen. [2]

Misty Krueger, in "From Marginalia to Juvenilia: Jane Austen's Vindication of the Stuarts", explores the juvenilia of Jane Austen entitled "The History of England: From the Reign of Henry the 4th to the Death of Charles the 1st". It focuses on how Austen supports the cause of the Stuarts and Jacobitism within her work, including her views on the martyrdoms of Mary, Queen of Scots and Charles I, King of Great Britain. Contemporary histories and political philosophies by

---

[1] Quinn M. "The Sensation of Language in Jane Austen's *Persuasion*". Eighteenth-Century Fiction, 2017, 30(2):243-263.

[2] Barchas J, Picherit E. "Speculations on Spectacles: Jane Austen's Eyeglasses, Mrs. Bates's Spectacles, and John Saunders in *Emma*". Modern Philology, 2017, 115(1):131-143.

authors including Edmund Burke, Mary Wollstonecraft, and Thomas Taylor are considered.①

Erin M. Goss, in "Homespun Gossip: Jane West, Jane Austen, and the Task of Literary Criticism", compares and contrasts the novels *A Gossip's Story* by Jane West as well as *Sense and Sensibility* and *Emma* by Jane Austen, offering the observation that West's 1796 story helped influence Austen's later works, especially *Sense and Sensibility*. An overview of the plot of West's novel is presented. Topics explored include gossip, narrators' roles, and the history of literary criticism.②

Chery A. Wilson, in "'Something like Mine': Catherine Hutton, Jane Austen, and Feminist Recovery Work", compares and contrasts the novels of early 19th century English women authors Janes Austen and Catherine Hutton, considering contemporary reception and criticisms of their novels. Hutton's novels *The Miser Married*, *The Welsh Mountaineer* and *Oakwood Hall* are considered against Austen's works including *Emma*, *Pride and Prejudice* and *Northanger Abbey*. Topics include books and reading in the early 19th century, the letters of Hutton, and narrative techniques.③

Megan Taylor, in "Jane Austen and 'Banal Shakespeare'", argues that while critics have long acknowledged Jane Austen's literary debt to William Shakespeare, little attention has been paid to her infrequent use of direct quotations from his work. Perhaps because these instances of quotation are so rare, most critics who take note of them classify them as purely ironic: Austen quotes the bard as a means by which to satirize the eighteenth-century vogue for Shakespeare epigrams,

---

① Krueger M. "From Marginalia to Juvenilia: Jane Austen's Vindication of the Stuarts". The Eighteenth Century: Theory & Interpretation, 2015, 56(2):243-259.

② Goss E M. "Homespun Gossip: Jane West, Jane Austen, and the Task of Literary Criticism". The Eighteenth Century: Theory & Interpretation, 2015, 56(2):165-177.

③ Wilson C A. "'Something like Mine': Catherine Hutton, Jane Austen, and Feminist Recovery Work". The Eighteenth Century: Theory & Interpretation, 2015, 56(2):151-164.

mocking other writers who ineptly or inaptly cite well-worn passages in a transparent bid for artistic legitimacy. While true to a certain extent, this conclusion does not do justice to Austen's admiration of Shakespeare nor to the range of her sophisticated irony. Opening up such a critical standpoint in this article, the author closely examines instances of direct quotations from Shakespeare in Austen's novels and argues that Austen does not simply mock those writers who misuse Shakespeare; her quotations also reinvigorate his most clichéd aphorisms and demonstrate both their continuing relevance and her own keen understanding of their complex original contexts. [1]

10. Thematic Study

Raisa Bruner, in "Home with Jane", compares her isolation experience with the experiences of Jane Austen's heroines in the books including *Persuasion*, *Sense and Sensibility*, and *Mansfield Park*. Topics discussed include description of Austen's style in writing which, according to the author, offered stability in times of isolation, the lack of freedom, among these women, in spite of a certain class in Regency England, and comparison to the challenges faced by Fanny Price, a character in the book *Mansfield Park*. [2]

---

[1] Taylor M. "Jane Austen and 'Banal Shakespeare'". Eighteenth-Century Fiction, 2014, 27(1): 105-125.

[2] Bruner R. "Home with Jane". Time Magazine, 2020, 195(19): 54.

Chapter 5

Charles Dickens

Charles Dickens(1812-1870)

The son of a feckless government clerk, Dickens was born in Portsmouth but came when he was ten to live in London with his family. When his father was prisoned for debt two years later, Dickens was forced to work in a blacking (shoe polish) warehouse. He later worked as an office boy and then a secretary, eventually finding work as a reporter covering debates in Parliament for *The Morning Chronicle* and contributing to a variety of journals and magazines. Some of these were collected into his first published volume, *Sketches by Boz*, which was accompanied by the serial publication of the phenomenally successful *The Pickwick Papers*. Other serialized works followed: *Oliver Twist*, *Nicholas Nickleby*, *The Old Curiosity Shop*, and *Barnaby Rudge*. An 1842 trip to America produced *American Notes* and influenced the composition of *Martin Chuzzlewit*. His best-known works include *A Christmas Carol*, *David Copperfield*, *Bleak House*, *Hard Times*, *Little Dorrit*, *A Tale of Two Cities*, *Great Expectations*, *Our Mutual*

Friend, and *The Mystery of Edurin Drood*. Indefatigable and prolific, perhaps the most influential and best-known writer of his day, Dickens also produced voluminous journalism and edited several periodicals, in addition to reading from his works in public to great acclaim.[1]

---

[1] Richetti J, Bender J, David D, et al. The Columbia History of the British Novel. New York: Columbia University Press, 1994.

Critical Perspectives

1. Thematic Study

Olga Y. Osmukhina, A. B. Tanaseichuk, E. A. Sharonova, et al., in "Urban Theme Embodiment in the Novels of Charles Dickens", analyze the features of London image and the representation of urban theme in Charles Dickens' novels *The Adventures of Oliver Twist*, *Dombey and Son*, and *Bleak House*. As anthropomorphic characters of novels, the city acts as a full-fledged artistic image. It is established that London is a center of plot nodes contraction and appears to be versatile and multifaceted. On the one hand, it is a city in which all provincial residents rush. They dream of finding themselves here and occupying a worthy position in life. On the other hand, Dickens portrays London as the personification of cold, deceitful relationships, alienation of people in high society. It combines contrasting pictures of luxury and poverty, grandeur and squalor. It lives by a separate independent life and affects the feelings and actions of heroes. The article notes that London is always accompanied by landscape sketches in Dickens' novels. Most often, these are stable and multifunctional images of fog and cold. In the novel *The Adventures of Oliver Twist*, fog and cold become symbols of the concealment of the dirty deeds of the cruel and criminal world of London, in which the protagonist is originally immersed. In the novel *Bleak House*, they are the personification of the Supreme Court, and in *Dombey and Son*, the descriptions of cold, foggy, and gray London represent the cold of human relations that reigns in the family of financial magnate Mr. Dombey. ①

Anita Breckbill, in "Dismal Sounds: Flute Playing in the Fiction of Charles Dickens", discusses presence of flute playing in the fiction of author Charles Dickens. Topics include different roles relating to flute used by Dickens, such as satire of the incompetent musician, a vent for passions, and an expression of a broken heart; view of music and musicians found in Dickens' work; and examples of flute music in his work like the novel *Martin Chuzzlewit*. ②

Stephen B. Dobranski, in "Names in Dickens: The Trouble with Dombey", offers criticism of the book *Dombey and Son* by Charles Dickens. It outlines the authorship and completion of the novel. The author discusses the thematic implications of the novel as demonstrated in Dickens' egregious and gothic icons. The depiction on the development of the individual characters of the novel is noted. ③

2. Comparative Study

Tom Hubbard, in "Heart and Soul: Dickens and Dostoevsky", documents both convergences and divergences in the works of Dickens and his admirer Dostoevsky. While many such comparisons have been made by earlier scholars, the field is a rich one and there is much relevant detail that has not been previously rehearsed. Both major and minor works are here elucidated to provide fresh perspectives on this endlessly explorable territory of comparative literary studies. ④

---

① Osmukhina O Y, Tanaseichuk A B, Sharonova E A, et al. "Urban Theme Embodiment in the Novels of Charles Dickens". Journal of History, Culture & Art Research, 2020, 9(1):468-476.

② Breckbill A. "Dismal Sounds: Flute Playing in the Fiction of Charles Dickens". Flutist Quarterly, 2017, 42(3):20-26.

③ Dobranski S B. "Names in Dickens: The Trouble with Dombey". Modern Philology, 2016, 114(2):388-410.

④ Hubbard T. "Heart and Soul: Dickens and Dostoevsky". Slavonica, 2020, 25(2):89-105.

Carla A. Arnell, in "'Love beyond Logic': On Cannons, Castles, and Healing Tomfoolery in Dickens's *Great Expectations* and Dostoevsky's *The Brothers Karamazov*", makes a literary criticism of books including *Great Expectations* by Charles Dickens and *The Brothers Karamazov* by Fyodor Dostoevsky. It mentions the working of Dickens and Dostoevsky regarding providing ethical vision through books. It also mentions that Dickens offers information about the character who was beaten and humiliated in a boarding school.①

Patricia M. Ard, in "Charles Dickens and Frances Trollope: Victorian Kindred Spirits in the American Wilderness", compares British authors Charles Dickens and Frances Trollope's views about America as shown in their books, *American Notes* and *Domestic Manners of the Americans*. Topics include shared critical view of America as a wilderness; reasons for the authors' dislike of the American landscape; and analysis of the authors' descriptions of Niagara Falls and the Mississippi River.②

3. New Historicism

Carolyn Vellenga Berman, in "Tracing Characters: Political Shorthand and the History of Victorian Writing", examines Charles Dickens's apprenticeship to political shorthand in order to reconsider the relationship between parliamentary representation and print culture. Shorthand was a crucial part of the ecosystem of news publication, but it was profoundly incompatible with print. It was at once a technology for breaching parliamentary privilege and a means of fostering secrecy through cryptography. Readers must examine the toggling between speech and

---

① Arnell C A. "'Love beyond Logic': On Cannons, Castles, and Healing Tomfoolery in Dickens's *Great Expectations* and Dostoevsky's *The Brothers Karamazov*". Renascence, 2017, 69(2):81-98.

② Ard P M. "Charles Dickens and Frances Trollope: Victorian Kindred Spirits in the American Wilderness". American Transcendental Quarterly, 1993, 7(4):293-306.

writing, handwriting and print, that resulted from this paradox in order to understand the dense political history of Victorian writing.①

Jonathan Daniel Wells, in "Charles Dickens, the American South, and the Transatlantic Debate over Slavery", argues that the complex relationship between Dickens and his readers in the American South is shaped by the novelist's views of slavery and capitalism. Neglected both by Dickens scholars as well as historians of the South, Dickens' views on slavery offer important insights into the transatlantic debate over bondage and free labour. In addition, the way in which Dickens was read by both black and white Americans and his popularity among southerners in particular virtually guaranteed he would figure prominently in domestic policy debates. While African-Americans employed Dickens to attack slavery, and criticized him when he failed to meet their antislavery expectations, white southerners rejected Dickens's criticism of slavery but embraced his depiction of the ill effects of industrial capitalism. In examining politics, literature and intellectual life between the 1830s and the 1860s, this essay joins two broad historiographies that rarely intersect: the economic and political history of slavery and the intellectual and literary culture in the Early Republic. In examining the interactions, both real and imagined, between Dickens and his southern readership, scholars join current historiographical debates over political economy with transatlantic literary history in ways that shed light on Dickens, the South and the debates on political economy that strained sectional harmony and led to the Civil War.②

Anna Neill, in "The Made Man and the 'Minor' Novel", argues that Bruno Latour identifies the "great novel" as a site for revealing the complex nature of agency in the Anthropocene. As it traces cause and effect through numerous, interrelated events, the "great novel" reveals a vast network of actors-entities,

---

① Berman C V. "Tracing Characters: Political Shorthand and the History of Victorian Writing". Victorian Studies, 2020, 63(1):57-84.
② Wells J D. "Charles Dickens, the American South, and the Transatlantic Debate over Slavery". Slavery & Abolition, 2015, 36(1):1-25.

human and non-human—that are neither pure subjects nor pure objects. This essay examines firstly how novels by Charles Dickens and George Eliot depict the agency of non-human things within a network of actors. It then discusses how a self-proclaimed "minor" novel, Samuel Butler's *Erewhon*, challenges readers to think about the colonial implications of the distributed, networked agency represented in "great" Victorian fiction. *Erewhon* shows how the imbrication of the human and the (in particular) non-human machinate underpins the entrepreneurial success of the colonial adventurer. ①

Jesse Rosenthal, in "The Untrusted Medium: Open Networks, Secret Writing, and *Little Dorrit*", investigates the ways in which changing communication networks in the middle of the nineteenth century forces people to entrust their most closely guarded secrets to unknown intermediaries as a matter of course. This shift introduces a number of pressing concerns that stay with us today, particularly a growing sense of the need for encryption. Looking at Charles Dickens's *Little Dorrit*, this essay also argues that this changing understanding of how people are connected requires a different way of visualizing character networks in novels. Instead of focusing only on named characters in private spaces, in *Little Dorrit*, Dickens consistently imagines characters connected through an unknown, and unknowable, public. ②

Raphael Samuel, in "Dickens on Stage and Screen", argues that film and stage treatments of works by Charles Dickens reflect changing attitudes to the legacy of 19th-century Britain. Topics include key film and stage productions of *Little Dorrit*, *Nicholas Nickleby*, and *Great Expectations*; and other works set to film and stage. ③

---

① Neill A. "The Made Man and the 'Minor' Novel". Victorian Studies, 2017, 60(1):53-73.
② Rosenthal J. "The Untrusted Medium: Open Networks, Secret Writing, and *Little Dorrit*". Victorian Studies, 2017, 59(2):288-313.
③ Samuel R. "Dickens on Stage and Screen". History Today, 1989, 39(12):44-51.

Siân Ellis, in "Charles Dickens & Portsmouth", presents a description of the English port-city of Portsmouth, particularly in relation to its historical connection to the 19th-century British author Charles Dickens. Anecdotes describing the ways in which the author was connected to the city of Portsmouth are provided. Further historical features of the city are noted, such as its naval garrison which has operated prominently since the 16th century. Advice for tourist visits is also included. ①

4. Biographical Study

I. C. McManus, in "Charles Dickens: A Neglected Diagnosis", discusses author Charles Dickens and his various illnesses. Topics include hypothesis that Dickens had a right parietal or parietal-temporal disorder; description of his symptoms; illnesses which he suffered from, including possible frostbite of the foot; denial of Dickens that he was ill; and analysis of his symptoms. ②

5. Cultural Studies

Pablo Ruano San Segundo, in "Revisiting the Dickensian Echo of the HBO TV Series *The Wire*", analyzes the alleged Dickensian echo of the highly-acclaimed HBO TV series *The Wire*. Charles Dickens is probably the literary author to whom the series has most frequently been likened. This correspondence is scrutinized here, as it seems to have been built upon impressionistic references, rather than on methodical intertextual analyses of both the series and the Victorian author. The analysis throws new light on the Dickensian ambience of *The Wire*, which seems to

---

① Ellis S. "Charles Dickens & Portsmouth". British Heritage, 2011, 32(5):28-35.
② McManus I C. "Charles Dickens: A Neglected Diagnosis". Lancet, 2001, 358(9299):2158-2161.

be different than previous critical appreciations of the series have suggested.①

Dehn Gilmore, in "Pigmies and Brobdignagians: Arts Writing, Dickensian Character, and the Vanishing Victorian Life-Size", argues that Charles Dickens's "larger than life" characters were critically shaped by the Victorians' increasing doubts about the life-size as a visual standard in painting and sculpture. Departing from a tendency to read Dickens's excesses as the products of larger thematic design or as the results of structural exigency, this essay proposes instead that his famously "static" and "flat" characters were significantly influenced by debates about state and flat forms of art. In novels like *Bleak House* and *Little Dorrit*, Dickens investigated contemporary commentators' assertions that the perception of the "size of life" was a trick of the eye. Ultimately, his investigations went beyond exploration and were transformed into practice. What scholars have long taken as characterological exaggeration should in fact be reread as an effort to encapsulate lived visual experience.②

6. Theology Study

Mary Lenard, in "The Gospel of Amy: Biblical Teaching and Learning in Charles Dickens' *Little Dorrit*", argues for a revised view of Charles Dickens as a more mature and profound Christian thinker than his reputation has suggested. The author disputes critic Janet Larson's view that *Little Dorrit* increasingly reflects a "broken scripture", a Bible that has lost meaning in an industrialized world. In contrast, this article argues that the figure of Amy Dorrit is one intended to engage the reader in addressing the moral and ethical concerns of this world, not to present

---

① San Segundo P R. "Revisiting the Dickensian Echo of the HBO TV Series *The Wire*". International Journal of English Studies, 2019, 19(1):151-166.

② Gilmore D. "Pigmies and Brobdignagians: Arts Writing, Dickensian Character, and the Vanishing Victorian Life-Size". Victorian Studies, 2015, 57(4):667-690.

the ominous shadow of a failed apocalypse. Dickens' work represents not a decline in theology, but the development of a new kind of theology. ①

Scott Dransfield, in "Charles Dickens and the Victorian 'Mormon Moment'", argues that the growth of Mormonism in England in the middle of the nineteenth century presents a number of challenges relating to the cultural status of the new religion and its followers. Dickens's "uncommercial traveller" sketch describing a group of 800 Mormon converts preparing to emigrate to the Unites States, *Bound for the Great Salt Lake*, represents the challenge effectively. While Mormons were quickly identified by their heresies and by those qualities that characterized cultural and religious otherness, they were also observed to possess traits of Englishness, reflecting the image of a healthy working class. This article considers the tensions among these contradictory qualities and traces them to a middle-class "secular gospel" that Dickens articulates in his novels. Dickens utilizes this "gospel"—an ethic that valorizes work and domestic order as bearing religious significance—to perceive the followers of the new religion. ②

Geoffrey Rowell, in "Dickens and the Construction of Christmas", focuses on *A Christmas Carol*, by Charles Dickens, and discusses its appeal and its powerful religious and social overtones. Topics include Dickens' own reaction to the book; the story as the vehicle of Christian truths; Dickens' advice to his children regarding the *New Testament*; and the musical transformation of Christmas in the nineteenth century. ③

Miguel Mota, in "The Construction of the Christian Community in Charles Dickens's *Bleak House*", offers a literary critique of Charles Dickens's novel *Bleak House* in which the author examines the narrative structure of the representation of the

---

① Lenard M. "The Gospel of Amy: Biblical Teaching and Learning in Charles Dickens' *Little Dorrit*". Christianity & Literature, 2014, 63(3):337-355.

② Dransfield S. "Charles Dickens and the Victorian 'Mormon Moment'". Religion & the Arts, 2013, 17(5):489-506.

③ Rowell G. "Dickens and the Construction of Christmas". History Today, 1993, 43(12):17-24.

19th-century Christian society and community. Topics include Dickens's understanding of Christian ethics, the role of dialogue in the novel and its representation of community and open society, as well as the novel's projection of moral goodness. [1]

7. Canonization Study

Radhika Jones, in "Charles in Charge", looks at Charles Dickens, noting his contributions to literature on the eve of his bicentenary in 2012. Topics discussed include the relative lack of novels written before the Victorian period of 1837-1901, Dickens' early career as a journalist, and his love of acting, including giving dramatic readings of his novel *Oliver Twist*. This essay also discusses how his work was influenced by his readers' opinions, the systemic nature of evil and corruption as the negative forces in his later novels, and how he shocked readers by admitting in his posthumous biography that as a child he worked in a factory, an event that influenced his fiction. [2]

David Gates and Jac Chebatoris, in "Back from the Dead", discuss the posthumous publishing of unfinished works and what survivors should do with close-to-finished projects whose creators have died. A book entitled "A Miracle of Catfish" by Larry Brown, is being published in the spring of 2007 with its final page containing Brown's notes on how he planned to finish it. Charles Dickens book, *The Mystery of Edwin Drood*, is also briefly mentioned. [3]

---

[1] Mota M. "The Construction of the Christian Community in Charles Dickens's *Bleak House*". Renascence, 1994, 46(3):187-198.
[2] Jones R. "Charles in Charge". Time Magazine, 2012, 179(4):52-55.
[3] Gates D, Chebatoris J. "Back from the Dead". Newsweek, 2007, 149(21):70-72.

8. Narrative Study

Andrew Bedford and Bonnie Meekums, in "Narrating Attachment: Some Lessons Learned from Charles Dickens' Novel *Little Dorrit*", consider attachment from a post-modern, narrative and psychosocial perspective. Charles Dickens' *Little Dorrit* is used as a case study from which to explore these perspectives. The received wisdom that attachment styles are almost exclusively derived from the caregiver-infant relationship is critiqued, making use of the personal history of one of the authors to illustrate the importance of unintentional and unforeseen childhood experiences in generating attachment narratives. Attachment is treated not merely as a psychological phenomenon, but impacted on by social forces and occurring within social frameworks including identity. Literary sources offer one lens through which such psychosocial phenomena can be examined. Dickens' story illustrates the difficulties faced by boys and men in terms of gendered attachment behaviours, but does so without falling into the trap of portraying either men or women in stereotypical ways. The authors propose that avoidant attachment is a defence against the possibility of extreme dependency, and that the underlying fear is therefore the same for both avoidant and ambivalent internal working models, namely that the loved one will disappear. The therapeutic relationship is conceptualized as one in which personal narratives are re-authored within a collaborative and co-creative framework, but the possibility of re-authoring is also considered possible without the intervention of a psychotherapist, and the arts in particular are considered as media in which reflective function is fostered. Conclusions are drawn for how literature can act as research data in order to enhance understanding of the psychosocial complexity within which individuals negotiate issues of attachment.①

Kathleen Pacious, in "Misdirections, Delayed Disclosures, and the Ethics of the Telling in Charles Dickens's *Our Mutual Friend*", explores the ethics of the telling of Charles Dickens's *Our Mutual Friend* from a rhetorical perspective to demonstrate the ethical implications of misdirections and delayed disclosures, which create a multi-layered author-audience relationship. *Our Mutual Friend* has received much critical attention but very little has focused on the ethical implications of form for the relationship between Dickens and his audience. By examining the techniques of synthetic functions of character, double communication, misdirections, delayed disclosures, and narratorial devices of uncertainty, this essay demonstrates the consequences (for the genre of realism, the ethics of readerly judgment, the ethics of performance and play) and the rewards of reconfiguring the novel through attention to the synthetic dimension of acts of reading, themes, and characters. The author of this essay offers some new directions for understanding Dickens's multi-layered relationships with his readers in *Our Mutual Friend*, including a focus on perception, interpretation, and judgment; the cognitive pleasure of dealing with techniques that offer both immersion and defamiliarization; and the explicit awareness of the metafictional engagement offered by Dickens as designer. The author also offers a new argument about the nuances of implied author-narrator relationships in heterodiegetic narration, about the significance of mimetic and synthetic components of readerly and textual dynamics and their implications for genre, and about the ethics of the telling in narratives whose effects depend on misdirection and reconfiguration.②

Tzu Yu Allison Lin, in "Images of Spatial Representations in Charles Dickens's New York", claims that Charles Dickens came back from America,

---

① Bedford A, Bonnie M. "Narrating Attachment: Some Lessons Learned from Charles Dickens' Novel *Little Dorrit*". Psychodynamic Practice, 2010, 16(4): 431-444.
② Pacious K. "Misdirections, Delayed Disclosures, and the Ethics of the Telling in Charles Dickens's *Our Mutual Friend*". Narrative, 2016, 24(3):330-350.

"heartily disillusioned". In this paper, through reading *American Notes*, the author finds the image of spatial representation in the city of New York. On the surface, the city shows Dickens's eye of observation, revealing the dark side of the city. And yet, Dickens's writing expresses more than what he sees. Dickens's image of New York, the author argues, is not only a "realistic" account of what things look like, but a true realisation of how he feels about himself, and about the country in which he was situated in. ①

9. Feminism Study

Theresa Atchison, in "Accessories to the Crime: Mapping Dickensian Trauma in *Great Expectations* and *A Tale of Two Cities*", delves into Charles Dickens's nuanced use of fashion accessories in two of his later works. The author of this essay argues that because of nineteenth-century conventions, Dickens has to intimate certain aspects of his characters' interiority by creating a performative exterior. Such analyses, particularly regarding female accessories concerning mobility, reveal censored subjects and illustrate Dickens as a more compassionate writer regarding the female sex. ②

David Kaplin, in "Transparent Lies and the Rearticulation of Agency in *Our Mutual Friend*", presents criticism on the novel *Our Mutual Friend* by Charles Dickens. Particular focus is given to the work's exploration of lies and agency. Additional topics discussed include an examination of a widow depicted in the book, Lady Tippins, the Victorian taxonomy of status and the book's character, Jenny

---

① Allison Lin T Y. "Images of Spatial Representations in Charles Dickens's New York". Journal of History Culture and Art Research, 2013, 2(2):175-182.

② Atchison T. "Accessories to the Crime: Mapping Dickensian Trauma in *Great Expectations* and *A Tale of Two Cities*". Fashion Theory: The Journal of Dress, Body & Culture, 2016, 20(4):461-473.

Wren.①

Judith Newton, in "Historicisms New and Old: 'Charles Dickens' Meets Marxism, Feminism, and West Coast Foucault", focuses on the relation between characteristic tendencies in materialist-feminist literary criticism in feminist New Historicism, and some tendencies that characterize the New Historicism influenced by critical reading of Michel Foucault. Topics discussed include links with Marxist criticism; 1980's surge of feminist writing on Dickens; world of power in *Bleak House*; Dickens' representation of gender conflict within the family; and nature of dominant masculine ideologies.②

10. Reader-response Study

Philip Collins, in "Dickens and His Readers", examines the writing style of British author Charles Dickens. Topics discussed include influence of the reformists in the 1830s on the writings of Dickens; themes of his works; and comparison of the themes and styles of Dickens and poet Alfred Tennyson.③

11. Eco-criticism Study

Ann Haley MacKenzie, in "An Analysis of Environmental Issues in 19th Century England Using the Writings of Charles Dickens", discusses the use of literature written by the 19th century author Charles Dickens to examine environmental and social issues. The author states that by using such literature,

---

① Kaplin D. "Transparent Lies and the Rearticulation of Agency in *Our Mutual Friend*". Papers on Language & Literature, 2015, 51(3):244-268.

② Newton J. "Historicisms New and Old: 'Charles Dickens' Meets Marxism, Feminism, and West Coast Foucault". Feminist Studies, 1990, 16(3):449-470.

③ Collins P. "Dickens and His Readers". History Today, 1987, 37(7):32-40.

Chapter 5　Charles Dickens

students can understand that environmentalist issues do not merely belong to the 21st century. Several relevant passages from Dickens' literature are presented and examined including his books *Hard Times* and *Bleak House*. Topics include Dickens' commitment to sanitary living conditions amongst the poor, infectious diseases, and pollution. Also discussed is the industrial revolution. [1]

---

[1] MacKenzie A H. "An Analysis of Environmental Issues in 19th Century England Using the Writings of Charles Dickens". American Biology Teacher, 2008, 70(4):202-204.

Chapter 6

William Makepeace Thackeray

William Makepeace Thackeray(1811-1863)

Born in India, Thackeray was raised and educated in England from the age of six. After attending Trinity College, Cambridge, he went to France and Germany, and then he returned to London to study law. After working as a journalist for a time, he studied art in Paris and continued to work as a journalist upon his return to England in 1837. As a popular satirist in journals, he began to publish his best-known novels serially in 1848 with *Vanity Fair*, followed by *Pendennis*, *Henry Esmond*, and *The Newcomes*. A lecture tour to Armorica in 1852 led to another novel, *The Virginians*, published serially. [1]

---

[1] Richetti J, Bender J, David D, et al. The Columbia History of the British Novel. New York: Columbia University Press, 1994.

Critical Perspectives

1. Canonization

Carol Iannone, in "All's Fair in Love and War?", discusses some of the film and television adaptations of the novel *Vanity Fair* by William Makepeace Thackeray. Topics discussed include film version by director Mira Nair starring Reese Witherspoon, the play *Becky Sharp* by Langdon Mitchell and the title of the book took by Thackeray from John Bunyan's *The Pilgrim's Progress*. [1]

Edgar F. Harden, in "Thackeray and His Publishers: Two Uncollected Letters Concerning *Vanity Fair* and *Esmond*", focuses on the degree of control exercised by novelist William Makepeace Thackeray regarding the printed text of the title page of his works *Vanity Fair* and *Henry Esmond*. Topics discussed include development of the original titles of the two novels by Thackeray; advertisements and title page design which appeared in the literary works; and background on Thackeray's career. [2]

Joseph Cunneen, in "From Page to Screen", focuses on the film adaptations of novels by William Makepeace Thackeray, Evelyn Waugh and Andre Dubus. The author especially discusses the film adaptation of *Vanity Fair*. [3]

Richard Schickel, in "Lots of Flair, not Enough Fire", discusses the role of actress Reese Witherspoon as the character of Becky Sharp in the film adaptation of William Makepeace Thackeray's *Vanity Fair*. Topics discussed include suggestion

---

[1] Iannone C. "All's Fair in Love and War?". Academic Questions, 2019, 32(3):435-437.
[2] Harden E F. "Thackeray and His Publishers: Two Uncollected Letters Concerning *Vanity Fair* and *Esmond*". Papers on Language & Literature, 1976, 12(2): 167-176.
[3] Cunneen J. "From Page to Screen". National Catholic Reporter, 2004, 40(42):19.

that the film is not as deep as the novel; development of a colorful set and unique costumes by director Mira Nair; and how Nair chose to depict the colonial empire of England in the film differently than it was portrayed in the book. ①

2. New-historicism

Cristina Richieri Griffin, in "Experiencing History and Encountering Fiction in *Vanity Fair*", argues that William Makepeace Thackeray's *Vanity Fair* puts forward a theory of historical experience. Though the novel revolves around the Napoleonic wars, the narrator famously avoids recounting this military history as it occurs. This essay argues that the narrator finally encounters history in a way that he can both narrate and experience, and in the five chapters from the end of the novel, he appears as a character in the fictional town of Pumpernickel, which belatedly rehearses the Napoleonic wars through its aesthetic representations. With the narrator's appearance, *Vanity Fair* offers a self-reflexive historiography that trumpets belated aesthetic revivals—the fictional town, the fictional novel—as the best and perhaps the only ways to confront not only military but even personal, domestic history. ②

Hedi Abdel-Jaouad, in "The Sands of Rhyme: Thackeray and Abd al Qadir", focuses on novelist and satirist William Makepeace Thackeray's denunciation of French colonial adventurism in Algeria and his siding with the Emir Abd al Qadir. Topics discussed include failure of Thackeray's critics to note his admiration and support of the Emir; examination of the novelist's motives in writing about the Emir; personal background; and interpretation of Thackeray's works. ③

---

① Schickel R. "Lots of Flair, not Enough Fire". Time Magazine, 2004, 164(10):86.
② Griffin C R. "Experiencing History and Encountering Fiction in *Vanity Fair*". Victorian Studies, 2016, 58(3):412-435.
③ Abdel-Jaouad H. "The Sands of Rhyme: Thackeray and Abd al Qadir". Research in African Literatures, 1999, 30(3):194-206.

Ruth M. McAdams, in "Clothing Napoleonic History in *Vanity Fair* and *The Trumpet-Major*", argues that William Makepeace Thackeray's *Vanity Fair* and Thomas Hardy's *The Trumpet-Major* use the temporal multiplicity and ambiguity of fashion to depict historical time as striated and multidimensional. It challenges the critical paradigm that has long maligned conspicuous clothing in historical fiction as a kind of facile historicism. Such an approach fails to acknowledge the complex temporalities of fictional clothing. In emphasizing the persistence of older styles, offering multiple interpretations of apparently fashionable garments, and depicting the unsynchronized life cycles of clothes, *Vanity Fair* and *The Trumpet-Major* undermine the idea that to be historically situated is to keep pace with rapid linear progress. The essay also links these novels' attention to clothing to their shared historical setting during the Napoleonic wars. [1]

Robert Eaglestone, in "Waterloo in Fiction: A Tale of Two Sharp(e)s", discusses literary characters from fiction associated with the history of the Battle of Waterloo which include Lieutenant-Colonel Richard Sharpe from the novels of Bernard Cornwell and Rebecca Sharp from the novel *Vanity Fair*, by William Makepeace Thackeray. Emphasis is given to topics such as depictions of the character in films by actors Sean Bean and Reese Witherspoon, military metaphors, and the influence of the diaries of author Frances Burney on Thackeray's work. [2]

3. Narrative Study

Dianne F. Sadoff, in "Thackeray, Catherine Gore, and Harriet Martineau: Genres of Fashionable and Domestic Fiction", addresses the emergence of the

---

[1] McAdams R M. "Clothing Napoleonic History in *Vanity Fair* and *The Trumpet-Major*". Victorian Studies, 2017, 60(1):9-28.

[2] Eaglestone R. "Waterloo in Fiction: A Tale of Two Sharp(e)s". History Today, 2015, 65(8): 4-5.

Victorian novel. Rather than assuming the genre's natural or inevitable occurrence, the author examines the ways in which William Makepeace Thackeray borrows from his predecessors, Catherine Gore and Harriet Martineau, whose respective exploitation of the silver fork genre and the domestic novel enables Thackeray to seize a historical moment in which fashionable fiction undergoes its demise and the domestic novel emerges. This pivotal moment in literary history also witnesses the historical shift from consanguineal to conjugal family form; alterations in ideologies of marriage, gender, and property; and the possibility of generic transformation and reinvention. Given the instability of generic forms in the 1830s and 1840s, Thackeray also repurposed and hybridized fashionable and domestic fiction, as he modernized both for the Victorian novel in the 1840s.①

Robert Bledsoe, in "Fitz-Boodle among the Harpies: A Reading of *Dennis Haggart's Wife*", explores the narrative in the book *Dennis Haggarty's Wife*, by William Makepeace Thackeray. Topics discussed include representation of women in the writings of Thackeray; impact of the narrator's total hostility towards the characters on the story; and analysis of the narrator's savagely misogynistic point of view.②

Alexandra Mullen, in "*Vanity Fair* and Vexation of Spirit", focuses on the life and works of author William Makepeace Thackeray. Topics discussed include details on several misfortunes in life; theme of several novels; and description of characters in the novel *Vanity Fair*.③

Victor R. Kennedy, in "Pictures as Metaphors in Thackeray's Illustrated Novels", argues that traditional literary criticism concerns itself with metaphors in texts. There is a long tradition, however, of illustrated literature—texts with

---

① Sadoff D F. "Thackeray, Catherine Gore, and Harriet Martineau: Genres of Fashionable and Domestic Fiction". Victorian Studies, 2019, 61(4):629-652.

② Bledsoe R. "Fitz-Boodle among the Harpies: A Reading of *Dennis Haggart's Wife*". Studies in Short Fiction, 1975, 12(2):181-184.

③ Mullen A. "*Vanity Fair* and Vexation of Spirit". Hudson Review, 2002, 54(4):581-589.

accompanying pictures. This article examines the relationship between pictures and texts in the works of William Makepeace Thackeray, a 19th-century English novelist who illustrated his own works and whose pictures are more than merely decorative. They provide visual explanation and ironic commentary on the text through a subtle system of related metaphors. The metaphors in the illustrations range from simple to highly complex, and close analysis shows them to be an integral part of the narrative, adding depth and meaning. ①

4. Biographical Study

Richard Mullen, in "Thackeray: Man of Letters", discusses the book *The Letters and Private Papers of William Makepeace Thackeray*, edited by Gordon Norton Ray. Topics discussed include problems faced by the author in compiling the letters of Thackeray; range of letters included in the supplement; and insight that the letters give on Thackeray's life. ②

Brooke Allen, in "Sadness Balancing Wit: Thackeray's Life & Works", focuses on William Makepeace Thackeray's professional life. Topics discussed include comparison of Thackeray's work with author Charles Dickens; family history of Thackeray; and description of Thackeray's behavior at work. ③

Nancy Caldwell Sorel, in "William Makepeace Thackeray and James T. Fields", recounts incidents that suggest a close friendship between London, England-based novelist William Makepeace Thackeray and Boston, Massachusetts-based publisher James T. Fields. The author discusses Fields' visits to London and Thackeray's visits to Boston. Additional topics include Thackeray's job as an editor

---

① Kennedy V R. "Pictures as Metaphors in Thackeray's Illustrated Novels". Metaphor & Symbolic Activity, 1994, 9(2):135-147.

② Mullen R. "Thackeray: Man of letters". Contemporary Review, 1995, 266(1551):187-192.

③ Allen B. "Sadness Balancing Wit: Thackeray's Life & Works". The New Criterion, 2001, 19(5):19-28.

of *The Cornhill Magazine* and Fields' job as an editor of *The Atlantic Monthly*.①

5. Cultural Study

Christoph Lindner, in "Thackeray's Gourmand: Carnivals of Consumption in *Vanity Fair*", focuses on the novel *Vanity Fair*, by William Makepeace Thackeray. Topics discussed include representation of runaway consumption; views on commodity in the context of the Victorian culture; and fascination on the spectacular and performative aspects of commodity culture.②

6. Gender Study

Brian Mccuskey, in "Fetishizing the Flunkey: Thackeray and the Uses of Deviance", provides an alternative to the dominant model of reading Victorian fiction as an open secret for homosexuality and to discover what ways the representation of deviance might be useful for a writer. Topics discussed include discussion on the fetishizing of male servants in the novel *The History of Pendennis*, by William Makepeace Thackeray, and how the obsession of the author with figures and accessories of male servants complicated the issue of male sexuality.③

7. Feminism Study

Phyllis Susan Dee, in "Female Sexuality and Triangular Desire in *Vanity Fair*

---

① Sorel N C. "William Makepeace Thackeray and James T. Fields". The Atlantic, 2001, 287(5):87.

② Lindner C. "Thackeray's Gourmand: Carnivals of Consumption in *Vanity Fair*". Modern Philology, 2002, 99(4):564-581.

③ Mccuskey B. "Fetishizing the Flunkey: Thackeray and the Uses of Deviance". Novel: A Forum on Fiction, 1999, 32(3):384-400.

and *The Mill on the Floss*", deals with female sexuality and triangular desire in the novels *Vanity Fair*, by William Makepeace Thackeray and *The Mill on the Floss*, by George Eliot. Topics discussed include description of Rene Girard's paradigm of triangular desire, storylines, and interpretation of triangular desire. [1]

8. Translation Study

Andreea-Mihaela Tamba, in "Translating vs. Rewriting during the Romanian Communist Period—Prefaces to Translations of *Vanity Fair* and *Tess of the d'Urbervilles*", argues that the Communist period represents a turning point in the evolution of translation within the Romanian socio-cultural space. The author of this essay argued that the Communist Party had instilled in Romania throughout the second half of the 20th century, and the education reform was intimately liaised with the need for enhancing the access of the Romanian public to world's literary masterpieces. Hence emerged a new generation of highly competent translators, who provided an impressive number of high-quality translations. The setting up of specialized publishing houses and magazines dealing with translations testifies to an institutionalization of translation in Romania during the communist period. However, there also was a flipside of the Romanian communist translation boom, given that books, one of the main informational resources at the time, could have also contained elements that were ideologically unacceptable to the Communist Party. Therefore, censorship became a most powerful political tool for a social and literary phenomenon which could have threatened the ideological communist system. Ideologically offensive books had to comply with the communist doctrine, otherwise they were banned altogether. This paper focuses on presenting the extent to which

---

[1] Dee P S. "Female Sexuality and Triangular Desire in *Vanity Fair* and *The Mill on the Floss*". Papers on Language & Literature, 1999, 35(4):391-416.

the Romanian communist translation campaign represented an ambitious plan aimed at responding to the need for a literary, social and cultural synchronization, as well as a highly fertile ground for ideological manipulative intrusions or rewritings, as André Lefevere put it. Prefaces to Romanian translations of novels such as William Makepeace Thackeray's *Vanity Fair* and Thomas Hardy's *Tess of the d'Urbervilles* that came out during the communist years are referred to in order to illustrate the thesis.①

---

① Tamba A-M. "Translating vs. Rewriting during the Romanian Communist Period—Prefaces to Translations of *Vanity Fair* and *Tess of the d'Urbervilles*". Philologica Jassyensia, 2013, 9(2):261-270.

Chapter 7

Emily Bronte

Emily Bronte(1818-1848)

For a short time, Emily Bronte(also known as Emily Brontë) was schooled at Cowan Bridge with her sister Charlotte, but most of her education was carried out at home. Emily was a governess at Law Hill, but only briefly. Afterward she went to Brussels with Charlotte to study languages. Most of her remaining years were spent at Haworth. In 1846, Emily's poems were published as a joint publication between her, Anne, and Charlotte, under the title "Poems, by Currer, Ellis and Acton Bell". Her best-known work, *Wuthering Heights*, was published in 1847.[1]

---

[1] Richetti J, Bender J, David D, et al. The Columbia History of the British Novel. New York: Columbia University Press, 1994.

Critical Perspectives

1. Narrative Study

Sarah Wootton, in "Emily Brontë's Darkling Tales", examines light and dark as coalescing and contradictory opposites in Emily Brontë's *Wuthering Heights*. The resonant interplay of light and dark in the novel, as captured and reworked to startling effect in Rosalind Whitman's series of etchings *Black and White in Wuthering Heights*, is conceived in the shadow of Romanticism. Subjecting Romantic ideals and anxieties to the pressure of Victorian prose darkens, if not quite eclipses, Keats's "truth of magination", thereby situates the novel at an interpretative crossroads. *Wuthering Heights* is poised on a literary fault-line, as an heir to the Romantic tradition that simultaneously heralds the advent of Modernism. Readers of Emily Brontë's novel, like the gaunt thorns and stunted firs that cling to the landscape surrounding the Heights, are hardened by the inhospitable terrain of the text and yearn for the light amidst a dense and disorientating post-Romantic darkness.[①]

Bette London, in "*Wuthering Heights* and the Text between the Lines", focuses on the double-handedness of the narrative of *Wuthering Heights*, a novel written by Emily Bronte. Topics discussed include commentary on the secondary tales in the novel in the love story between Cathy and Heathcliff; analysis of the novel's narrative marginality; and information on its double texts and double

---

① Wootton S. "Emily Brontë's Darkling Tales". Romanticism, 2016, 22(3):299-311.

narrators.[1]

Ismail Khalaf Salih, Danear Jabbar Abdul Kareem, and Omar Najem Abdullah, in "Monomaniac Revenge in Melville's *Moby Dick* and Bronte's *Wuthering Heights*", argue that revenge can be one of consequences of bad feeling towards others. This feeling of anger, hatred and prejudice could be based on traumatic visible or invisible experience. On the one hand, the level of that anger and hatred depends on the volume of damage caused by the action or judgment; on the other hand, it depends on man's endurance and tolerance upon that action or judgment. Revenge can be individual or collective as well. Individually, it is driven personally as a reaction of other's perceived harm when the individual desire is set to retaliate for bringing justice and satisfying his need. Collectively, most of ancient wars and conflicts were based on the concept of revenge which mostly brought collective devastation. This study utilizes rereading of the canonical texts—*Moby Dick* by Herman Melville and *Wuthering Heights* by Emily Bronte—to make better understanding of the "monomaniac revenge" by highlighting and analyzing the main characters in the two novels above Ahab and Heathcliff, respectively, and their destructive revenge under the light of psychological theory. Ahab was isolated from his family. Heathcliff was dismissed by his family. Later on they both lost their lives. Melville and Bronte prove that destructive revenge brings destructive results. The top focus of the study is on how Ahab and Heathcliff's excessive desire of revenge develops and then brings them and people around to death.[2]

2. Psychological Study

Gazi Abdulla-hel Baqui, and Nishat Tasneem, in "Emily Bronte's *Wuthering*

---

[1] London B. "*Wuthering Heights* and the Text between the Lines". Papers on Language & Literature, 1988, 24(1):34-52.

[2] Salih I K, Abdul Kareem D J, Abdullah O N. "Monomaniac Revenge in Melville's *Moby Dick* and Bronte's *Wuthering Heights*". e-BANGI Journal, 2021, 18(10):107-116.

Heights: An Unconventional Victorian Masterpiece", argue that *Wuthering Heights* by Emily Bronte is a novel which is windswept and weather-beaten both in the world outside and in the world inside of human emotion. The total book leaves a deep impression of an intense but dreary romantic view of life and of an unusual mystery and conflict. None of the Victorian novelists has been able to create these traits. Some of Emily's characters appear like creatures of their autonomous, unreal world. This paper shows that the novel is an expression of Emily's rare sense of imagination that is absent in many other contemporary novelists. It also shows that Emily paints an unusual love before which the demonic passion melts. So, this novel stands far apart from other Victorian masterpieces. Not only this, *Wuthering Heights* does not portray Victorian realism which is the focal point of most of the Victorian great novels. [1]

Kevin A. Morrison, in "'Whose Injury Is like Mine?' Emily Brontë, George Eliot, and the Sincere Postures of Suffering Men", provides a discussion of the gestural and rhetorical modes of male suffering as suffering while recognizing them as calculated strategies at the same time, as figured by novelists Emily Brontë and George Eliot. It is inferred that they were able to acknowledge the violence that men inflict on women emotionally, and its cause which is outside men's individual control. It is also mentioned that the conclusion of Eliot's novel *The Mill on the Floss* suggests that modern conjugality is based on psychic pain. [2]

Emily M. Baldys, in "Hareton Earnshaw and the Shadow of Idiocy: Disability and Domestic Disorder in *Wuthering Heights*", discusses how a disability studies approach in Emily Bronte's novel *Wuthering Heights* can be productively applied to decipher the ideological anxieties and motives of 19th century narrative. It uses the term disability to refer to the condition of idiocy with an understanding that 19th-

---

[1] Abdulla-hel Baqui G, Tasneem N. "Emily Bronte's *Wuthering Heights*: An Unconventional Victorian Masterpiece". ASA University Review, 2014, 8(2):251-258.

[2] Morrison K A. "'Whose Injury Is like Mine?' Emily Brontë, George Eliot, and the Sincere Postures of Suffering Men". Novel: A Forum on Fiction, 2010, 43(2):271-293.

century concept of idiocy is a nebulous one that does not overlap with a modern conception of cognitive disability. It notes that disability lurks in the shadows to trouble the novel's resolution.①

Graeme Tytler, in "'Nelly, I Am Heathcliff!': The Problem of 'Identification' in *Wuthering Heights*", explores the problem of identification involving the characters, Heathcliff and Catherine, of the novel *Wuthering Heights* by Emily Bronte. The extent to which identification is a kind of domination in the literature is noted. The words expressed by Heathcliff that are considered as a travesty of the notion of sympathy as a concern to identify with others in their weal or woe are analyzed. The propensity of Catherine for domineering with others and her apparent fascination with machismo are also discussed.②

3. New-historicism

Claire O'Callaghan, in "The Weirdest of the 'Weird Sisters'", explores the myths and uncertainties of biographies of English author Emily Bronte. It talks about the lack of source material available written by Emily detailing her life in Haworth, England, contemporary critical response to her novel *Wuthering Heights*, and the biographical information related by her sister in her *Biographical Notice of Ellis and Acton Bell* which debunked the aliases of her sisters Emily and Anne respectively after their deaths by tuberculosis.③

Christopher Heywood, in "A Yorkshire Background for *Wuthering Heights*", examines the relationship between Yorkshire Dale in England and Emily Bronte's novel *Wuthering Heights*. Topics discussed include Charlotte Bronte's description

---

① Baldys E M. "Hareton Earnshaw and the Shadow of Idiocy: Disability and Domestic Disorder in *Wuthering Heights*". Philological Quarterly, 2012, 91(1): 49-74.

② Tytler G. "'Nelly, I Am Heathcliff!': The Problem of 'Identification' in *Wuthering Heights*". Midwest Quarterly, 2006, 47(2): 167-181.

③ O'Callaghan C. "The Weirdest of the 'Weird Sisters'". History Today, 2018, 68(8): 36-43.

of sister Emily's novel as a portrayal of a remote and unclaimed region and its dwellers whose stories Emily had mastered; novel as an invocation of the history and society contained in the Craven landscape in Yorkshire; and novel's reflection of Whitaker's "Deanery of Craven". ①

4. Eco-criticism Study

Maureen B. Adams, in "Emily Brontë and Dogs: Transformation within the Human-Dog Bond", examines the bond between humans and dogs as demonstrated in the life and work of Emily Brontë. The nineteenth-century author, publishing under the pseudonym, Ellis Bell, evinced, both in her personal and professional life, the complex range of emotions explicit in the human-dog bond: attachment and companionship to domination and abuse. In *Wuthering Heights*, Brontë portrays the dog as scapegoat, illustrating the dark side of the bond found in many cultures. Moreover, she writes with awareness of connections—unknown in the nineteenth century—between animal abuse and domestic violence. In her personal life, Brontë's early power struggles with her companion animal mastiff, Keeper, evolve into a caring relationship. In a human-dog bond transformation that survives Brontë's death, Keeper, becomes both bridge and barrier to other human relationships. A dog may, and in this case Keeper does, take on a comprehensive role in which he both mourns his own loss and comforts others in their collective grief. ②

Anne Williams, in "Natural Supernaturalism in *Wuthering Heights*", suggests that Emily Bronte's *Wuthering Heights* is a quintessential example of natural

---

① Heywood C. "A Yorkshire Background for *Wuthering Heights*". Modern Language Review, 1993, 88(4): 817-830.
② Adams M B. "Emily Brontë and Dogs: Transformation within the Human-Dog Bond". Society & Animals, 2000, 8(2):167-181.

supernaturalism. Topics discussed include evocations of two traditional tales; varieties of human love; movement from novel into romance; and literary incarnations of the Tristan myth. ①

5. Thematic Study

James Como, in "On the Depth of *Wuthering Heights*", presents a criticism of the English novel *Wuthering Heights* by Emily Bronte. He discusses the themes of love and revenge, considers which is the more predominant of the two, and how revenge is transcended by the ending. ②

6. Feminism

Yeşim Sultan Akbay, in "The Mighty Voice of the Silenced: The Victorian Sappho's Literary Painting", argues that women in the nineteenth-century have no free will and chance to express themselves through writing, and they are studied in the academic field. Women writers were locked out of mainstream literature, for "literature cannot be the business of a woman's life, and it ought not to be". Today's readers find it is hard to believe that it was claimed by the Victorian poet laureate Robert Southey in his letter to Charlotte Brontë. The literary field, especially poetry, which has always been a holy occupation, was considered as a serious career for the male only. So how women were expected to bring voice to their literary paintings? Through text analysis, this paper aims to seek the "Judith Shakespeare" in the field of poetry through an analysis of Emily Brontë's poetry skills. It was she, who, despite the long held Angel in the House image, had her

---

① Williams A. "Natural Supernaturalism in *Wuthering Heights*". Studies in Philology, 1985, 82 (1):104-127.
② Como J. "On the Depth of *Wuthering Heights*". The New Criterion, 2018, 37(3):34-36.

mighty voice heard regardless all the prejudices against women writers. Likened to the Greek Sappho by Janet Gezari, the image of Emily Brontë is carried out not as a protesting one but as bringing voice to the pleasing silence of the nineteenth-century parsonage where she lived. Modern-day critics are surprised by her "pure cry of genuine poetry" and this paper aims to show how unique Brontë's poetry skills in a male-dominated world are, surpassing even those of her male-contemporaries. ①

  Abbie L. Cory, in "'Out of My Brother's Power': Gender, Class, and Rebellion in *Wuthering Heights*", reports on the literary criticism of author Emily Brontë's novel *Wuthering Heights*. This criticism seems to demonstrate that literary works are not produced in vacuums but are reflections of the author's life, culture, and ideological beliefs. Brontë's novel captures in a microcosm many aspects of the radical sociopolitical movements in England in the 1840s, both metaphorically and literally disrupting dominant structures of power. In this macrocosm of radicalism, chartism was a resistance to state power. Chartism was remarkable for the number of women involved. ②

---

  ① Akbay Y S. "The Mighty Voice of the Silenced: The Victorian Sappho's Literary Painting". Journal of Suleyman Demirel University Institute of Social Sciences, 2017, 28(3):371-381.
  ② Cory A L. "'Out of My Brother's Power': Gender, Class, and Rebellion in *Wuthering Heights*". women's Studies, 2005, 34(1):1-26.

Chapter 8

Thomas Hardy

Thomas Hardy (1840-1928)

Born near Dorchester, as a son of a stonemason, Hardy went to school until the age of sixteen, when he began an apprenticeship with an architect. When he was twenty-two, he went to London to work, and upon returning to work in Dorchester he began his first novel, *The Poor Man and the Lady*. During this period as an architect he produced his first published novels: *Desperate Remedies*, *Under the Greenwood Tree*, *A Pair of Blue Eyes*, and *Far from the Madding Crowd*. In the period between 1874 and 1895, Hardy was extremely productive, writing short stories, poems, and the following novels: *The Hand of Ethelberta*, *The Return of the Native*, *The Trumpet-Major*, *A Laodicean*, *Two on a Tower*, *The Mayor of Casterbridge*, *The Woodlanders*, *Wessex Tales*, *Tess of the d'Urbervilles*, *A Group of Noble Dames*, *Life's Little Ironies*, and *Jude the Obscure*. Hardy gave up writing fiction late in life and devoted himself to poetry. [1]

---

[1] Richetti J, Bender J, David D, et al. The Columbia History of the British Novel. New York: Columbia University Press, 1994.

Critical Perspectives

1. Ecocriticism

John MacNeill Miller, in "Mischaracterizing the Environment: Hardy, Darwin, and the Art of Ecological Storytelling", reads Hardy's representation of Egdon Heath in *The Return of the Native* against the ecology and environmental history of English heathland to challenge a growing consensus that sees Hardy as an ecological thinker. Hardy's writings fall short of ecological understanding, the author argues, because his vision of humans is entangled with an animated but deeply inhuman landscape which creates affective and scalar tensions that falsely cast interspecies interdependence as ominous and alienating. [1]

2. Feminism Study

Shazia Ghulam Mohammad, and Abdus Salam Khalis, in "Archetypal Patterns in Thomas Hardy's Depiction of Women", argue that the novels of Thomas Hardy, having the inherent potential to be evaluated and re-evaluated in accordance with emerging standards of literary criticism, are rightly considered both rich and complex in themes and characters. This paper builds on the aforementioned qualities, contending that the existence of archetypal pattern in Hardy's art of characterization brings to limelight his affinity with psychologists, particularly Freud

---

[1] Miller J M. "Mischaracterizing the Environment: Hardy, Darwin, and the Art of Ecological Storytelling". Texas Studies in Literature & Language, 2020, 62(2):149-177.

and Carl Jung. Though these archetypes exist in both male and female characters, the authors' focus here is on exploring and analyzing these unconscious complexes with particular reference to women. These complexes have been presented here as the motives due to which they behave in a particular way and which render them as a markedly distinct species in the works of art and worlds of literature, probably in line with their actual roles in life.①

Donguk Kim, in "Thomas Hardy's *The Well-Beloved*: A 'Ghost' Story", argues that *The Well-Beloved* attends to the complexities and anxieties of creative consciousness. The artist hero Jocelyn Pierston is an explorer feeling his way in an effort to reveal some unknown beauty. It is his desire to find the ideal of woman(the Well-Beloved) and translate her beauty into a sculptural form that impels him to wander. So among Hardy's preoccupations in the novel is a need to register the notion of wandering as a metaphorical referent for the hero's journey in search of ideal beauty, which is in fact beyond the limits of his own power. This essay invites the reader to consider the nature of Pierston's wandering, thereby aiming to underline that *The Well-Beloved* reflects Hardy's aesthetic and mores beyond his own fin de siècle, which could be described as distinctively postmodern.②

Shazia Ghulam Mohammad, and Abdus Salam Khalis, in "Thomas Hardy's Tess: A Seductive Eve or a Blemished Woman?", argue that despite the fact that the character Tess Durbeyfield in Thomas Hardy's *Tess of the d'Urbervilles* has aroused bitter criticism from many critics and readers, she is considered as one of the most fascinating and charming fictional characters. Notwithstanding her inadequacies, Hardy remains emotionally committed to her to the last page of the book and never withdraws his inherent sympathy for her. Invested with tremendous strength, irresistible physical attraction and sensuality, she is an epitome of human

---

① Mohammad S G, Khalis A S. "Archetypal Patterns in Thomas Hardy's Depiction of Women". Putaj Humanities & Social Sciences, 2014, 21(1):9-15.

② Kim D. "Thomas Hardy's *The Well-Beloved*: A 'Ghost' Story". College Literature, 2014, 41(3):95-113.

frailties. Hardy presents her as an amalgamation of diverse impulses which complicates her situation. This paper aims at focusing on those aspects in her constitution which perplex readers as well as critics; hence making it difficult for them to determine whether she can be termed as "Seductive Eve" or she was just a passive victim of circumstantial conspiracies/compulsions. ①

Laura Green, in "'Strange [in] Difference of sex': Thomas Hardy, the Victorian Man of Letters, and the Temptations of Androgyny", presents information on Thomas Hardy, and his work and how he was perceived. Topics discussed include discussion on his last novel *Jude the Obscure* which relates to the Victorian perceptions of woman and man; background information on Hardy including his burial and cremation; distinction of gender in relation to the disagreement between Florence Dugdale Hardy, widow of Thomas Hardy and Sydney Cockerell; and exemplification of the self-made man including the origins of femininity and masculinity. ②

Tracy Hayes, in "Thomas Hardy's *Far from the Madding Crowd*", presents the highlights of the third annual Thomas Hardy Society Study Day held at the Corn Exchange in Dorchester, Dorset, England on April 13, 2019. Topics include Hardy's novel *Far from the Madding Crowd*; the book's reputation as the 10th greatest love story of all time; and the gender role issues tackled by the novel. ③

3. Theological Study

Stephen Platten, in "'They Know Earth-Secrets': Thomas Hardy's Tortured

---

① Mohammad S G, Khalis A S. "Thomas Hardy's Tess: A Seductive Eve or a Blemished Woman?". The Dialogue, 2013, 8(2):218-225.

② Green L. "'Strange [in] Difference of sex': Thomas Hardy, the Victorian Man of Letters, and the Temptations of Androgyny". Victorian Studies, 1995, 38(4):523-549.

③ Hayes T. "Thomas Hardy's *Far from the Madding Crowd*". Papers on Language & Literature, 2020, 56(2):210-219.

Vocation", believes that Thomas Hardy is often read as a quintessential example of the classical Victorian agnostic, or more likely atheist. To counter such a view, this article cites evidence from Hardy's poetry and prose as well as his life experience and influences, including the Dorset dialect poet William Barnes, Henry Moule, a son of the rectory and a great friend of Hardy's in his youth, and Arthur Shirley, the incumbent of Stinsford when Hardy was a boy. The culture, mores, and philosophical climate of his time challenged Hardy's faith in God and persuaded him of a more ethically focused religion, sometimes dubbed "evolutionary meliorism". This article argues that Hardy's continual movement in and out of religious faith with a sense of religious vocation directed his literary creativity. Readers encounter Hardy's continued fascination, indeed almost obsession, with religion in his literary work and in his introductory essays to collections of poetry. He refers to the (Roman) Catholic Modernists and to the true nature of the Church of England's vocation as a "national church". The creativity produced by this vocational tension and religious uncertainty bears fruit in Hardy's understanding of how religious thought and belief are carried through key controlling images. In this way, Hardy effectively preempts some of the creative work of Austin Farrer, the twentieth-century Anglican theologian and philosopher of religion. In sum, Thomas Hardy's literary achievement cannot be understood outside of his tortured religious belief and the tensions it created in his intellectual output. [1]

4. Biographical Study

Alexandra Mullen, in "Thomas Hardy Goes to Town", discusses the physical and imaginative movement of poet and novelist Thomas Hardy based on the analysis of scholar, poet and essayist Mark Ford. Hardy was believed to have been traveling

---

[1] Platten S. "'They Know Earth-Secrets': Thomas Hardy's Tortured Vocation". Religion & Literature, 2013, 45(3):59-79.

between Dorset and London in England according to his earliest surviving literary works *Dream of the City Shopwoman* and *Tess of the d'Urbervilles*. His residence in London, England in 1862 to work as an architect for ecclesiastical architecture is also mentioned. ①

Dana Huntley, in "Thomas Hardy's Wessex Country: Still Far from Madding Crowds", focuses on the region of Wessex, England, including the towns of Dorset and Dorchester, as depicted by British author Thomas Hardy in his novels *Far from the Madding Crowd* and *The Mayor of Casterbridge*. The author discusses Hardy's life in the region, explores the fictional landscape he created called Casterbridge, and presents travel information for the area. ②

Suzanne R. Johnson, in "Thomas Hardy the Obscure: Hardy's Final Fiction", analyzes the autobiographical books of Thomas Hardy. Topics discussed include two-volume biography book that Hardy began compiling around 1915; problems surrounding autobiography as a genre and the autobiographical act as a process; and association between Hardy's decision to write an authorized biography and his theories about fiction, reality and narrative which had developed during his writing career. ③

Floyd Skloot, in "Into a Maelstrom of Fire on Having a Feeling for Thomas Hardy", presents a personal narrative which explores the author's experience relating to projects about the novels of Thomas Hardy. ④

Genevieve Abravenel, in "Hardy's Transatlantic Wessex: Constructing the Local in *The Mayor of Casterbridge*", explores Thomas Hardy's *The Mayor of Casterbridge*. This essay points out that in today's society, there is often a

---

① Mullen A. "Thomas Hardy Goes to Town". The Hudson Review, 2017, 70(1):43-55.
② Huntley D. "Thomas Hardy's Wessex Country: Still Far from Madding Crowds". British Heritage, 2015, 36(4):24-29.
③ Johnson S R. "Thomas Hardy the Obscure: Hardy's Final Fiction". English Literature in Transition, 1880-1920, 1992, 35(3):300-308.
④ Skloot F. "Into a Maelstrom of Fire on Having a Feeling for Thomas Hardy". The Sewanee Review, 2008, 116(4):618-629.

discussion about globalization and its detriments, while others argue that globalization is not a modern construction. But in studying global policies, there has been a growth in recognizing what it means to be local. Hardy's novel emphasizes this, and through it, Hardy offers his criticism of England trading with North America. [1]

5. Narrative Study

Abdur Razaq, in "Symbolic Significance of Bird in Thomas Hardy's *The Mayor of Casterbridge*", investigates Hardy's employment of symbolism in *The Mayor of Casterbridge*, a masterpiece of Thomas Hardy. Hardy is primarily an artist and only incidentally a philosopher, so it is natural that he would present his philosophy artistically. He uses various artistic techniques to make his philosophy enriched. One of these techniques is the use of bird as a symbol. Thomas Hardy has used this symbol very skillfully. Through the use of bird imagery, he elucidates his philosophy as well as adds special artistic charm to his style. So far, his critics have only cursorily analyzed this symbol and have never applied it to an analysis of his philosophy. This study is an interpretation of this artistic technique and can be viewed as a new approach to an understanding of Hardy's philosophy. [2]

Lesley Goodman, in "Rebellious Identification, or, How I Learned to Stop Worrying and Love Arabella", discusses the concept of rebellious identification by reviewing Thomas Hardy's *Jude the Obscure*, a paradigmatic case of the term. It outlines two facets of the term, namely the emotional logic that exists outside of fiction and a relationship that is unique to fictional texts, between reader, character

---

[1] Abravenel G. "Hardy's Transatlantic Wessex: Constructing the Local in *The Mayor of Casterbridge*". Novel: A Forum on Fiction, 2005, 39(1):97-117.

[2] Razaq A. "Symbolic Significance of Bird in Thomas Hardy's *The Mayor of Casterbridge*". The Dialogue, 2011, 6(2):187-195.

and author. It reviews several other books depicting the meaning of the term, such as Judith Fetterley's *The Resisting Reader: A Feminists Approach to American Fiction*.①

6. New-historicism

Adam Grener, in "Hardy's Relics", focuses on novelist Thomas Hardy's discovery with the Dorset Natural History and Antiquarian Field Club in a speech entitled "Some Romano-British Relics Found at Max Gate". Topics discussed include his fascination with relics; his principle of his poetry; and his historicism. Also mentioned are the antiquarian perspective, processes of modernity, and historicity.②

Claire Senior, in "Shades of Gray: A Diachronic Reading of Thomas Hardy's *Neutral Tones*", notes that Thomas Hardy is one of the first writers to benefit from the knowledge of philology that becomes current in England in the 1860s, as seen in his poem *Neutral Tones*.③

Shannon L. Rogers, in "'The Historian of Wessex': Thomas Hardy's Contribution to History", argues that the struggle between content and form is one that has plagued historians for more than a century. In many ways, the field of history—and of historiography—was in its infancy during the Victorian era. Concurrent with its development was that of the historical novel. Inspired by the commercial and popular success of these novels, many historians attempted to make their accounts read more like fiction. This blurring of the line between history and fiction appears to have given more authority to pure fiction as historical source. Thus

---

① Goodman L. "Rebellious Identification, or, How I Learned to Stop Worrying and Love Arabella". Narrative, 2010, 18(2):163-178.

② Grener A. "Hardy's Relics". Modern Philology, 2016, 114(1):106-129.

③ Senior C. "Shades of Gray: A Diachronic Reading of Thomas Hardy's *Neutral Tones*". Victorian Poetry, 2006, 44(2):213-233.

it becomes fruitful to examine the works of these "unconscious historians" in order to reveal another side to history. Thomas Hardy, in particular, is an extremely valuable source for the history of life in southwestern England during the nineteenth century. He achieves the creation—usually unconscious—of historical documents through the medium of fictionalized social commentary. This is to create a record of rural society for later generations to examine as both a work of deliberate fiction and as a historical creation. His novels, informed as they are by his own experiences rather than simply by book-knowledge, is an accurate account of rural life through all of the century's developments, one which provides us with an alternative to academic cultural histories. ①

Felicia Bonaparte, in "The Deadly Misreading of Mythic Texts: Thomas Hardy's *Tess of the d'Urbervilles*", argues that Thomas Hardy's *Tess of the d'Urbervilles* is a novel much misread when it is taken, as it is, as a realistic narrative. But misreading of this kind is what Hardy is writing about. Both the characters and the story reenact, in modern dress, the classical myth of Persephone. Each of the characters in the novel misapprehends both his/her own identity and the meaning of the events, and does so each time with deadly consequences. But Hardy is not only illustrating in the errors of his characters the misconceptions of his age, he is making a substantive point about the act of reading itself. And our readings also have consequences. To read the story of Tess as a myth is to celebrate her fertility—both her physical fertility as well as her more mystical power to bring a spiritual rebirth. To see her as a fallen woman is to drive her to her death as a sinful social outcast. ②

Shannon L. Rogers, in "Medievalism in the Last Novel of Thomas Hardy: New Wine in Old Bottles", discusses the concept of medievalism in the novels of Thomas

---

① Rogers S L. "'The Historian of Wessex': Thomas Hardy's Contribution to History". Rethinking History, 2001, 5(2):217-232.

② Bonaparte F. "The Deadly Misreading of Mythic Texts: Thomas Hardy's *Tess of the d'Urbervilles*". International Journal of the Classical Tradition, 1999, 5(3):415-431.

Hardy. Topics discussed include significance of the Victorian era to Hardy; characteristics of the literary works of Hardy; and reason for the use of the element of the past on literature.①

John Halperin, in "Leslie Stephen, Thomas Hardy, and *A Pair of Blue Eyes*", focuses on the literary works of Thomas Hardy, a renowned novelist and poet. Much has been written about the famous scene in Hardy's novel *A Pair of Blue Eyes* in which the Knight slips over the edge of a cliff and, while dangling over a deep chasm, reviews several thousand years of world history before being rescued by a rope of lady's underwear. Carl J. Weber, a renowned author, says the scene was adapted by Hardy from an incident that occurred during a picnic he went on in August 1870 with his future first wife, Emma Lavinia Gifford, who lost an ear-ring during the day in a rocky crevice and asked Hardy, despite the heavy rain, to look for it. According to Weber, Hardy sketched two pictures of the scene and afterwards wrote a poem, *Where the Picnic Was*, recalling the day's events. The fictionalized version is the first indication in the novels of Hardy's ability to sustain interest in a tense situation by the sheer power of vivid description. Among Hardy's critics, Robert Gittings, as might be expected, comes closest to the truth. Gittings is pretty sure that some of the realistic details described in *A Pair of Blue Eyes* were based on an essay by Leslie Stephen titled "A Bad Five Minutes in the Alps".②

Aaron Matz, in "Hardy and the Vanity of Procreation", argues that it is difficult to ignore, in the fiction and poetry of Thomas Hardy, a persistent skepticism concerning the moral implications of procreation. In Hardy, having children seems an ethical dilemma; the infanticide scene in *Jude the Obscure* is only the most spectacular representation of this doubt. This essay asks how such a tendency can be accommodated within the form of the novel, typically understood

---

① Rogers S L. "Medievalism in the Last Novel of Thomas Hardy: New Wine in Old Bottles". English Literature in Transition, 1880-1920, 1999, 42(3):298-316.

② Halperin J. "Leslie Stephen, Thomas Hardy, and *A Pair of Blue Eyes*". Modern Language Review, 1980, 75(4):738-745.

as giving life rather than denying it. How can fiction represent a wish not to be—indeed, not to have been created in the first place? This is not only a representational question; it is a question about sexuality in Hardy's fiction (where contraception is absent), and it is a philosophical one, connecting Hardy to contemporary procreative ethics, especially the extreme position of antinatalism.①

Benjamin Cannon, in "'The True Meaning of the Word Restoration': Architecture and Obsolescence in *Jude the Obscure*", situates *Jude the Obscure* in the context of the Victorian architectural restoration debate, a pitched battle of ideas in which Thomas Hardy (a former architect and preservation activist) was deeply involved. For Hardy, architectural restoration threatens historical continuity by approaching history as a traumatic process that must be reversed. In *Jude the Obscure*, this restorationist vision is disastrously triumphant, trapping the novel's characters in cycles of meaningless repetition. In response, Hardy explores how the novel might serve as a compensatory medium, emplacing and connecting its characters in ways that material architecture no longer can. At the same time, Hardy imagines the printed text as a material object not unlike architecture, potentially opening up his work to contingent and unanticipated meanings.②

Jeffrey Meyers, in "Thomas Hardy & the Warriors", discusses the influence of the English author and poet Thomas Hardy on younger writers including D. H. Lawrence, Robert Graves, and Siegfried Sassoon. The personal relationships between Hardy and the other writers are examined, and the argument that the bleak, realistic nature of Hardy's poetry appealed to writers who fought in the World War Ⅰ is explored.③

---

① Matz A. "Hardy and the Vanity of Procreation". Victorian Studies, 2014, 57(1):7-32.
② Cannon B. "'The True Meaning of the Word Restoration': Architecture and Obsolescence in *Jude the Obscure*". Victorian Studies, 2014, 56(2):201-224.
③ Meyers J. "Thomas Hardy & the Warriors". The New Criterion, 2002, 21(1):34-40.

7. Ethical Study

Annette Federico, in "Thomas Hardy's *The Well-Beloved*: Love's Descent", presents literary criticism which offers literary criticism for the novel *The Well-Beloved*, by novelist Thomas Hardy. The author focuses on the main character Jocelyn Pierston, who is seeking individual fulfillment through both art and love. The author discusses the issue of human transcendence in relation to Pierston and compares her attempts at transcendence with the philosophical theories of philosopher Iris Murdoch concerning moral philosophy and metaphysics.[①]

Caroline Sumpter, in "On Suffering and Sympathy: *Jude the Obscure*, Evolution, and Ethics", links Thomas Hardy's exploration of sympathy in *Jude the Obscure* to contemporary scientific debates over moral evolution. Tracing the relationship between pessimism, progressivism, and determinism in Hardy's understanding of sympathy, it also considers Hardy's conception of the author as enlarger of "social sympathies"—a position, the author argues, that was shaped by Leslie Stephen's advocacy of novel writing as moral art. Considering Hardy's engagement with writings by Charles Darwin, T. H. Huxley, Herbert Spencer, and others, the author explores the novel's participation in a debate about the evolutionary significance of sympathy and its implications for Hardy's understanding of moral agency. Hardy offered a stronger defence of morality based on biological determinism than Darwin, but this determinism was linked to an unexpected evolutionary optimism.[②]

[①] Federico A. "Thomas Hardy's *The Well-Beloved*: Love's Descent". English Literature in Transition, 1880-1920, 2007, 50(3):269-290.

[②] Sumpter C. "On Suffering and Sympathy: *Jude the Obscure*, Evolution, and Ethics". Victorian Studies, 2011, 53(4):665-687.

8. Thematic Study

Jeanette Roberts Shumaker, in "Abjection and Degeneration in Thomas Hardy's *Barbara of the House of Grebe*", explores Thomas Hardy's gothic tale *Barbara of the House of Grebe*, which dramatizes the horrid consequences of belief in the Victorian myth of degeneration. Topics discussed include explanation on the popularity of degenerationism during Hardy's era; description of the character Barbara; and investigation on the abjection of Barbara and the degeneration of Uplandtowers. [1]

9. Psychological Study

Margaret Kolb, in "Plot Circles: Hardy's Drunkards and Their Walks", argues that Thomas Hardy's Wessex novels move in circles: characters retrace their steps, and history repeats itself. The limited geography registers and reflects both movements. At the same time, the novels repeatedly figure choice as binary—limited to two seemingly equivalent alternatives. This essay argues that these apparently disparate features of Hardy's plots are, in fact, structurally linked. Circular movement and binary choice echo through contemporary cultural artifacts, ranging from popular board games to mathematical and biological theories. Drawing on developments in the mathematical study of probability—the drunkard's walk and the Markov chain—this essay claims that Hardy's binary choices generate his

---

[1] Shumaker J R. "Abjection and Degeneration in Thomas Hardy's *Barbara of the House of Grebe*". College Literature, 1999, 26(2):1-16.

characters' roundabout geographic trajectories, transforming Victorian models for human motion and choice into a formal principle for the novel.①

10. Gender Study

Karin Koehler, in "Late-Victorian Polemics about Sexual Knowledge in Thomas Hardy and Sarah Grand", explores the relationship between literary fiction and sexual knowledge in late Victorian Britain, arguing that far from existing in a simply contextual relationship to the making and consumption of the period's literature, late Victorian polemics about sexual knowledge were refracted in the content and narrative form of popular fiction. Despite the volume and diversity of Victorian publications offering sexual information and advice, historic states of knowledge remain a subject of conjecture. Focusing on Thomas Hardy's *Tess of the d'Urbervilles* and Sarah Grand's *The Heavenly Twins*, two bestselling novels with heroines who occupy the "borderland" between child- and adulthood, this discussion considers how writers of fiction respond to issues of sexual epistemology in their plots and narrative methods. Hardy's novel is informed by a radical endorsement of sexual knowledge, while Grand's work is characterized by a more careful consideration of how sexual information should be communicated.②

---

① Kolb M. "Plot Circles: Hardy's Drunkards and Their Walks". Victorian Studies, 2014, 56(4):596-623.
② Koehler K. "Late-Victorian Polemics about Sexual Knowledge in Thomas Hardy and Sarah Grand". English Literature in Transition, 1880-1920, 2020, 63(2):211-233.

Chapter 9

D. H. Lawrence

D. H. Lawrence (1885-1930)

Lawrence was born in a family of five children in Nottinghamshire, as the son of a schoolteacher and a miner. Amid often brutal poverty, Lawrence managed with the love and help of his mother to excel in school; he won a scholarship to attend high school until he was forced to find a job. After a period of working, he resumed his education at the University of Nottingham with the aim of earning a teaching certificate. It was at this point that he began writing, mostly poetry and short stories. His first novel, *The White Peacock*, was followed by *The Trespasser* and then by his great autobiographical novel *Sons and Lovers*. Having eloped with Frieda Weekley in 1912, Lawrence embarked on a turbulent marital life that included an enormous amount of travel to such places as Ceylon, Australia, the United States, and Mexico. *The Rainbow* marked the beginning of his persistent troubles with censorship, a problem that dogged the publication of *Women in Love* for five years and would later make *Lady Chattertey's Lover* notorious. His other works include *The Lost Girl*, *Aaron's Rod*, *Kangaroo*, and *The Plumed Serpent*.[①]

---

① Richetti J, Bender J, David D, et al. The Columbia History of the British Novel. New York: Columbia University Press, 1994.

Critical Perspectives

1. Narrative Study

Viana da Silva, and Carlos Augusto, in "*The Fox*: D. H. Lawrence's Short Novel in Mark Rider's Film", investigate the particular reading of the modern short novel *The Fox*, by the English writer D. H. Lawrence in Mark Ryder's film, analyzing the theme of completeness, its rewriting on screen through the characters' love affair, and its fit into the parameters of the cinematographic system, with a new narrative configuration closer to the social and cultural discursive claims of the reception context. [1]

Earl G. Ingersoll, in "D. H. Lawrence's *Mr. Noon* as a Postmodern Text", analyzes the book *Mr. Noon*, by D. H. Lawrence as a postmodern text. At the center of contemporary discussion of Postmodernism, or perhaps more precisely Postmodernisms, is a disagreement over which writers and even which works by those writers represent the beginnings of the movement. *Mr. Noon* is eligible for interpretation as a postmodern text not because it appeared long after what everyone considers the end of modernism but because it contains elements which violate the tenets of a modernism to which, perhaps, Lawrence never fully subscribed. Since *Mr. Noon* appeared only a few years ago, some discussion of the circumstances of its composition and delayed publication may be in order. According to the diary of Lawrence, he began work on *Mr. Noon* in May 1920, only months after he and his wife Frieda had finally managed to escape from England, following the long ordeal of

---

[1] Da Silva V, Augusto C. "*The Fox*: D. H. Lawrence's Short Novel in Mark Rider's Film". Revista FSA, 2020, 17(7):239-252.

the Great War which he and their marriage had barely survived. After Lawrence's death in 1930, the typescript of Part 1 of *Mr. Noon* was returned to Frieda, and it appeared in 1934 as the long short story *Mr. Noon* in the collection *A Modern Lover*. The lost manuscript of the much longer Part 2 passed through various hands until it appeared on the auction block in 1972.①

2. Cultural Study

Kyle Smith, in "Foreign Accents", focuses on the works on English writer D. H. Lawrence. It mentions that Lawrence eschews pressing a point about the exploitation of workers in favor of honest portraiture of the kinds of people he knew in his hometown of Eastwood. It also mentions that the musical *Space Dogs* made by Nick Blaemire and Van Hughes has the frisky spirit of an undergraduate fringe show.②

3. Comparative Study

Susie Gharib, in "The Interweaving of Color and Theme: Purple and Blue in the Works of D. H. Lawrence and Virginia Woolf", argues that both Virginia Woolf and D. H. Lawrence are considered great colorists. Many critics have studied the visual quality of these painterly writers, but this essay attempts to show how they similarly interweave color with theme in the fabric of their literary works.③

Deanna Wendel, in "'There Will Be a New Embodiment, in a New Way': Alternative Posthumanisms in *Women in Love*", places *Women in Love* in dialogue

---

① Ingersoll E G. "D. H. Lawrence's *Mr. Noon* as a Postmodern Text". Modern Language Review, 1990, 85(2):304-309.

② Smith K. "Foreign Accents". The New Criterion, 2022, 40(8):55-58.

③ Gharib S. "The Interweaving of Color and Theme: Purple and Blue in the Works of D. H. Lawrence and Virginia Woolf". Pennsylvania Literary Journal, 2019, 11(2):182-189.

with posthumanism in order to understand what kind of a nonhuman world the novel might be imagining when Rupert Birkin declares that "humanity is a dead letter", and when characters alternately degrade and idealize what they identify as the inhuman, superhuman, or extra-human. The author argues that Lawrence's array of prefixes does not graft easily onto the "post" of posthumanism, and that *Women in Love* constantly invokes, but never settles on a definitive answer to Katherine Hayles's question: "What kind of posthumans will we be?" Instead, the novel enacts a series of alternative posthumanisms that, through their vexed encodings of the human and humanist, direct us to reflect on the merits and limitations of our own contemporary theorizations. ①

Anca Mihaela Dobrinescu, in "A Realist Modernist's Challenge to Readers' Expectations", focuses on how D. H. Lawrence, one of the most controversial figures of modernism, succeeds in challenging his audience's expectations by a subtle combination of conventional and innovative elements. *Women in Love*, deceivingly constructed as a realist novel, turns out to be nothing but a novel in which all the anxieties and uncertainties of the modern individual at the beginning of the twentieth century are brought to the fore. Lawrence's main interest in *Women in Love* is the modern individual, socially and individually perceived, whose identity is built up out of the fragmentary, sometimes unequivocal identities of the various characters of the novel. ②

Paul Eggert, in "The Dutch-Australian Connection: Willem Sibenhaar, D. H. Lawrence, *Max Havelaar* and *Kangaroo*", looks at the link between authors D. H. Lawrence and Willem Sibenhaar in the Australian literary field. Topics discussed include career and social background of Sibenhaar; differences in the opinions of Lawrence and Sibenhaar on politics; ideas of Sibenhaar reflected in Lawrence's

---

① Wendel D. "'There Will Be a New Embodiment, in a New Way': Alternative Posthumanisms in *Women in Love*". Journal of Modern Literature, 2013, 36(3):120-137.

② Dobrinescu A M. "A Realist Modernist's Challenge to Readers' Expectations". Petroleum-Gas University of Ploiesti Bulletin, Philology Series, 2010, 62(2):163-168.

book *Kangaroo*; and contributions of Sibenhaar to the Australian literary field.①

4. Psychological Study

Peter Balbert, in "From Relativity to Paraphrenia in D. H. Lawrence's *The Man Who Loved Islands*: Speculations on Einstein, Freud, Gossamer Webs, and Seagulls", argues that the development of D. H. Lawrence's *The Man Who Loved Islands* through Cathcart's consecutive ownership of three islands engages the consequences of Cathcart's intense isolation from humanity. In the process of charting the steps in this character's collapse of body, mind, and spirit, Lawrence employs metaphors that explicitly connect to Einstein's notions of relativity and spacetime. In addition to this fictionalized adaptation of contemporary research in astrophysics, Lawrence cumulatively relates the palpable decline of Cathcart's equilibrium, the pattern of his anxiety, and the context of his depression to precise pathologies outlined in Freud's work the previous decade about obsessional neurosis, melancholia, and ultimately, paraphrenia. Lawrence's awareness of the work of an innovative psychiatrist and writer, Trigant Burrow, provides additional insight into Lawrence's personal preoccupations and doctrinal emphasis in the tale.②

Armando Pereira, in "D. H. Lawrence. México, la utopía imposible", notes that Lawrence finds in Mexico the country where he could realize one of the more important desires in his life: to buy a ranch and build there a sort of commune, where he, his wife and his closest friends could live in a creative way and free of the oppressive rationality, anxiety of technique and obsession of progress that had

---

① Eggert P. "The Dutch-Australian Connection: Willem Sibenhaar, D. H. Lawrence, *Max Havelaar* and *Kangaroo*". Australian Literary Studies, 2003, 21(1): 3-19.

② Balbert P. "From Relativity to Paraphrenia in D. H. Lawrence's *The Man Who Loved Islands*: Speculations on Einstein, Freud, Gossamer Webs, and Seagulls". Journal of Modern Literature, 2020, 43(2): 60-79.

swallowed Europe up. That project he could only realize not in life, but in a novel *The Plumed Serpent*. In this essay, the author tries to analyze this novel and other short stories, in which Lawrence exposes his variegated, contradictory and disillusioned points of view about Mexico and its people. ①

5. Gender Study

Sam Halliday, in "Electricity and Homosexuality: From 19th-century American Sexual Health Literature to D. H. Lawrence", surveys a range of scientific, popular scientific and literary texts from the late-19th- to the early 20th-centuries in order to demonstrate electricity's importance within theories of sexuality, in general, and homosexuality, in particular. ②

N. S. Boone, in "D. H. Lawrence's Theology of the Body: Intersections with John Paul II's *Man and Woman He Created Them*", examines the philosophical foundations of both D. H. Lawrence's sexual ethics and the "theology of the body" developed by Pope John Paul II. Although Lawrence is often viewed, rightly in most cases, as a critic of Christianity, and even though his work has been scorned or outright banned by Christian groups over the years, Lawrence's overarching view of life in his later years was remarkably amenable to Catholic Christianity. Linking Lawrence with Christian and even Catholic thought is not unique, as two books from the 1950s make claims very similar to the author. But these critical works are almost six decades past, and this article primarily contributes to this earlier criticism by aligning Lawrence with the theology of sexuality developed by Pope John Paul II. Though Pope and Lawrence do differ on

---

① Pereira A. "D. H. Lawrence. México, la utopía imposible". Literatura Mexicana, 2013, 24(1):65-90.

② Halliday S. "Electricity and Homosexuality: From 19th-century American Sexual Health Literature to D. H. Lawrence". Centaurus, 2015, 57(3):212-228.

some points, they do not differ substantially in their philosophical stances regarding the mind/body relationship or the absolute necessity of full reciprocity in sexual intercourse. This essay does not claim that Lawrence was a Catholic, or even a Christian, or that if he had lived longer he would have converted to Catholicism. In his own mind, he had made a clean break with Christianity. But as some of his late essays extol the virtues of the Catholic Church's development of the sacrament of marriage, Lawrence may not have been surprised to see how thoroughly his thoughts on sex and marriage align with those of the late Pope.①

Judith P. Saunders, in "Female Mate-Guarding in Lawrence's *Wintry Peacock*: An Evolutionary Perspective", argues that D. H. Lawrence's 1921 story *Wintry Peacock* presents a vivid example of female mate-guarding behavior, along with the male counter-strategies it provokes. Employing an elaborate yet subtle allusion to a tale from classical mythology, Lawrence underlines the archetypal—and, indirectly, the Adaptationist—significance of the male-female conflict he depicts. The allusion explains the otherwise puzzling presence of the title peacock, moreover, a non-human character who serves as a magnet for the fierce emotions of the battling husband and wife. Conflict between the sexes is inevitable, as the story indicates, and men and women are caught up in a contest neither sex can win definitively. Evolutionary theory helps to identify the causes of this conflict, which is rooted in innate biological differences. Deeply ingrained in evolved adaptations, male and female behavioral tactics are bound to collide, creating mutual frustration. Instead of demanding sympathy for either the male or female point of view, Lawrence's story encourages readers to view the vicissitudes of intersexual competition with detachment.②

---

① Boone N S. "D. H. Lawrence's Theology of the Body: Intersections with John Paul II's *Man and Woman He Created Them*". Religion & the Arts, 2014, 18(4):498-520.
② Saunders J P. "Female Mate-Guarding in Lawrence's *Wintry Peacock*: An Evolutionary Perspective". College Literature, 2012, 39(4):69-83.

6. Ethical Study

N. S. Boone, "D. H. Lawrence between Heidegger and Levinas: Individuality and Otherness", presents the art ethics used by novelist D. H. Lawrence which highlights its relationship with philosophers Martin Heidegger and Emmanuel Levinas. It offers a discussion of the ethical discourse between Heidegger's individual authenticity ontology and Levinas's radical alterity. The author also discusses the use of Heideggerian posture in his novels.[①]

Peter Balbert, in "From Panophilia to Phallophobia: Sublimation and Projection in D. H. Lawrence's *St. Mawr*", presents literary criticism of the book *St. Mawr* by D. H. Lawrence. Particular focus is given to the psychosexual aspects of the novel and to the roles of sublimation and projection in the text. Details on Lawrence's relationship with his wife, Frieda, are presented. Other topics include gender, the Greek god Pan, and narration.[②]

7. New-historicism

Geoffrey Robertson, in "Trial of the Century", discusses the British censorship court case of 1960 in which Penguin Books defended their right to publish *Lady Chatterley's Lover* by D. H. Lawrence in a jury trial against charges of obscenity. Some of the subjects considered include the British Obscene Publications Act of 1959; literature and social classes; and the use of expert witnesses by Penguin's defense lawyer Michael Rubinstein. The author considers how the jury's decision to

---

① Boone N S. "D. H. Lawrence between Heidegger and Levinas: Individuality and Otherness". Renascence, 2016, 68(1):49-69.

② Balbert P. "From Panophilia to Phallophobia: Sublimation and Projection in D. H. Lawrence's *St. Mawr*". Papers on Language & Literature, 2013, 49(1):37-69.

allow Penguin to publish the book allowed for later liberalization of British social laws including those covering divorce, birth control, and film censorship. ①

Nils Clausson, in "Practicing Deconstruction, Again: Blindness, Insight and the Lovely Treachery of Words in D. H. Lawrence's *The Blind Man*", argues that at a time when the turn to history and various forms of cultural studies frames the practice of literary studies as an either/or choice between a cultural/historical criticism of political engagement with issues of race, gender and ethnicity, or a retreat into formalism and aesthetic, we are in danger of losing sight of the most valuable lesson of deconstruction: that whatever else literary critics do we must read texts closely. Taking D. H. Lawrence's aphorism "the proper function of the critic is to save the tale from the artist who created it" as its starting point, this paper offers an analysis of D. H. Lawrence's short story *The Blind Man* to demonstrate that the charges most frequently levelled against deconstruction—that is leads to relativism, anarchy, conservatism, meaninglessness and paralyzing undecidability—are not supported by a deconstructionist reading of Lawrence's story. ②

Duane Edwards, in "Locating D. H. Lawrence in *The Plumed Serpent*", discusses aspects of novelist D. H. Lawrence's beliefs and sensibilities as revealed in his letters and essays. It notes that they espouse opinions which differ from those of fictional characters in his novels. It, therefore, argues that Lawrence should not be judged personally by traits of his fictional characters, and his novels should not be taken as positions taken by the author. It cites Lawrence's novel *The Plumed Serpent*, which was subjected to harsh criticism for being barbaric, as an impetus for criticism which called Lawrence racist, sexist, fascist and anti-Christian. It notes that Lawrence did seek to disturb his readers and sought a fuller relationship with

---

① Robertson G. "Trial of the Century". History Today, 2010, 60(11):41-44.
② Clausson N. "Practicing Deconstruction, Again: Blindness, Insight and the Lovely Treachery of Words in D. H. Lawrence's *The Blind Man*". College Literature, 2007, 34(1):106-128.

oneself, humanity and the universe.[①]

A. Banerjee, in "D. H. Lawrence's Discovery of American Literature", focuses on the distinctive quality of the American literature as described by writer D. H. Lawrence. According to him, the American literature expresses a new experience in an accent which belonged to the American continent and nowhere else. It comments that his observations on the life of the people living in America gave him a new perspective on the American people and their literature.[②]

Catherine Brown, in "The Russian Soul Englished", argues that the reception of Russian literature in English translation lowered self-consciousness in the use of the term "soul" by English authors. Virginia Woolf and D. H. Lawrence provide evidence of an opposite effect. Russian literature has a significant and enduring impact on its use in English literary production.[③]

John Rodden, in "Paul Morel's Second Home: The Role of the Factory Employees in *Sons and Lovers*", presents literary criticism of the book *Sons and Lovers* by D. H. Lawrence. It highlights the journey of character Paul Morel from his home to the Jordans's surgical appliances factory in Nottingham, England, owned by character Mr. Jordan. The author focuses on the role of the factory employees in the novel, comparing Paul's factory relationships with the major friendships and relationships of his childhood. His relationships with men and women factory workers are compared.[④]

[①] Edwards D. "Locating D. H. Lawrence in *The Plumed Serpent*". Midwest Quarterly, 2010, 51(2):183-199.

[②] Banerjee A. "D. H. Lawrence's Discovery of American Literature". The Sewanee Review, 2011, 119(3):469-475.

[③] Brown C. "The Russian Soul Englished". Journal of Modern Literature, 2012, 36(1):132-149.

[④] Rodden J. "Paul Morel's Second Home: The Role of the Factory Employees in *Sons and Lovers*". Papers on Language & Literature, 2011, 47(1):26-44.

8. Biographical Study

Jeffrey Meyers, in "The Quest for D. H. Lawrence", describes how the author goes about in uncovering new information about poet and novelist D. H. Lawrence for his biography. Topics discussed include comparison between Lawrence's and Ernest Hemingway's biography; desire to write an analytical and interpretive narrative; and Lawrence's relationship with journalist Esther Andrews. [1]

Brooke Allen, in "D. H. Lawrence in Decline", reflects on the life and works of D. H. Lawrence, poet and preacher, and his diminishing reputation. Scholar John Worthen wrote in his biography of Lawrence and pointed out that the titanic reputation of Lawrence had already diminished and many English departments in the United States and Great Britain had stopped teaching him. [2]

John Worthen, in "'Wild Turkeys': Some Versions of America by D. H. Lawrence", argues that D. H. Lawrence's desire to go to the United States in 1917-1918 leads to his planning and then writing of the essays, which is finally published as *Studies in Classic American Literature* (1923), and all of them were conceived and written with ambivalence. He revised the essays for the last time in New Mexico in the autumn and early winter of 1922, and "Americanized" them for his new American market. In particular, his essay on Walt Whitman now refused to allow the great writer to be an iconic figure. Lawrence's satirical version of Whitman set out to undermine the seriousness with which Whitman took himself and with which he was generally taken. Lawrence was attacked for his ignorance of American writing, but he had set out to track the American obsession with power and death, satirically; he remained in an uneasy and finally unresolved relationship

---

[1] Meyers J. "The Quest for D. H. Lawrence". Virginia Quarterly Review, 1990, 66(2): 249-261.

[2] Allen B. "D. H. Lawrence in Decline". The New Criterion, 2006, 24(9): 4-9.

with American writing. ①

John Turner, in "'Reducing Down': D. H. Lawrence and Captain Scott", presents information on a letter written by author D. H. Lawrence in response to extracts from Captain Scott's journal in 1913. Topics discussed include background on racial degeneration in Great Britain; views of Lawrence on heroism and decadence; and details on the short story *New Eve and Old Adam*. ②

9. Reader-response Criticism

Michael Ragussis, in "The False Myth of *St. Mawr*: Lawrence and the Subterfuge of Art", presents a literary critique of the novella *St. Mawr*, by D. H. Lawrence, focusing on how its aesthetic principles violate the very writings which the author presents in his criticism. Topics addressed include the notion of artistic work as subterfuge; the prevalence of bluffing and false pretenses throughout the plot of the story; and the extent to which the reader identifies or disassociates with the main protagonist. ③

10. Aesthetical Study

Andrew Kalaidjian, in "Positive Inertia: D. H. Lawrence and the Aesthetics of Generation", argues that "inertia" becomes a key term for D. H. Lawrence's understanding of energy and materiality, leading him to a unique environmental aesthetics that stresses the body's constant engagement with its surroundings. His

---

① Worthen J. "'Wild Turkeys': Some Versions of America by D. H. Lawrence". European Journal of American Culture, 2005, 24(2):91-103.
② Turner J. "'Reducing Down': D. H. Lawrence and Captain Scott". 2002, 14(3): 14-27.
③ Ragussis M. "The False Myth of *St. Mawr*: Lawrence and the Subterfuge of Art". Papers on Language & Literature, 2014, 50(3): 352-364.

articulation of "positive inertia" as an attention to the limits, needs, and fragility of human life serves as an important counterpoint to modernism's obsession with autonomy, excess, and limitless production. Lawrence fully develops this critique in *The Rainbow*, where the negative inertia of industrialism and coal mining is juxtaposed to the positive inertia of familial generation and personal growth. This aesthetics of generation leads to a model of community based on ecological dependencies rather than hierarchical power structures. ①

11. Philosophical Study

Desmond Manderson, in "Between the Nihilism of the Young and the Positivism of the Old: Justice and the Novel in D. H. Lawrence", discusses the philosophy of nihilism and the works of English novelist D. H. Lawrence. It appreciates Lawrence's novel *Kangaroo* as something like a Gesamtkunstwerk. It analyzes Lawrence's painterly writing in *Kangaroo*, which is essentially performative and is a gramaphone type of novel. ②

Peter Balbert, in "Courage at the Border-Line: Balder, Hemingway, and Lawrence's *The Captain's Doll*", discusses the characterization of attitude as depicted in the book *The Captain's Doll* by D. H. Lawrence. The work by Lawrence has been viewed as a supreme example of his genius in conveying the shifts of poise and tone defining a delicate complexity of attitude. The subtle changes in character development and narrative perspective are considered to reflect nothing less than the range of a great dramatic poet. ③

---

① Kalaidjian A. "Positive Inertia: D. H. Lawrence and the Aesthetics of Generation". Journal of Modern Literature, 2014, 38(1):38-55.

② Manderson D. "Between the Nihilism of the Young and the Positivism of the Old: Justice and the Novel in D. H. Lawrence". Law & Humanities, 2012, 6(1):1-23.

③ Balbert P. "Courage at the Border-Line: Balder, Hemingway, and Lawrence's *The Captain's Doll*". Papers on Language & Literature, 2006, 42(3):227-263.

Erwin Ray Steinberg, in "D. H. Lawrence: Mythographer", discusses D. H. Lawrence's use of myth in his novels to serve his own purposes. Topics discussed include ways in which Lawrence pulls references from a variety of resources and molds them to a pattern to suit his own needs; use of allusions from Greek mythology, the Old and New Testament, and other sources; and use of a variety of books which dealt with various religions and showed how religion functioned within certain cultures. ①

Thomas L. Jeffers, in "'We Children Were the In-betweens': Character(De) Formation in *Sons and Lovers*", discusses the problem of transcendence that confronts the character of Paul Morel in D. H. Lawrence's book *Sons and Lovers*. Topics discussed include how the web of circumstance within which Morel struggles is mediated by the micro-society of his family; effects of Morel's relationship with his mother; and the therapeutic aspect of the novel. ②

12. Eco-criticism Study

Annaon Barcz, in "On D. H. Lawrence's *Snake* that Slips out of the Text: Derrida's Reading of the Poem", confronts and compares Derrida's "close reading" of the poem *Snake* (by D. H. Lawrence) with questions about the philosopher's speculations in the interest of animal ethics. Discussion focuses on how the animal in *Snake* is represented and how Derrida combines ethics with aesthetics in his ninth lecture of *The Beast and the Sovereign*. The text, according to Derrida, leads to an old biblical statement in front of a real beast: "Thou shalt not kill". What does it mean that the snake was before man, and that the scene takes

---

① Steinberg E R. "D. H. Lawrence: Mythographer". Journal of Modern Literature, 2001, 25(1): 91-108.

② Jeffers T L. "'We Children Were the In-betweens': Character(De) Formation in *Sons and Lovers*". Texas Studies in Literature & Language, 2000, 42(3):290-313.

place near a water source? Why is the snake a beast that becomes a sovereign, an uncrowned king in the underworld? Finally, Derrida's understanding that the snake is a victim from the Garden of Eden is discussed. ①

13. Cultural Study

Gertrude Schwartzman, in "D. H. Lawrence's *The Daughter-in-law*: Transforming a Family System", argues that D. H. Lawrence's play *The Daughter-in-law*, written in 1912, explores underlying, implicit conflict within a family. Set in a small mining town in England, the family consists of Mrs. Gascoyne, her sons Luther and Joe, and her daughter-in-law, Minnie, Luther's wife. The central conflict is between Mrs. Gascoyne and Minnie, who challenges her mother-in-law's control over her sons, who also compete with each other for the love and recognition of their mother. Joe, the youngest son, perturbs the family system and acts as a mediator, functioning as a family therapist. He sets a process in motion through which the rigid family alliances are challenged and ultimately realigned. Mrs. Gascoyne's self-image as a perfect, self-sacrificing, self-righteous mother ultimately is transformed, and she accepts Minnie as a family member. Brandchaft's concept of "pathological accommodation" explicates how enmeshed family members can collide, and thereby stultify their personal development. As Joe plays his role of "family therapist", the family dynamic changes. Through the process of rupture and repair, each family member begins to recognize the needs of the other, and thereby a path for differentiation, individuation, and autonomy becomes possible for them. ②

---

① Barcz A. "On D. H. Lawrence's *Snake* that Slips out of the Text: Derrida's Reading of the Poem". Brno Studies in English, 2013, 39(1):167-182.

② Schwartzman G. "D. H. Lawrence's *The Daughter-in-law*: Transforming a Family System". International Forum of Psychoanalysis, 2011, 20(3):176-182.

Chapter 10

James Joyce

James Joyce(1882-1941)

Joyce was born in Dublin. Disgusted with Irish provincialism and Roman Catholic bigotry, he left Ireland for Paris in 1902. Except for two brief visits, he lived with his wife, Nora Barnacle, in Europe for the rest of his life, in Paris, Trieste, and Zurich. The publication of his collection of short fiction, *Dubliners*, occasioned his last visit to Ireland, and his autobiographical novel, *A Portrait of the Artist as a Young Man* was published serially in the celebrated journal *The Egoist* in 1914 and 1915. Hampered by a severe case of glaucoma, Joyce survived through the support of patrons like Harriet Shaw Weaver. Joyce published his greatest work, *Ulysses*, in Paris in 1922. Although banned in the United States as obscene, it was immediately hailed by many as a modernist masterpiece that revolutionized the art of the novel. His last work, *Finnegans Wake*, has drawn much critical attention, but its forbidding complexity has discouraged most readers. [1]

---

[1] Richetti J, Bender J, David D, et al. The Columbia History of the British Novel. New York: Columbia University Press, 1994.

Critical Perspectives

1. Psychological Study

Zennure Köseman, in "James Joyce's Manifestation of Epiphany in Ernest Hemingway's *Big Two-Hearted River*", highlights that Ernest Hemingway's main character, Nick Adams, acquires an epiphany of natural healing by returning to his childhood fishing terrains. Hemingway specifies the terrifying reality of World War I through Nick Adams' having a psychological disturbance from the war by reflecting nature's profound healing source in *Big Two-Hearted River*. Following his return, Nick Adams overcomes the battle disturbances psychologically by diving into the natural fishing area. When he visits his previous fishing environment, he revives himself from terrible war memories. His escape into nature implies that he, thereby, is the lover of nature. Through the acquisition of natural healing in his childhood fishing areas, Hemingway, concurrently, manifests James Joyce's epiphany in his target short story. Nick Adams becomes relaxed while possessing a peaceful mind in natural living. Therefore, this article, being interested in Nick Adams' thinking and diving into his previous living areas, focuses on how he has a maturity within himself in nature.[①]

Louis Armand, in "'He Proves by Algebra': James Joyce's Post-Literary Incest Machines", asserts that Richard Ellmann's well-known assertion that "we are still learning to be James Joyce's contemporaries" carries with it a number of proscriptive implications for how we view the very possibility of a "writing after Joyce". We see these refracted not only within the Joyce industry, but also in the

---

① Köseman Z. "James Joyce's Manifestation of Epiphany in Ernest Hemingway's *Big Two-Hearted River*". Gaziantep University Journal of Social Sciences, 2021, 20(4):1795-1804.

persistent haunting of contemporary (experimental) literature by what we might call a modernist false-consciousness. ①

Genevieve Sartor, in "A Joycean Interface: Re-Territorializing between Deleuze and Lacan", argues that aspects of Jacques Lacan's late seminar on James Joyce supplements his failed attempt to work with Gilles Deleuze. Lacan's *Seminar XXIII* was presented shortly after the publication of Deleuze and Felix Guattari's *Anti-Oedipus*, and he asserts that Joyce's use of language, particularly in *Finnegans Wake*, exemplifies how creative and potentially psychotic self-naming can operate as an Oedipal traversal, transforming the symptom into what Lacan terms the sinthome. This article argues that Lacan's theory of the sinthome significantly reconfigures his prior psychoanalytic frameworks due to engagement with concepts found in *Anti-Oedipus*. Critically fortifying this correlation provides the means for etching out a theoretical intersection between Deleuze, Guattari, and Lacan, and it consequently provides an innovative interpretation of Lacan's late work. ②

Mary Adams, in "The Beauty of *Finnegans Wake*: Remembering and Re-Imagining: A Return to the Father", considers James Joyce's immersion in *Finnegans Wake* as his way of controlling his imagination and holding together emotionally. As a sensitive, bright and impressionable child, he had much to contend with, including being a "replacement child", born into his parents' grief at losing other children. This can create lasting guilt and confusion in the surviving child: do they have the right to an existence of their own, or should they, like Joyce, go into exile? The author describes the fears that plagued Joyce and how a proleptic imagination, and his phenomenal memory, gave him a sense of control. Placing *Finnegans Wake* in a timeless dream world gave Joyce space, but within a carefully boundaried structure. Joyce's love affair with language enables him to produce his own elaborate *Book of Kells* playfully, in which punning and parody

---

① Armand L. "'He Proves by Algebra': James Joyce's Post-Literary Incest Machines". Journal of Modern Literature, 2021, 44(3):63-75.

② Sartor G. "A Joycean Interface: Re-Territorializing between Deleuze and Lacan". University of Toronto Quarterly, 2018, 87(2):1-15.

distract from the grief which underlies the work. At the centre is a Dublin family in a story which loosely parallels Sophocles' Oedipus, playing out the internal world of the "replacement child" who fears he was responsible for the siblings' deaths. The beauty of *Finnegans Wake* is the extraordinary way that Joyce stays afloat, producing a unique masterpiece of levity and poetry. ①

Robert Kaplan, in "Madness and James Joyce", considers the association between the author James Joyce and madness. Joyce lived closer to the state of madness than he would have preferred. His mother died in a state of delirium. His daughter Lucia developed hebephrenic schizophrenia and was permanently hospitalised. His son married a manic depressive. Joyce, an acute observer of the world around him, portrayed different states of madness in his writings, most famously in the Nighttown chapter of *Ulysses*. Critics of his works accused him of being mad, interpreting his use of the stream-of-consciousness and other unique literary techniques as the product of a disordered mind. A psychiatrist referred to him as the schizoid origin of his daughter's insanity. Yet Joyce, who displayed an extraordinary discipline in writing his works, always had a clear idea of his intentions and believed his approach would ultimately be vindicated. ②

Mike Harding, in "James Joyce's Concept of the Underthought", presents a discourse delivered by Mike Harding in the 19th Annual Conference of the Society for Existential Analysis regarding James Joyce's concept of underthought and some of its similarities with the work of philosopher Ludwig Wittgenstein. It explores the images or metaphors of language use in Joycean studies. It examines the similarities of underthought in Joyce's novel *Ulysses* with the ideas of Wittgenstein. ③

J. B. Lyons, in "James Joyce: Steps towards a Diagnosis", makes pronouncements on James Joyce's health. A publication in this genre claims he had tabes dorsalis. One

---

① Adams M. "The Beauty of *Finnegans Wake*. Remembering and Re-Imagining: A Return to the Father". British Journal of Psychotherapy, 2018, 34(3):467-483.

② Kaplan R. "Madness and James Joyce". Australasian Psychiatry, 2002, 10(2):172-176.

③ Harding M. "James Joyce's Concept of the Underthought". Existential Analysis: Journal of the Society for Existential Analysis, 2008, 19(1):2-16.

feels that an authoritative comment, accepting or rejecting a diagnosis of neurosyphilis, should be provided by *Journal of the History of the Neurosciences*. [1]

2. New-historicism

Richard Barlow, in "James Joyce and Walter Scott: Incest, Rivers of History, and 'Old Useless Papers'", examines a number of significant references to Scott and his texts in *Dubliners*, *A Portrait of the Artist as a Young Man*, *Ulysses*, and *Finnegans Wake*. In Joyce's texts, readers of Scott are associated with incest and onanistic self-absorption, as well as familial and racial decline. However, both writers present models or structures of historical progress in their work. Scott's view of history is reflected in texts such as *Waverley* while Joyce's use of the theories of Giambattista Vico(1668-1744) is demonstrated in *Finnegans Wake*. In addition to studying the function of references to Scott and his texts in Joyce's work, this article analyses the different configurations of history offered by Scott and Joyce, and considers how these models relate to the use of river imagery by the two authors. The article also charts Joyce's personal reading of Scott's work, from his encounter with *Ivanhoe* as a student in 1899 to his attempt to memorise *The Lady of the Lake* while recovering from an eye operation in 1924. [2]

James Alexander Fraser, in "The Exile and the University in Exile: Betrayal as Work in the Writings of James Joyce", discusses the writings of novelist James Joyce, which is based on betrayal and his play, *Exiles*, in which the protagonist, Richard Rowan, is faced with the same kinds of ethical and political choices. Topics discussed include information on Joyce's works in connection to conceptions of "freedom", particularly academic freedom; Joyce's interest in the structures

---

[1] Lyons J B. "James Joyce: Steps towards a Diagnosis". Journal of the History of the Neurosciences, 2000, 9(3):294-306.

[2] Barlow R. "James Joyce and Walter Scott: Incest, Rivers of History, and 'Old Useless Papers'". Scottish Literary Review, 2020, 12(1):1-18.

and forms of betrayal; and Joyce's analysis of intellectual freedom.①

Charles Travis, in "Visual Geo-Literary and Historical Analysis, Tweetflickrtubing, and James Joyce's *Ulysses*(1922)", argues that situated at the intersection of the arts and sciences, Humanities GIS(HumGIS) is contributing to new knowledge systems emerging in the digital, spatial, and geo-humanities. This article discusses the conceptualization and operationalization of two HumGIS models which engage the cartographical and discursive tools employed by James Joyce to compose *Ulysses*(1992). The first model is used to perform a visual geo-literary historical analysis by transposing Homeric and Dantean topologies on a spatialized narrative of Joyce's work. The second model integrates *Ulysses* within a social media map to interpret Bloomsday 2014 digital ecosystem spatial performances in Dublin and globally. This article suggests that HumGIS models reflecting human contingency, idiosyncrasy, and affect, drawing on literary, historical, and social media tools, sources, and perceptions, might offer neogeography, and big data studies alternative spatial framings and modeling scenarios.②

3. Narrative Study

Daniel Ryan Morse, in "Sounding Dismodernism in James Joyce's *Ulysses*", argues that James Joyce's use of a wide variety of methods to read and write (including audiobooks, dictation, and enlarged print) provides a new way to understand the representation of disability in *Ulysses*. Focusing in particular on the role of dictation in versions of *Ulysses*(both by Joyce and later readers), the article recuperates the novel's various challenges to a culture of silent reading. Written texts and audiobooks supposedly serve separate audiences, deserve different levels of cultural prestige, and create divergent means of consuming literature. This article

---

① Fraser J A. "The Exile and the University in Exile: Betrayal as Work in the Writings of James Joyce". Social Research, 2019, 86(3):743-764.

② Travis C. "Visual Geo-Literary and Historical Analysis, Tweetflickrtubing, and James Joyce's *Ulysses*(1922)". Annals of the Association of American Geographers, 2015, 105(5): 927-950.

connects this false binary with that between the disabled and normal body to demonstrate how both combine to enforce a culture of compulsory able-bodiedness. Joining the methods and insights of textual criticism and disability studies, the article makes the case for a more capacious account of the novel's writing that could serve as a model for research on other writers with disabilities and non-print versions of books. [1]

Noel Arthur Davies Glover, in "Portraits in Development: James Joyce, the Artist, and the Human Condition of Creativity", focuses on James Joyce's novel *Stephen Hero* and body's limits seem to have a constitutive relationship to limits in understanding. It mentions subject of human development itself as a creative relation between what matters and what is missing and artist's problem of meaning is a process of symbolization. It also mentions that symbolic register is the artist's developmental resource as a paradoxical play with presence and absence. [2]

Christopher Michael Elias, in "What Makes Them Dubliners? James Joyce's *An Encounter* and the Foundations of Masculinist Nationalism in Ireland", performs a close reading of James Joyce's *An Encounter*, the second story in *Dubliners*, in an effort to examine a key aspect of the story that has been heretofore overlooked: Joyce's commentary on the role of masculinity in the construction of Irish identity. Since prior critical readings of *An Encounter* have focused almost exclusively on the final scenes of the narrative, the rest of the story has been given short shrift. By concentrating on only the perverted and homophobic aspects of the narrative, critics largely fail to recognize the themes of the story that are developed over the entirety of the text, not just its climax. The boys' journey to the field and the other elements that Joyce uses to set the scene should not be seen as mere prologue; particularly noteworthy are the literary, pop-cultural, and religious references that pepper the first half of the text. A more holistic look at the events in *An Encounter* reveals a

---

[1] Morse D R. "Sounding Dismodernism in James Joyce's *Ulysses*". Journal of Literary & Cultural Disability Studies, 2018, 12(4): 459-475.

[2] Glover N A D. "Portraits in Development: James Joyce, the Artist, and the Human Condition of Creativity". English Studies in Canada, 2017-2018, 43/44(4/1):131-149.

commentary not only on homosexuality and perversion but also on broader topics such as masculinity, coming of age, the dissemination of sociocultural knowledge, and the construction of Irish national identity. In bringing those themes to the fore, the author of this essay intends to explicate the way in which the experience of the English colonization of Ireland was written onto every aspect of an Irishman's life, even the process of sexual maturation and gendered citizenship.[①]

Elizabeth M. Bonapfel, in "Joyce's Punctuation and the Evolution of Narrative in *Finnegans Wake*", argues that many innovations in James Joyce's *Finnegans Wake*, often considered a limit case for literature, derive from Joyce's punctuation decisions. These decisions include using dashes to mark the boundaries of speech, removing hyphens from compound words and employing parentheses for multiple interrupting voices. By drawing upon manuscript material, revisions, and printed versions of Joyce's texts, the author of this paper compares the punctuation of Joyce's earlier works to that of *Finnegans Wake* in order to show how Joyce's use of experimental punctuation indicates the boundaries between thought, speech, and voice in *Finnegans Wake*, thus establishing a new narrative mode.[②]

Stephanie J. Brown, in "The Great Criminal, the Exception, and Bare Life in James Joyce's *Ulysses*", outlines the characters and explores the symbolic significance of these characters. It highlights that the book opposes the grammatical mode of thinking in future anterior. It also mentions the metaphors, symbols, and overtones used by Joyce in the book.[③]

David W. Janzen, , in "Potential Unfettered: Narrative Transformation as Historical Transition in *Ulysses*", presents a literary criticism of the book *Ulysses*. It discusses narrative transformation as historical transition in the book. The book is stated to be less concerned with historical particulars (political figures, and

---

① Elias C M. "What Makes Them Dubliners? James Joyce's *An Encounter* and the Foundations of Masculinist Nationalism in Ireland". Journal of Men's Studies, 2016, 24(3):229-240.

② Bonapfel E M. "Joyce's Punctuation and the Evolution of Narrative in *Finnegans Wake*". Journal of Modern Literature, 2019, 42(4):54-73.

③ Brown S J. "The Great Criminal, the Exception, and Bare Life In James Joyce's *Ulysses*". Criticism, 2014, 56(4): 781-805.

symbols) and more concerned with the formal conditions of politico-historical change. Its engagement with social transformation is not merely representative, and it maps the historical transition from the waning masters of Irish Catholicism. [1]

John McIntyre, in "Far from the Centre: Robertson Davies and a Provincial Encounter with James Joyce", argues that Robertson Davies' significant role in promoting and disseminating the work of James Joyce in the pages of *The Peterborough Examiner* is exemplified in his claim to have introduced Joyce's work to the emerging literary critic Hugh Kenner. As an advocate of Joyce and of modernist literature more broadly, Davies sought, against the backdrop of a provincial setting that both frustrated and motivated him, to soften some of modernism's difficult edges for his readers and to dispel charges of inaccessibility. In both *The Peterborough Examiner* and *Saturday Night*, he argued for Joyce's universality—of relevance to readers everywhere. Such claims follow from Davies' larger belief in the importance of fostering literary culture in Canada, the ultimate success of which could be seen in the work of figures such as Kenner. The view of Joyce and of literary modernism that Davies framed for his readers has considerable implications not only for our understanding of Davies, but also for Joyce studies. [2]

4. Comparative Study

Andy Merrifield, in "A Commodius Vicus of Recirculation: Encountering Marx and Joyce", discusses the works and similarities between philosopher Karl Marx and author James Joyce. Also cited are Marx's *Capital*, Joyce's *Finnegans Wake*, the stateless persona non grata situation experienced by Marx in countries like Belgium

---

[1] Janzen D W. "Potential Unfettered: Narrative Transformation as Historical Transition in *Ulysses*". English Studies in Canada, 2017, 43(2/3):13-32.

[2] McIntyre J. "Far from the Centre: Robertson Davies and a Provincial Encounter with James Joyce". University of Toronto Quarterly, 2009, 78(4): 967-978.

and France, and the self-imposed exile of Joyce in Paris, France and Trieste, Italy.①

5. Canonization Study

Kevin P. Reilly, in "Get a Job and Get a Life—with James Joyce: Why Reading the 'Jocoserious' Joyce Is Useful Fun", offers information on development of the University of Wisconsin System and the University of Wisconsin-Madison. It presents essential learning outcomes included ethical reasoning, international knowledge and competence, critical and creative thinking. It focuses on the reference of author James Joyce's works such as *A Portrait of the Artist as a Young Man*. This essay also discusses Joyce's work in the ancient Greek epic poem.②

6. Cultural Study

Georgina Binnie, in "'Photo Girl He Calls Her': Re-Reading Milly in *Ulysses*", argues that Milly Bloom, James Joyce's "photo girl" in *Ulysses*, is read typically by critics as a whimsical and overtly-sexualized figure, despite the more progressive aspects of her role in the photographic industry. In *Ulysses*, photography is depicted as a hereditary pursuit. Joyce's relationship with his daughter, Lucia, was frequently mediated by photography. In 1935, he purchased a new camera for Lucia after encouraging her to pursue this medium. In re-reading Milly's role via George Eastman's *Kodak Girl*, and the emergence of Irish and Triestine visual culture, new light is shed on the relationship between female photography and

---

① Merrifield A. "A Commodius Vicus of Recirculation: Encountering Marx and Joyce". Monthly Review: An Independent Socialist Magazine, 2021, 72(10): 47-54.

② Reilly K P. "Get a Job and Get a Life—with James Joyce: Why Reading the 'Jocoserious' Joyce Is Useful Fun". Liberal Education, 2020, 106(1/2) 58-63.

familial duty.①

Benjamin Dwyer, in "Joycean Aesthetics and Mythic Imagination in the Music of Frank Corcoran", explores points of convergence and difference in Irish composer Frank Corcoran's relationship to author James Joyce as a method of assessing the music of one of Ireland's most radical and individual composers.②

Neil R. Davison, in "*Ivy Day*: Dublin Municipal Politics and Joyce's Race-Society Colonial Irish Jew", introduces Albert Altman, an Irish-Jewish politician of Joyce's era, as an absent center of the *Dubliners* story *Ivy Day in the Committee Room*. The author shows how the text's representations of post-Parnell Irish nationalism become more historically accurate, localized, and nuanced. Altman's position as a left-leaning liberal Dublin corporation councilor is illustrative of the precarious position of "the Jew" in colonialized countries during the era when race and race-societies transforms outposts of late Empire. Leopold Bloom's future politics appear to draw on Joyce's memories of Altman, and *Ivy Day in the Committee Room* is the earliest piece in which Altman's career influenced Joyce's interest in labor as a promising route toward colonial independence. This was also the moment Joyce first recognized what Hannah Arendt would later examine as the Jewish third racial-space between the colonized and colonizer, which she argued eventually became a germ of totalitarianism, when racialized imperial politics "boomeranged" back to the Continent.③

7. Theological Study

Thomas Merton, in "Aesthetic and Contemplative Experience—James Joyce",

---

① Binnie G. "'Photo Girl He Calls Her': Re-Reading Milly in *Ulysses*". Journal of Modern Literature, 2019, 42(4): 39-53.

② Dwyer B. "Joycean Aesthetics and Mythic Imagination in the Music of Frank Corcoran". Musical Times, 2019, 160(1948): 33-48.

③ Davison N R. "*Ivy Day*: Dublin Municipal Politics and Joyce's Race-Society Colonial Irish Jew". Journal of Modern Literature, 2019, 42(4): 20-38.

outlines the reaction of Joyce against the Irish Catholicism of his time. The author believes that this is a reaction against an external and shallow form of Christianity. It highlights the use of Catholic terminology by Joyce in discussing aesthetic experience and the little stories in *Dubliners* as epiphanies. ①

Martin Brick, in "Death, Resurrection, and Meaning in *Finnegans Wake*: A Process Theology Approach", explores the death and mourning of the main character Tim Finnegan and outlines the symbolic significance of other characters. An overview of the story and representation of the Catholic Church teaching and Irish ideology is also given. ②

Zennure Köseman, in "Spiritual Paralysis and Epiphany: James Joyce's *Eveline* and *The Boarding House*", intends to highlight James Joyce's ironical outlook for the existence of epiphanies in women's lives to be released from their spiritual paralysis and stagnation as indicated in *Eveline* (1904) and *The Boarding House* (1906) in *Dubliners*. In *Eveline* and *The Boarding House*, Joyce portrays women who are in a struggle for setting aside the inequalities and miseries of their social environment through their representative wish for emancipation in their lonely and alienated state of minds. Trapped in a web of social expectations and constraints, women intend to escape from the strict patriarchal society of Dublin in these short stories. Structured and controlled by the issue of femininity, James Joyce writes about the effects of the Irish society on female adolescents. *Eveline* and *The Boarding House* offer two portrayals of women who are enclosed by the dominance of the rigid patriarchal society which ends up the need for emancipation from social rigid rules. In these stories, however, the women characters portray a continuation of the choice of their domestic female roles, i. e. , their struggle for emancipation turns out to be useless. *Eveline* is the story of a young teenager who faces a dilemma—she has to choose either to live with her father or escape with her

---

① Merton T. "Aesthetic and Contemplative Experience—James Joyce". Merton Annual, 2014 (27):35-44.

② Brick M. "Death, Resurrection, and Meaning in *Finnegans Wake*: A Process Theology Approach". Renascence, 2018, 70(3): 171-186.

boyfriend. In *The Boarding House*, Mrs. Mooney, a working woman who has rooms to be rented by the young male lodgers, is also in a struggle for supporting herself and her two children. She is in search for emancipation from her drunken abusive husband who has social prejudices. Hence, both of these stories highlight women's tendency for exploring their selfhood and free will because of the inequalities and struggles of patriarchal society of the time in which they are spiritually paralyzed. Thus, James Joyce hints at women's wish for emancipation from the oppressions of patriarchal social environment in the first quarter of the twentieth century. [1]

Gregory Erickson, in "Arius and the Vampire: Figures of Heresy and Disruption in James Joyce's *Ulysses*", focuses on two figures in James Joyce's *Ulysses*, the heretic Arius and the vampire, who are examined together to address issues of anxiety over the body and artistic creation. Stephen's early musings on Arius lead directly into his primary act of artistic creation, a poem he writes that begins with "He comes, pale vampire". Like the heretic, the vampire recedes into the background, but continues to haunt the novel, offering troubling and disruptive commentary on the narrative. Joyce's less literal vampires have the ability to change forms—a rat in the cemetery, a bat flying over a church, ghosts of deceased characters, and a "black panther vampire"—and along with his paradigmatic heretic, Arius, they seem to float from the mind of character to character, forcing them to question received wisdom about creation, procreation, authority, succession, and the relationship of body to mind. Throughout the novel, heretics and vampires work as figures of disruption, as symbols of an alternative taxonomy, and as reminders of the threat or promise of undeserved births and unnatural death. Ultimately, readers will see that vampire narratives, classical heresy, and *Ulysses* share a common central project: questioning and rethinking the act of creation itself. [2]

---

[1] Köseman Z. "Spiritual Paralysis and Epiphany: James Joyce's *Eveline* and *The Boarding House*". Gaziantep University Journal of Social Sciences, 2012, 11(2):587-600.

[2] Erickson G. "Arius and the Vampire: Figures of Heresy and Disruption in James Joyce's *Ulysses*". Religion & the Arts, 2016, 20(4): 442-458.

8. Feminism

Seth Hadley, in "A Representation of Patriarchal Society's Response to Feminism", explores the theme of feminism within James Joyce's *The Dead*. It emphasizes the focal character, Gabriel Conroy, being a representation of cultural norms within a patriarchal society. This essay also discusses the way in which repetition is used within the night's events to highlight social change within gender roles. Specifically, it looks at how Gabriel interacts with Lily, the serving girl; Miss Ivors, his contemporary; and Gretta, his wife. These three encounters take place over the course of the night and work together to slowly, but surely, replace Gabriel's incorrect stigmas and stereotypes concerning women with the current truths that the women surrounding him have to offer through their experiences. All while this takes place, there is a snowstorm over Ireland. At the very end of the night, Gabriel finally has his feminist epiphany as he stares outside at the snow: the snow is a physical embodiment of the feminist change that is taking place in Ireland and within Gabriel. This essay primarily uses the source material itself, but it refers to two other scholars' works in passing for historical context within the topic of gender in *The Dead*.[1]

Marian Eide, in "James Joyce's Magdalenes", presents the short story *Clay* by James Joyce in which the author explores an allusion of the story's protagonist Maria Magdalene, a prostitute. The essay argues that James Joyce presents social hypocrisies of love, family, and community for women. Topics include the social conditions of women in Dublin, Ireland; Joyce's exploration of private and civic roles of single women; and the Catholic Irish asylums for sexually promiscuous women called Magdalene Laundries.[2]

---

[1] Hadley S. "A Representation of Patriarchal Society's Response to Feminism." Logos: A Journal of Undergraduate Research, 2017(10): 28-34.

[2] Eide M. "James Joyce's Magdalenes". College Literature, 2011, 38(4): 57-75.

Michael Wainwright, in "Female Suffrage in Ireland: James Joyce's Realization of Unrealized Potential", presents the issue of women empowerment in Ireland. It highlights the struggle of Irish women for emancipation, stressing the efforts of Charlotte Matilda Stoker in Irish activism. The author also tackles the Irish novelist James Joyce's delineation of self-empowerment which has been crucial for the liberation of Irish women. [1]

9. Philosophical Study

Aleksandar Stević, in "Stephen Dedalus and Nationalism without Nationalism", argues that while recent critics often downplay the significance of Joyce's attack on the Gaelic Revival in *A Portrait of the Artist as a Young Man*, the novel actually enacts nothing less than a systematic repudiation of nationalist tropes from the position of liberal cosmopolitanism. As a detailed comparison of Joyce's text with the turn-of-the-century revivalist discourse shows, *A Portrait of the Artist as a Young Man* undermines each of the key revivalist preoccupations (including both linguistic nationalism and ethnic essentialism), finally deconstructing the project of nation building in toto. This radical critique of nationalism suggests that, after twenty years in which Joyce studies have been dominated by attempts to displace the once-prevalent vision of Joyce as an apolitical and internationalist aesthete with a version of Joyce as, above all, a colonial Irish intellectual, it is time to once again take his commitment to aestheticism and cosmopolitanism seriously. [2]

10. Spatial Study

Carlos Menéndez-Otero, in "Making James Joyce's Life into a Graphic Novel.

---

[1] Wainwright M. "Female Suffrage in Ireland: James Joyce's Realization of Unrealized Potential". Criticism, 2009, 51(4): 651-682.

[2] Stević A. "Stephen Dedalus and Nationalism without Nationalism". Journal of Modern Literature, 2017, 41(1): 40-57.

An Interview with Alfonso Zapico", argues that "Alfonso Zapico was born in Blimea, Asturias, Spain, in 1981. He started working as a professional illustrator and cartoonist in 2006 and has since published four graphic novels: *La guerre du professeur Bertenev*(2006), set in the Crimean War; *Café Budapest*(2008), about the Israeli-Palestinian conflict; *Dublinés*(2011), a biography of James Joyce, and *La ruta Joyce*(2011), a kind of 'making of' of *Dublinés*. His works have received several prestigious awards and been published in Spain, France, Belgium, Switzerland, Poland, Germany and Ireland, where The O'Brien Press released the English version of *Dublinés*". The Niemeyer Center in Avilés, Asturias, opened "an exhibition focused on his career and, more particularly, on *Dublinés* and *La ruta Joyce*. He will soon be publishing his fifth graphic novel, *Elotro mar*, about Vasco Núñez de Balboa and the expedition that led·to the European discovery of the Pacific Ocean in 1513. We interviewed Zapico at the Niemeyer Center on June 29th, 2013". ①

---

① Menéndez-Otero C. "Making James Joyce's Life into a Graphic Novel. An Interview with Alfonso Zapico". Estudios Irlandeses, 2014(9): 121-127.

Chapter 11
Virginia Woolf

Virginia Woolf(1882-1941)

Virginia Woolf, original name in full Adeline Virginia Stephen, is the daughter of the English essayist and historian Sir Leslie Stephen. Virginia Woolf was educated at home and read widely in her father's huge library. After she married the critic Leonard Woolf in 1912, they moved to the London district called Bloomsbury, and their home became a center for the artists, thinkers, and writers who have come to be called the Bloomsbury Group. She and Leonard founded the Hogarth Press in 1917. Woolf's first novel, *The Voyage Out*, was relatively conventional, but the works that followed such as *Night and Day* and *Jacob's Room* featured an innovative lyricism and complex narrative structure. With the publication of *To the Lighthouse* and *The Waves*, Woolf perfected her radical departures from the traditional English novel and established herself as one of the central figures of the modernist movement. In spite of serious psychological problems that had led to mental breakdowns in 1895 and 1915, Woolf wrote many essays and book reviews, as well as more conventional, lighter novels such as *Orlando* and *The Years*.

Among her most important critical volumes are the classics of modern feminism *A Room of One's Own* and *Three Guineas*. Shortly after finishing her final novel, *Between the Acts*, Woolf committed suicide. [①]

---

① Richetti J, Bender J, David D, et al. The Columbia History of the British Novel. New York: Columbia University Press, 1994.

Critical Perspectives

1. Narrative Study

Tali Banin, in "He Winged Creatures of *The Waves* and Virginia Woolf's Figurations of 'The One'", argues that "When she originally conceived *The Waves*, Virginia Woolf declared that 'It is to be a love story: she is finally to let the last great moth in.' The unlikely association of this novel with a 'love story' is illuminated only when the text's nonhuman figuration is brought into play. Woolf's consideration of the real-life behaviors of winged creatures, namely moths and birds, facilitates the novel's revision of romantic convention. This revision manifests in the bird sections of the novel's famous interludes, where the depiction of Song Thrush feeding behavior brushes against echoes of nineteenth-century romance poetry. The as-yet unexplored link between the interludes and Woolf's discussion of Christina Rossetti and Alfred Tennyson in *A Room of One's Own* reveals Woolf's invention of a new approach to the romantic ideal of 'the one.'"[1]

Alexandra Edwards, in "*Orlando*: A Fanfiction; or, Virginia Woolf in the Archive of Our Own", argues that Virginia Woolf's *Orlando* models a type of female gift exchange that resurfaces in places we might not expect—for instance, contemporary digital literatures like fanfiction. Though ontologically indeterminate, *Orlando* can be at least provisionally understood as both a gift and an archive, and it inspires several pieces of fanfiction that are posted freely on the Woolfishly-titled website Archive of Our Own. Reading one of these stories, *The Wretch Takes to Writing*, alongside the novel makes their commonalities apparent, across the divide

---

[1] Banin T. "He Winged Creatures of *The Waves* and Virginia Woolf's Figurations of 'The One'". Journal of Modern Literature, 2021, 45(1):56-73.

of nearly 100 years, and across the supposed distinctions between modernism and popular culture, and between professional and amateur writing. *Orlando* plays with literary tradition exactly as fanfiction writers have come to do.①

Leah Toth, in "Re-listening to Virginia Woolf: Sound Transduction and Private Listening in *Mrs. Dalloway*", presents a literary criticism of the book *Mrs. Dalloway* by Virginia Woolf. Focus is given to the topics of sound transduction and private listening by exploring how characters in the story listen in different ways. It argues that the narrative method of the book is evident in early twentieth-century phonograph listening methods and suggests that innovation in the story lies in its relay between external events and their internal reflections.②

Anna Jones Abramson, in "Beyond Modernist Shock: Virginia Woolf's Absorbing Atmosphere", argues that "Shock has long been the dominant paradigm for theorizing urban modernism. Virginia Woolf's representations of the city demand an adjusted framework: absorption is also a critical point of intersection between Woolf's historical, psychological, and formal concerns. *Mrs. Dalloway* (1925) tells the story of a post-war metropolis that has absorbed the shocking blows of recent history. The novel also turns absorptive processes into a distinct narrative procedure: Woolf's free indirect discourse allows the narrator to absorb and be absorbed by the novel's extensive cast of characters. Woolf moves beyond the matter of how the psyche absorbs shock and trauma to consider how the urban atmosphere itself functions as shock absorber, a kind of affective repository for the past. Form and history meet in Woolf's understanding of what is 'in the air.'"③

Mihaela-Alina Ifrim, in "Representations of Virginia Woolf", argues that the postmodern culture exploits the multifaceted Woolfian text extensively and intensively. Numerous films, plays and written texts have emerged. Although

---

① Edwards A. "*Orlando*: A Fanfiction; or, Virginia Woolf in the Archive of Our Own". Journal of Modern Literature, 2021, 44(3): 49-62.

② Toth L. "Re-listening to Virginia Woolf: Sound Transduction and Private Listening in *Mrs. Dalloway*". Criticism, 2017, 59(4): 565-586.

③ Abramson A J. "Beyond Modernist Shock: Virginia Woolf's Absorbing Atmosphere". Journal of Modern Literature, 2015, 38(4): 39-56.

acknowledged while alive, Edward Albee's *Who's Afraid of Virginia Woolf?* contributed prodigiously to her fame. It is not an exaggeration to say that now, literally, Virginia Woolf is everywhere. The internet abounds in Virginia Woolf societies, blogs and forums debating her works and life, in pictures and documentaries and, just as any respectable celebrity, she even has a Facebook account made on her name. The motivation for this noticeable presence on the World Wide Web and on the postmodern stage is unquestionably the magnetism exerted by her experimental writing and tumultuous life. Therefore, in the context thus formulated, the name Virginia Woolf denominates the writer, and develops a certain textuality indicating her various and multiple instances. This paper sets out to investigate how impersonators of Virginia Woolf, such as Eileen Atkins(*A Room of One's Own*) and Nicole Kidman(*The Hours*), make use of this textuality in their attempt to portray different facets of a troubled yet very resourceful mind. [1]

Irina-Ana Drobot, in "The Hero's Isolation in Virginia Woolf's and Graham Swift's Lyrical Novels", analyses comparatively the theme of isolation in Woolf's and Swift's lyrical novels. The theme the two authors have in common is also part of Romanticism; it reminds of Romantic lyric poetry. The way in which isolation as a trope in Romantic lyric poetry works to create the lyrical aspect in Woolf's and Swift's novels is explored. The characters' difficulty with communication makes them retreat into themselves and, if the novel is composed of lyrical monologues, it reveals this idea through its very form. The characters' isolation is always connected to a poetic view of life. Sometimes, it is also connected, at the same time, with tragic view of life. For the Romantics, solitude was, however, coupled with the idea of sociability, in the sense that a balance was supposed to be achieved between public and private lives. Here characters such as Rachel, Septimus or Lucrezia in Woolf's novels, fail. Delgado Garcia suggests a narratological interpretation: the level of the story presents disconnected, isolated characters, while the level of narration shows that common memories about the war connect them. The characters'

---

[1] Ifrim M-A. "Representations of Virginia Woolf". Philologica Jassyensia, 2014, 1(19): 573-579.

solitude is tied in with parts of their personalities. One significant aspect of Orlando's personality is his preference for solitude, which casts him in the role of a Romantic poet. Characters sometimes talk without actually having something meaningful to say, without connecting to those they talk to. For Swift's characters, conflictual relationships lead to the characters' isolation. The isolated characters talk, yet the others do not connect with them. The Romantic ideal of connecting private with public lives leads to a tragic result of being isolated from the others.①

Anis Shivani, in "Character in Fiction: Virginia Woolf's *Mr. Bennett and Mrs. Brown* Reconsidered", explores Woolf's views on Edwardian writers and an anecdote wherein she encountered a train passenger who she calls Mrs. Brown. It tackles Woolf's dismissal of the Edwardian realist and the validity of her assessments. It is the author's view that characters in fiction is not a matter of working on the perceptions of sensitive minds.②

Rosemary Luttrell, in "Virginia Woolf's Emersonian Metaphors of Sight in *To the Lighthouse*: Visionary Oscillation", highlights parallels and differences between Woolf's philosophy of sight and that of Ralph Waldo Emerson in order to advance understanding of Woolf's epistemology and, collaterally, to offer new perspectives on *To the Lighthouse*. The argument thus diverges from Woolf scholarship that focuses primarily on her move from Impressionism to Post-Impressionism. Emerson's metaphors of vision rest on the claim that in the natural world we are afforded glimpses of universal laws. *To the Lighthouse* similarly implies that manipulating distance and vision in observing the external world can provide "illuminations" of something, but Woolf teases us with the ambiguity of what that something is. Through this framework, a reading of Mrs. Ramsay is developed, which moves beyond the more traditional take on her character as a domestic artist or mystic; she provides, additionally, a paradigm of visionary illumination resonant

---

① Drobot I-A. "The Hero's Isolation in Virginia Woolf's and Graham Swift's Lyrical Novels". Philologica Jassyensia, 2014, 10(1): 147-158.

② Shivani A. "Character in Fiction: Virginia Woolf's *Mr. Bennett and Mrs. Brown* Reconsidered". Texas Review, 2012, 33(1/2): 80-93.

with Lily Briscoe's project of negotiating space to create art. ①

Jane Goldman, in "'Had There Been an Axe Handy': Transatlantic Modernism, Virginia Woolf and Jean Toomer", looks at transatlantic modernist intertextuality and identifies African American influences and voices in the writing of Virginia Woolf. While comparisons between Woolf and the Harlem Renaissance writer Jean Toomer have occasionally been made in transatlantic studies of the matrix of modernism, little attention has been paid to the possibility of more direct or precise connections and intertexts. This essay offers a reading of a precise intertext between Woolf and Toomer and suggests further citations by Woolf of African American writing. ②

Elicia Clements, in "Transforming Musical Sounds into Words: Narrative Method in Virginia Woolf's *The Waves*", discusses various issues related to transformation of musical sounds into words. The article makes specific reference to narrative method used in the book *The Waves*, by Virginia Woolf. Woolf was fascinated by the connections between literature and music. Often Woolf explores the different reactions of the audience members to the sounds of the music or the behavioral expectations of such events. In her fiction, Woolf frequently uses traditional Western music figuratively. Her early essays deal with music as subject-matter and address its affect on community. From *The Waves* onward, Woolf deliberately attempts to reconstitute novelistic methods by looking to the classical tradition of music as a potential model. In *The Waves*, the connections among music, novelistic form, and character are vivid and fundamental. More specifically, Woolf utilizes a particular piece of music, to which she was listening while creating the novel, to reconfigure her compositional methods. Critics have argued for Woolf's politicized notion of narrative structure, making an additional link to music. The method for *The Wave* is as much about reconstituting human interaction

---

① Luttrell R. "Virginia Woolf's Emersonian Metaphors of Sight in *To the Lighthouse*: Visionary Oscillation". Journal of Modern Literature, 2013, 36(3): 69-80.

② Goldman J. "'Had There Been an Axe Handy': Transatlantic Modernism, Virginia Woolf and Jean Toomer". European Journal of American Culture, 2009, 28(2): 109-123.

as it is about formulating new narrative structures.[1]

Lorraine Sim, "Virginia Woolf Tracing Patterns through Plato's Forms", discusses the concept of patterns in the author Virginia Woolf's life and work, with particular focus given to their relationship to Woolf's emphasis on everyday life in books including *A Room of One's Own*, *Night and Day* and *The Years*. The influence of the idea of forms defined by the philosopher Plato on Woolf's patterns is also explored.[2]

Steven Putzel, in "Virginia Woolf and 'the Distance of the Stage'", examines Virginia Woolf's performance theory as delineated in her writings, and applies it to some adaptations of her book for performances on stage. Topics discussed include nature of theater; lament that a play needs external action; incorporation of the evocative power and immediacy of drama into her work; plays include *To the Lighthouse*, by the Empty Space Theater Co.; and musical version of *Orlando*.[3]

Anna Snaith, in "Virginia Woolf's Narrative Strategies: Negotiating between Public and Private Voices", discusses the narrative strategies of the writer Virginia Woolf. Topics discussed include quote from the diary of Woolf on January 26, 1940; information on the relation of a public or private dialectic to the life and writing of Woolf; and details on the use of indirect interior monologue in some of Woolf's novels.[4]

Robin Gail Schulze, in "Design in Motion: Words, Music, and the Search for the Coherence in the Works of Virginia Woolf", discusses coherence in the works of writer Virginia Woolf in relation to the music of Arnold Schoenberg. Topics discussed include Woolf's distaste for the constraints of the chronological novel;

---

[1] Clements E. "Transforming Musical Sounds into Words: Narrative Method in Virginia Woolf's *The Waves*". Narrative, 2005, 13(2): 160-181.

[2] Sim L. "Virginia Woolf Tracing Patterns through Plato's Forms". Journal of Modern Literature, 2005, 28(2): 38-48.

[3] Putzel S. "Virginia Woolf and 'the Distance of the Stage'". Women's Studies, 1999, 28(4): 435-470.

[4] Snaith A. "Virginia Woolf's Narrative Strategies: Negotiating between Public and Private Voices". Journal of Modern Literature, 1996, 20(2): 133-148.

study of the novels *Mrs. Dalloway* and *To the Lighthouse*; Woolf's aesthetic longing for music in the novel *The Waves*; and Schoenberg's experiments in conventional tonal music. ①

Elizabeth Steele, in "*A Haunted House*: Virginia Woolf's Noh Story", discusses the adaptation of the short story *A Haunted House*, by Virginia Woolf into a Noh play. Topics discussed include basic functions of protagonist, protagonist's companion, priest or wise man, and Chorus; concessions to modern times that have been made; and suitability of Woolf's tale in the Noh canon. ②

2. Feminism

Višnja Krstić, in "Gendered Geographies of Power: London in Virginia Woolf's *Mrs. Dalloway* and Jean Rhys's *Voyage in the Dark*", poses a parallel analysis of Virginia Woolf's *Mrs. Dalloway* and Jean Rhys's *Voyage in the Dark*, two novels set in London around the World War I that complement one another with regard to representation of women in the city. In focus are Woolf's and Rhys's heroines who belong different social classes. With a view to producing a fuller picture of the London strata of the time, the paper concentrates on a dual front: it examines the position the protagonists enjoy in respect to their gender as well as in respect to their social status. While Rhys's Anna is a young woman from a distant colony, that is an outsider with no permanent residence in London, Woolf's Clarissa Dalloway, however seemingly privileged, is greatly disadvantaged by her restricted experience of the metropolis. The paper argues that in these two novels London is a source of double marginalisation—a city unjust to the colonial subjects and women of all strata. As a theoretical background, the paper uses the concept of gendered geographies of power, which is supposed to help us reveal how

---

① Schulze R G. "Design in Motion: Words, Music, and the Search for the Coherence in the Works of Virginia Woolf". Studies in the Literary Imagination, 1992, 25(2):5-22.

② Steele E. "*A Haunted House*: Virginia Woolf's Noh Story". Studies in Short Fiction, 1989, 26(2):151-161.

different power structures affect the cityscape on both macro and micro level.①

Francisco José Cortés Vieco, in "(Im) Perfect Celebrations by Intergenerational Hostesses: Katherine Mansfield's *The Garden Party* and Virginia Woolf's *Mrs. Dalloway*", focuses on *The Garden Party* and *Mrs. Dalloway*. Katherine Mansfield and Virginia Woolf nourished a peculiar stream of parallel foreignness and kinship with each other as coetaneous writers. This article explores the likenesses and dialogues between Mansfield's story *The Garden Party* and Woolf's *Mrs. Dalloway* to detect and depict how bourgeois women, like Laura Sheridan and Clarissa Dalloway, albeit from two different generations, are indoctrinated by social etiquette, class consciousness and the prevailing archetype of domestic femininity inherited from Victorian times. Integrated into their compulsory roles as angelic daughters and wives, Laura and Clarissa gladly perform the role of the hostess to organise (im) perfect parties at home until death knocks at the door. Paradoxically that uninvited guest precipitates escapades of self-discovery and mental emancipation, leading to transient or enduring transformations in the lives of these two women.②

Kayte Stokoe, in "Fucking the Body, Rewriting the Text: Proto-Queer Embodiment through Textual Drag in Virginia Woolf's *Orlando* (1928) and Monique Wittig's *Le Corps lesbian* (1973)", develops the conceptual frame of "textual drag" in order to define and examine the relationship between parody, satire and gender. The author of this essay tests this frame by reading two seminal feminist works, Virginia Woolf's *Orlando* (1928) and Monique Wittig's *Le Corps lesbien* (*The Lesbian Body*) (1973). Both texts lend themselves particularly persuasively to analysis with this frame, as they each use strategies to facilitate proto-queer satirical critiques of reductive gender norms. *Orlando* deploys an exaggerated nineteenth-century biographical style, which foregrounds the

---

① Krstić V. "Gendered Geographies of Power: London in Virginia Woolf's *Mrs. Dalloway* and Jean Rhys's *Voyage in the Dark*". Annual Review of the Faculty of Philosophy, 2021, 46(2): 35-49.

② Cortés Vieco F J. "(Im) Perfect Celebrations by Intergenerational Hostesses: Katherine Mansfield's *The Garden Party* and Virginia Woolf's *Mrs. Dalloway*". International Journal of English Studies, 2020, 20(1): 93-111.

protagonist's gender fluidity and her developing critique of the norms and systems that surround her, while *Le Corps lesbien* rewrites canonical romance narratives from a lesbian perspective, challenging the heterosexism inherent in these narratives and providing new modes of thinking about gender, desire and sexual interaction. ①

Margarita E. Sánchez Cuervo, in "The Appeal to Audience through Figures of Thought in Virginia Woolf's Feminist Essays", discusses the presence of figures of thought in some well-known feminist essays by Virginia Woolf. Virginia Woolf tries to make readers aware of her feminist views by using expressive resources like figures of speech or schemes, tropes and figures of thought in her writing. Figures of thought can be defined as those specific gestures which are designed to interact with the audience. Their use is connected with the functional use of language in the sense that they may draw readers' attention away from the textual content and toward the context. This essay also explores financial desires of women, along with social constraints imposed on them. ②

Susie Gharib, in "Billowing Frocks and Velvets: A Sartorial Study of *The Waves* and *Madame Bovary*", attempts to show how Virginia Woolf and Gustave Flaubert similarly employ sartorial allusions in their fictions to portray the sexuality of their characters. In *The Waves*, Woolf dresses the promiscuity of Jinny with translucent and billowing dresses as Flaubert in *Madame Bovary* tailors for adulterous relationships the most alluring of outfits. ③

Ali Smith, in "Virginia and Her Sisters", discusses the exhibition "Virginia Woolf: An Exhibition Inspired by Her Writings", displayed at the Pallant House Gallery in Sussex, England and then at Fitzwilliam Museum in Cambridge, England

---

① Stokoe K. "Fucking the Body, Rewriting the Text: Proto-Queer Embodiment through Textual Drag in Virginia Woolf's *Orlando*(1928) and Monique Wittig's *Le Corps lesbien*(1973)". Paragraph, 2018, 41(3): 301-316.

② Cuervo M E S. "The Appeal to Audience through Figures of Thought in Virginia Woolf's Feminist Essays". Renascence, 2016, 68(2): 127-143.

③ Gharib S. "Billowing Frocks and Velvets: A Sartorial Study of *The Waves* and *Madame Bovary*". Pennsylvania Literary Journal, 2019, 11(1): 185-191.

in 2018.①

Jennifer Barker, in "Indifference, Identification, and Desire in Virginia Woolf's *Three Guineas*, Leni Riefenstahl's *The Blue Light* and *Triumph of the Will*, and Leontine Sagan's *Maedchen in Uniform*", seeks to deepen understanding of the complex and unique position of women fascist ideology by examining Virginia Woolf's ideas on resistance from *Three Guineas* in relation to Leni Riefenstahl's *The Blue Light* and *Triumph of the Will*, and Leontine Sagan's *Maedchen in Uniform*. It states that Virginia Woolf focuses on the relationship between gender, patriarchy, and fascism. It notes that Virginia Woolf describes the differences between British men and women in the 1930s and explores the possibilities of resistance to women. It also mentions that Virginia Woolf addresses the contemporary psychoanalytical and religious theories.②

Victoria L. Smith, in "'Ransacking the Language': Finding the Missing Goods in Virginia Woolf's *Orlando*", contends that Virginia Woolf's peculiar and fantastical "biography" of Vita Sackville-West effects a double compensation. By attending to the tensions between the real and the fictional/fantastic and the public and private, the author of this essay suggests that the text restores lost loves and lost objects to both Vita Sackville-West and Virginia Woolf. The other compensation the novel effects is located at the level of representation. *Orlando* is a complex interplay between Woolf and Sackville-West that produces not only Sackville-West's "biography". It is also Woolf's own story of the inadequacy of language to name the "thing itself" and to represent women, a story that nevertheless self-consciously conveys through language the very things she suggests language is incapable of.③

Alice Staveley, in "Marketing Virginia Woolf: Women, War, and Public Relations in *Three Guineas*", discusses the history of marketing efforts by publishing

---

① Smith A. "Virginia and Her Sisters". The New Statesman, 2018, 147(5420): 38-41.

② Barker J. "Indifference, Identification, and Desire in Virginia Woolf's *Three Guineas*, Leni Riefenstahl's *The Blue Light* and *Triumph of the Will*, and Leontine Sagan's *Maedchen in Uniform*". Women in German Yearbook: Feminist Studies in German Literature & Culture, 2010, 26(1): 73-96.

③ Smith V L. "'Ransacking the Language': Finding the Missing Goods in Virginia Woolf's *Orlando*". Journal of Modern Literature, 2006, 29(4): 57-75.

companies for the book *Three Guineas*, by Virginia Woolf. It describes the feminist themes, the socio-political commentary related to the World War Ⅰ, and the criticisms of politicians that forced publishers to market Woolf as a public intellectual. Woolf's correspondence with friends that reveal her social and political views are discussed, along with her understanding of pacifism, fascism, and the professionalization of women. ①

Jane de Gay, in "Virginia Woolf's Feminist Historiography in *Orlando*", discusses how author Virginia Woolf's novel *Orlando: A Biography*, reflects Woolf's concepts of female literary history. She comments that the book explores conditions for writers and the rewriting of history. Woolf's essay *A Room of One's Own* proposes an alternate history of female literature. The author suggests Woolf's novel parodies the patriarchal views of her father, Sir Leslie Stephen, on literary history. ②

Chloë Taylor, in "Kristevan Themes in Virginia Woolf's *The Waves*", argues that Julia Kristeva describes three patterns of psychic identification: identification with the father and the symbolic, identification with the mother and the semiotic, and a refusal of either identification which results in a precarious balance in between. It is in the latter manner that a writer can access the paternal symbolic, or language, while nevertheless recalling and introducing the maternal semiotic into his or her writing. According to Kristeva, it is in this prevarication that a writer can revolutionize language. Based on readings from "French feminists" such as Irigaray to interpret Virginia Woolf's work, this article explores Kristeva's theory through a reading of *The Waves*. It argues that the characters in Woolf's book adhere to Kristeva's discussion of the relations to language, and, in particular, each of the three female characters can be understood as one of the patterns of psychic

---

① Staveley A. "Marketing Virginia Woolf: Women, War, and Public Relations in *Three Guineas*". Book History, 2009(12): 295-339.

② De Gay J. "Virginia Woolf's Feminist Historiography in *Orlando*". Critical Survey, 2007, 19 (1): 62-72.

identification as Kristeva describes them. ①

Karin E. Westman, in "'For her generation the newspaper was a book': Media, Mediation, and Oscillation in Virginia Woolf's *Between the Acts*", discusses on the literary works of author Virginia Woolf during the 19th century in the U. S. It emphasizes that during Woolf's period, newspaper was a popular means of literary media. For her, the journal *The Times*, has played a formative role in developing her feminism. The influence of newspaper has been demonstrated in her last novel *Between the Acts*. ②

Elicia Clements, in "Virginia Woolf, Ethel Smyth, and Music: Listening as a Productive Mode of Social Interaction", argues that the correspondence between Virginia Woolf and Ethel Smyth reveals that Woolf's interactions with her friend reverberate in her thinking about cultural meaning. Aesthetic and social ideas that circulate around notions of music, subjectivity, difference, and community emerge from an examination of the relationship. In turn, these concepts resurface in her final novel, *Between the Acts*, when Woolf's thematic depiction of music becomes especially conspicuous. Woolf's representations of the sonorous art enable her to explore alternative models of social organization. ③

Lorraine Sim, in "No 'Ordinary Day': *The Hours*, Virginia Woolf and Everyday Life", examines the representation of the relationship of author Virginia Woolf to everyday life in the motion picture *The Hours*. Topics discussed include plot of the film; suggestion that the feminist agenda of Woolf was centrally concerned with escaping her everyday life; and antipathy of Woolf towards food in the film. ④

Vassiliki Kolocotroni, in "'This Curious Silent Unrepresented Life': Greek

---

① Taylor C. "Kristevan Themes in Virginia Woolf's *The Waves*". Journal of Modern Literature, 2006, 29(3):57-77.

② Westman K E. "'For her generation the newspaper was a book': Media, Mediation, and Oscillation in Virginia Woolf's *Between the Acts*". Journal of Modern Literature, 2006, 29(2): 1-18.

③ Clements E. "Virginia Woolf, Ethel Smyth, and Music: Listening as a Productive Mode of Social Interaction". College Literature, 2005, 32(3): 51-71.

④ Sim L. "No 'Ordinary Day': *The Hours*, Virginia Woolf and Everyday Life". Hecate, 2005, 31(1):60-70.

Lessons in Virginia Woolf's Early Fiction", argues that Virginia Woolf famously identifies with the culturally disenfranchised. As a young woman and aspiring writer, she was irked by her exclusion from formal training in the classics, and especially Greek, a language and a literature in which, she would later argue, "the stable, the permanent, the original human being is to be found". Yet Woolf's knowledge of classical Greek is remarkable and inflects early efforts such as *The Voyage Out* and its original version, entitled in a Greek manner. This article offers a reading of Woolf's deployment of Greek motifs in her early work, identifies previously overlooked subtleties in her borrowings from the classical lexicon, and argues that, in her use of Greek, Woolf formulates precise responses to the need to reflect critically on women's intellectual development, cultural participation, and emotional patronage. [1]

Ellen Carol Jones, in "The Flight of a Word: Narcissism and the Masquerade of Writing in Virginia Woolf's *Orlando*", examines the use of metaphors to hide the sexuality and the transvestite nature of Virginia Woolf's book *Orlando*. Topics discussed include proliferation of metaphors as a sign of narcissism; mask of sex and text; representation of the concept of androgyny; materiality of the sexual body of the book; guarding against losing of the woman when writing fiction; and flight of the metaphor. [2]

Jane Elizabeth Fisher, in "The Seduction of the Father: Virginia Woolf and Leslie Stephen", interprets the father-daughter relationship between Virginia Woolf and her father, and how it influences her development as a feminist writer. Topics discussed include women's relationship to literary tradition; creation of a feminist literary and critical tradition; and women's alienation from linguistic and cultural authority in patriarchal society. [3]

---

[1] Kolocotroni V. "'This Curious Silent Unrepresented Life': Greek Lessons in Virginia Woolf's Early Fiction". Modern Language Review, 2005, 100(2): 313-322.

[2] Jones E C. "The Flight of a Word: Narcissism and the Masquerade of Writing in Virginia Woolf's *Orlando*". Women's Studies, 1994, 23(2): 155-174.

[3] Fisher J E. "The Seduction of the Father: Virginia Woolf and Leslie Stephen". Women's Studies, 1990, 18(1): 31-48.

Julie Robin Solomon, in "Staking Ground: The Politics of Space in Virginia Woolf's *A Room of One's Own* and *Three Guineas*", explores Virginia Woolf's use of spatial metaphors in her essays *A Room of One's Own* and *Three Guineas*. Topics discussed include women's social and political existence; women's needs in the context of capitalist patriarchy; and female version of possessive individualism. [1]

Chris Steyaert, in "Three Women. A Kiss. A Life. On the Queer Writing of Time in Organization", relates a queer approach of feminine writing to the development of new female subject positions through conceiving of other understandings of time. To conceptualize this relationship, the novel *The Hours* by Michael Cunningham is analysed and interpreted as a queer story of how women—writing, reading and enacting a novel—acquire an opening to a life that breaks with the heteronormative conception of time. This one-day novel that interweaves the lives of three women in a multiple assemblage offers the "formula" of the triptych, which can be considered a primary form of life as multiplicity. Interconnecting the writings of Virginia Woolf, Michael Cunningham, Gilles Deleuze and Félix Guattari, the cartographic analysis zooms in on three aspects of time by addressing respectively the motifs of the party, the kiss and the day: time as pause, time as exquisite moment and time as affect. By re-establishing the relationship between writing, time and the becoming-woman of life, the paper aims to indicate that queer writing can help to re-imagine new possibilities for(work) life. [2]

Shazia Ghulam Mohammad, and Mohammad Farooq, in "*To the Lighthouse*: A Sequel to *Night and Day*", argue that Virginia Woolf is a modernist writer who primarily concerns herself with the technical side of novel writing with a definite goal in her mind. Keeping in view the above fact, we have reason to believe that her amateur novel *Night and Day* shows flashes of what she intends to do in future by writing *To the Lighthouse*. *To the Lighthouse* is culmination of the journey initiated

---

[1] Solomon J R. "Staking Ground: The Politics of Space in Virginia Woolf's *A Room of One's Own* and *Three Guineas*". women's Studies, 1989, 16(3/4): 331-347.

[2] Steyaert C. "Three Women. A Kiss. A Life. On the Queer Writing of Time in Organization". Gender, Work & Organization, 2015, 22(2): 163-178.

by Virginia Woolf in *Night and Day*. The striking similarities between the two novels manifest themselves not only in the choice of subject matter but also in the art of characterization. Katherine stands as a prototype to Lily Briscoe while Ralph anticipates Mr. Ramsey in his frustration over not being able to sustain himself in the wilderness of the world unless aided by Mary Dachet who protects him from the bleakness that surrounds him. *To the Lighthouse* is a substantial reality towards which Virginia Woolf's imagination aspires to present the duality of life—night and day. Lily's and Katharine's preference for abstractions and angular shapes sets them in contrast with Mrs. Ramsey who considers her femininity a powerful weapon to be used against men. She lets men step in the feminine zone for comfort through a partial access of windows. This paper examines the two novels to highlight the similarities between *To the Lighthouse* and *Night and Day*, and to prove that *To the Lighthouse* is a sequel of *Night and Day*. [1]

3. Philosophical Study

Veronika Krajickova, in "Virginia Woolf's 'Ontoethics' in Her Late Oeuvre from the Perspective of Alfred North Whitehead's Philosophy of Organism", argues that in *A Sketch of the Past*, Virginia Woolf introduces her personal philosophy, her own ontology, based on the idea that all human and nonhuman beings are interconnected in a single work of art. This idea is foregrounded in her novels, *The Waves*, *Between the Acts*, and the pacifist manifesto *Three Guineas*, where Woolf fully develops her "ontoethics", which consists in ontological interconnection of human beings and recognition of value of every human and nonhuman being. This article discusses this universal relationality via Alfred North Whitehead's philosophy of organism, which emphasizes the interrelatedness of all constituents of reality and

---

[1] Mohammad S G, Farooq M. "*To the Lighthouse*: A Sequel to *Night and Day*". Putaj Humanities & Social Sciences, 2013(20): 283-289.

solidarity that springs from this ontological bond.①

Graham Fraser, in "Solid Objects/Ghosts of Chairs: Virginia Woolf and the Afterlife of Things", argues that abandoned and broken objects fascinate Virginia Woolf. Her attention to such things is so exquisite that Michel Serres writes that in her work "inanimate objects have a soul". The author of this essay traces the progress of these inanimate souls across three texts from their life in human service to their afterlife as debris, reading Woolf's attention to these objects through the lens of New Materialism and theories of decay and haunting. Household objects, having outlived their usefulness, are abandoned to a spectral process of decay and re-asserted materiality. Woolf reveals that the afterlife of these things is an uncanny transformation toward an ontological illegibility, which ultimately troubles anthropocentric subjectivity.②

Yiğit Sümbül, in "A Plotinian Reading of Virginia Woolf's *To the Lighthouse*", argues that Virginia Woolf is one of the precursors of modernist English fiction and a master of the technique of stream-of-consciousness. One of her masterpieces, *To the Lighthouse*, basically reflects her literary technique and her vision of life as a female writer at the beginning of the 20th century. Woolf's portrayal of the three major characters in the novel, Mrs. Ramsay, Mr. Ramsay and Lily Briscoe, offers the reader an understanding of fulfillment of desires on personal, aesthetic and intellectual levels. Mrs. Ramsay's search for harmony in nature and the household, and her role as a mediator between God's creations can be associated with Plotinus's philosophy of reaching the God through contemplation on godly creations. Thus, in this article, the character Mrs. Ramsay in Woolf's *To the Lighthouse* can be analyzed in the light of Plotinian philosophy in question.③

---

① Krajickova V. "Virginia Woolf's 'Ontoethics' in Her Late Oeuvre from the Perspective of Alfred North Whitehead's Philosophy of Organism". Process Studies, 2021, 50(2):222-241.

② Fraser G. "Solid Objects/Ghosts of Chairs: Virginia Woolf and the Afterlife of Things". Journal of Modern Literature, 2020, 43(2): 80-97.

③ Sümbül Y. "A Plotinian Reading of Virginia Woolf's *To the Lighthouse*". Journal of Graduate School of Social Sciences, 2013, 17(1): 87-94.

Graham Fraser, in "The Fall of the House of Ramsay: Virginia Woolf's Ahuman Aesthetics of Ruin", argues that "Time Passes", the middle section of Virginia Woolf's *To the Lighthouse*, is an experiment in making the invisible visible. Woolf narrates the collapse into ruin of an abandoned house, showing how time passes not by but through its material structure. Woolf presents the consequent ruination of the empty house as beautiful—as an aesthetic event in itself, independent of human action or witness. Her attention, however, falls not on the ruins themselves but on the architectonics of ruin that unfolds through them, an aesthetic perspective that challenges a static and anthropocentric history of ruin-gazing. This central scene of beautiful ruin is bookended by the more celebrated, anthropocentric artistic triumphs of Mrs. Ramsay's party in part 1 and Lily Briscoe's painting in part 3. Rather than the conventional reading of time and ruin as an antagonist to art, "Time Passes" offers a vision of an alternative (and inevitable) beauty of change and loss in the world without us, and an image of time which has nothing to do with a human art that needs to transcend it. [1]

James Harker, in "Misperceiving Virginia Woolf", argues that "The longstanding critical refrain that Virginia Woolf's fiction represents a turn 'inward' to the vagaries of the inner life has more recently been countered with an 'outward' approach emphasizing Woolf's interest in the material world, its everyday objects and their social and political significance". Yet one of the most curious and pervasive features of Woolf's works is that characters are so frequently wrong in their perceptions. This essay consolidates the inward and outward approaches by tracing the trope of misperception in Woolf's fiction as well as in her conceptions of the work of author and reader. For Woolf, the modern literary experience derives from the nature of the faculties of perception, the tenuous points of connection—and disjunction—between the inner and the outer worlds. [2]

---

[1] Fraser G. "The Fall of the House of Ramsay: Virginia Woolf's Ahuman Aesthetics of Ruin". Criticism, 2020, 62(1):117-141.

[2] Harker J. "Misperceiving Virginia Woolf". Journal of Modern Literature, 2011, 34(2):1-21.

Ann-Marie Priest, in "Between Being and Nothingness: The 'Astonishing Precipice' of Virginia Woolf's *Night and Day*", presents a critical analysis of Virginia Woolf's book *Night and Day*, which projects a precipice between the two worlds of being and nothingness. Topics discussed include presence of the everyday world of social life and constraint, and a shadowy other realm of liberation; attempt to recreate identity in ways not circumscribed by any existing models of the character Katharine Hilbery; and *Night and Day*, as precursor to the experiments with identity by Virginia Woolf in her later novels.①

4. Psychological Study

Susie Gharib, in "Physiognomical Depiction in Virginia Woolf's *The Waves*", attempts to demonstrate Virginia Woolf's significant use of physiognomical details in her most sophisticated novel *The Waves*.②

Zülal Ayar, in "Integrating *The Mark on the Wall* into an EFL Lesson to Teach Reading and Vocabulary", argues that "As the literature strikes interest and arouses the curiosity of learners, it is widely acknowledged that it has an undeniable impact on language education. In this sense, a lesson plan was developed focusing on the reading skill and vocabulary, and aimed at getting learners to discuss and make a critical analysis of a story". Accordingly, Virginia Woolf's one of the well-known short stories, *The Mark on the Wall*, was incorporated into the plan as an intensive reading resource. "In light of constructivism theory and eclectic method, this plan was designed for the instructors teaching English to learners enrolled in the English philology department and taking one-year compulsory preparatory education at schools of foreign languages. As it is grounded upon synchronization, orchestration and symbiotic existence of the language teaching techniques, this short course plan

---

① Priest A-M. "Between Being and Nothingness: The 'Astonishing Precipice' of Virginia Woolf's *Night and Day*". Journal of Modern Literature, 2003, 26(2): 66-80.

② Gharib S. "Physiognomical Depiction in Virginia Woolf's *The Waves*". Pennsylvania Literary Journal, 2021, 13(2): 55-65.

would stimulate students' self-discovery, creativity, learner-centeredness, and reading analyses via pair-work and group activities". ①

Rebecah Pulsifer, in "'Contemplating the idiot' in Virginia Woolf's *Between the Acts*", argues that *Between the Acts* (1941) tests modernism's aesthetic investment in exploring interiority through the figure of a "village idiot". For Woolf, so-called idiocy represents an unreadable form of mental privacy that resists incorporation into social systems of meaning. Imagined as a peculiarly inaccessible form of cognition, idiocy halts Woolf's exploration of interiority and registers private thoughts as potentially isolating rather than narratively instigating. This reticent, as opposed to exploratory, approach to the mind points to an awareness of the closeness between being captivated by others' minds and desiring to capture others, something Woolf became especially wary of at the end of her life. ②

Michael R. Schrimper, in "The Eye, the Mind & the Spirit: Why 'the look of things' Held a 'great power' over Virginia Woolf", argues that "Virginia Woolf was fixated on vision, the actual act of seeing and the concentrated observation of objects and surroundings, so much so that she professed, 'The look of things has a great power over me'". Utilizing a psychoanalytic framework put forth by Charles Mauron—adapted from Freud for Charles Mauron's book *Introduction to the Psychoanalysis of Mallarmé*—and examining predominantly but not solely moments of observation in *To the Lighthouse*, *Mrs. Dalloway*, and the diaries, the author of this essay analyzes moments in which Woolf's preoccupation with seeing makes itself visible, and explore why, precisely, the look of things held a great power over her. ③

Alexander Venetis, in "Jamesian and Freudian Rhetoric and Themes in Virginia Woolf's Literary Manifestos", argues that in her seminal work *Modern*

---

① Ayar Z. "Integrating *The Mark on the Wall* into an EFL Lesson to Teach Reading and Vocabulary". Journal of Graduate School of Social Sciences, 2021, 25(4): 1793-1808.

② Pulsifer R. "'Contemplating the idiot' in Virginia Woolf's *Between the Acts*". Journal of Modern Literature, 2019, 42(2): 94-112.

③ Schrimper M R. "The Eye, the Mind & the Spirit: Why 'the look of things' Held a 'great power' over Virginia Woolf". Journal of Modern Literature, 2018, 42(1):32-48.

Fiction (1925), Virginia Woolf asserts that the most interesting and fruitful way for the modernist novelist to proceed is to appropriate what she calls "the dark places of psychology" into literary writing. The image of "dark places", especially when put into the context of the psychology of the 1920s, almost immediately conjures up a Freudian perspective. However, as this paper argues, in addition to the Freudian overtones, there is more to a full appreciation of Woolf's psychology-related assertions in *Modern Fiction*. Taken in conjunction with her previous text, *Character in Fiction* (1924), it seems possible to read Woolf's manifestos through the lens of the empiricist psychology of William James. Primarily relying on rhetorical analysis of Woolf's vocabulary, this paper aims to disentangle the dynamic relationship between the distinct Jamesian and Freudian psychological schools influencing Woolf's programmatic writings. ①

Margrét Gunnarsdóttir Champion, in "Crowd Psychology and the Heterotopic Imaginary in Virginia Woolf's *Mrs. Dalloway*", argues that as nuanced as Freud's own investigations in *Group Psychology and the Analysis of the Ego*, *Mrs. Dalloway* shows an awareness of the oscillation in group mentality between narcissistic desire and ethical self-transcendence. Taking its cue from the parameters set up in the early scenes, one of a conformist group, the other of a creative, self-determining one, this essay examines how the novel intimates the psychoanalytic Real as ontological ground to the work of mourning, empathy and ethics. Aiming to intertwine the worlds "seen by the sane and the insane side by side", Woolf imbues signification with a tragic identity. How suffering is sutured into the signifier can be productively investigated by conflating Foucault's conception of heterotopia with the Lacanian mirror. As the novel's creative apex, *Mrs. Dalloway*'s party resembles Foucault's "ship of the imagination", imbricating the Symbolic with ethical tropes of the Real. ②

---

① Venetis A. "Jamesian and Freudian Rhetoric and Themes in Virginia Woolf's Literary Manifestos". PsyArt, 2017(21): 20-37.

② Champion M G. "Crowd Psychology and the Heterotopic Imaginary in Virginia Woolf's *Mrs. Dalloway*". PsyArt, 2017(21): 198-224.

Katherine Dalsimer, in "Virginia Woolf: Thinking Back through Our Mothers", explores the complexities of Virginia Woolf's ongoing internal relationship with her mother, Julia Stephen, who had died when her daughter was 13. The author of this essay draws on Woolf's memoirs, one written when she was 25 and the other toward the end of her life; on her autobiographical novel, *To the Lighthouse*; on her early essays and book reviews; and on *A Room of One's Own*. The author concludes by considering some writings of Julia Stephen's—writings overlooked by her daughter. [1]

Michael Lackey, in "Modernist Anti-Philosophicalism and Virginia Woolf's Critique of Philosophy", argues that Woolf is one of many modernists who lead an assault on philosophy. Given her anti-philosophical orientation, scholars who use philosophy to interpret Woolf are implicitly at odds with her aesthetics. Crucial to the author's augument is Woolf's conception of what the author refers to as the semiotic unconscious, which predetermines the conceptual systems scholars use to systematize human's experiences of the world. Based on the findings, the author of this essay suggests an alternative frame for understanding Woolf's treatment of philosophy and, more generally, modernist anti-philosophicalism. Instead of assuming that philosophy signifies intellectual depth, as many scholars do, the author suggests approaching Woolf, as well as many modernists, in terms of their scathing critique of philosophy. What readers need are more studies that use a new frame to discuss the literary modernist assault on philosophy. As for Woolf, the author concludes: to have an intimate understanding of her work, scholars and readers must first banish philosophy and the philosopher. [2]

Michael Lackey, in "The Gender of Atheism in Virginia Woolf's *A Simple Melody*", considers the gender of atheism in Virginia Woolf's 1925 short story *A Simple Melody*. Topics discussed include feature of a main character who is an

---

[1] Dalsimer K. "Virginia Woolf: Thinking Back through Our Mothers". Psychoanalytic Inquiry, 2004, 24(5): 713-730.

[2] Lackey M. "Modernist Anti-Philosophicalism and Virginia Woolf's Critique of Philosophy". Journal of Modern Literature, 2006, 29(4): 76-98.

atheist; Woolf's first effort to give a sympathetic picture of a male atheist; and clarification of why Woolf considers atheism necessary for the development of healthy human relationships. ①

Emily Dalgarno, in "Ideology into Fiction: Virginia Woolf's *A Sketch of the Past*", analyzes the development of women's ideology of gender in Virginia Woolf's memoir *A Sketch of the Past*. Topics discussed include challenges on the ideology of patriarchy; imaginary identification with the mother; desire for social change; and suppression of memories of child abuse. ②

5. Thematic Study

Athena Androutsopoulou, Eugenia Rozou and Mary Vakondiou, in "Voices of Hope and Despair: A Narrative-Dialogical Inquiry into the Diaries, Letters, and Suicide Notes of Virginia Woolf", argue that reading the last diary entries and letters of British author Virginia Woolf, readers are intrigued and puzzled by her melancholic thoughts. Even though the study of written residues (diaries, letters, and suicide notes) can provide useful insights into persons' experience before death, existing research findings concerning positive/negative mood before dying often appear contradictory. In the present study, readers use the conceptualization of polyphonic/multivoiced self as theoretical lens. Readers studied all diary entries written in the last two months of Virginia Woolf's life and up to four days before her suicide, and conducted a thematic narrative analysis in which themes—each seen as sustained by a different voice—were traced across diary entries. The strength of voices was monitored based on the space each covered in the narrative. Findings were triangulated with letters and suicide notes. The authors of this essay monitored a struggle between at least two opposite inner voices, the voice of "despair" and the

---

① Lackey M. "The Gender of Atheism in Virginia Woolf's *A Simple Melody*". Studies in Short Fiction, 1998, 35(1): 49-63.

② Dalgarno E. "Ideology into Fiction: Virginia Woolf's *A Sketch of the Past*". Novel: A Forum on Fiction, 1994, 27(2): 175-195.

voice of "hope". Following a period of balance between voices, the voice of hope covered more space in the entry before last, but the voice of despair gained ground in the last entry. The idea that suicidal patients may be struggling with opposite inner voices until the end has interesting implications for prevention therapy and for the process of meaning making for suicide survivors. [1]

Susie Gharib, in "Infernal, Erotic and Divine Flames: The Fire-Motif in the Work of Stephen Crane, Virginia Woolf, D. H. Lawrence and May Sinclair", attempts to examine the significance of the recurrent fire-motif in the writing of Stephen Crane, Virginia Woolf, D. H. Lawrence, and May Sinclair. [2]

Cheryl Hindrichs, in "Reading 'Moments of Being' between the Lines of Bach's Fugue: Lyric Narrative in Virginia Woolf's *Slater's Pins Have No Points*", provides a guide for reading the lyric narrative experiments in Virginia Woolf's short story *Moments of Being: Slater's Pins Have No Points*, which is said to capture her fondness for Johannes Bach's fugue. It proposes a dialectic relationship of love between theme and content in the story. It examines two parallel structures in the narrative progression, and how the mimetic and synthetic dimensions work together to enlist readers in the lyric narrative. [3]

Joyce Van Tassel-Baska, in "Study of Life Themes in Charlotte Bronte and Virginia Woolf", explores the inner and outer force that energized the lives of Charlotte Bronte and Virginia Woolf and accounted for their creative productivity. Similarities in their lives and works are also discussed. [4]

---

[1] Androutsopoulou A, Rozou E, Vakondiou M. "Voices of Hope and Despair: A Narrative-Dialogical Inquiry into the Diaries, Letters, and Suicide Notes of Virginia Woolf". Journal of Constructivist Psychology, 2020, 33(4): 367-384.

[2] Gharib S. "Infernal, Erotic and Divine Flames: The Fire-Motif in the Work of Stephen Crane, Virginia Woolf, D. H. Lawrence and May Sinclair". Pennsylvania Literary Journal, 2020, 12(1): 69-76.

[3] Hindrichs C. "Reading 'Moments of Being' between the Lines of Bach's Fugue: Lyric Narrative in Virginia Woolf's *Slater's Pins Have No Points*". Studies in Short Fiction, 2012, 37(1): 1-25.

[4] Van Tassel-Baska J. "Study of Life Themes in Charlotte Bronte and Virginia Woolf". Roeper Review, 1995, 18(1): 14-19.

6. Biographical Study

Christopher Wiley, in "Music and Literature: Ethel Smyth, Virginia Woolf, and 'The First Woman to Write an Opera'", discusses the intellectual dialogue between musician Ethel Smyth and author Virginia Woolf. Smyth was born in 1858 and Woolf in 1882, and historical records of correspondence suggest an intimate friendship between the two. The highlights of their career are discussed. It also mentions some of their works including *Three Guineas*, *A Room of One's Own*, and *Impressions that Remained*.[1]

Peter Gay, in "On not Psychoanalyzing Virginia Woolf", profiles Virginia Woolf, a novelist. Topics discussed include description of the biography of Woolf by Hermione Lee; information on the book *Virginia Woolf: The Impact of Childhood Sexual Abuse on Her Life and Work*; and implication of the plaint of an unidentified speaker in Woolf's novel *Between the Acts*.[2]

Maria Ippolito, and Ryan Tweney, in "The Journey to *Jacob's Room*: The Network of Enterprise of Virginia Woolf's First Experimental Novel", examine aspects of the early career of the English novelist Virginia Woolf, drawing primarily on Howard Gruber's approach to the understanding of creativity that views the individual as a unique "evolving system" engaged in a series of goal-directed activities. The various enterprises Woolf engaged in preceding the publication of her first experimental novel, *Jacob's Room*, in 1922 are detailed—including her early literary influences and activities, family background, "organization of affect", development of expertise, and network of writing enterprises. The method utilized here was a blending of the idiographic account of Woolf's resolution of the problem she set for herself of re-forming the English novel (in a departure from the realism

---

[1] Wiley C. "Music and Literature: Ethel Smyth, Virginia Woolf, and 'The First Woman to Write an Opera'". The Musical Quarterly, 2013, 96(2): 263-295.

[2] Gay P. "On not Psychoanalyzing Virginia Woolf". The American Scholar, 2002, 71(2): 71-75.

of, for example, Hardy, Austen, and Dickens) to capture the stream of human consciousness. This idiographic account and nomothetic findings of germane psychological research (e. g. , expertise and the psychology of writing) provide a network of constraints that serve as a kind of framework for an analysis of aspects of the creative process.[1]

7. New Historicism

Imola Nagy-Seres, in "Malleable Sculptures in Virginia Woolf's *Jacob's Room* and Early Travel Diaries", argues that the body in Virginia Woolf's works has often been regarded as absent, a void filled with the flickering impressions of the psyche. Woolf's representations of flesh in *Jacob's Room* and her 1906 travel diaries in Greece demand an adjusted perspective: the body comes into existence at the intersections of hard matter and soft malleability. Instead of representing a hole, the flesh becomes a "hollow", defined by phenomenologist Maurice Merleau-Ponty as the mutually created meeting space between subject and other. Woolf's preoccupation with the semi-soft bodies of sculptures in her early journals and first experimental novel throws fresh light on her literary aesthetics. Distancing herself from a male tradition based on hardness and painstaking physical descriptions, Woolf proposes a more empathetic way of knowing others: the vulnerable and incomplete body acquires shape under its creator's fingers, whose touch gently redraws its boundaries without annihilating its individuality.[2]

Riley H. Floyd, in "'I Must Tell the Whole World': Septimus Smith as Virginia Woolf's Legal Messenger", focuses on the character Septimus Smith in *Mrs. Dalloway* and how he reflects Woolf's views on killing in war and the legal aspects. Particular attention is given to the relationship between law and conscience

---

[1] Ippolito M, Tweney R. "The Journey to *Jacob's Room*: The Network of Enterprise of Virginia Woolf's First Experimental Novel". Creativity Research Journal, 2003, 15(1): 25-43.

[2] Nagy-Seres I. "Malleable Sculptures in Virginia Woolf's *Jacob's Room* and Early Travel Diaries". Journal of Modern Literature, 2019, 42(2): 149-166.

as it relates to war and killing.①

Emily James, and Rachel M. Busse, in "The Forms of War: Pocket Diaries and Post Cards in *Jacob's Room*", argue that in Virginia Woolf's *Jacob's Room* (1922), ephemeral forms popular during World War I—pocket diaries and post cards—inflect the style of soldiers and civilians alike. The novel's diaries and letters anticipate the rhetorical demands of war, which were no doubt shaped by new and uniquely bureaucratic forms, namely the Field Service Post Card and the War Diary, as well as related commercial products that promised to insure the soldier's body and life. These forms encouraged and often enforced a concise style and cheery voice, which strategically muted the war's gruesome realities in service of optimistic national narratives. Woolf's novel pays homage to these forms at the same time that it shows how ordinary writers learned to navigate the censor's gaze and circumvent these formal strictures.②

Casey M. Walker, in "Marcel Proust Meets *Mrs. Dalloway*", presented a literary criticism of the 20th century English fictional book *Mrs. Dalloway* by Virginia Woolf. Particular focus is given to the literary influence that French author Marcel Proust had on the book. An overview of the book's characters, including in regard to the interaction between the modern character and urban space, is provided.③

8. Canonization

Sofia Kostelac, in "*Mrs. Dalloway* in Johannesburg: Reconceptualizing Literariness in Woolf's Novel after FeesMustFall", describes the experience teaching Virginia Woolf's *Mrs. Dalloway* as part of a third-year English Literature

---

① Floyd R H. "'I Must Tell the Whole World': Septimus Smith as Virginia Woolf's Legal Messenger". Indiana Law Journal, 2016, 91(4): 1473-1492.

② James E, Busse R M. "The Forms of War: Pocket Diaries and Post Cards in *Jacob's Room*". Journal of Modern Literature, 2018, 42(1): 1-18.

③ Walker C M. "Marcel Proust Meets *Mrs. Dalloway*". Raritan, 2014, 34(1): 35-56.

course during the FeesMustFall protests in South Africa and the calls for curriculum transformation across the academy that ensued. In particular, it discusses students' heightened awareness of "the social function of difficulty", and the critical doubt to which activist readings of Woolf's aesthetic were subsequently subjected. It then explains how the introduction of neuro-cognitive approaches to Woolf's writing provided a surprisingly enabling approach to the novel in this context by illuminating both the intuitive and "transforming" version of literariness that *Mrs. Dalloway* explicitly promotes, as well as the specialized and arguably elitist one that Woolf's difficult and "multiply embedded" aesthetic implicitly inscribes. The conclusion is a largely speculative one: the author proposes that the cognitive approach has some efficacy in this context because it helps students translate their intuitive and affective responses to Woolf's difficulty into analytical terms and, moreover, legitimizes the feelings of alienation that her work often engenders. [1]

9. Traumatic Study

Sabiner Sautter-Leger, in "Railed in by a Maddening Reason: A Reconsideration of Septimus Smith and His Role in Virginia Woolf's *Mrs. Dalloway*", presents the character Septimus Smith in his post-war traumatized state. The author of this essay argues that the character Septimus symbolizes creative rebellion associated with stifling society. His obsession with everyday phenomena and his emotional response to them are also discussed. [2]

Hillis J. Miller, in "*The Waves* as Exploration of (An) aesthetic of Absence", argues that Virginia Woolf's *The Waves* demonstrates how an (an) aesthetic of absence might be dramatized in a work of fiction. It presupposes a vast impersonal memory bank that stores everything that has ever happened, every thought or feeling

---

[1] Kostelac S. "*Mrs. Dalloway* in Johannesburg: Reconceptualizing Literariness in Woolf's Novel after FeesMustFall". English in Africa, 2020, 47(1): 7-24.

[2] Sautter-Leger S. "Railed in by a Maddening Reason: A Reconsideration of Septimus Smith and His Role in Virginia Woolf's *Mrs. Dalloway*". Papers on Language & Literature, 2017, 53(1): 3-31.

of every person. This data bank, however, is absent, inaccessible to direct experience. The thoughts and feelings it stores, moreover, are always already turned into appropriate language, complete with figures of speech for sensations and feelings that cannot be said literally. These vivid memories are involuntary, to borrow a word from Henri Bergson's memory theory. They have been forgotten completely and suddenly "come to the top" and begin re-enacting themselves as present occurrences in vivid detail before the mind's eye. All the characters in *The Waves*, to different degrees and in different ways, are haunted with the sense of a secret absent centre to which they are attached and that they glimpse but cannot reach. ①

10. Space Theory

Sławomir Kozioł, in "The Logic of Visualization in Virginia Woolf's *Mrs. Dalloway*", analyses the way in which Virginia Woolf shows the importance of the visual in the social space of London in the third decade of the 20th century, which she represents in her novel *Mrs. Dalloway*. The analysis draws on the terminology and theory developed by Henri Lefebvre, who claims in *The Production of Space* that one of the main characteristics of the social space of modern society is the logic of visualization. According to Lefebvre, this logic has two aspects: metaphoric, which treats writing and visual signs in general as focal points of human life, and metonymic, which transforms the visible into totality. The article argues that Woolf shows in her novel how the logic of visualization in both its aspects is used as a mechanism helping to implant proper models and values in members of society and how it is responsible for the emptiness of human life which is limited to its surface value. ②

---

① Miller H J. "*The Waves* as Exploration of (An) aesthetic of Absence". University of Toronto Quarterly, 2014, 83(3): 659-677.
② Kozioł S. "The Logic of Visualization in Virginia Woolf's *Mrs. Dalloway*". Bulletin of the Transilvania University of Brasov, Series IV: Philology & Cultural Studies, 2015, 8(2): 79-94.

Paul Tolliver Brown, in "The Spatiotemporal Topography of Virginia Woolf's *Mrs. Dalloway*: Capturing Britain's Transition to a Relative Modernity", argues that Virginia Woolf entangles time and topography in *Mrs. Dalloway* to reveal that her characters inhabit a relative London. Woolf creates characters who spend the day reminiscing about their youth before the war or who still suffer the lingering effects of mechanized combat. While they navigate an increasingly complex and commercialized environment, she locates them at specific landmarks as Big Ben and St. Margaret's chime the hour, creating a dynamic, interactive setting aligned with her characters thoughts. Woolf styles a narrative that unfolds from a diversity of viewpoints, contrasting a Victorian period that adhered to the ideas of the Enlightenment with a modern period in which individuals experience a relationship between space and time in accord with Albert Einstein's special and general theories of relativity. ①

Sheheryar B. Sheikh, in "The Walls that Emancipate: Disambiguation of the 'Room' in *A Room of One's Own*", argues that "Critics have often understood Virginia Woolf's *A Room of One's Own* (1929) as an anti-patriarchy essay, and the limited understanding of that approach positions the work at one end of a dichotomous relationship. My essay argues that the purpose of her persuasive work is to transcend binary oppositions in her dialectical argumentation rather than find a home within the room. I use examples from Woolf's exploration of interior and exterior spaces in *A Room of One's Own* and *Mrs. Dalloway*, as well as critical approaches to understanding the concept of 'room' as simultaneously an abstract and physical space—and much more". ②

Paul Tolliver Brown, in "Relativity, Quantum Physics, and Consciousness in Virginia Woolf's *To the Lighthouse*", argues that *To the Lighthouse* demonstrates Woolf's understanding of the connections between space, time, objectivity, and

---

① Brown P T. "The Spatiotemporal Topography of Virginia Woolf's *Mrs. Dalloway*: Capturing Britain's Transition to a Relative Modernity". Journal of Modern Literature, 2015, 38(4): 20-38.

② Sheikh S B. "The Walls that Emancipate: Disambiguation of the 'Room' in *A Room of One's Own*". Journal of Modern Literature, 2018, 42(1): 19-31.

consciousness, and reveals the degree to which her ideas both resemble and diverge from those expressed by Einstein. Whereas Woolf's notions of space and time are intimately linked with the preeminent scientist's, her ideas of fluid subject-object boundaries offer a holistic conception of the world that proves far more compatible with the controversial assertions made by quantum physicists such as Bohr and Heisenberg in the early 1900s than with Einstein's adamant belief in objective realism. The author discusses how Mrs. Ramsey embodies key elements of the special and general theories of relativity at the same time as she supersedes them via her conscious connections to people and objects around her. Mrs. Ramsay's unique worldview is counterbalanced by her husband's traditional, representational logic, and dramatized through their interpersonal conflicts. Lily Briscoe's artistic development reveals Woolf's own complex beliefs and mirrors the dramatic shifts that occurred in modern scientific epistemologies. [1]

Marc D. Cyr, in "A Conflict of Closure in Virginia Woolf's *The Mark on the Wall*", discusses Virginia Woolf's short story *The Mark on the Wall*. Topics discussed include readers' reactions to the first paragraph of the story, and definition of the mark in the story. [2]

11. Eco-criticism Study

Vicki Tromanhauser, in "Eating Animals and Becoming Meat in Virginia Woolf's *The Waves*", argues that "Long treated as a novel of unsurpassed interior depth, Virginia Woolf's *The Waves* (1931) also acts as an extended meditation upon the food that sustains such a conceptual model of human inwardness and subjectivity. While depicting rituals of meat eating, Woolf's novel internalizes and challenges the conventional narratives of becoming human by animating the

---

[1] Brown P T. "Relativity, Quantum Physics, and Consciousness in Virginia Woolf's *To the Lighthouse*". Journal of Modern Literature, 2009, 32(3): 39-62.

[2] Cyr M D. "A Conflict of Closure in Virginia Woolf's *The Mark on the Wall*". Studies in Short Fiction, 1996, 33(2):197-205.

nonhuman world that surrounds and infuses them. The text's many scenes of ingestion expose the violence that inheres in transforming the substance of others into the tissue of the exceptional human subject. Such scenes mark a 'postanthropocentric shift' in Woolf's fiction, prompting readers to consider the connections between epistemological and consumptive practices. In doing so, *The Waves* tests the limits of existing cultural, ontological, and gastronomical categories in order to give voice to the stuff of life". ①

12. Linguistic Study

Roberta Rubenstein, in "'I Meant Nothing by *The Lighthouse*': Virginia Woolf's Poetics of Negation", argues that "Virginia Woolf's recurrent 'glooms' and the experience of 'non-being' (her terms)—the dark aspect of her lifelong struggle with bipolar mental illness—are reflected in her fiction through a distinct and recurrent negative vacabulary". The author of this essay argues that the marked meanings of nothing and its variants occur frequently and across a number of epistemological registers in her now-canonical *To the Lighthouse*. Negative diction functions not simply as a syntactical element that appears to a greater or lesser extent in all discourse, literary and otherwise, but as a concentration of linguistic cues that underscore and advance the narrative's thematic concerns. What the author terms the poetics of negation may be understood in semantic, psychological, historical, and formal senses, not only exemplifying Woolf's close acquaintance with negation but further securing her semantic links to modernist preoccupations. ②

Clare Morgan, in "Vanishing Horizons: Virginia Woolf and the Neo-Romantic Landscape in *Between the Acts* and 'Anon'", explores, through a concentration on Woolf's treatment of landscape, how Woolf's vision of art and of England comes to

---

① Tromanhauser V. "Eating Animals and Becoming Meat in Virginia Woolf's *The Waves*". Journal of Modern Literature, 2014, 38(1): 73-93.

② Rubenstein R. "'I Meant Nothing by *The Lighthouse*': Virginia Woolf's Poetics of Negation". Journal of Modern Literature, 2008, 31(4): 36-53.

be grounded in the inter-war zeitgeist of Neo Romanticism, a grounding that significantly alters our perception of the role both nation and community play in her work.①

13. Gender Study

Suzan Harrison, in "Playing with Fire: women's Sexuality and Artistry in Virginia Woolf's *Mrs. Dalloway* and Eudora Welty's *The Golden Apples*", examines women's sexuality and artistry in literary works *Mrs. Dalloway*, by Virginia Woolf and *The Golden Apples*, by Eudora Welty. Topics discussed include narrative strategies of intertextual play with masculine texts; critical reticence about sexuality in the work of fiction; and link between sexuality and artistic creativity.②

14. Sociology Study

Helen Southworth, in "Correspondence in Two Cultures: The Social Ties Linking Colette and Virginia Woolf", presents information on the social ties linking English writer Virginia Woolf and her French contemporary Sidonie-Gabrielle Collette. Topics discussed include list of the mutual acquaintances and network of friends shared by both Woolf and Collette; details of the novels written and published by Woolf; and excerpts of letters by Woolf in contrast to her French contemporary.③

Ferhat Ordu and Murat Karakaş, in "Gender Politics in *To the Lighthouse*", try to solve the gender identity problem in *To the Lighthouse* and focus upon the

---

① Morgan C. "Vanishing Horizons: Virginia Woolf and the Neo-Romantic Landscape in *Between the Acts* and 'Anon'". Worldviews: Global Religions, Culture and Ecology, 2001, 5(1): 35-57.

② Harrison S. "Playing with Fire: women's Sexuality and Artistry in Virginia Woolf's *Mrs. Dalloway* and Eudora Welty's *The Golden Apples*". Mississippi Quarterly, 2003, 56(2): 289-314.

③ Southworth H. "Correspondence in Two Cultures: The Social Ties Linking Colette and Virginia Woolf". Journal of Modern Literature, 2003, 26(2): 81-99.

struggle of the modern woman against the dominant patriarchal male characters and submissive female characters trying to find their way out. ①

Clare Hanson, in "Virginia Woolf in the House of Love: Compulsory Heterosexuality in *The Years*", argues for a re-reading of one of Virginia Woolf's neglected novels, *The Years*, in the light of theoretical work on the performance of gender. Topics discussed include Woolf's offer of a powerful analysis and critique of the production of gender identity within the matrix of family life, and passages from the novel. ②

---

① Ordu F, Karakaş M. "Gender Politics in *To the Lighthouse*". Journal of History Culture and Art Research, 2015, 4(3): 69-77.

② Hanson C. "Virginia Woolf in the House of Love: Compulsory Heterosexuality in *The Years*". Journal of Gender Studies, 1997, 6(1):55-62.

Chapter 12
Martin Amis

Martin Amis (1949-)

Martin Amis is probably the most widely acclaimed writer in contemporary Britain. He was born in Oxford on 25th August, 1949 and was educated in Britain, Spain and the USA, attending a lot of schools and then a series of crammers (a special school that prepares people quickly for an examination) in London and Brighton. He received his formal university education at Exeter College, Oxford, graduating with distinctions. For some time, he was an editorial assistant for *Times Literary Supplement* and was a literary editor of *The New Statesman* from 1977 to 1979. He then worked as a special writer for *The Observer*. Ever since the early 1970s, he has published several novels: *The Rachel Papers* (1973), which won the 1974 Somerset Maugham Award, *Dead Babies* (1975), *Success* (1978), *Other People: A Mystery Story* (1981), *Money: A Suicide Note* (1984), *London Fields* (1989), *Time's Arrow* (1991), *The Information* (1995), *Night Train* (1997), and a story-collection called *Einstein's Monsters* (1986). His non-fictional writings include *Visiting Mrs. Nabokov* (1993).[①]

[①] 罗经国, 阮炜. 新编英国文学选读(下). 4版. 北京大学出版社2016年版.

Critical Perspectives

1. Narrative Study

Will Norman, in "Killing the Crime Novel: Martin Amis's *Night Train*, Genre and Literary Fiction", explores the encounter between autonomous aesthetics, mass genre and the publishing category of literary fiction in Martin Amis's *Night Train*. Taking the confused critical response to the novel as a starting point, the author of this essay argues that the novel confounds the conventions governing the writing, circulation and consumption of contemporary literary fiction. In analyzing the narrative and stylistic strategies Amis deploys in exploiting the conventions of crime writing, the author of this essay gives an account of the relationship between high autonomous aesthetics and mass genre that makes *Night Train* inimical to the category of literary fiction. Putting Amis's term "postmodern decadence" to use as a way of conceptualizing this relationship historically, readers are able to reorientate their sense of Amis's place in the cultural field and understand the set of factors that have determined his vexed reputation in contemporary literature. ①

Ali Gunes, in "The Deconstruction of 'Metanarrative' of Traditional Detective Fiction in Martin Amis's *Night Train*: A Postmodern Reading", examines the view of "unreliable" or "little narrative" or "incredulity toward metanarrative" in Martin Amis's novel *Night Train* as an anti-detective novel. The paper falls into two parts. The first part focuses upon the convention of traditional "reliable" or

---

① Norman W. "Killing the Crime Novel: Martin Amis's *Night Train*, Genre and Literary Fiction". Journal of Modern Literature, 2011, 35(1):37-59.

"metanarrative" in a typical traditional detective story, in which Mike Hoolihan as a detective investigates Jennifer Faulkner's suicide by collecting all the possible evidences and then examining them in a chronological linear way to solve her enigmatic death. Who has killed her? Why was she murdered? If it is suicide, why has she ended her life? However, the paper also discusses that the way Mike passionately attempts to solve Jennifer's mysterious death is not possible due not only to lack of evidences but also to the fact that there occurs various interpretations about her death, which, after a while, turns into a psychological evaluation of the case with her own emotional involvement. Hence Jennifer's death remains a mystery from the beginning to the end in the novel. This situation obviously defies the expectation of her father Tom as in the traditional sense because why Tom hires Mike as an "exceptional interrogator" with an outstanding "paperwork" in the past is to clarify the case and then appease his anxiety, as well as the mystery of his daughter's death. Through his representation of Mike in such a condition, Amis apparently illuminates that it is almost impossible to create a detective story with a final legitimate total meaning in an age based on fragmentation, uncertainty, doubt, interruption, lack of authority, and self-expression.[①]

2. Feminism Study

Mustafa Güneş, in "The Mystery in the Eye of the Beholder: An Analysis of the Gaze and Power in Martin Amis' *London Fields* and *Night Train*", argues that Amis's novels dating the 1980s and 1990s and portraying mostly the lives of the modern English, more specifically the Londoners, are provocative for the way they represent women. They are sometimes classified as the "ladlit" or at times

---

① Gunes A. "The Deconstruction of 'Metanarrative' of Traditional Detective Fiction in Martin Amis's *Night Train*: A Postmodern Reading". Journal of History Culture and Art Research, 2018, 7(2): 216-229.

dismissed all together out of the canon because they confine women mostly in patriarchal cliché female figures, or silence them to an extent that would discard the very existence of women in these texts. Among these ladlits, *London Fields* strikes the reader at first glance as the ladlit par excellence; yet, the protagonist in the novel is an extraordinary woman, Nicola Six, and her representation in the novel is exceptional in Amis's oeuvre. When this novel is read in relation to another woman-starring Amisian novel, *Night Train*, which features a hardboiled female detective, the result would be thought-provoking for gender studies across Amis's works. Therefore, the way Amis portrays Nicola Six is studied together with another fictional female figure, Mike Hoolihan of the novel *Night Train*, and the focus of the study is limited to the analysis of the characterization of the protagonists in relation to the concepts of "seeing" and "being seen" together with such mediums of power and the ideology as "the authority" "the author", and "the reality". [1]

3. Psychological Study

Cristina Ionica, in "Masculinism as Global Psychosis: A Cognitive-Enactivist Reading of Martin Amis's 'Men'", focuses on novels of Martin Amis which enact stories' participation in universal masculinist circuits of power in ways that denounce masculinist societal frameworks' malignity. It mentions non empathic-to-sadistic protagonist-narrators are allowed to spin outrageous guilt-deflecting fables to the point of self-incrimination. It also mentions peculiar modes of questioning textual authority that enacts the narrative nature of cognitive processes and subsumptions of breed violence. [2]

---

[1] Güneş M. "The Mystery in the Eye of the Beholder: An Analysis of the Gaze and Power in Martin Amis' *London Fields* and *Night Train*". Journal of History Culture and Art Research, 2021, 10(4):18-31.

[2] Ionica C. "Masculinism as Global Psychosis: A Cognitive-Enactivist Reading of Martin Amis's 'Men'". English Studies in Canada, 2017(44):67-89.

4. Thematic Study

Tamás Juhász, in "Murderous Parents, Trustful Children: The Parental Trap in Imre Kertész's *Fatelessness* and Martin Amis's *Time's Arrow*", offers a literary comparison of the novels *Fatelessness* by Imre Kertész and *Time's Arrow* by Martin Amis. It states that the key narrative idiosyncrasies of both novels is the verbal representations produced under the effect of trauma. Moreover, both novels exemplifies the overriding theme of abused trust.[①]

5. Biographical Study

William H. Pritchard, in "Amis as Critic", focuses on the work of author Martin Amis which provide collection of essays such as *The War against Cliché* and memoir *Experience* and interval between his serious fall and his death. It mentions necessity of working hard to erase the "incidental grit and lint and sweat" that accumulates around words and moments of enthusiasm for a writer and becomes more exploratory and poetic.[②]

6. New Historicism

Sam Tanenhaus, in "The Electroshock Novelist", discusses British novelist Martin Amis, focusing on his book *Lionel Asbo: State of England*, as well as Amis' fascination with U.S. politics and cultural excesses. Amis' first novel *The Rachel

---

① Juhász T. "Murderous Parents, Trustful Children: The Parental Trap in Imre Kertész's *Fatelessness* and Martin Amis's *Time's Arrow*". Comparative Literature Studies, 2009, 46(4): 645-666.
② Pritchard W H. "Amis as Critic". The Hudson Review, 2018, 71(2):303-308.

Papers is also mentioned, along with his relationship with fellow author Christopher Hitchens. ①

Boris Johnson, in "Staggers Envy, Being Rejected by Martin Amis, and Why the Left Hated Maggie So Much", discusses a series of topics relevant to readers of the magazine *The New Statesman*. The author of this essay explores topics including his attempt to convince writer Martin Amis to write for his periodical, *The Spectator*; the psychological difference between right wing and left wing politicians; and why members of the Labour Party should read *The New Statesman*. ②

7. Canonization

Victoria N. Alexander, in "Martin Amis: Between the Influences of Bellow and Nabokov", features British novelist Martin Amis. Topics discussed include stances towards narrative; influences of authors Saul Bellow and Vladimir Nabokov; views on the role of novelists; and concepts on literary elements like voice, narrative, structure and epistemology. ③

8. Traumatic Study

Olga A. Dzhumaylo, in "Martin Amis's *The Pregnant Widow* as a Postmodern Confessional Novel", reads Martin Amis's *The Pregnant Widow* as a confessional novel in relation to the profound postmodern skepticism about the language of truthfulness and format constrains of consummated confession. In addition to the

---

① Tanenhaus S. "The Electroshock Novelist". Newsweek, 2012, 160(1/2):50-53.
② Johnson B. "Staggers Envy, Being Rejected by Martin Amis, and Why the Left Hated Maggie So Much". The New Statesman, 2013, 142(5153/5154): 23.
③ Alexander V N. "Martin Amis: Between the Influences of Bellow and Nabokov". The Antioch Review, 1994, 52(4):580-590.

contemporary discourse about confessional writing, the author of this essay applies Jacques Derrida's idea of restructuring of personal memory traces and Mikhail Bakhtin's idea of confession with a loophole. The author argues that in his autobiographical and self-reflexive novel, Amis addresses his fictional doubles in wish to make sense of his personal traumatic experience and doubts multiple narrative and analytical frames directed towards closure and consummation of the Self. [1]

9. Post-colonial Study

Sean Seeger, in "Martin Amis, Neo-Orientalism, and Hubris", puts forward a reading of Martin Amis's 2008 book *The Second Plane* with an emphasis on its cultural politics. It reconsiders Amis's book from a distance of almost a decade in light of global developments, including the rise of ISIS in the Middle East, the resurgence of acute Islamophobia in Europe and the US, and Tony Blair's public acknowledgement of the shortcomings of the 2003 invasion of Iraq. With these factors in mind, the essay argues that it is possible to detect in Amis's book early warning signs of how the West's relationship with both Islamism and Islam would develop in the period following its publication. [2]

---

[1] Dzhumaylo O A. "Martin Amis's *The Pregnant Widow* as a Postmodern Confessional Novel". Brno Studies in English, 2019, 45(1):77-89.

[2] Seeger S. "Martin Amis, Neo-Orientalism, and Hubris". Postcolonial Studies, 2017, 20(4):494-509.

Chapter 13

George Orwell

George Orwell(1903-1950)

Burn in Bengal, Orwell was brought to England and educated at St. Cyprian's School and Eton College. His experience with the Indian Imperial Police in Burma provided the material for his first novel, *Burmese Days*(1928). After resigning in disgust over the degradations of imperialism, he moved to Paris where he struggled to publish some of his early novels. A trip to northern England in 1936 inspired the impassioned documentary piece *The Road to Wigan Pier*, and a stint with the Republican fighters in the Spanish civil war resulted in his enduring paean to antifascist struggle, *Homage to Catalonia*. As a fiercely independent democratic socialist, Orwell is perhaps best known for his satirical novels, *Animal Farm* and *Nineteen Eighty-Four*.[1]

---

[1] Richetti J, Bender J, David D, et al. The Columbia History of the British Novel. New York: Columbia University Press, 1994.

Critical Perspectives

1. Narrative Study

Danny Heitman, in "A New Column about an Old Craft", discusses lack of time to focus on how to use written language with skill and grace, and mentions argument of author George Orwell. Topics discussed include concern of professional writers, and experience as a journalist of the author.①

Tony E. Jackson, in "Oceania's Totalitarian Technology: Writing in *Nineteen Eighty-Four*", presents a literary criticism of the 1949 book *Nineteen Eighty-Four* by George Orwell. The novel is set in 1984 and in Oceania where people were plagued with war, government surveillance, and public manipulation. Also examined are the main characters and the symbolic significance of these characters, a handwritten diary that is central to the story, and the novel's themes.②

Thomas Dilworth, in "Erotic Dream to Nightmare: Ominous Problems and Subliminal Suggestion in Orwell's *Nineteen Eighty-Four*", presents a literary critique of the novel *Nineteen Eighty-Four*, by George Orwell, highlighting its aesthetic weaknesses and arguing that they are deliberately interpretive elements of the story's message. Questions raised include the notion of whether the main characters ever had a chance of succeeding, interpretation of the erotic elements of the story, and the metaphors of dreams and games seen throughout the narrative.③

---

① Heitman D. "A New Column about an Old Craft". Phi Kappa Phi Forum, 2021, 101(3): 4.

② Jackson T E. "Oceania's Totalitarian Technology: Writing in *Nineteen Eighty-Four*". Criticism, 2017, 59(3): 375-393.

③ Dilworth T. "Erotic Dream to Nightmare: Ominous Problems and Subliminal Suggestion in Orwell' *Nineteen Eighty-Four*". Papers on Language & Literature, 2013, 49(3): 296-326.

2. Gender Study

Blu Tirohl, in "We are the dead... you are the dead': An Examination of Sexuality as a Weapon of Revolt in Orwell's *Nineteen Eighty-Four*", examines sexuality as a weapon of revolt in Orwell's *Nineteen Eighty-Four*. The sexual relationship between Winston and Julia is scrutinized in terms of its effectiveness as a means of mutiny against the omnipresent Party surveillant mechanisms and the underpinning thought-control and sex-control exercised by the Party. Some discrepancy is noted in Orwell's depiction of women, and an attempt is made to contextualise this within Orwell's own experiences as described through various biographers. [1]

3. Philosophical Study

Peter Wilkin, in "George Orwell: The English Dissident as Tory Anarchist", examines the nature of George Orwell's Tory anarchism, a term that he used to describe himself until his experiences in Spain in 1936. The argument developed here says that the qualities that Orwell felt made him a Tory anarchist remained with him throughout his life, even after his commitment to democratic socialism. In fact, many of those qualities (fear of an all-powerful state, respect for privacy, support for common sense and decency, patriotism) connect the two aspects of his character. The article explains what the idea of a Tory anarchist means, describing it as a practice rather than a coherent political ideology, and moves on to examine the relationship between Eric Blair, the Tory anarchist, and George Orwell, the

---

[1] Tirohl B. "'We are the dead... you are the dead': An Examination of Sexuality as a Weapon of Revolt in Orwell's *Nineteen Eighty-Four*". Journal of Gender Studies, 2000, 9(1): 55-63.

democratic socialist. It makes the case for his Tory anarchism by drawing out recurring themes in his work that connect him to other Tory anarchist figures such as his contemporary Evelyn Waugh. Thus Tory anarchism is presented as a conservative moral critique of the modern world that can connect figures who hold quite radically different political beliefs.①

William Hunt, in "Orwell's Commedia: The Ironic Theology of *Nineteen Eighty-Four*", focuses on theology in the George Orwell's book *Nineteen Eighty-Four*. Orwell's book contains several references to Dante's "Inferno". The author of this essay explains that the title for the book was chosen by Orwell late into his composition and was based on the year G. K. Chesterton set his own antiauthoritarian fantasy *The Napoleon of Notting Hill*.②

Anthony Lock, "Prick the Bubbles, Pass the Mantle: Hitchens as Orwell's Successor", discusses critic and public intellectual Christopher Hitchens and the degree to which he can be identified with author George Orwell whom Hitchens admired. The author discusses Hitchens' resemblance to Orwell in his quest to challenge totalitarianism, as well as the representation in totalitarianism in Orwell's book *Nineteen Eighty-Four* and Newspeak, the book's portrayal of a totalitarian language. Topics include language and thought and Hitchens' views on the Iraq War.③

Liam Julian, "Orwell's Instructive Errors", examines the cultural and political insight inherent in the writings of 20th century English author George Orwell. It discusses the ways that U. S. President Barack Obama uses rhetoric to craft metaphors and redefine words and likens this tendency to Orwell's musings

---

① Wilkin P. "George Orwell: The English Dissident as Tory Anarchist". Political Studies, 2013, 61(1):197-214.

② Hunt W. "Orwell's Commedia: The Ironic Theology of *Nineteen Eighty-Four*". Modern Philology, 2013, 110(4): 536-563.

③ Lock A. "Prick the Bubbles, Pass the Mantle: Hitchens as Orwell's Successor". The Humanist, 2012, 72(4): 26-30.

about hyperbole in language. Two collections of Orwell's essays were released in 2008, titled "Facing Unpleasant Facts" and "All Art is Propaganda". The latter volume contains a piece that examines the English language within politics. Prominent themes in the author's works include imperialism, poverty and oppression. Numerous quotes and excerpts from Orwell's works are presented. [1]

Naomi Jacobs, in "Dissent, Assent, and the Body in *Nineteen Eighty-Four*", presents a literary criticism of the novel *Nineteen Eighty-Four* by George Orwell. In the book, several bodies marked the progression from hope to despair and together, these bodies reflected a persuasive anatomy of the powers and limitations of the human body and of the human being. Central to utopian literature, the body attempts to address the desires of individual bodies with the needs of the body politic. The concept of the body has been central to Orwell's explorations of the workings of power. The context of the body among the novel's characters is also explored. [2]

4. Psychological Study

Simon B. Eickhoff and Robert Langner, in "Neuroimaging-based Prediction of Mental Traits: Road to Utopia or Orwell?", argue that predicting individual mental traits and behavioral dispositions from brain imaging data through machine-learning approaches is becoming a rapidly evolving field in neuroscience. Beyond scientific and clinical applications, such approaches also hold the potential to gain substantial influence in fields such as human resource management, education, or criminal law. Although several challenges render real-life applications of such tools difficult, future conflicts of individual, economic, and public interests are preprogrammed,

---

[1] Julian L. "Orwell's Instructive Errors". Policy Review, 2009(155): 47-58.
[2] Jacobs N. "Dissent, Assent, and the Body in *Nineteen Eighty-Four*". Utopian Studies, 2007, 18(1):3-20.

given the prospect of improved personalized predictions across many domains. In this paper, the authors thus argue for the need to engage in a discussion on the ethical, legal, and societal implications of the emergent possibilities for brain-based predictions and outline some of the aspects for this discourse. Advances in machine learning on neuroimaging data have opened up the possibility of objectively predicting individual traits like intelligence, personality, or clinical risks from brain scans. This article discusses the methodological and ethical challenges arising from these advances. ①

Zennure Köseman, in "Psychoanalitical Outlook for Orwell's *Coming up for Air*, *Animal Farm* and *Nineteen Eighty-Four*", highlights a psychoanalytical approach while assessing how world wars cause mental and psychological disorders in human beings in respect to George Orwell's *Coming up for Air* (1939), *Animal Farm* (1945) and *Nineteen Eighty-Four* (1949). Rising global risks results in different forms of tension in financial, economic, and social respects. The atmosphere of perpetual crisis is influential on human psychology and personal values in worsening socio-economic circumstances. The role of psychoanalysis in literary criticism cannot be disregarded because of the rising global risks' influence on human beings. The chaos of World Wars is the reason for Orwell to portray an apocalyptic analysis in his fictional works. Orwell's aforementioned three novels in question here reveal a dark undertone of war and conflicts and manifest Orwell's tendency to portray individuals having anxiety, uncertainty, meaninglessness, alienation, and isolation in the modern world. Moreover, Orwell indirectly depicts that such psychological tensions end up rebellious activities of human beings in his novels. ②

---

① Eickhoff S B, Langner R. "Neuroimaging-based Prediction of Mental Traits: Road to Utopia or Orwell?". PLOS Biology, 2019, 17(11):1-6.

② Köseman Z. "Psychoanalitical Outlook for Orwell's *Coming up for Air*, *Animal Farm* and *Nineteen Eighty-Four*". Gaziantep University Journal of Social Sciences, 2016, 15(3):867-880.

5. Biographical Study

David Fitzpatrick, in "Records of the Times: Layers of Creation in the George Orwell Archive", argues that the Canadian archivist Jennifer Douglas has highlighted six layers of archival creation which she argues shape the ways in which a writer's archive is formed, appraised, enhanced, arranged and interpreted over time. This article applies Douglas's notion of the six layers of creation to the George Orwell archive, which is held at University College London, by showing the ways in which the archive has been shaped and interpreted over time by various contributors. It discusses not only the value of these contributions, but also how typical such contributions are. The article also discusses the challenge that collections like the Orwell archive pose to our understanding of the concept of the fonds. In agreement with Geoffrey Yeo's writings on the subject, this article concludes that a collection such as the Orwell archive, which has been supplemented with additional material over time, is best understood as a collection of items that reflects the contributions of a number of different creators and custodians, something that is distinct from its main creator's "conceptual" fonds, which is dispersed across a number of collections. [1]

Danny Heitman, in "George Orwell, Outdoorsman: A Keen Observer of Human Depravity, the Author of *1984* Found Respite in Natural Settings", focuses on the late English novelist, essayist, journalist and critic George Orwell, whose alertness to the excesses of official power informed *Animal Farm* and *1984*, his two masterpiece books about totalitarianism. His fascination by how language could be distorted and abstracted to promote any number of atrocities is explored. Information

---

[1] Fitzpatrick D. "Records of the Times: Layers of Creation in the George Orwell Archive". Archives & Records, 2016, 37(2):188-197.

about his life and works and the challenges in the completion of the book *1984* is also tackled.①

6. New Historicism

James F. Penrose, in "War as an Art Form", focuses on several best writers of the twentieth century including George Orwell, Vladimir Nabokov, and John Hersey. Topics include histories that have supplemented and occasionally corrected the factual material in *The African Trilogy* and *Eclipse* by John Shirley; and impressionistic descriptions of dying institutions, resistance to change, and human foibles show.②

Chris Nashawaty, in "George Orwell, Budway Joe and Ling Ling the Impolitic Panda", discusses the historical relationship between television advertising and the National Football League's (NFL's) Super Bowl championship game of 2016, and it mentions the 50-year history of television commercials that aired during various Super Bowl games. Computer company Apple Inc.'s advertisement is addressed in relation to the late author George Orwell. A 1980 commercial featuring then-football player Mean Joe Greene is examined, along with pandas in advertising.③

Peter Firchow, in "Homage to George Orwell", presents an examination into the life, works and historic reception of the 20th-century English author George Orwell. The author focuses on the question of whether or not Orwell was a "genius". Comments that highlight the various characteristics of Orwell's literary output are given. Further discussion is given to reflect on his personal life and opinions. Concluding statements asserting that he was both an intellectual and an

---

① Heitman D. "George Orwell, Outdoorsman: A Keen Observer of Human Depravity, the Author of *1984* Found Respite in Natural Settings". Humanities, 2019, 40(1): 1.
② Penrose J F. "War as an Art Form". The New Criterion, 2020, 39(2): 12-19.
③ Nashawaty C. "George Orwell, Budway Joe and Ling Ling the Impolitic Panda". Sports Illustrated, 2016, 124(5): 34-40.

"ordinary fellow" who deserves the recognition he's been given within the literary canon are offered. ①

Peter Stansky, in "Utopia and Anti-Utopia: William Morris and George Orwell", features utopian authors William Morris and George Orwell. Topics discussed include their attributes; personal information on Morris and Orwell; and information on some of their written works. ②

John Rodden, in "The 'Orwellian' Night of December 12", argues that although it is rare that one can pinpoint an historical moment in which a writer's public reputation is "launched", the day of destiny is clear in George Orwell's case: Sunday, 12 December 1954. BBC-TV's adaptation of *Nineteen Eighty-Four* that night, and especially the debates in the British press that ensued for three weeks thereafter, ignited controversy that permanently boosted sales of his dystopian novel and made his very name as proper adjective—"Orwellian"—a household word. The iconic figure of "Orwell"—the mythic bogeyman rather than a writer or literary figure—became one of the first examples of a celebrity created by modern television. George Orwell's posthumous fame owes less to his strictly literary achievement than to the Zeitgeist's embrace of his work in the era of the telescreen. ③

John Rodden, in "The Intellectual as Critic and Conscience", discusses intellectuals George Orwell and Albert Camus. According to the author, both of these men were distinguished by their ability to speak out against oppression and to critique other leftist intellectuals. Details on their moral and political stances regarding fascism, imperialism, Communism, and religious belief are presented. ④

---

① Firchow P. "Homage to George Orwell". Midwest Quarterly, 2011, 53(1): 77-94.
② Stansky P. "Utopia and Anti-Utopia: William Morris and George Orwell". History Today, 1983, 33(2):33-38.
③ Rodden J. "The 'Orwellian' Night of December 12". Society, 2015, 52(2):159-165.
④ Rodden J. "The Intellectual as Critic and Conscience". Midwest Quarterly, 2014, 56(1):86-102.

John Rodden, in "Homage to My Intellectual Big Brother", discusses the author's personal feelings of affinity to writer George Orwell and his relationships with other people who feel connected to Orwell and his works. Reading Orwell's works inspired the author to research the lives of other people in Orwell's generation and the history of that period. Details on his studies of the history of East Germany are also presented.①

John Rodden, in "The Orwell Century?", focuses on the influences of historian and political writer George Orwell. The entire twentieth century was dubbed as the Orwell Century. The centennial of his death is furnishing cultural and intellectual historians as well as media broadcasters with renewed occasion for staking his title to such claim, just as news commentators on the war on terrorism find increasing and urgent reason to evoke his dystopian vision. Tributes suggests that commentators and critics have exalted Orwell in terms far greater than those commonly applied to a writer. The intellectual legacy and cultural impact of George Orwell, the foremost political writer of the century and the contemporary master of plain English prose, was given consideration.②

Thomas E. Ricks, in "We Are (Still) Living in an Orwellian World", reports on the resurgence of the popularity of the totalitarianism book *Nineteen Eighty-Four* by George Orwell in the 21st century. Topics discussed include the countries where the book has enjoyed a resurgence of popularity, the factors that make Orwell's book politically and socially significant for the 21st century, and the parallelism between the totalitarian government in the book and the global social and political conditions of the 21st century. Also discussed are the ways in which the global counterterrorism efforts and drone warfare of the 21st century parallel Orwell's book.③

---

① Rodden J. "Homage to My Intellectual Big Brother". Midwest Quarterly, 2014, 56(1): 46-54.
② Rodden J. "The Orwell Century?". Society, 2003, 40(5): 62-65.
③ Ricks T E. "We Are (Still) Living in an Orwellian World". Foreign Policy, 2017(225): 80-81.

7. Canonization

John Rodden and John Rossi, in "*Animal Farm* at 70", explores the 70th anniversary of the publication of the book *Animal Farm* by George Orwell in 2016. *Animal Farm* is reportedly published on August 26, 1946 in the U. S., and it is regarded as a hybrid of Menippean satire, historical allegory, and Aesopian fable. Also discussed are several world event in 1945, the political conditions in the U. S., Great Britain, and Germany, and Orwell's occupational achievements. ①

John P. Rossi, in "The Enduring Revelance of George Orwell", reports on the centenary commemoration of the birth of George Orwell, an English author considered to be one of the most read and most quoted authors of the 20th century. Topics discussed include books written by Orwell; influences of Orwell's political writings and insights to politicians, critics and ordinary readers; and background of Orwell's personal life. ②

John Rodden, in "Appreciating *Animal Farm* in the New Millennium", examines how the changes in historical conditions have altered the reception of the book *Animal Farm*, by George Orwell in the 21st century. Topics discussed include the film adaptation of the book; information on how the book was categorized by the U. S. publishing industry in 1945; and the theme of the *Animal Farm*. ③

8. Post-colonial Study

Edward King, in "What Muck & Filth Is Normally Flowing through the Air",

---

① Rodden J, Rossi J. "*Animal Farm* at 70". Modern Age, 2016, 58(4):19-27.
② Rossi J P. "The Enduring Revelance of George Orwell". Contemporary Review, 2003, 283 (1652): 172-176.
③ Rodden J. "Appreciating *Animal Farm* in the New Millennium". Modern Age, 2003, 45(1): 67-76.

argues that criticism has tended to view George Orwell's radio career in terms of his relationship to imperial politics or his relationship to late modernism. Orwell, however, had a longer and more complex relationship to radio than his BBC years. His views on radio changed significantly between the late 1930s and the end of his BBC career in 1943. His earlier work rejected the radio as a form of cultural and national pollution. In his later work, Orwell develops a media theory that starts to think of the airwaves as a cultural environment. Where radio had once stood for the polluted "muck & filth" of modernity's bad air, in his later work, it becomes a vehicle that might just bring poetry back into the national culture.[①]

Jutta Paczulla, in "'Talking to India': George Orwell's Work at the BBC, 1941-1943", discusses the tensions between Orwell's wartime service for the BBC and his position on behalf of Indian independence, a stance he had adopted earlier in his career. Orwell attempted to reconcile these contradictions by elevating the demands of what he conceived of as an anti-fascist war to the highest importance. Exploring these and related issues, the author draws on Orwell's own writings, both publicized and private, available in *The Complete Works of George Orwell*.[②]

9. Comparative Study

David Pryce-Jones, in "The Visions of Orwell & Waugh", presents information on the works of English writers George Orwell and Evelyn Waugh. It cites that Orwell and Waugh were conspicuously different, going against the grain of the times by holding uncompromisingly to unpopular opinions. According to the

---

① King E. "What Muck & Filth Is Normally Flowing through the Air". Journal of Modern Literature, 2018, 41(2):60-76.

② Paczulla J. "'Talking to India': George Orwell's Work at the BBC, 1941-1943". Canadian Journal of History, 2007, 42(1): 53-70.

article, the two are both geniuses with unchallenged places in the field of literature that justifies England to posterity. ①

10. Ethical Study

Gerald Frost, in "All is Orwell", examines the enduring interest in the life and work of English essayist, journalist and critic George Orwell. Topics discussed include several contradictions in his character which contributed to his popularity, the reason behind his participation in the Spanish Civil War, and his reputation as a moral influencer as well as his difficulty in recognizing unpalatable truths. ②

D. J. Taylor, in "Orwell & the Totalitarian Mind", offers information on the novelist George Orwell's obsession with the totalitarian mind, which are strewn all over his life in the late 1930s and the early 1940s. It mentions his understanding of the totalitarian mindset and, in particular, its mystical and well-nigh religious underpinning. ③

Anna Vaninskaya, in "The Bugle of Justice: The Romantic Socialism of William Morris and George Orwell", considers three possible applications of the concept of justice to the work of William Morris and George Orwell. It begins with a brief look at the treatment of criminals in Morris's utopian writing: a specific issue which anticipates some of the points of the modern restorative justice model. The bulk of the essay is devoted to the elaboration of four interconnected elements of the utopia of romantic socialism in Morris and Orwell: elements that provide the positive building blocks of the just society of human well-being. The roles of the past, of nationality, of the natural environment, and of the demechanization of labor in the creation of the community of the future are considered. The final section, by

---

① Pryce-Jones D. "The Visions of Orwell & Waugh". The New Criterion, 2008, 27(1): 4-8.
② Frost G. "All is Orwell". The New Criterion, 2021, 39(10):17-21.
③ Taylor D J. "Orwell & the Totalitarian Mind". The New Criterion, 2019, 38(2):27-30.

drawing on several other specimens of socialist utopianism, examines the insufficiency of emotional ethical responses to injustice in producing a convincing version of ideal arrangements, and thereby highlights the value of the romantic visions of Morris and Orwell. ①

Dan Hitchens, in "Orwell and Contraception", expounds on English novelist George Orwell's belief in the evil of contraception. Topics include discussion of passages from Orwell's poem, *Saint Andrew's Day, 1935*, showing his antipathy to birth control, Orwell's disdain for Catholicism's description of contraception as a kind of doublethink, and why the works of Orwell, who did not consider himself a moral theologian, have all the answers for a couple who wonder how a decent life is possible without contraception. ②

11. Cultural Study

John Michael Roberts, in "How Are George Orwell's Writings a Precursor to Studies of Popular Culture?", argues that George Orwell is known as an acclaimed novelist, essayist, documentary writer, and journalist. But Orwell also wrote widely on a number of themes in and around popular culture. However, even though Orwell's writings might be considered as a precursor to some well-known themes in studies of popular culture, his contribution to this area still remains relatively unacknowledged by others in the discipline. The aim of this article is simply, therefore, to provide a basis to begin to rethink Orwell's contribution to contemporary studies of popular culture. It does so by demonstrating some comparable insights into culture and society. These insights are also related to four

---

① Vaninskaya A. "The Bugle of Justice: The Romantic Socialism of William Morris and George Orwell". Contemporary Justice Review, 2005, 8(1):7-23.

② Hitchens D. "Orwell and Contraception". First Things: A Monthly Journal of Religion & Public Life, 2016(262): 19-21.

main areas of discussion: debates in contemporary cultural studies about the contested pleasures of popular culture and experiences; the relationship between language and culture; how social class needs to be defined not just economically but also culturally; and how one might escape cultural relativism when writing about popular culture. The article concludes by suggesting that Orwell is a precursor to contemporary studies of popular culture insofar that some of the cultural themes he explores have become established parts of the discipline's canon. [1]

John Rodden, in "Big Rock (Sugar) candy Mountain? How George Orwell Tramped toward *Animal Farm*", presents literary criticism of the book *Animal Farm* by George Orwell, also known by his birth name, Eric Blair. The author discusses the possible role of the song *The Big Rock Candy Mountain*, which was made popular when recorded by a homeless man in the 1920s, in Orwell's decision to include the song *Beasts of England*, created by the character Old Major in the book. The article also explores the presence of the song in the book *Down and Out in Paris and London*. [2]

David L. Kirp, in "Standing in the Shadows", focuses on the book *Down and Out in Paris and London*, by George Orwell. Orwell speaks of the Paris slums as one might speak of the streets of New York or San Francisco, as topsy-turvy, sometimes violent, a gathering-place for eccentric people—people who have fallen into solitary, half-mad grooves of life and given up trying to be normal or decent. While Orwell's account surprised its readers, there is now more news from nowhere than we are prepared to digest. [3]

---

[1] Roberts J M. "How Are George Orwell's Writings a Precursor to Studies of Popular Culture?". Journal for Cultural Research, 2014, 18(3): 216-232.

[2] Rodden J. "Big Rock (Sugar) candy Mountain? How George Orwell Tramped toward *Animal Farm*". Papers on Language & Literature, 2010, 46(3): 315-341.

[3] Kirp D L. "Standing in the Shadows". The Nation, 1994, 258(14): 490-495.

12. Socialism Study

Richard White, in "George Orwell: Socialism and Utopia", discusses how George Orwell's writing is acquainted with the basic values of socialism, including fraternity and liberty. It examines the possibility of ethical socialism and its relationship to Marxism. Moreover, it explores the meaning of equality, liberty and fraternity. It describes the general possibility of ethical socialism as an ongoing tradition of thought. Furthermore, particular example of George Orwell as one of the most effective supporters of the said position is presented.[①]

Tony Shaw, in "'Some Writers Are More Equal than Others': George Orwell, the State and Cold War Privilege", argues that George Orwell's *Animal Farm* and *Nineteen Eighty-Four* are widely regarded as two of the best known and most influential novels in English of the Cold War. By 1989, the novels had sold almost 40 million copies in more than 60 languages, more than any other pair of books by a serious or popular post-war author. This article concentrates on the role official western propagandists played in lifting Orwell's profile during the first decade or so of the Cold War. It examines why *Animal Farm* and *Nineteen Eighty-Four* were appropriated by the British and American governments and what financial assistance was given to foreign publishers in order to make books more accessible.[②]

Rob Breton, in "Crisis? Whose Crisis? George Orwell and Liberal Guilt", examines George Orwell's approach to the failure of middle-class liberals to connect with the working class, during the twentieth-century. Topics discussed include complaints stated in his *Down and Out in Paris and London*, from the working-class perspective; reasons for his rejection of liberal organicism and socialist collectivism;

---

① White R. "George Orwell: Socialism and Utopia". Utopian Studies, 2008, 19(1): 73-95.
② Shaw T. "'Some Writers Are More Equal than Others': George Orwell, the State and Cold War Privilege". Cold War History, 2003, 4(1):143-170.

and argument presented in Orwell's *The Road to Wigan Pier*, regarding middle-class socialists. ①

John P. Rossi, in "George Orwell's Concept of Patriotism", examines the importance of patriotism to writer George Orwell. Topics discussed include description of his work *Down and Out in Paris and London* published in 1993; distinction between patriotism and nationalism; and argument for patriotism contained in Orwell's *The Lion and the Unicorn: Socialism and the English Genius*. ②

John Rodden and John Rossi, in "Jean Malaquais: A French Orwell?", discuss the uncanny parallels, paradoxes, and puzzles in the lives and careers of the author of *Nineteen Eighty-Four*, the famous George Orwell, and the virtually unknown French writer and political radical, Jean Malaquais. The striking affinities between Orwell and Malaquais, both of whom came to literary maturity in the 1930s, involve both their themes and genres. Both men fully engaged the issues of their times as independent leftists. Both also wrote political novels, documentary reportage and war diaries that addressed the conditions of the poor and working class (especially miners), the agonies of war-torn Europe, and the dangers of a totalitarian dystopia in the near future. Their remarkable affinities even extended to participation as volunteer soldiers in the same militia during the Spanish Civil War, the POUM(United Marxist Workers' Party). Yet no biographer or scholar has ever compared the two men or even noted their numerous, arresting similarities. The divergent "afterlives" of Orwell and Malaquais raise large questions about cultural memory, the literary Zeitgeist, and Clio's caprice. ③

John Newsinger, in "The American Connection: George Orwell, 'Literary Trotskyism' and the New York Intellectuals", examines some of the contributions

---

① Breton R. "Crisis? Whose Crisis? George Orwell and Liberal Guilt". College Literature, 2002, 29(4): 47-66.
② Rossi J P. "George Orwell's Concept of Patriotism". Modern Age, 2001, 43(2):128-132.
③ Rodden J, Rossi J. "Jean Malaquais: A French Orwell?". Society, 2015(52):360-371.

made by British Labour Party supporter George Orwell to U. S. journals and their reciprocal influence on his own thinking. Orwell developed his political ideas as part of a continuing dialogue with the non-Communist Left. His involvement with the literary Trotskyists of the U. S. -based *Partisan Review* was an important part of this dialogue. Orwell's reputation rests so much on his being an exponent of Englishness that his U. S. connection has been virtually ignored. His "London Letters" are often treated as part of his literary canon, rather than as deliberate and self-conscious interventions in a particular political milieu. But Orwell's contributions to *Partisan Review* were those of a literary Trotskyist, a person influenced by revolutionary socialist ideas and arguments, but always drawing his own conclusions. He always maintained a critical and independent position, and he contributed to and was influenced by debates on the U. S. Far Left. Clear examples are his attitude towards the war and debates on the class nature of the Soviet Union.[①]

Ferdinand Mount, in "Orwell and the Oligarchs: George Orwell Memorial Lecture, 26 November 2010", argues that the unique quality of George Orwell's political journalism is to force us to examine not just the utterances of our opponents, but what we say ourselves, in particular how we deceive ourselves as well as deceiving others. What would Orwell diagnose as our major self-deception if he were alive today? He agreed with the idea that the predominant drift in modern society was towards oligarchy, and not towards democracy as we like to flatter ourselves. Whether in business or politics, decisions today rest in fewer hands. Power is concentrated, not dispersed. As in Russia, the emerging system enables oligarch to collar a disproportionate share of the rewards. Management becomes a self-remunerating elite. Inequality of income increases sharply as a result. Oligarchy is a perversion of liberal capitalism and not a natural development of it. It can be

---

① Newsinger J. "The American Connection: George Orwell, 'Literary Trotskyism' and the New York Intellectuals". Labour History Review, 1999, 64(1): 23-43.

reversed. The Coalition government has set out in a liberal and localist direction. It remains to be seen whether these promising signs will develop into a sustained and effective programme. ①

John Rodden, in "How Orwell Became 'a Famous Author'", discusses writer George Orwell, with a particular focus on his literary reception, influence, and reputation. Details on the effects of his political beliefs and his death at the age of 46 are presented. Other topics include historical context, contingency, and Orwell's books *Animal Farm* and *Nineteen Eighty-Four*. ②

John Rodden, in "Introduction, or Orwell into the Twenty-First Century", discusses various reports within the issue on topics including writer George Orwell, literary reputation, socialism in East Germany, and writer Albert Camus. ③

Jennie Yabroff, in "Why We Need to Call a Pig a Pig (with or without Lipstick)", discusses Eric Blair, who is best known by his pseudonym George Orwell, and the relevance of his writings, including the book *Animal Farm*. Topics include a brief biography of Blair, and how his ideas have been distorted and simplified over time. ④

Robert Colls, in "Homage to Caledonia", explores 20th-century British author George Orwell's view on Scottish independence, in the context of upcoming referendum on the issue. The author outlines the arguments for Scottish independence made by the Scottish National Party (SNP) under party leader Alex Salmond and suggests how Orwell would view them. Topics include national

---

① Mount F. "Orwell and the Oligarchs: George Orwell Memorial Lecture, 26 November 2010". Political Quarterly, 2011, 82(2): 146-156.

② Rodden J. "How Orwell Became 'a Famous Author'". Midwest Quarterly, 2014, 56(1): 26-45.

③ Rodden J. "Introduction, or Orwell into the Twenty-First Century". Midwest Quarterly, 2014, 56(1): 5-25.

④ Yabroff J. "Why We Need to Call a Pig a Pig (with or without Lipstick)". Newsweek, 2008, 152(19): 58-60.

identity, the dominance of London, England, in British politics, and economic shifts. ①

John Rodden, in "A Young Scholar's Encounter with Russell Kirk", presents the author's experience of meeting conservative political theorist Russell Kirk. The author comments on the impact of Kirk's book *The Conservative Mind* on his life. He discusses Kirk's thoughts about author George Orwell and his influence on political thought via the literary works *Nineteen Eighty-Four* and *Animal Farm*. He compares commonalities shared between Orwell and Kirk. ②

John Rodden, in "Lessons from Brother Orwell", presents a letter focusing on the lessons learned from George Orwell, a political writer and intellectual. Lessons are presented below. Do not ride along with the intellectual herd. Refuse to accede to coterie politics. Become a freelance writer. Risk becoming the conscience of your reference group, indeed a public conscience. Look to your own failings, your own self-righteous anger and intolerance. Resist the bewitching attractions of court patronage and courtly politicos. Keep a distance from power. Renounce the alluring, merely oppositional role of critic and skeptic. Commit to a constructive vision. Be both a skeptic and a dreamer, a realist and an idealist. Break the intelligentsia's lazy, knee-jerk habit of lining up people in categories. Avoid addressing primarily the cultural elite. Address the informed lay person. ③

Jim Sleeper, in "Orwell's 'Smelly Little Orthodoxies'—And Ours", discusses George Orwell's difficulties in securing a publisher for *Animal Farm*. Topics discussed include satire of the Soviet example of socialism; ways in which British socialists and communists condemned the book as treasonous for the left;

---

① Colls R. "Homage to Caledonia". The New Statesman, 2014, 143(5221): 30-33.
② Rodden J. "A Young Scholar's Encounter with Russell Kirk". Modern Age, 2007, 49(3): 290-298.
③ Rodden J. "Lessons from Brother Orwell". Society, 2005, 42(6): 69-73.

condemnation of the book's leftwing sensibility by liberals and conservatives. ①

Matthew McCoy, in "Outsider on the Inside", argues that George Orwell claims that the inherent political criticism in his work is determined by the age he lives in. This is partially true. While his work is ostensibly determined by the political developments of the 1930s and 1940s, it is overwhelmingly subjective, influenced by his own experiences and his emotional reactions to them. It might be more accurate to say that the content of his work is determined by how he lives in the age he lives in. Orwell's five-year stint as an Imperial Policeman in Burma immeasurably influenced his career as a writer. Besides giving him a first-hand look at effects of imperial policy on native populations, Orwell's job left him with a guilty conscience. ②

John Rodden, in "My Orwell, Right or Left", comments on British author George Orwell, and what his possible political views might have been during his life. Topics discussed include difficulty of figuring out his possible allegiances; comments on the Cold War; and comments on his book *1984* and its implications. ③

V. C. Letemendia, in "Revolution on *Animal Farm*: Orwell's Neglected Commentary", analyzes revolutionary allegories in the novel *Animal Farm*, by George Orwell. Topics discussed include betrayal of socialist ideals by the Soviet regime; despair and pessimism of the tale; dimension of democracy in the proletarian struggle; and alternatives to capitalism and dictatorship. ④

Stephen Ingle, in "A Note on Orwellism", examines two lines of criticism of political writer George Orwell, which purport to explain the ambiguities of his

---

① Sleeper J. "Orwell's 'Smelly Little Orthodoxies'—And Ours". Journal of the Historical Society, 2004, 4(2): 141-165.

② McCoy M. "Outsider on the Inside". Peace Review, 2003, 15(2): 223-231.

③ Rodden J. "My Orwell, Right or Left". Canadian Journal of History, 1989, 24(1): 1-15..

④ Letemendia V C. "Revolution on *Animal Farm*: Orwell's Neglected Commentary". Journal of Modern Literature, 1992, 18(1): 127-138.

legacy. Topics discussed include problems with Orwellism; his establishment of a moral system based upon the Christian virtues; analysis of Orwell's works; model used by Orwell in portraying the values of the working class lifestyle; and claims that Orwell sought consistently to characterize socialism as a moral system based upon the values of the stable working class. ①

Anthony Daniels, in "Orwell's 'Catalonia' Revisited", comments on the character and reputation of George Orwell as a writer. The author asserts that Orwell is the modest and egocentric writer of the 20th century. According to the author, his writings are lucid and essays are best among the best English prose of the century. The author admired him for his decency in writing anti-totalitarian books. ②

Jeffrey Meyers, in "Orwell on Writing", focuses on the life and works of writer George Orwell in Great Britain. Topics discussed include principle of Orwell to provide advocated direct language and unambiguous expression in communication; Orwell's educational background; and his interest in sharing political awareness to readers. ③

13. Biographical Study

Beth Ann Fennelly, in "All in Favor, Say 'I'", offers literary criticism on the use of writing style by memoirists. The essays *Shooting an Elephant* by George Orwell and *Cutty, One Rock* by August Kleinzahler are addressed. The short story *A Rose for Emily* by William Faulkner, the use of punctuation by Kleinzahler, and the views of writer Eileen Pollack on memoir-writing are analyzed. ④

---

① Ingle S. "A Note on Orwellism". Political Studies, 1980, 28(4): 592-598.
② Daniels A. "Orwell's 'Catalonia' Revisited". The New Criterion, 2007, 25(6): 11-19.
③ Meyers J. "Orwell on Writing". The New Criterion, 2003, 22(2): 27-33.
④ Fennelly B A. "All in Favor, Say 'I'". Virginia Quarterly Review, 2014, 90(3): 182-186.

Chapter 13　George Orwell

Robert Pearce, in "Orwell Now", features George Orwell on *The Collected Essays, Journalism and Letters* which is published by Penguin in 1970. This book is among the most well-thumbed paperbacks on many modern historians' shelves. Topics discussed include reasons why historians are interested in Orwell's works; Orwell's documentary writings; and Orwell's more general contemporary relevance. ①

Henri Astier, in "Spilling the Beans in Paris and London: George Orwell and Jean-Francois Revel", focuses on the works of philosopher turned journalist Jean-Francois Revel, France's most influential political analysts. Topics discussed include parallelisms between writer George Orwell and Revel; career highlights; Revel's revival of pamphleteering, a style of political writing; styles of both writers; objection to communism; replies to charge of absolutism; and comments on Revel's works. ②

Paul Delany, in "Orwell on Jura: Locating *Nineteen Eighty-Four*", claims that George Orwell's biographers have been divided about his move to the island of Jura in the last years of his life. Some have seen it as a refuge from the trials of London life during the war; others have viewed it as a bleak and inaccessible place, chosen in one of Orwell's masochistic gestures. The ordeal of writing *Nineteen Eighty-Four* on Jura has been described as a suicidal project. But Orwell wanted to be "a farmer who wrote" after the war, for both sentimental and practical reasons. Life on Jura was in some ways healthier and more comfortable than that in London, and Orwell certainly was happier there than in most other places he lived. If he had survived, he probably would have continued to live in the countryside—still producing his books, and also cultivating his vegetables. ③

---

① Pearce R. "Orwell Now". History Today, 1997, 47(10): 4-6.
② Astier H. "Spilling the Beans in Paris and London: George Orwell and Jean-Francois Revel". Contemporary Review, 1994, 264(1541): 292-302.
③ Delany P. "Orwell on Jura: Locating *Nineteen Eighty-Four*". University of Toronto Quarterly, 2011, 80(1): 78-88.

Stephen Miller, in "Orwell Once More", presents literary criticism about English writer George Orwell. "His essays are often found in freshman college readers and in anthologies of English writers, and two of his novels—*Animal Farm* and *1984*—have been translated into many languages". Why biographers are interested in Orwell is understandable because he led a life that was unusual for a writer. He was a British policeman in Burma, a dishwasher in Paris, and an investigative journalist in England; he was also a bookstore assistant, schoolmaster, grocer, and foreign correspondent. Orwell's interest in military affairs is apparent in his essays and reviews, many of which touch on military questions. ①

14. Theological Study

Lawrence Dugan, in "Orwell and Catholicism", deals with the work of George Orwell on Roman Catholicism. Orwell's ideas focus on the Catholicism, its importance to British literature of the 1920s and 1930s, the political influence of the Church in British, Irish and international affairs, and the impact of Church as a universal institution. His view of Catholicism is a reactionary-force and not a moral force sharing a unique doctrine. ②

Paul J. Griffiths, in "Orwell for Christians", presents a critique of the work of author George Orwell. Topics discussed include Orwell's vestigial affection for the rites and buildings of the Church of England; Orwell's opposition to almost everything about Christianity, and especially to Catholicism; books published about Orwell, such as *The Complete Works of George Orwell*, by George Orwell, edited by

---

① Miller S. "Orwell Once More". The Sewanee Review, 2004, 112(4): 595-618.
② Dugan L. "Orwell and Catholicism". Modern Age, 2006, 48(3): 226-240.

Peter Davison, with Ian Angus and Sheila Davison, *Inside George Orwell*, by Gordon Bowker, and *Why Orwell Matters*, by Christopher Hitchens. ①

15. Linguistic Study

Lawrence Davidson, in "Orwellianism and the Kafkaesque in the Israeli-Palestinian Discourse", argues that Israeli perceptions and Palestinian conditions of life can be understood in terms of the literary worlds created by George Orwell and Franz Kafka. For Israel, the relevant literary environment is that of George Orwell's novel *1984*. Here Orwell pictures a community psychologically closed in by the twisted use of language and an incapacity for critical self-analysis. In the case of the Palestinians, the relevant literary world is that created in many of the novels of Franz Kafka. Kafka's literary world is characterised by unpredictability. It depicts oppressed societies in which the individual is subject to the arbitrary will of a greater power. This essay demonstrates how Orwellian and Kafkaesque depictions define current Israeli perceptions of the Palestinians, and Palestinian life under Israeli occupation. ②

---

① Griffiths P J. "Orwell for Christians". First Things: A Monthly Journal of Religion & Public Life, 2004(148): 32-40.

② Davidson L. "Orwellianism and the Kafkaesque in the Israeli-Palestinian Discourse". Holy Land Studies: A Multidisciplinary Journal, 2004, 3(2): 195-211.

Chapter 14

William Golding

William Golding(1911-1993)

Golding was born in Cornwall and was graduated from Brasenose College, Oxford. He has been an actor, theater producer, teacher, and aviator in the Royal Navy. His first novel, *Lord of the Flies*, is popular and lasting. This was followed by *Pincher Martin*, *The Brass Butterfly* (a play, 1958), *Free Fall*, *The Spire*, *The Pyramid*, *Darkness Visible*, *Rites of Passage*, and *The Paper Men*. Golding won the Nobel Prize in Literature in 1983. [1]

---

[1] Richetti J, Bender J, David D, et al. The Columbia History of the British Novel. New York: Columbia University Press, 1994.

Chapter 14　William Golding

Critical Perspectives

1. Philosophical Study

Eric Wilson, in "Warring Sovereigns and Mimetic Rivals: On Scapegoats and Political Crisis in William Golding's *Lord of the Flies*", explores the theme of the book which traces the Society's defects back to the human nature's defects. The author reads the novel as a satire of the theory of the State of Nature and the Social Contract by philosopher Thomas Hobbes. It argues that the boys in Golding's novel do not regress to the mimetic logic of cultural formation. [1]

2. Thematic Study

Sergios Paschalis, in "Intertextual Sparagmos: Euripides, Ovid and *Lord of the Flies*", discusses the intertextual relationship between William Golding's 1954 novel *Lord of the Flies* and Euripides' *Bacchae*. Topics include the similar themes of the works like ritual, irrational violence, hunting and sacrifice, how Golding used the concept of sparagmos (dismemberment) in his novel, and a study by Justine McConnell on the appropriation of Greek tragedy. [2]

---

[1] Wilson E. "Warring Sovereigns and Mimetic Rivals: On Scapegoats and Political Crisis in William Golding's *Lord of the Flies*". Law & Humanities, 2014, 8(2): 147-173.

[2] Paschalis S. "Intertextual Sparagmos: Euripides, Ovid and *Lord of the Flies*". International Journal of the Classical Tradition, 2021, 28(2): 183-215.

3. Canonization

Katie Porteus, in "Easing the Pain of the Classics", discusses ways of teaching of classic English literature to young adults. It notes that many books were written for well-educated adults with leisure time, not for young adults with busy schedules and other interests. It also notes that reading classics is good preparation for college reading, for it helps expand vocabulary and increase cultural literacy. Methods for making the classics more relevant to teens are given, including pairing of a classic novel with a contemporary one, such as *Lord of the Flies* by William Golding with *Gone* by Michael Grant. Other pairings include Shakespeare's *Romeo and Juliet* and *Saving Juliet* by Suzanne Selfors, and *Ringside 1925: Views from the Scopes Monkey Trial* by Jen Bryant with the play *Inherit the Wind* by Jerome Lawrence and Robert E. Lee.[①]

Christine McGovern, in "Will *Survivor* Replace *Lord of the Flies*?", focuses on a literature teacher's concerns about the impact of the television program *Survivor* on students' reading of William Golding's novel, *Lord of the Flies*. Topics discussed include required reading material at Georgetown Visitation Preparatory School in Washington, D. C.; pre-reading activity; and a glimpse into the evil that lurks in the hearts of the characters.[②]

4. Post-colonial Study

Matthew R. Kay, in "Seeing the Curriculum with Fresh Eyes: Race Can Be an Important—And Enriching—Lens to Apply to Any Unit of Study", discusses the

---

① Porteus K. "Easing the Pain of the Classics". Young Adult Library Services, 2009, 7(4):16-18.
② McGovern C. "Will *Survivor* Replace *Lord of the Flies*?". Independent School, 2001, 60(2): 12.

importance of discussing race in the classroom to make sure that antiracism is at the forefront of students' experience. The author of this essay considers the books *Lord of the Flies* by William Golding and Homer's *The Odyssey* as important sources about race. The author also examines the subject of race as a curricular lens. [1]

5. Ethical Study

Nabil A. Jalil, et al., in "The Absurd Rebel on an Imaginary Rock", argue that in his novel *Pincher Martin*, William Golding places his protagonist, Pincher Martin, in an extreme situation where the lines between reality and imagination are blurred. The result is that the protagonist's struggles for his existence verges on the absurd. Still it is not a story for mere fantasy. Golding is known to convey a moral lesson in his novels, and *Pincher Martin* is certainly no exception. The struggle of the protagonist can be seen as a story about human existence and the absurd struggle in life against death. The protagonist becomes a representative of the human individual faced with the realization of his own mortality and the absurdity of his life. These are themes which existentialist writers like Jean-Paul Sartre and Albert Camus address in their philosophy, as Whitehead points out. However, Whitehead's approach is to look at the novel through the Sartrean psychological concept of imagination which makes the protagonist struggle an outcome of mere fantasy. To examine the existential dilemma of the protagonist and his absurd struggle against death, this paper proposes to uses Albert Camus' philosophical concepts of the absurd and absurd rebellion to look at the novel in a new light. [2]

---

[1] Kay M R. "Seeing the Curriculum with Fresh Eyes: Race Can Be an Important—And Enriching—Lens to Apply to Any Unit of Study". Educational Leadership, 2021, 78(5): 78-79.

[2] Jalil N A, et al. "The Absurd Rebel on an Imaginary Rock". The International Journal of Interdisciplinary Social Sciences, 2011, 6(4):187-196.

Charles Travis, in "The Morphology of Prometheus, Literary Geography and the Geoethical Project", explores mappings, musings and "thought experiments" in literary geography to consider how they may contribute to geoethical pedagogy and research. Representations of Prometheus from the fourteenth century onwards have traveled along three broad symbolical roads: first, as the creator, and bringer of fire; second, as a bound figure in chains; and thirdly, unbound. As the geophysicist Professor Michael Mann observes, global warming and loss of biodiversity constitute an ethical problem. The remediation of the Prometheus myth in Mary Shelley's *Frankenstein, or the modern Prometheus*, Jonathan Fetter-Vorm's *Trinity: A Graphic History of the First Atomic Bomb* and William Golding's novel *Lord of the Flies* provides the means to explore the geographical, historical and cultural contingencies of geoethical dilemmas contributing to the framing of the Anthropocene and Gaia heuristics. This paper argues for the necessity of scholars in the arts, humanities and geosciences to share and exchange idiographic and nomothetic perspectives in order to forge a geoethical dialectic that fuses poetic and positivistic methods into transcendent ontologies and epistemologies to address the existential questions of global warming and loss of biodiversity as we enter the age of the Anthropocene.[①]

6. Cultural Study

Aniela Toma, in "Tribal Organisation in *Lord of the Flies*. An Anthropological Perspective", argues that a man can develop from a peaceful, fruit-picking being into a violent, carnivorous one. A similar development can be seen in William Golding's *Lord of the Flies*, where a group of children gradually separates into two tribes, each being organized based on a different set of principles. As such, placing

---

① Travis C. "The Morphology of Prometheus, Literary Geography and the Geoethical Project". Geosciences, 2021, 11(8): 340.

the text into the broader context of anthropological studies and analyzing the way in which the theme is constructed from a narrative point of view, the author of this essay argues that the tribal organisation on the island closely resembles that of the primitive man. It is quite clear that there is something in our collective consciousness that makes one act and develop in a similar manner. ①

Zoltan Varga, et al., in "We Are Invited to Imagine: Using a Literary Text to Encourage Cross-cultural Dialogue about Citizenship", argue that researchers from Norway, Pakistan and the United Kingdom explore the potential of a literary text to encourage intercultural dialogue by using William Golding's *Lord of the Flies* as a stimulus. The innovative research method used is to combine Literature Circles and Google Documents to provide a platform for asynchronous online exchange between three cohorts of students in higher education. The authors' analysis of the data suggests the differences between those students who regard the text as a living document that is related directly to their personal experiences of citizenship issues. The authors contend that this research can contribute original and significant insights to the literature on teaching citizenship through literary texts such as the relationship between text choice and context, models of international collaboration at the higher education level and contrasting approaches towards citizenship and reading. ②

7. Socialism Study

Gary Watt, in "The Law of Dress in *Lord of the Flies*", offers the author's insights regarding the book *Lord of the Flies*, by William Golding. Topics discussed include the concept of clothing-nakedness cluster, the importance of civilized

---

① Toma A. "Tribal Organisation in *Lord of the Flies*. An Anthropological Perspective". Bulletin of the Transilvania University of Brasov, Series IV: Philology & Cultural Studies, 2017, 10(1): 179-188.

② Varga Z, et al. "We Are Invited to Imagine: Using a Literary Text to Encourage Cross-cultural Dialogue about Citizenship". Cambridge Journal of Education, 2020, 50(4): 501-519.

culture, and the mutability of laws and government policies concerning social systems. It also mentions the primal state which impulses civil society and symbolism of clothing.①

David P. Barash, in "Red in Tooth, Claw, and Trigger Finger", focuses on homo sapiens with reference to an exhibit at the Bronx Zoo. Homo sapiens has much to answer for that, including a gory history of murder and mayhem. An unruly, ingrained savagery, verging on bloodlust, has been a favorite theme of fiction, including, for example, Joseph Conrad's *Heart of Darkness* and William Golding's book *Lord of the Flies*, while Robert Louis Stevenson's book *The Strange Case of Dr. Jekyll and Mr. Hyde* developed an explicit notion of duality: that a predisposition to violence lurks within the most outwardly civilized and kindly person. Human beings are a violent, murderous lot, destructive of each other no less than of their environment.②

8. Linguistic Study

Natalia Vladimirova, and Yekaterina Nagornaya, in "The Semiotics of a Ship and Its Modelling Features in the Novels of William Golding, Julian Barnes, and Gregory Norminton", study the semiotics of the ship as an image of the world in cases of the novels *To the Ends of the Earth* by William Golding, *A History of the World in $10^{1/2}$ Chapters* by J. Barnes, and *The Ship of Fools* by Gregory Norminton. The ship is considered as a new version of the Biblical Noah's Ark—a miniature society. The authors believe that the avantext integrates the new "generative model"

---

① Watt G. "The Law of Dress in *Lord of the Flies*". Law & Humanities, 2014, 8(2): 174-191.
② Barash D P. "Red in Tooth, Claw, and Trigger Finger". Chronicle of Higher Education, 2005, 51(49): B19-B20.

creating at the same time new forms of fictional conditionality and types of literary generalization.①

9. Theological Study

James Clements, in "'The Thing in the Box': William Golding's *Miss Pulkinhorn* as Apophatic Literature", analyzes the short story *Miss Pulkinhorn* by William Golding. Topics include the characters and plot of the story, the nature of religious symbols in the story, such as depiction of darkness as an image of the unknown God in the story, and the story *Miss Pulkinhorn* as an apophatic literature.②

David Troupes, in "Ted Hughes and the Biological Fall", argues that the British poet Ted Hughes offers an undeniably religious vision of the world, combining devotion to a Robert Graves-style goddess figure with an enduring fascination with Christian cosmology and biblical stories. He pursues science, particularly anthropology and palaeontology, with equal interest. These interests intersect in an essay Hughes wrote, ostensibly about William Golding's novel *The Inheritors*, in which he attempts to unite a lapsarian reading of the human condition with the (at the time) latest scientific developments concerning human evolution. Taking Hughes's article as a starting point, the author of this essay explores the ways in which this lapsarian-evolutionary perspective on humanity informs Hughes's own creative output, locating resonant *Old Testament* passages which appear to underwrite his project and providing a critique of his ideas along both scientific and theological lines.③

---

① Vladimirova N, Nagornaya Y. "The Semiotics of a Ship and Its Modelling Features in the Novels of William Golding, Julian Barnes, and Gregory Norminton". *Vestnik IKBFU*, 2013(8): 146-150.

② Clements J. "'The Thing in the Box': William Golding's *Miss Pulkinhorn* as Apophatic Literature". Religion & Literature, 2014, 46(1): 93-115.

③ Troupes D. "Ted Hughes and the Biological Fall". Religion & Literature, 2018, 50(1/2): 153-176.

Chapter 15

Doris Lessing

Doris Lessing (1919-2013)

Born in Persia to British parents, Lessing moved with her family at the age of five to a farm in Southern Rhodesia. After dropping out of school at fifteen, she worked as a nursemaid, secretary, and telephone operator. When her first marriage ended, she became active in leftist politics. In 1949, Lessing went to England with her youngest child and published her first novel, *The Grass Is Singing*. Her great quintet of novels, Children of Violence, comprises the somewhat autobiographical life from her youth in Rhodesia to the year 2000: *Martha Quest*, *A Proper Marriage*, *A Ripple from the Storm*, *Landlocked*, and *The Four-Gated City*. Her most famous and perhaps most political novel is *The Golden Notebook*, a work that has become a feminist classic. Her late novels include *Briefing for a Descent into Hell* and *The Memoirs of a Survivor*.[1]

---

[1] Richetti J, Bender J, David D, et al. The Columbia History of the British Novel. New York: Columbia University Press, 1994.

Critical Perspectives

1. Narrative Study

Katherine Fishburn, in "The Manichean Allegories of Doris Lessing's *The Grass Is Singing*", discusses the Manichean allegories in the book *The Grass Is Singing*, by Doris Lessing. Topics discussed include realism and vividness of Lessing's portrayal of colonialism; colonialist's need to perpetuate racial differences; transition in colonized Africa from the dominant phase to the hegemonic; and plurality of meaning. [①]

Carol Franko, in "Authority, Truthtelling, and Parody: Doris Lessing and 'the Book'", provides a critical interpretation of writer Doris Lessing's fiction. Topics discussed include Lessing's ambivalence toward canonical authorities; the heroine's subjectivity as battleground of discourses in *Martha Quest*; power of language to construct experience; and difference of genre and setting in *The Sun between Their Feet* and *The Golden Notebook*. [②]

Maureen Corrigan, in "Improbably Star-crossed", discusses the book *Love, Again*, by Doris Lessing. Lessing's high seriousness, her intellectual chilliness, and her stern lack of sentimentality cause people to esteem rather than embrace her books, and make them suspect that Lessing and they would not hit it off. Lessing is a notorious scold who routinely swats down the interpretations of her novels proffered

---

① Fishburn K. "The Manichean Allegories of Doris Lessing's *The Grass Is Singing*". Research in African Literatures, 1994, 94(25): 1-14.

② Franko C. "Authority, Truthtelling, and Parody: Doris Lessing and 'the Book'". Papers on Language & Literature, 1995, 31(3): 255-285.

by academic supplicants, literary journalists and naive fans. *Love, Again* is Lessing's exhilarating and disquieting meditation on old age.①

Tonya Krouse, in "Freedom as Effacement in *The Golden Notebook*: Theorizing Pleasure, Subjectivity, and Authority", examines Doris Lessing's novel *The Golden Notebook* as a crucial transitional text between modernist and postmodernist periods. In situating the novel between these two periods, special attention is paid to the way that the narrative seems to construct authorial and female subjectivity through intermittent effacements of the physical self, which the text constitutes as a gesture toward "freeing" writing from the constraints of embodied expression. Engaging the theories of Roland Barthes, Michel Foucault, and Helene Cixous, the article looks at Lessing's representations of pleasure, subjectivity, and the author-figure's authority to examine how Lessing's novel both borrows from and reacts against its modernist predecessors James Joyce, D. H. Lawrence, and Virginia Woolf, as well as how it imagines potential possibilities for authorial and female subjectivity in the postmodern era.②

Herbert Marder, in "Borderline Fantasies: The Two Worlds of *Briefing for a Descent into Hell*", presents information on the book *Briefing for a Descent into Hell*, by Doris Lessing. Topics discussed include other books written by Lessing; problems of classification that arise from differing attitudes to the implied comparison between estranged and ordinary realities; and arrangement of the interpreting layers of the book.③

---

① Corrigan M. "Improbably Star-crossed". The Nation, 1996, 262(18): 62-66.
② Krouse T. "Freedom as Effacement in *The Golden Notebook*: Theorizing Pleasure, Subjectivity, and Authority". Journal of Modern Literature, 2006, 29(3): 39-56.
③ Marder H. "Borderline Fantasies: The Two Worlds of *Briefing for a Descent into Hell*". Papers on Language & Literature, 1983, 19(4): 427-448.

2. Feminism Study

Niger Afroz Islam, and Sharifa Akter, in "Kristevan Exploration of Abjection in Doris Lessing's *The Grass Is Singing*", attempt to identify to what extent the psychological portrayal of Mary Turner's fragmented subjectivity and failure of individuation justifies Doris Lessing's *The Grass Is Singing* as a powerful analysis of Julia Kristeva's theory of abjection. For Kristeva, abjection is the process of identity formation experiencing the separation from the mother and entry into language that blurs the boundaries between self and other, hence creates a disturbing, horrible and repulsive generative power of the self within the phallocentric systems of thought. *The Grass Is Singing* is replete with such tropes of abjection where the female protagonist, Mary Turner, is exposed to decode the conventional features of femininity. She encounters Kristeva's imaginary boundary into the realm of death and horror; experiences the transition between psychoanalysis and the subconscious mind; and manipulates the boundaries, laws, and rules of her existence to a point where meaning is undermined. Even the concept of death is defamiliarized by portraying Mary as a "willing victim". This article demonstrates how the theory of abjection by Kristeva serves to parody the binary oppositions and effectively deconstructs the reader's expectations of archetypal, naive, passive female role endorsed with patriarchal ideology. This essay explores how in Doris Lessing's *The Grass Is Singing* (1950), Mary Turner is portrayed as neither a subject nor an object, but as a perverse, narcissist, ambivalent and willing victim to subvert the conventional representation of femininity. [1]

Roberta Rubenstein, in "Going on Fifty: Doris Lessing's *The Golden Notebook*", critiques Doris Lessing's novel *The Golden Notebook*. The author

---

[1] Islam N A, Akter S. "Kristevan Exploration of Abjection in Doris Lessing's *The Grass Is Singing*". ASA University Review, 2017, 11(1): 43-50.

discusses Lessing's portrayal of the social and political conditions of women in the novel, including discussions of patriarchal male-female relationships and the protagonist's involvement in liberal politics. The historical significance of the novel is also discussed.①

Linda H. Halisky, in "Redeeming the Irrational: The Inexplicable Heroines of *A Sorrowful Woman* and *To Room Nineteen*", discusses Gail Godwin's short story *A Sorrowful Woman* and Doris Lessing's short story *To Room Nineteen*. Topics discussed include similarities of the stories; one marked difference of the stories; Lynn Sukenick's view about Lessing's stories in Sukenick's book *Feeling and Reason in Doris Lessing's Fiction*; chief concern of much feminist criticism; and views about each author's heroines.②

David Pryce-Jones, in "Doris Lessing Wins", presents views on British writer Doris Lessing and her winning of the Nobel Prize for Literature. Her early days as a Communist and anti-nuclear activist are criticized, but her later repudiation of Communism and even feminism, and her two-volume autobiography, are viewed more charitably.③

3. Psychological Study

Rosario Arias, in "'All the world's a Stage': Theatricality, Spectacle and the Flâneuse in Doris Lessing's Vision of London", argues that Doris Lessing has lived in London since she first arrived there in 1949, from Southern Rhodesia (now Zimbabwe). Lessing has always expressed her passion for the city of London, which has been turned into the setting for most of her novels and short stories. In addition,

---

① Rubenstein R. "Going on Fifty: Doris Lessing's *The Golden Notebook*". women's Review of Books, 2012, 29(5): 24-26.

② Halisky L H. "Redeeming the Irrational: The Inexplicable Heroines of *A Sorrowful Woman* and *To Room Nineteen*". Studies in Short Fiction, 1990, 27(1): 45-54.

③ Pryce-Jones D. "Doris Lessing Wins". National Review, 2007, 59(20): 28-30.

in her fictional and autobiographical texts, the author reveals her love for theatregoing and play-acting, as well as her perception of life as a stage. This article strives to link these two ideas (the city and the theatre) in Lessing's fiction, which shows an increasing interest in the image of London as a theatre, whereby the female protagonist happens to become a spectator of snippets and sketches of real-life scenes, as she strolls around the city. In the act of observing these scenes from everyday life, these twentieth-century female flâneurs render London as a potential space, a space of creativity, where mutual bonds are established between the flâneuse/spectator and the performers. In this sense, psychoanalytic criticism—for example, the concept of transitional space as defined by D. W. Winnicott—can prove to be useful in the analysis of Lessing's fiction. [1]

A. Rahman and S. G. Mohammad, in "*Two Potters*: A Tale of Unknown Fears and Uncertain Desires", argue that Doris Lessing is a contemporary novelist and short story writer whose work deals primarily with female psyche, and her independence has profound appeal and tremendous challenge for female readership. There are diverse approaches applied to her fiction to unveil the mystery that surrounds it. Keeping in view Lessing's preoccupation with issues related to women and their situation in the twentieth century, this study focuses on one of her short stories, *Two Potters*. Doris Lessing's *Two Potters* abounds with dreams, shapes and colours. Preoccupation with a particular shape or colour has its roots in the unconscious. The text contains all the elements which are vital requisites for Freudian dream analysis. Our preference for one color over the other is unconscious and psychological. Why one prefers pink over blue or brown over pale needs a thorough psychological analysis. In order to probe into psychological reasons for colour preference, we need to decode the dreams in the text by interpreting repetitions, gaps and missing links. Mary Tawnish has been represented as the

---

[1] Arias R. "'All the world's a Stage': Theatricality, Spectacle and the Flâneuse in Doris Lessing's Vision of London". Journal of Gender Studies, 2005, 14(1): 3-11.

object of author's uncertain desires. The narrator herself seems to be uncertain about her own desires. This paper traces the elements of fear and uncertainty of desires by decoding the text. Freud's interpretation of dreams provides a viable foundation for the discussion as it involves dream analysis and focuses on the centrality of the unconscious. These dreams show a slow growth or progress towards maturity—from vagueness to clarity. Moreover, it focuses on the play of colours in the text. Different recurring shapes and colours are clues to the Freudian interpretations of the text. [①]

4. Thematic Study

Karen Schneider, in "A Different War Story: Doris Lessing's Great Escape", focuses on Doris Lessing's views on the World War II. Topics discussed include how World War II enables us to "live differently"; description of specific themes that highlighted in Children of Violence Series; and Lessing's aim for the provision of tools for the re-examination of history. [②]

Lisa Tyler, in "Our Mothers' Gardens: Doris Lessing's *Among the Roses*", analyzes Doris Lessing's short story, *Among the Roses*. Topics discussed include use of dialectic in presenting the mode of thought and narrative strategy; emphasis on cycles; and examination of the mother-daughter relationship. [③]

Virginia Pruitt, in "The Crucial Balance: A Theme in Lessing's Short Fiction", examines the theme of crucial balance in Doris Lessing's short fiction. Topics discussed include list of the short stories; emphasis on false dichotomies and

---

① Rahman A, Mohammad S G. "*Two Potters*: A Tale of Unknown Fears and Uncertain Desires". Putaj Humanities & Social Sciences, 2014, 21(1): 17-26.

② Schneider K. "A Different War Story: Doris Lessing's Great Escape". Journal of Modern Literature, 1995, 19(2): 259-272.

③ Tyler L. "Our Mothers' Gardens: Doris Lessing's *Among the Roses*". Studies in Short Fiction, 1994, 31(2):163-173.

divisions; and description of the characters with maintaining self-control. ①

5. Biographical Study

Aaron S. Rosenfeld, in "Re-membering the Future: Doris Lessing's 'Experiment in Autobiography'", explores the use of future history or speculative description in the book *The Memoirs of a Survivor*, by Doris Lessing. Topics discussed include characterization of the future histories; main categories of future history that constitute the bulk of the genre; and representation of dystopia in the book. ②

Jeanne Schinto, in "Lessing in London", appraises the book *Walking in the Shade: Volume Two of My Autobiography, 1949-1962*, by Doris Lessing. *Walking in the Shade* is chock full of piquant accounts of her friendships with numerous writers and artists, especially those in the theater arts. In this book, Kenneth Tynan is described as being fragile, vulnerable, like an elegant gray silky moth, with his large prominent greeny eyes and his bony face. She also tells many stories of political friends and foes. ③

Ellena Savage, in "Would Crikey Pay Doris Lessing?", offers an insight on the death of British author and Nobel laureate Doris Lessing. The author discusses the life of Lessing, her writings such as the novel *The Golden Notebook*, and her literary accomplishments. The author says that the life of Lessing represents the profound seriousness of how writers approach their works and the kind of risks they take. ④

---

① Pruitt V. "The Crucial Balance: A Theme in Lessing's Short Fiction". Studies in Short Fiction, 1981, 18(3): 281-285.

② Rosenfeld A S. "Re-membering the Future: Doris Lessing's 'Experiment in Autobiography'". Critical Survey, 2005, 17(1): 40-55.

③ Schinto J. "Lessing in London". The Nation, 1997, 265(11): 31-33.

④ Savage E. "Would Crikey Pay Doris Lessing?". Eureka Street, 2013, 23(23): 32-33.

S. Saraçoğlu, in "A New Form Derived out of Formlessness in Doris Lessing's *The Golden Notebook*", argues that *The Golden Notebook*, Doris Lessing's most famous novel published in 1962, is now considered one of the major works of twentieth-century literature. It is the story of Anna Wulf, a single woman living with her young daughter in a flat. Following the great success of her autobiographical novel about a group of Communists in colonial Africa, Anna struggles to write again, but she is blocked. So she tries to find a way to integrate the multiple selves that fragment her personality by deciding to keep four notebooks, one for each component of her life—black for her experiences in Africa, red for current politics, yellow for a fictionalized version of herself, and blue for a diary. By viewing her life from these different angles, going over her experiences, and revising her responses, Anna eventually manages to unify her identity in one notebook which is the very title of the novel analyzed in this study.[①]

6. New Historicism

C. G. Navarro, in "'Oh, There Are So Many Things I Want to Write': Becoming an Author: Doris Lessing and the Whitehorn Letters from 1944 to 1949", explores the narrative process identified in the Whitehorn Letters, written by Doris Lessing from 1944 to 1949, as historical documents that form a single, coherent whole. Their significance is assessed by means of an epistemological reflection that sheds light on the path by which the young Lessing established her identity as an author. In the letter-writing process, Lessing declares her aim to become a writer. The letters also characterise the writer as a historical subject, and describe the relationship between this historical subject and the individual who writes the correspondence. Since the letters formulate a coherent discourse about Lessing's

---

[①] Saraçoğlu S. "A New Form Derived out of Formlessness in Doris Lessing's *The Golden Notebook*". Ekev Academic Review, 2006, 10(26): 141-146.

authorial identity, the author of this essay investigates whether using a model for reading them may be beneficial. The author believes that additional nuances could be detected in her narratives by revisiting Lessing and examining, in the centenary of her birth, some hitherto unknown parts of her writings, as these letters represent.①

Susan Watkins, in "Second World Life Writing: Doris Lessing's *Under My Skin*", argues that the first volume of Doris Lessing's official autobiography, *Under My Skin*, returns her to memories of her African childhood, and necessitates that she reassess the status of official and "fictionalised" accounts of the past, especially her own story of the impact of colonisation and Empire on her family, herself and the African population in Southern Rhodesia. In the 1990s, feminist critics were working out the distinctive features of women's autobiographical writing, and much more recently those of postcolonial life writing have been identified by critics such as Bart Moore-Gilbert. This article considers whether categories such as feminist autobiography, autobiography of empire or postcolonial autobiography are helpful in reading *Under My Skin*, and investigates whether or not it is more appropriate to consider the text as an example of second world life writing. As a second world writer, to use Stephen Slemon's 1990 term, Lessing's ambivalence about issues of gender, race, empire and nation, and her complicity with colonialism as the daughter of white invader settlers and her resistance to it, become easier to analyze. In order to understand how this ambivalence plays out in the text, the article investigates whether the trope Helen Tiffin identifies as particular to second world women's life writing—dispersive citation—is useful in reading Lessing's autobiography and making sense of her intervention in the genre of life writing.②

---

① Navarro C G. "'Oh, There Are So Many Things I Want to Write': Becoming an Author: Doris Lessing and the Whitehorn Letters from 1944 to 1949". International Journal of English Studies, 2019, 19(2):19-36.

② Watkins S. "Second World Life Writing: Doris Lessing's *Under My Skin*". Journal of Southern African Studies, 2016, 42(1):137-148.

Joseph Hynes, in "Dorris Lessing's Briefing as Structural Life and Death", presents an examination of the structure and techniques used by Doris Lessing in her novel *Briefing for a Descent into Hell*, which demonstrates two stylistic emphases of Lessing's career. Subjects addressed include comparison of the novel with Lessing's other works, analysis of literary realism in the works prior to it, and the Romantic tendencies in the novels written afterward.①

7. Canonization

Sean French, in "Doris Lessing Thinks Kids Can Learn to Read from the Bible. Has She Seen the Illiteracy Rates for the 17th Century?", ponders on the assertion of writer Doris Lessing that British children in the 1990s lack the ability to read long books and understand difficult words, specifically that of the Bible. Topics discussed include role of grandparents and forebears in the issue; children's literacy in the 1990s; and types of books being read by children.②

8. Post-colonial Study

Bill Schwarz, in "The Fact of Whiteness: Doris Lessing's *The Grass Is Singing*—A Historian's Notebook", approaches Doris Lessing's famous 1950 novel, *The Grass Is Singing*. *The Grass is Singing*, as an engaging and sophisticated exploration of gendered racial whiteness, manifest in the settler colony of Southern Rhodesia towards the end of colonial rule. The author of this essay suggests that central to Lessing's novelistic project is a thinking that how it might be possible to

---

① Hynes J. "Dorris Lessing's Briefing as Structural Life and Death". Renascence, 1994, 46(4): 225-245.
② French S. "Doris Lessing Thinks Kids Can Learn to Read from the Bible. Has She Seen the Illiteracy Rates for the 17th Century?". The New Statesman, 1999, 128(4466): 28.

envisage knowledge (truth) if it were to be freed from race. Arguably, the novel is a fictional embodiment of the thesis that the dismantling of racial whiteness provides the precondition for new thought to happen, both in an epistemological and ethical sense. The article situates knowledge in relation to the emotions and psychic life of characters. In opposition to the imperatives of instrumental reason, *The Grass Is Singing* arguably champions an ethics of "principled unknowability", in which the location of the unconscious is never far away, and the Manichaean certainties of colonial-era whiteness are revealed as pathologically overdetermined. [1]

9. Cultural Study

Katherine Fishburn, in "Back to the Preface: Cultural Conversations with *The Golden Notebook*", comments on the writings of Doris Lessing. Topics discussed include hermeneutical instruction in the preface for the Bantam edition of *The Golden Notebook*; man's lack of a true self; Lessing's autobiographical fiction; the politicized male theorists; and political work of intellectuals. [2]

10. Socialism Study

James Arnett, in "What's Left of Feelings? The Affective Labor of Politics in Doris Lessing's *The Golden Notebook*", argues that in *The Golden Notebook*, Doris Lessing's fragmented narrative, invocations of Sisyphean labor, and characterization of political work demonstrate that the most effective route to progressive political change is through embodying an optimism that may seem naive. Progressive politics is

---

[1] Schwarz B. "The Fact of Whiteness: Doris Lessing's *The Grass Is Singing*—A Historian's Notebook". Journal of Southern African Studies, 2016, 42(1): 127-136.

[2] Fishburn K. "Back to the Preface: Cultural Conversations with *The Golden Notebook*". College Literature, 1990, 17(2/3): 183-195.

the prey to what Wendy Brown calls "left melancholy", a political and affective paralysis, a mood that is grappled with from within an experience of political depression. The question posed by Lessing is: what can to be done facing such disempowering affective responses to the apparently inevitable defeat of progressive politics.①

11. Theological Study

Matthew Fike, in "C. G. Jung's *Memories, Dreams, Reflections* as a Source for Doris Lessing's *Briefing for a Descent into Hell*", argues that Doris Lessing is conversant in Jungian psychology, and her novel *Briefing for a Descent into Hell* includes more Jungian elements than previous critics have identified. In particular, it is likely that she borrowed from Jung's *Memories, Dreams, Reflections* when crafting her protagonist Charles Watkins's descent into madness and return to sanity. This essay argues that the autobiography's chapter 6, "Confrontation with the Unconscious", and chapter 10, "Visions"—Jung's encounter with madness and his near-death experience—provided Lessing with a series of images that she reworked in the novel. Considered in light of *Memories, Dreams, Reflections*, *Briefing for a Descent into Hell* conveys a sense of lost potential: Watkins regains his memory but, unlike Jung, forgets his vision of the collective unconscious.②

Anthony Chennells, in "*The Sweetest Dream*: Lessing, Zimbabwe and Catholicism", argues that Lessing refers frequently, if in passing, to Roman Catholicism, often as part of her growing interest in spirituality, which begins while she was writing. Some of these references are in the accounts of her travels in

---

① Arnett J. "What's Left of Feelings? The Affective Labor of Politics in Doris Lessing's *The Golden Notebook*". Journal of Modern Literature, 2018, 41(2): 77-95.

② Fike M. "C. G. Jung's *Memories, Dreams, Reflections* as a Source for Doris Lessing's *Briefing for a Descent into Hell*". Journal of Jungian Scholarly Studies, 2016, 11(1): 18-28.

Zimbabwe, but they are also to be found in her autobiographies, reviews and occasional journalism. Because of their frequency, she cannot be regarded as entirely indifferent to the church. A valid line of enquiry into Lessing's work asks whether her dislike for the church, formed during her traumatic four years as a young child in the Salisbury convent, remained her dominant impression, or whether in later life she found in Catholicism, particularly in Zimbabwe, an institution that invited more complex responses. An answer is provided in *The Sweetest Dream*, her last long novel that deals directly with Africa. The novel is partly set in Zimlia, a country that clearly suggests Zimbabwe. It avoids representing Catholicism and traditional spirituality as antagonistic; the complex plotting at its end rejects a confident division between the sacred and the secular, and suggests that, although Catholicism is on the whole a force for good, its powers in Zimlia are limited, confronted as the church is by the literal epidemic of AIDS and the power of traditional spirituality. One possible reading suggests that this latter power prevails. [1]

---

[1] Chennells A. "*The Sweetest Dream*: Lessing, Zimbabwe and Catholicism". Journal of Southern African Studies, 2016, 42(1):111-125.

Chapter 16

Iris Murdoch

Iris Murdoch (1919-1999)

Iris Murdoch was born in Dublin, Ireland and grew up in the suburbs of London. While still at Oxford, she began to help edit periodicals. She was a radical and joined the Communist Party at one time. Later she worked in the United Nations and traveled to Europe, where she met Satre, the French existentialist author-philosopher and came under his influence. She devoted herself wholly to writing in 1963, and has been very prolific. So far she has written over twenty novels such as *Under the Net*, *The Sandcastle*, *The Bell*, *A Severed Head*, *The Black Prince*, and *The Sea, the Sea*. Murdoch is a philosopher-writer.[1]

---

[1] 常耀信. 英国文学简史. 南开大学出版社 2006 年版.

Critical Perspectives

1. Narrative Study

S. F. Nejad, in "The Crisis of Interpretation in the Allegorical Reading of Iris Murdoch's *The Unicorn*", presents a literary criticism of the book *The Unicorn* by Iris Murdoch. Topics include the crisis of interpretation in the allegorical reading of the book. *The Unicorn* is stated to be an amalgam of various genres and allusive references to other texts, that turn out to be self-conflicting in purpose. ①

2. Feminism Study

M. García-Avello, in "Romantic Love, Gender Imbalance and Feminist Readings in Iris Murdoch's *The Sea, the Sea*", notes that Iris Murdoch's novels depict a profoundly patriarchal society. Most scholars have generally failed to identify any feminist aspirations in her work. This article aims to reassess her legacy as a writer by analyzing from a feminist perspective one of her most acclaimed novels, *The Sea, the Sea*. The tension between the androcentric approach of a self-deluded male narrator and a female author whose worldview is strongly influenced by her gender results in a feminist critique which is not based on the recovery of a female voice, but on the exploration of patriarchy within the novel and the production of a feminist epistemology derived from a dialogue between Murdoch's

---

① Nejad S F. "The Crisis of Interpretation in the Allegorical Reading of Iris Murdoch's *The Unicorn*". Papers on Language & Literature, 2018, 54(4): 381-401.

fiction and philosophy.①

Sissela Bok, in "Simone Weil and Iris Murdoch: The Possibility of Dialogue", investigates the possibility of a philosophical dialogue between women writers Simone Weil and Iris Murdoch. An overview of the physical sufferings of Weil and the course of her near-starvation is presented. It offers information on the self-indulgent lifestyle of Murdoch. It also explores how Murdoch considers the views of Weil based on her novels and philosophical writings.②

David J. Fine, in "'What a Fuss about Probably Nothing': Iris Murdoch's Ordinary Queerness", focuses on ordinary queerness of Irish-British novelist Iris Murdoch. It reports on her moral philosophy and realist fictions and her association with Platonism and poststructuralism which influences her work from feminism and Queer Studies. It analyzes the representation of queer desire challenges in the novel *A Fairly Honourable Defeat*.③

3. Philosophical Study

Lesley Jamieson, in "The Case of M and D in Context: Iris Murdoch, Stanley Cavell and Moral Teaching and Learning", argues that Iris Murdoch's famous case of M and D illustrates the moral importance of learning to see others in a more favourable light through renewed attention. Yet if we do not read this case in the wider context of Murdoch's work, we are liable to overlook the attitudes and transformations involved in coming to change one's mind as M does. Stanley Cavell offers one such reading and denies that the case represents a change in M's sense of

---

① García-Avello M. "Romantic Love, Gender Imbalance and Feminist Readings in Iris Murdoch's *The Sea, the Sea*". Critical Survey, 2022, 34(1): 27-44.

② Bok S. "Simone Weil and Iris Murdoch: The Possibility of Dialogue". Gender Issues, 2005, 22(4): 71-78.

③ Fine D J. "'What a Fuss about Probably Nothing': Iris Murdoch's Ordinary Queerness". Studies in the Literary Imagination, 2018, 51(2): 115-135.

herself or the possibilities for her world of the kind exemplified by Nora in Ibsen's *A Doll's House*. In this essay, the author challenges Cavell's reading, suggesting that the case, while it may not be an exemplar of the perfectionist outlook as described by Cavell, can and should be interpreted in perfectionist terms. To see this, the author reflects on Murdoch's views on the endless perfectibility of language, the importance of humility, and the role of love and attention in moral learning. The author concludes that Murdoch's work uniquely sheds light on how we might cultivate a perfectionist outlook in ourselves and others, and describes the distinctive role that some novels can play in moral education. [1]

David Robjant, in "Nauseating Flux: Iris Murdoch on Sartre and Heraclitus", observes Iris Murdoch's distinctive use of the word "flux" in discussion of Sartre's *Nausea*, and shows that her usage is persuasive and revolutionary, first as Sartre exegesis, second as Heraclitus exegesis, and throughout as a contribution to the philosophy of language. Murdoch's usage of "flux" frames a comparison of Sartre's Roquentin with other figures who have had similarly flowing experience but without nausea. Roquentin's plight is shown to be "a philosopher's plight" precipitated by a defective theory of descriptive success. The author of this essay then shows how the Heraclitean fragments support Murdoch's treatment of "flux". "Flux" is not a variety of change, and the river image cannot be analyzed into non-metaphorical components without a loss of substance. [2]

Sara Soleimani Karbalaei, in "Iris Murdoch's *The Black Prince*: A Valorization of Metafiction as a Virtuous Aesthetic Practice", argues that having a self-conscious narrator who is obsessed by the question of art-truth relationship, *The Black Prince* is the paradigm of metafiction among Iris Murdoch's works. As a discourse about the problems of writing fiction, the novel actually exposes the

---

[1] Jamieson L. "The Case of M and D in Context: Iris Murdoch, Stanley Cavell and Moral Teaching and Learning". Journal of Philosophy of Education, 2020, 54(2):425-448.

[2] Robjant D. "Nauseating Flux: Iris Murdoch on Sartre and Heraclitus". European Journal of Philosophy, 2014, 22(4): 633-652.

ontological status of all literary fiction, i.e. its quasi-referentiality, its indeterminacy and its existence as a linguistic world. This paper argues that more than being a thematic concern, metafiction is the integral part of *The Black Prince*, whose fragmented form mirrors the complexity of reality. It concludes that such a full-fledged metafictional project does not resonate with the anti-fictional convictions but aspires to validate metafiction as the perfect moral form of fiction. ①

David Robjant, in "Is Iris Murdoch a Closet Existentialist? Some Trouble with Vision, Choice and Exegesis", points out that Richard Moran believes Iris Murdoch is an Existentialist who pretends not to be. Moran's view depends on his attempt to assimilate Iris Murdoch's discussion of moral "vision" in the parable of the Mother in Law to Sartre's thought on "choice" and "orientation". Discussing both Moran's Murdoch exegesis and Sartre's Being and Nothingness, the author of this essay develops the Sartrean view to which Moran hopes to assimilate Murdoch, before pointing out how Moran's assimilation fails. The author of this essay also develops this point of disagreement between Murdoch and Sartre, and argues that Murdoch has not as Moran claims made a misattribution to Sartre of an unsituated will, but has instead offered a penetrating critique of the central theme of Sartre's epistemology. ②

Tony Milligan, in "Iris Murdoch and the Broders of Analytic Philosophy", argues that Iris Murdoch's philosophical texts depart significantly from familiar analytic discursive norms. This may lead us to adopt one of two strategies. On the one hand, an assimilation strategy involves translation of Murdoch's claims into the more familiar terms of property-realism (the terminology of ethical naturalism and non-naturalism). On the other hand, there is the option of adopting a crossover strategy and reading Murdoch as (in some sense) a philosopher who belongs more

---

① Karbalaei S S. "Iris Murdoch's *The Black Prince*: A Valorization of Metafiction as a Virtuous Aesthetic Practice". Brno Studies in English, 2014, 40(2): 91-107.
② Robjant D. "Is Iris Murdoch a Closet Existentialist? Some Trouble with Vision, Choice and Exegesis". European Journal of Philosophy, 2013, 21(3): 475-494.

properly to the continental tradition. This article argues that if familiar Quinean claims about ontological commitment and Murdoch's account of metaphor are both broadly correct, then the assimilation strategy must fail to produce a faithful translation. Nonetheless, Murdoch's connection to the analytic tradition is more than genealogical, and it is more than a matter of her writing(initially) in response to analytic contemporaries. While she departs from familiar analytic discursive norms, she continues to accept most of the epistemic values(such as clarity and simplicity) that the norms embody. [1]

Clare Mac Cumhaill, in "Getting the Measure of Murdoch's Good", presents a literary criticism of the book *The Sovereignty of Good* by Iris Murdoch. Topics include acquiring structure over time, their interrelations shift and ramifying but always in ways being personal; involving the continuous reassessment of past events, relationships, and individuals; and Murdoch's conception of the concrete universal being inflected more by British Idealism. [2]

David Bakhurst, in "Analysis and Transcendence in *The Sovereignty of Good*", presents a literary criticism of the book *The Sovereignty of Good* by Iris Murdoch. Topics include challenging the moral-philosophical orthodoxies of the day; opposing the view that myth and metaphor playing an ineliminable role in moral consciousness; and philosophers of an analytic cast of mind being prone in thinking of historical texts as resources mined for arguments relevant to contemporary questions. [3]

Margaret Guise, in "On the Failure of Philosophy to 'Think Love': Iris Murdoch as Phenomenologist", focuses on the philosophy of Irish-British novelist

---

[1] Milligan T. "Iris Murdoch and the Broders of Analytic Philosophy". Ratio, 2012, 25(2): 164-176.

[2] Cumhaill C M. "Getting the Measure of Murdoch's Good". European Journal of Philosophy, 2020, 28(1): 235-247.

[3] Bakhurst D. "Analysis and Transcendence in *The Sovereignty of Good*". European Journal of Philosophy, 2020, 28(1): 214-223.

Iris Murdoch. It reports on her inspirations on multifarious manifestations from Platonism, Neo-Platonism, Christianity and Buddhism. It examines the selection of phenomenologies of love depicted in her major novels including *The Bell*, *The Sacred and Profane Love Machine* and *The Black Prince*.①

Tony Milligan, in "Iris Murdoch's Mortal Asymmetry", points out that Iris Murdoch holds that the best sort of life is a figurative death of the self. This figurative death is informed by an acceptance of real mortality. A recognition of mortality is supposed to help redirect our attention away from self and towards others. Yet these others are also mortal but(unlike the self) remain worthy of love, care and consideration. That is to say, the significance of mortality for Murdoch depends on whose mortality is at issue. The author's rejection of two ways of making sense of this self/other asymmetry is used to motivate the view that her attitude towards death requires a prior commitment to unselfing. And this is a problematic moral project.②

David Robjant, in "The Earthy Realism of Plato's Metaphysics, or: What Shall We Do with Iris Murdoch?", argues Iris Murdoch is against the Separation of the Forms not as a correction of Plato but in order to keep faith with him. Plato's *Parmenides* is not a source book of accurately targeted self-refutation but a catalogue of student errors. The testimony of Aristotle and Gilbert Ryle about Plato's motivations in the Theory of Forms is not an indubitable foundation from which to denounce Iris Murdoch's treatment of Plato as inaccurate but a rival reading of dubious charity. If Iris Murdoch's version of the Theory of Forms strikes Newton Garver as an incoherent mix of influences from Wittgenstein and Plato, this is not because Iris Murdoch is herself confused, but because, in important respects, the

---

① Guise M. "On the Failure of Philosophy to 'Think Love': Iris Murdoch as Phenomenologist". Studies in the Literary Imagination, 2018, 51(2): 1-19.
② Milligan T. "Iris Murdoch's Mortal Asymmetry". Philosophical Investigations, 2007, 30(2): 156-171.

orthodoxy has wronged Plato. ①

4. Psychological Study

David Robjant, in "As a Buddhist Christian: the Misappropriation of Iris Murddoch", focuses on the misconception on the exegesis of Saint Anselm reflected on the book *Metaphysics as a Guide to Morals*, by British author Iris Murdoch, and the inclination of her being either a reformist Christian theist or a Buddhist. It mentions the confusion on the attempt of extending the definition of the word God in the spiritual reality by defending Saint Anselm. It states that despite the confusion, Murdoch only extends the meaning of God's name to merely a supernatural being. ②

Tony Milligan, in "Exile from Perfection in Iris Murdoch's Philosophical Texts", argues that Iris Murdoch's philosophical texts set out the egocentric dangers of guilt but still endorse an account of original sin. This might seem like an unstable combination as these two are in tension, but the author of this essay argues that Murdoch manages to use this tension in a productive manner. The human condition is treated as one of fallenness, in the sense of an exile from perfection. We are aware of moral failure and also aware of the standard by which we fail. Guilt is reined in, however, by the fact that such failure is a matter of commonplace flawed moral vision and not an Augustinian perversity of the will. This reining in of guilt is still accompanied by a recognition of our unbridgeable remoteness from perfection. ③

---

① Robjant D. "The Earthy Realism of Plato's Metaphysics, or: What Shall We Do with Iris Murdoch?". Philosophical Investigations, 2012, 35(1): 43-67.

② Robjant D. "As a Buddhist Christian: the Misappropriation of Iris Murddoch". The Heythrop Journal, 2011, 52(6): 993-1008.

③ Milligan T. "Exile from Perfection in Iris Murdoch's Philosophical Texts". The Heythrop Journal, 2010, 51(1): 22-33.

Bran Nicol, in "Iris Murdoch's Aesthetics of Masochism", discusses the aesthetics presented in Murdoch's essays. It emphasizes that Murdoch's theory of her work is also a theory of ethics. Her works also describe a range of theories of authorship from romanticism to modernism and poststructuralism. Murdoch's theory of artistic production is compared with the principles used by Sigmund Freud's writings on aesthetics. ①

Rebecca Moden, in "Colors of Consciousness in the Novels of Iris Murdoch", focuses on the colors of consciousness in the novels of Irish-British novelist Iris Murdoch. It reflects on the paintings on experience of being in love by color theorist Denis Paul and artist Harry Weinberger which permeate in the novels of Murdoch. It also analyzes the explorations of colors in the novel *The Sandcastle* which render the inner psychology of characters. ②

5. Thematic Study

William Slaymaker, in "Myths, Mystery and the Mechanisms of Determinism: The Aesthetics of Freedom in Iris Murdoch's Fiction", discusses the use of classical myths, mystery and mechanisms of determinism in the interpretations of human freedom in the fiction of Iris Murdoch. Topics discussed include opinion on the relationship between love and freedom; description on human freedom in Murdoch's essays; and position of Murdoch on marriage. ③

Jeffrey Meyers, in "Iris Murdoch's 'Marsyas'", presents criticism on several novels by the British author Iris Murdoch including *Jackson's Dilemma*, *The Black*

---

① Nicol B. "Iris Murdoch's Aesthetics of Masochism". Journal of Modern Literature, 2006, 29(2): 148-165.

② Moden R. "Colors of Consciousness in the Novels of Iris Murdoch". Studies in the Literary Imagination, 2018, 51(2): 79-94.

③ Slaymaker W. "Myths, Mystery and the Mechanisms of Determinism: The Aesthetics of Freedom in Iris Murdoch's Fiction". Papers on Language & Literature, 1982, 18(2): 166-180.

Prince and *A Fairly Honourable Defeat*. Particular focus is given to how the works were influenced by Murdoch's appreciation for art, most notably the painting *The Flaying of Marsyas*, by Titian. Various aspects of Murdoch's life are also discussed including her death from Alzheimer's disease. ①

Farisa Khalid, in "*The Bell* and *The Time of the Angels*: The Philosophy of Love and Virtue in Iris Murdoch's Ecclesiastical Fiction", reflects on the philosophy of love and virtue in the books. It reports on the inspiration of Murdoch from the concept and practice of organized religion. It analyzes the sensual rituals of the Catholic Mass depicted in the novels. ②

6. Ethical Study

Rachael Wiseman, in "What if the Private Linguist Were a Poet? Iris Murdoch on Privacy and Ethics", presents a literary criticism of the book *The Sovereignty of Good* by Iris Murdoch. Topics include the anxiety and the conceptual resources available to moral philosophy; moral philosophy of good and evil, piety and salvation, and humility and love; and choosing public universal rules for action based on utility-calculations and determining the most rational course of action. ③

Mark Hopwood, in "'The Extremely Difficult Realization that Something Other than Oneself Is Real': Iris Murdoch on Love and Moral Agency", argues that in the last few years, there has been a revival of interest in the philosophy of Iris Murdoch. Despite this revival, however, certain aspects of Murdoch's views remain poorly understood, including her account of a concept that she famously described as "central" to moral philosophy, i. e. , love. In this paper, the author argues that the

---

① Meyers J. "Iris Murdoch's 'Marsyas'". The New Criterion, 2013, 31(6): 31-35.

② Khalid F. "*The Bell* and *The Time of the Angels*: The Philosophy of Love and Virtue in Iris Murdoch's Ecclesiastical Fiction". Studies in the Literary Imagination, 2018, 51(2): 137-156.

③ Wiseman R. "What if the Private Linguist Were a Poet? Iris Murdoch on Privacy and Ethics". European Journal of Philosophy, 2020, 28(1): 224-234.

concept of love is essential to any adequate understanding of Murdoch's work. The attempts by Kieran Setiya and David Velleman to assimilate Murdoch's account of love to neo-Aristotelian or neo-Kantian theories of moral agency are misconceived. We can't understand what Murdoch is trying to do unless we understand her position as a radical alternative to such theories. Here, the author of this paper presents a reading of Murdoch's account of love as a form of Platonic eros directed toward two objects: the Good and the particular individual. It is in navigating the tension between these two objects that we find ourselves facing what Murdoch famously described as "the extremely difficult realization that something other than oneself is real". When properly understood, Murdoch's account of love opens up conceptual space for an alternative approach to some of the central questions in contemporary moral theory.[①]

Maria Silvia Vaccarezza, in "Saving the Contingent. A Dialogue between Iris Murdoch and Aquinas", explores the commonalities between philosophers Iris Murdoch and Saint Thomas Aquinas in terms of their moral philosophy. Topics covered include Murdoch's critique of the Natural Law moralists, her act of distancing herself from a group of people identifying themselves as Thomists, Hegelians or Marxists in order to save the contingent, and the notions of attention and imagination. Also discussed is Aquinas's analysis of moral perception to save the contingent.[②]

James K. A. Smith, in "The Moral Vision of Iris Murdoch", discusses the thought of novelist and philosopher Iris Murdoch. Topics include the moral philosophy of Murdoch's book *The Sovereignty of Good*, the notion of the self in relation to moral formation in Murdoch's work, and her thinking about God and

---

① Hopwood M. "'The Extremely Difficult Realization that Something Other than Oneself Is Real': Iris Murdoch on Love and Moral Agency". European Journal of Philosophy, 2018, 26(1): 477-501.

② Vaccarezza M S. "Saving the Contingent. A Dialogue between Iris Murdoch and Aquinas". New Blackfriars, 2016, 97(1067): 22-38.

religion in relation to the work of philosopher Charles Taylor. ①

Cristian Popescu, in "Ethical Readings of Iris Murdoch's Novels", discusses ethical challenges occurring in the interpretation of Iris Murdoch's novels. Due to her role as an academic who taught moral philosophy at Oxford and to the writings that she produced from such a position, Murdoch's novels have also been consistently treated as vehicles for philosophical ideas, despite her constant warnings that her literary work and her philosophy are not interrelated. According to Murdoch, any philosophical mixture in her novels is purely accidental and should not be given any attention whatsoever. However, critics have not ceased to look into Murdoch's novels for her philosophy. In this article, the author questions the limits of interpretation as far as three of Iris Murdoch's novels are concerned. ②

David Robjant, in "Symposium on Iris Murdoch", highlights the contentions of author and philosopher Maria Antonaccio about Murdoch in her book *A Philosophy to Live by: Engaging Iris Murdoch*. It emphasizes the response of Antonaccio to the interpretation of void by philosopher Stephen Mulhall. ③

Yoshiaki Michael Nakazawa, in "Iris Murdoch's Critique of Three Dualisms in Moral Education", explicates Murdoch's arguments against a moral education that aims at autonomy, showing that this kind of moral education is ensnared in problematic dualisms: a fact and value dualism (sometimes discussed as a dualism between metaphorical concepts and empirical concepts); a dualism of moral and non-moral human nature; and a dualism of philosophising and moralising (or form and content). If the dualisms go unacknowledged, the author contends, the moral educator is left with the confused task of providing the foundation of moral autonomy in a morally neutral way. The author of this essay argues, drawing on Murdoch's

---

① Smith J K A. "The Moral Vision of Iris Murdoch". America, 2019, 220(9): 8-13.
② Popescu C. "Ethical Readings of Iris Murdoch's Novels". Philobiblon: Transylvanian Journal of Multidisciplinary Research in Humanities, 2019, 24(2): 277-286.
③ Robjant D. "Symposium on Iris Murdoch". The Heythrop Journal, 2013, 54(6): 1012-1020.

work, that there is another kind of moral education that is free of such dualisms. On this view, moral education is basic and ubiquitous. It does not aim at moral autonomy, but instead aims at the development of moral vision, a capacity to see reality more clearly. While Murdoch's conception of moral education throws moral autonomy out of the picture, Murdoch's conception of moral education is attractive because it is not beset by dubious dualisms. [1]

William Evans, in "Iris Murdoch, Liberal Education and Human Flourishing", argues that articulating the good of liberal education—what we should teach and why we should teach it—is necessary to resist the subversion of liberal education to economic or political ends and the mania for measurable skills. The author of this essay argues that Iris Murdoch's philosophical writings enrich the work of contemporary Aristotelians, such as Joseph Dunne and Alasdair MacIntyre, on these issues. For Murdoch, studies in the arts and intellectual subjects, by connecting students to the inescapable contingency and finitude of human existence, contribute to the cultivation of intellectual and moral virtues and thus to human flourishing. [2]

Maria Antonaccio, in "The Virtues of Metaphysics: A Review of Iris Murdoch's Philosophical Writings", argues that Iris Murdoch's moral philosophy has long influenced contemporary ethics, yet it has not, in general, received the kind of sustained critical attention that it deserves. *Metaphysics as a Guide to Morals* provides new access to most of Murdoch's philosophical writings and makes possible a deeper appreciation of her contribution to current thought. After assessing the recent critical reception of Murdoch's thought, this review places her moral philosophy in the context of contemporary trends in ethics by tracing her influence

---

[1] Nakazawa Y M. "Iris Murdoch's Critique of Three Dualisms in Moral Education". Journal of Philosophy of Education, 2018, 52(3): 397-411.

[2] Evans W. "Iris Murdoch, Liberal Education and Human Flourishing". Journal of Philosophy of Education, 2009, 43(1): 75-84.

on the work of Charles Taylor, highlights the distinctive features of her moral philosophy(especially her analysis of consciousness), and suggests future directions for Murdochian ethics.①

Athanasios Dimakis, in "Making Love to Apollo: The Agalmatophilia of Iris Murdoch's Athenian Lovers in *A Fairly Honourable Defeat*", presents a literary criticism for the book *A Fairly Honourable Defeat* by Iris Murdoch. It reflects on the Apollonian love depicted in the book. It analyzes the idiosyncratic, quixotic conception of moral vision and philosophical idealism and spiritualism of Murdoch. It also highlights the theorizing of virtuous love by Murdoch in her novels.②

Hank Spaulding, in "The Just and Erotic Gaze: Iris Murdoch's Moral Ontology", focuses on the moral ontology of Irish-British novelist Iris Murdoch. It defines the parameters of understanding of Athenian philosopher Plato on philosophy of love and friendship. It explores the depiction of moral life in Murdoch's novel *The Nice and the Good*. It also discusses the impact of moral life on necessities of the world.③

Hannah Marije Altorf, in "Talk of Lovers in a Great Hall of Reflection: Rereading Iris Murdoch's *The Fire and the Sun* and *The Bell*", reflects on the views of Athenian philosopher Plato on art and beauty and analyses the importance of art and beauty in love. It also examines the understanding of loving attention of Murdoch and the impact of love on humanity.④

---

① Antonaccio M. "The Virtues of Metaphysics: A Review of Iris Murdoch's Philosophical Writings". Journal of Religious Ethics, 2001, 29(2): 309-335.
② Dimakis A. "Making Love to Apollo: The Agalmatophilia of Iris Murdoch's Athenian Lovers in *A Fairly Honourable Defeat*". Studies in the Literary Imagination, 2018, 51(2): 95-114.
③ Spaulding H. "The Just and Erotic Gaze: Iris Murdoch's Moral Ontology". Studies in the Literary Imagination, 2018, 51(2): 37-55.
④ Altorf H M. "Talk of Lovers in a Great Hall of Reflection: Rereading Iris Murdoch's *The Fire and the Sun* and *The Bell*". Studies in the Literary Imagination, 2018, 51(2): 21-36.

7. Theological Study

Jenifer Spencer Goodyer, in "The Blank Face of Love: The Possibility of Goodness in the Literary and Philosophical Work of Iris Murdoch", explores the value of Iris Murdoch's metaphysical ethics for the theologian. Although, in many ways, Murdoch does appeal to the theologian, a subtle form of nihilism underlies her thought insofar as human goodness—in the form of loving attention—is only possible once the individual has overcome his/her ego by staring into the void and accepting the ultimate meaninglessness of reality. As this article demonstrates, Murdoch's replacement of transcendence with void rules out any form of real love or human goodness: only a dualistic exchange of gazes remains possible. Real, selfless love is only possible when the ego understands itself in the context of theological transcendence. ①

Christopher J. Insole, in "Beyond Glass Doors... The Sun no Longer Shining: English Platonism and the Problem of Self-love in the Literary and Philosophical Work of Iris Murdoch", provides richly suggestive indications of what can happen to Platonism when it is brought into interaction with a mechanical and deterministic model of the physical universe. Murdoch's work acts as a particularly perspicuous theological flash-point, showing the intrinsic difficulties with combining demanding features of Platonism. This is illuminated through a comparison with a strand of neo-Lutheran theology. ②

F. B. A. Asiedu, in "Intimations of the Good: Iris Murdoch, Richard Swinburne and the Promise of Theism", argues that perhaps no one in the English

---

① Goodyer J S. "The Blank Face of Love: The Possibility of Goodness in the Literary and Philosophical Work of Iris Murdoch". Modern Theology, 2009, 25(2): 217-237.

② Insole C J. "Beyond Glass Doors... The Sun no Longer Shining: English Platonism and the Problem of Self-love in the Literary and Philosophical Work of Iris Murdoch". Modern Theology, 2006, 22(1): 111-143.

speaking world has carried on a philosophical defence of theism like Richard Swinburne. Yet in all of Swinburne's work, there is little use of a long-standing view in the Christian tradition that God is good, and that his goodness is interchangeable with his being. While Swinburne does little with the idea of goodness, Iris Murdoch proposes an anti-theistic view that insists on the Good without God. In this paper, the author's argument is that both Swinburne's indifference to the notion of the Good and Murdoch's "Good without God" take away from the promise of theism. The author suggests an Augustinian alternative that insists on the equation of God and the Good without falling into the problems inherent in Swinburne's and Murdoch's views. [①]

8. Gender Study

Alicia Muro Llorente, in "The Modernisation of William Shakespeare's *Hamlet*: Identity and Gender in Iris Murdoch's *The Black Prince*", reads Iris Murdoch's *The Black Prince* as a retelling of William Shakespeare's *Hamlet*, paying special attention to the changes that the original play has gone through in order to render it more apt for a contemporary audience. Even if Murdoch also adapts the male hero, the most interesting changes she introduces are related to gender, since the female figures resembling Ophelia and Gertrude bear little resemblance to their Shakespearean counterparts. Gender is also linked to how the novel is written, especially regarding the narrator and his unreliability. Murdoch's views on women will thus be juxtaposed to those of her (male) narrator. The rest of Murdoch's characters are also crafted in Shakespearean fashion, given that almost

---

① Asiedu F B A. "Intimations of the Good: Iris Murdoch, Richard Swinburne and the Promise of Theism". The Heythrop Journal, 2001, 42(1): 26-49.

all of them have a counterpart in the original play.①

Alexander G. Gonzalez, in "Joyce's Presence in Iris Murdoch's *Something Special*", examines the connection of *Dubliners*, a collection of short stories by James Joyce to the short story *Something Special*, by Iris Murdoch. It explores the story's treatment of the conflict between romantic illusion and reality from the perspectives of the male and female characters. It looks into the link between the stories, including appearance of the moon, similarity of the protagonists' thought, marriage, and geographical connections.②

Leo Robson, in "Iris the Insoluble", profiles British author Iris Murdoch. Topics covered include critical response to her novels such as *Under the Net*, *The Black Prince*, and *The Philosopher's Pupil*, her sexuality, and her depiction of London, England in her literary works.③

---

① Llorente A M. "The Modernisation of William Shakespeare's *Hamlet*: Identity and Gender in Iris Murdoch's *The Black Prince*". Estudios Irlandeses, 2018, 13(2): 90-102.

② Gonzalez A G. "Joyce's Presence in Iris Murdoch's *Something Special*". Studies in Short Fiction, 2012, 37(1): 69-85.

③ Robson L. "Iris the Insoluble". The New Statesman, 2019, 148(5479): 42-47.

Chapter 17
John Fowles

John Fowles (1926-2005)

Fowles is at once a popular and a serious novelist. He never fails to fascinate his readers; reading him can always be an enjoyable experience. His stories are basically traditional in nature, or love stories in its various forms, that present little or no obscurity in comprehension. However, the way he writes his novels merits particular attention. There seems to be some kind of pattern that underpins his stories: the hero undertakes a quest, with the guidance of some wise man, and finds the woman he loves and becomes spiritually whole. Fowles' major novels include *The Collector*, *The Magus*, *The French Lieutenant's Woman*, *The Ebony Tower*, *Daniel Martin*, and *Mantissa*. Fowles has also written a miscellany of other things such as poetry, short fiction, essays, and philosophy.[①]

---

① 常耀信. 英国文学简史. 南开大学出版社 2006 年版.

Critical Perspectives

1. Narrative Study

Carla Arnell, in "Chaucer's *Wife of Bath* and John Fowles's Quaker Maid: Tale-Telling and the Trial of Personal Experience and Written Authority", examines the medieval influence of Chaucer's *Canterbury Tales* on John Fowles's postmodern novel, *A Maggot*. In this essay, the author argues that Fowles's fiction reimagines and ultimately transforms the *Wife of Bath*'s debate about experience and written authority through the novel's "Quaker Maid" Rebecca Lee, whose extraordinary spiritual experience allows her to "rewrite" her life as a free soul. For Fowles, this transformation of identity, which has its seeds in the medieval era, looks forward to the Shaker movement's full flourishing at the end of the eighteenth century and, more broadly, to the age of Romanticism, with its personal and political freedoms.[①]

Raymond J. Wilson, in "Allusion and Implication in John Fowles's *The Cloud*", focuses on the allusion and implication in the book *The Cloud* written by John Fowles. Topics discussed include negative symbolic impact of *The Ebony Tower* from the opening story; implications for Fowle's allusions; and literary context for the action of the story.[②]

[①] Arnell C. "Chaucer's *Wife of Bath* and John Fowles's Quaker Maid: Tale-Telling and the Trial of Personal Experience and Written Authority". Modern Language Review, 2007, 102(4): 933-946.

[②] Wilson R J. "Allusion and Implication in John Fowles's *The Cloud*". Studies in Short Fiction, 1983, 20(1): 17-22.

Susan E. Lorsch, in "Pinter Fails Fowles: Narration in *The French Lieutenant's Woman*", examines the screenplay and narrative technique of Harold Pinter used in the film adaptation of the novel *The French Lieutenant's Woman*, by John Fowles. Topics discussed include factors to consider in film adaptations of a novel; criticism of the use of a modern narrator for the Victorian England plot used in the film; and views by Fowles on the relationship between modern narrator and novelist to his story. [1]

2. Feminism Study

Gwen Raaberg, in "Against 'Reading': Text and/as Other in John Fowles' *The French Lieutenant's Woman*", criticizes the interplay of textuality and sexuality in the novel *The French Lieutenant's Woman* by John Fowles. Topics discussed include emphasis on the juxtapositions of the Victorian narrative and perspective of the narrator; confrontation of patriarchal traditions and conceptions of women; and narrative technique used in the novel. [2]

Jeffrey Roessner, in "Unsolved Mysteries: Agents of Historical Change in John Fowles's *A Maggot*", asserts that John Fowles' prologue to *A Maggot* redefines history literature as he promotes his democratic, feminist vision of social change. Topics discussed include metahistorical questions raised by the story, and sense of mystery established by Fowles from the beginning of the narrative. [3]

---

[1] Lorsch S E. "Pinter Fails Fowles: Narration in *The French Lieutenant's Woman*". Literature Film Quarterly, 1988, 16(3): 144-154.

[2] Raaberg G. "Against 'Reading': Text and/as Other in John Fowles' *The French Lieutenant's Woman*". women's Studies, 2001, 30(4): 521-542.

[3] Roessner J. "Unsolved Mysteries: Agents of Historical Change in John Fowles's *A Maggot*". Papers on Language & Literature, 2000, 36(3): 302-323.

3. Philosophical Study

Kelly Cresap, in "The World-Making Capacity of John Fowles's *Daniel Martin*", examines the engagement of post-modernism with realist and modernist elements as represented in the novel. This paper explores how Fowles draws readers' attention with the variety and intrigue of the novel's world-making capacity. An overview of the story is presented. ①

4. Psychological Study

Amanda Scott, in "Nostalgic Renderings of Victorian Clothing in John Fowles's *The French Lieutenant's Woman*, A. S. Byatt's *Possession*, and Neal Stephenson's *The Diamond Age*", argues that the Neo-Victorian fiction of Fowles, Byatt, and Stephenson relies heavily on the Victorian visual aesthetic in portraying characters' clothing. These representations, however, are tainted by modern stereotypes of the Victorians and manifest the sociocultural distinction the authors draw between the Victorians and modern civilization. ②

Wisam Kh. Abdul Jabbar, in "A Freudian Reading of John Fowles' *The Ebony Tower*", explores the two character-triangles in John Fowles's *The Ebony Tower*. Henry Breasley, Anne and Diana on one hand and David Williams, Beth and Diana on the other are respectively tied up to the Ego, Super Ego and Id. The paper negotiates how the novella can be seen as a fictionalization of the quest of the

---

① Cresap K. "The World-Making Capacity of John Fowles's *Daniel Martin*". Texas Studies in Literature & Language, 2013, 55(2): 159-183.

② Scott A. "Nostalgic Renderings of Victorian Clothing in John Fowles's *The French Lieutenant's Woman*, A. S. Byatt's *Possession*, and Neal Stephenson's *The Diamond Age*". Journal of the Utah Academy of Sciences, Arts & Letters, 2011(88): 416-427.

Ego to satisfy the artist's urge for creativity which can potentially be realized by romancing the Id drive. The artist's innovative elocution can either be hindered or helped by its inevitable contact with realm of the Id where repressed desires restlessly reside. In effect, not only does the Freudian conceptualization better illustrate the triangle character relationships but it uncovers the anxieties of the artist's psyche. [1]

5. Canonization

Marie-Claire Simonetti, in "The Blurring of Time in *The French Lieutenant's Woman*, the Novel and the Film", focuses on the significance of time span between the release of John Fowles' novel *The French Lieutenant's Woman* in the late 1960s and its film adaptation by screenwriter Harold Pinter and director Karel Reisz in the early 1980s. Topics discussed include novel's treatment of temporality; blending of past and present; and contrast of the fast-paced modern times with the slow-paced, well-ordered Victorian period. [2]

6. Cultural Study

Emine Akkülah Doğan, in "Neo-Victorian Materialisms in John Fowles's *The Collector*", argues that while John Fowles's *The French Lieutenant's Woman* is studied frequently as a neo-Victorian novel, his first published novel, *The Collector*, is ignored in the critical analyses of neo-Victorian studies. This is mostly due to the fact that *The Collector* is neither a re-writing of a Victorian novel nor sets in the

---

[1] Abdul Jabbar W K. "A Freudian Reading of John Fowles *The Ebony Tower*". PsyArt, 2014 (18):1-13.

[2] Simonetti M-C. "The Blurring of Time in *The French Lieutenant's Woman*, the Novel and the Film". Literature Film Quarterly, 1996, 24(3): 301-308.

nineteenth century. However, a critical reading of the novel demonstrates how Fowles explicitly manifests the continuation of the Victorian materialist obsession in this particular novel. In other words, albeit the contemporary setting of the novel and the critical appreciation of it as a feminist fiction, the protagonist Clegg's obsession with the material objects echoes Victorian cultural materialisation in a way that leads him to collect butterflies and women. Drawing an analogy between these two collections, it is mostly argued by the critics that Fowles discusses the issues on gender in this particular novel. From a different perspective, it is argued in this study that Fowles actually illustrates the obsession with the material objects with respect to both the dead butterfly collection and also to the commodification of the female body as the material object. From this vantage point, the aim of this study is to analyse *The Collector* as a neo-Victorian novel revisiting the material culture of the Victorian period and the repercussions of the traumatic relation between the human and the object in the twentieth century.[1]

7. Structuralism

Aleks Matosoglu, in "Decentred Centre in John Fowles's *The Magus*", argues that John Fowles' *The Magus* has been the focus of criticism for many years. This study regards the character Conchis as a decentred "centre" in the structure of the novel and in the experience of the contemporary humanity. Conchis becomes in the eyes of Nicholas an all-knowing figure, an accumulation of Western thought since the Greek civilization. He produces signs to be read as he himself becomes a body of various signs that construct him as the metaphysical centre that Western thinkers have relied upon. His narration becomes superior to Nicholas' and he himself becomes only a narrative voice. The voice from the times of Plato has been

---

[1] Akkülah Doğan E. "Neo-Victorian Materialisms in John Fowles's *The Collector*". Gaziantep University Journal of Social Sciences, 2019(18): 130-138.

considered as a direct expression of the thoughts in one's mind and thus superior to writing that is permeated with the undecidability of meaning in the absence of the speaker and the addressee. In the novel, words as an endless play of metaphors take the place of voice. There is no knowable reality outside the play words or metaphors, which is an endless chain of signifiers that lead to other signifiers. Every time Nicholas turns to Conchis to find the centre outside the play of the language, he finds other signifiers. Thus, Conchis as a meaning-making centre is dethroned. He is not the sole operator of the masks that divert from their presumed original target when they are read. Nicholas is just another production of the literary tradition who reads the signs only to produce other signs. Conchis in the beginning of the novel renounces fiction for science but along the course of the novel, we see that words are never reliable whether in fiction or in science. [1]

---

[1] Matosoglu A. "Decentred Centre in John Fowles's *The Magus*". Journal of History Culture and Art Research, 2015, 4(2): 158-168.

Chapter 18

Anthony Burgess

Anthony Burgess (1917-1993)

Born and educated in Manchester, Burgess spent six years as an education officer in Malaya and Borneo with the colonial service. From this experience came The Malayan Trilogy, consisting of the novels, *Time for a Tiger*, *The Enemy in the Blanket*, and *Beds in the East*. His most famous work, *A Clockwork Orange*, a harrowing story of fascism and youth culture, was made into the cult film classic by Stanley Kubrick in 1971. Other notable novels include *Inside Mr. Enderby*, *Enderby Outside*, *The Clockwork Testament*, and *Earthly Powers*.[1]

---

[1] Richetti J, Bender J, David D, et al. The Columbia History of the British Novel. New York: Columbia University Press, 1994.

Critical Perspectives

1. Narrative Study

Paul Murgatroyd, in "Anthony Burgess's *Aeneid*", argues that Anthony Burgess' first novel, *A Vision of Battlements* (written in 1949, published in 1965), is an extended engagement with Virgil's *Aeneid*. Burgess updates the action (to World War II) and provides a new Mediterranean setting (the island of Gibraltar, under British control). He takes from the epic the framework for his novel in the form of the overall plot and many individual episodes (with lots of comic and grotesque twists and additions) and the main characters (all of whom are deflated in some way). This article investigates the humour, ingenuity and inventiveness in this very creative adaptation of Virgil to provide an epic parody which is a subversive satire on British military service. [1]

2. Psychological Study

David Rudd, in "Willy Wonka, Dahl's Chickens and Heavenly Visions", reconsiders Roald Dahl's *Charlie and the Chocolate Factory* 50 years after its initial UK publication, and over a hundred years since Dahl's birth. It suggests that the book has often been misinterpreted, in that the work is more critical of modern capitalism than is often recognized, capturing a post-World War II shift in sensibilities from a culture of hard work and deferred gratification to one that

---

[1] Murgatroyd P. "Anthony Burgess's *Aeneid*". Ordia Prima, 2014(13): 163-177.

celebrated consumerism and instant enjoyment. The article explores this idea by taking a psychoanalytical perspective, drawing largely on the work of Jacques Lacan, especially his notions of the superego, enjoyment and desire. It suggests that Dahl was one of a number of writers (Anthony Burgess and Marshall McLuhan are also discussed) who responded to this shift in capitalist relations, not simply in terms of the content of his work but in the way in which he wrote.[①]

3. Biographical Study

Joseph Darlington, in "Anthony Burgess and William S. Burroughs: Shared Enemies, Opposed Friends", uses biographical research into the relationship between Anthony Burgess and William Burroughs, and provides new ways of reading their works. Investigating their relationship through their correspondence, the author of this paper teases out the misunderstandings that lie within their mutual admiration. Analyzing Burgess's Catholicism and Burroughs's libertarianism in relation to the satirical intentions behind *A Clockwork Orange* and *Naked Lunch* opens avenues for new readings of the texts, and helps us better understand the two writers' eventual disagreement.[②]

4. Post-colonial Study

Zulfiya Zinnatullina, Liliya Khabibullina, and Ivan Popp, in "The Opposition of East and West in 'The Long Day Wanes' Novel by Anthony Burgess", argue that the trilogy *The Long Day Wanes* is among early works of the author, and the

---

① Rudd D. "Willy Wonka, Dahl's Chickens and Heavenly Visions". Children's Literature in Education, 2020, 51(1): 125-142.

② Darlington J. "Anthony Burgess and William S. Burroughs: Shared Enemies, Opposed Friends". Journal of Modern Literature, 2020, 44(1): 59-76.

author considers perspective of the East and the West relationship in it. In the article, "we consider the main lines of the characters representing the mother country and colony, also we designate evolution of heroes in the trilogy and we draw a conclusion on as far as the writer departs from the traditional ways the East-common English literature depicting in the first half of the 20th century. It is possible to allocate two tendencies of the East assessment in the trilogy: image of Asians as slow-witted and silly and, on the contrary, strange, difficult representatives of an exotic mentality. There is no uniformity in the image of colonialists. Some Europeans and British feel 'at home', being in East space, like culture and mentality of the East, and some represent type of the colonialist treating everything as an object to study. The special attention is deserved by any representatives of 'false' identity having lost themselves in someone else's system of values". ①

5. Ethical Study

Ekaterina V. Smyslova and Liliya F. Khabibullina, in "Aesthetics as an Aspect of Good in Enderby Novels by Anthony Burgess", consider the interaction of ethics and aesthetics in Anthony Burgess's worldview. It is based on an analysis of the novels about the minor poet Enderby, who is interpreted as the writer's alter ego. The material for the article is represented by the novels *Inside Mr. Enderby*, *Enderby Outside*, *The Clockwork Testament*, and *Enderby's Dark Lady*. Particular attention is paid to the personality of the protagonist and his worldview. In the course of the analysis, the superficial interpretations of Enderby's image and the system of his relationships with the outside world are rejected in favor of deeper ones, arising from the system of the author's outlooks on creativity. The analysis of

---

① Zinnatullina Z, Khabibullina L, Popp I. "The Opposition of East and West in 'The Long Day Wanes' Novel by Anthony Burgess". Journal of History Culture and Art Research, 2017, 6(4): 623-630.

Burgess's search for faith, his path from congenital Catholicism through Manichaeism to the development of his own religious and ethical picture of the world has been performed in this paper. It has shown that according to Burgess, the beauty is of primary value and the writer is seen as the creator of such a world view where the original duality of reality can be overcome through the language. ①

Todd F. Davis and Kenneth Womack, in "'O my brothers': Reading the Anti-Ethics of the Pseudo-Family in Anthony Burgess's *A Clockwork Orange*", examine the anti-ethics of a pseudo family in the book *A Clockwork Orange*, by Anthony Burgess. Topics discussed include criticisms on the 21st chapter of the book; discussion on family system and morphogenesis; and analysis of the main character of the story. ②

6. Social Study

David Waterman, in "Bill the Symbolic Worker: Forced Syndicalism, Opposition and the Self in Anthony Burgess's *1985*", analyzes the authority of labor unions in the book *1985* written by Anthony Burgess. Topics discussed include consequence for refusal to accept union membership; consideration of a subject's identity as a function of union membership in a society of totalitarian syndicalism; confirmation of labor unions as guilty of dehumanization; and development of Islam as the major party of opposition to counter the union-induced dystopia of *1985*. ③

---

① Smyslova E V, Khabibullina L F. "Aesthetics as an Aspect of Good in Enderby Novels by Anthony Burgess". Journal of History Culture and Art Research, 2017, 6(5):7-12.
② Davis T F, Womack K. "'O my brothers': Reading the Anti-Ethics of the Pseudo-Family in Anthony Burgess's *A Clockwork Orange*". College Literature, 2002, 29(2): 19-36.
③ Waterman D. "Bill the Symbolic Worker: Forced Syndicalism, Opposition and the Self in Anthony Burgess's *1985*". Atenea, 2004, 24(1):105-118.

7. Biographical Study

Christopher Sandford, in "The Restless Soul Who Gave Us *A Clockwork Orange*", discusses the life of author Anthony Burgess, known for his novel *A Clockwork Orange*, in relation to the Roman Catholic Church. Topics include his identity as an unbeliever, his criticisms of purported dilutions of Catholic moral teachings, and religious aspects of Burgess's novel *Earthly Powers*. [1]

---

[1] Sandford C. "The Restless Soul Who Gave Us *A Clockwork Orange*". America, 2018, 219(2): 38-42.

Chapter 19

Ian McEwan

Ian McEwan(1948-)

Ian McEwan's works have earned him worldwide critical acclaim. He won the Somerset Maugham Award in 1976 for his first collection of short stories *First Love, Last Rites*; the Whitbread Novel Award (1987) for *The Child in Time*; and Germany's Shakespeare Prize in 1999. He has been shortlisted for the Man Booker Prize for Fiction numerous times, winning the award for *Amsterdam* in 1998. His novel *Atonement* received the WH Smith Literary Award(2002), National Book Critics' Circle Fiction Award (2003), Los Angeles Times Prize for Fiction (2003), and the Santiago Prize for the European Novel(2004). *Atonement* was also made into an Oscar-winning film. In 2006, Ian McEwan won the James Tait Black Memorial Prize for his novel *Saturday*, and his novel *On Chesil Beach* was named Galaxy Book of the Year at the 2008 British Book Awards where McEwan was also named Reader's Digest Author of the Year. *Solar* won the

Bollinger Everyman Wodehouse Prize for Comic Fiction in 2010 and *Sweet Tooth* won the Paddy Power Political Fiction Book of the Year award in 2012. Ian McEwan was awarded a CBE in 2000. In 2014 he was awarded the Bodleian Medal. ①

---

① http://www.ianmcewan.com/.

Critical Perspectives

1. Narrative Study

Elena Bandín, and Elisa González, in "Ian McEwan Celebrates Shakespeare: *Hamlet* in a *Nutshell*", analyze Ian McEwan's *Nutshell*, published in September 2016, as a modern rewriting of *Hamlet* in relation to the usual issues and themes previously tackled by the author throughout his narrative. The novel focuses on the love triangle involving Claude (Claudius), Trudy (Gertrude) and John Cairncross (King Hamlet), and narrates how the lovers plot the murder of the husband from the unusual perspective of a proto-Hamlet in the womb. Despite the fact that he is rewriting a Shakespearean work, Ian McEwan remains faithful to his style and favourite topics, displaying the function of the family as destructive rather than constructive, conditioning the later development of the children and rendering them devoid of the affection needed. Similarly, *Nutshell* also depicts his recurrent configuration of mothers as authoritative and destructive, especially for the natural growth of their offspring. [1]

Nathalie Jaëck and Arnaud Schmitt, in "Layers of Deception in Ian McEwan's *Atonement*: A Dialogue", analyze from two different perspectives the pivotal role of the last part of *Atonement*, "London, 1999", and its effect on readers' understanding of the novel, as well as the authorial motives for orchestrating such a late narrative upheaval. This paper shows that this narrative reconfiguration forces the readers to reassess their interpretations of the interplay

---

[1] Bandín E, González E. "Ian McEwan Celebrates Shakespeare: *Hamlet* in a *Nutshell*". Critical Survey, 2021, 33(2): 17-30.

between truth, error, and deception, and to ponder the respective functions of omniscience and interlocution (i. e., Briony's resorting to the imagined words of others to speak through them, to externalize and thus voice out, in these alternative fantasized narratives, her own repressed voice) in the reception process. In light of the coda, one realizes that Briony herself is the character-author, lying in ambush behind the frame narrator and composing the inner focalizations of the different characters. It thus becomes clear that interlocution, manipulative though it proves to be, is a way to accommodate, within Briony's novel, dialogic spaces of inner contradiction, and crucially to literally voice out, through fantasized others and indirect subjectivation, what she cannot bear to adjust to. But this realization also requires a consistent hermeneutical effort on the part of the readers who, depending on the nature of their expectations and emotional involvement in the narrative, may perceive "London, 1999" either as a playful gauntlet to be picked up—leading to an enhanced understanding of a complex narrator—or a major disruption of their reading experience. This article eventually presents two possible strategies of readjustment—of naturalization—in order to make sense of *Atonement*'s last chapter and, above all, its relation to the other parts of the novel. [1]

Maurizio Ascari, in "Beyond Realism: Ian Mcewan's *Atonement* as a Postmodernist Quest for Meaning", presents literary criticism of the book *Atonement*, by Ian McEwan. Topics discussed include plot and characters of the book, the book being emblematic of a mature kind of metafiction, and the theme of redemption, confession and miscarriage of justice in the book. An overview of the story is also given. [2]

Hannah Courtney, in "Narrative Temporality and Slowed Scene: The Interaction of Event and Thought Representation in Ian McEwan's Fiction",

---

[1] Jaëck N, Schmitt A. "Layers of Deception in Ian McEwan's *Atonement*: A Dialogue". Narrative, 2019, 27(3): 353-374.

[2] Ascari M. "Beyond Realism: Ian Mcewan's *Atonement* as a Postmodernist Quest for Meaning". Renascence, 2019, 71(1): 3-19.

discusses the relationship between plot action and characters' consciousness in the novels of Ian McEwan, such as *Saturday*, *The Child in Time*, and *Enduring Love*.①

P. Chalupský, in "Playfulness as Apologia for a Strong Story in Ian McEwan's *Sweet Tooth*", argues that Ian McEwan's penultimate novel, *Sweet Tooth* (2012), is a remarkable achievement, not only in the context of the contemporary British literary scene, but also within the body of its author's work. Although it is written in the form of a spy thriller, with an element of romance, the novel by far transcends the limits of this genre. It provides an intriguing exploration of McEwan's favourite themes, and contains a notable dimension of intertextual and metafictional playfulness, which in this case is highly self-reflective as he makes direct references to his own fiction, namely to his short stories from the collection *In Between the Sheets* (1978). Therefore, in terms of its thematic and narrative framework, *Sweet Tooth* can be especially linked with two of his earlier novels, *The Innocent* (1990) and *Atonement* (2001). This article argues that McEwan's use of playful narrative strategies is not a result of his intention to write an experimental text challenging the traditional notion of the story and the plot, but rather serves as a means of his defence of a strong story as a crucial factor of a quality narrative.②

2. Feminism Study

A. Agache, in "Ian McEwan's Literary Approach to Feminism: An Applied Analysis", explains how Ian McEwan's public and supportive feminist discourse is transplanted into the intricate configurations of his novels. The subsequent but

---

① Courtney H. "Narrative Temporality and Slowed Scene: The Interaction of Event and Thought Representation in Ian McEwan's Fiction". Narrative, 2013, 21(2): 180-197.

② Chalupský P. "Playfulness as Apologia for a Strong Story in Ian McEwan's *Sweet Tooth*". Brno Studies in English, 2015, 41(1): 101-115.

interesting transformations that such a relocation implies consist, in the author's view, in the challenging of feminism as an ideology but not in the critique of the women's rights to obtain a legitimate equality of chances. Far from representing an artistic unavoidable reversal or a more substantial retraction, the distancing from a dogmatic dimension through the epic facilitates a beneficial encounter between feminism and a version of reality not so amenable to its requests and ideals. ①

Margaret Thornton and Heather Roberts, in "Women Judges, Private Lives: (In) Visibilities in Fact and Fiction", focus on fictional representation of English High Court judge Fiona Maye in the book *The Children Act* by Ian McEwan and representation of an actual judge, Justice Sharon Johns, at her swearing-in ceremony in the Family Court of Australia. It mentions that struggle by women to enter the legal profession is a marked dimension of first wave feminism at the turn of the 20th century. It also mentions periodic anxiety about autism, adoption and surrogate mothers. ②

3. Philosophical Study

Randy Fertel, in "Saturn vs. Hermes: The Battle of the Hemispheres in Ian McEwan's *Saturday*", argues that Ian McEwan's *Saturday* explores the tension between fundamental human polarities: immediacy vs. mediation; freedom vs. necessity; spontaneity vs. care and craft; Hermes vs. Saturn; and right- vs. left-brain. McEwan's protagonist has opportunities to confront and resolve these dualities. The novel exhibits improvisation's formal conventions and thematic features, demonstrating their synergy. Seen through the lens of improvisation, the

---

① Agache A. "Ian McEwan's Literary Approach to Feminism: An Applied Analysis". Bulletin of the Transilvania University of Brasov, Series IV: Philology & Cultural Studies, 2015, 8(1): 43-52.

② Thornton M, Roberts H. "Women Judges, Private Lives: (In) Visibilities in Fact and Fiction". University of New South Wales Law Journal, 2017, 40(2): 761-777.

novel dramatizes the right-brain's pushback in the life of a man almost wholly dedicated to the rationalistic, analytic left-brain.①

4. Psychological Study

Aura Sibişan, in "Aspects of Representation with Illustration from Ian McEwan's *Atonement*", presents theoretical aspects of representation, definition and connected concepts, illustrated in a brief discussion of Ian McEwan's novel *Atonement*. The systems of representation do not only mirror reality, but construct the mechanisms through which humans understand and process the information coming from the exterior. Ian McEwan explores the diversity and power of impact of these mechanisms. His characters face, imagine and shape reality at the same time.②

Tim Gauthier, in "'Selective in Your Mercies': Privilege, Vulnerability, and the Limits of Empathy in Ian McEwan's *Saturday*", argues that since September 11, 2001, a number of critics, including Judith Butler and Gayatri Spivak, have outlined a greater need for empathy, most specifically from those who were targeted on that day. The logic of this argument is that those who were victimized should use their newfound vulnerability as a means of resonating with the other. Ian McEwan's *Saturday* problematizes precisely the scenario to which these theorists allude. The novel illuminates a desire to empathize, to recognize empathy's importance, while unintentionally demonstrating just how difficult it is to enact. The protagonist, already existing in a state of heightened alert, is confronted by others in whom he recognizes anger and hatred, but also suffering. Arguably, these should prove

---

① Fertel R. "Saturn vs. Hermes: The Battle of the Hemispheres in Ian McEwan's *Saturday*". Journal of Modern Literature, 2016, 39(2): 53-71.

② Sibişan A. "Aspects of Representation with Illustration from Ian McEwan's *Atonement*". Bulletin of the Transilvania University of Brasov, Series IV: Philology & Cultural Studies, 2014, 7(1): 109-116.

optimal conditions for the exercise of empathy. The novel, however, demonstrates the problematics of just such an exercise. While *Saturday* may declare the need for empathy and extol it as a cornerstone of Western secularized society, the text simultaneously reveals how easily its application can be perverted. The seemingly benign and benevolent actions of the novel's neurosurgeon emphasize the blind spots of privilege and the co-opting of empathy to assert a superior moral stance over that of the other. The dialectics of the novel thus suggest that a retrenchment of differences is a more probable response to violence than a recognition of shared vulnerability. [1]

Mark Edmundson, in "Imagination: Powers and Perils", discusses the role of imagination in everyday life, highlighting writer Ian McEwan's opinion on the relation of imagination. The psychologist Sigmund Freud, the philosopher Arthur Schopenhauer, and the poet Robert Frost are discussed. The relation of imagination to poetry and literature is also addressed. [2]

Daniel Zalewski, in "The Background Hum", discusses English novelist Ian McEwan and the amount of scientific research that he draws on when creating the characters of his books. While it is noted that McEwan's novels tend to be intellectual and that his prose is packed with "visual details", his main strength is creating suspense in books such as *The Comfort of Strangers* and *On Chesil Beach*. McEwan talks about a book that he is working on about climate change. [3]

5. Thematic Study

Shou-Nan Hsu, in "Truth, Care, and Action: An Ethics of Peaceful

---

[1] Gauthier T. "'Selective in Your Mercies': Privilege, Vulnerability, and the Limits of Empathy in Ian McEwan's *Saturday*". College Literature, 2013, 40(2): 7-30.

[2] Edmundson M. "Imagination: Powers and Perils". Raritan, 2012, 32(2): 144-157.

[3] Zalewski D. "The Background Hum". The New Yorker, 2009, 85(2): 46-61.

Coexistence in Ian McEwan's *Solar*", discusses the issue of climate change and embraces both interpersonal relationships and relationship to the natural world. This paper also reflects on human relationships as an essential part of an ecological ethics, and gives messages about truth, care, and love. ①

Helen Lewis, in "Ghost in the Machine", focuses on author Ian McEwan and his novel, *Machines Like Me*. It states that the novel is set in an alternative universe where artificial intelligence research is far more advanced. It discusses McEwan's liberal views and identity politics, and talks about how he was raised in a strict household. ②

Eric P. Levy, in "Postlapsarian Will and the Problem of Time in Ian Mcewan's *Enduring Love*", explores the problem of time in Ian McEwan's novel *Enduring Love*. It cites the notions of the fall and of time as the central concepts explored in the novel's text. With respect to the fall, the description of the fall of Satan and the notion of the Biblical Fall and the estrangement of Man are noted. The notion of time, on the other hand, focuses on the balloon passage and its aftermath. The passage of time has become the central focus of attention as the narrator of the story attempts to rescue a terrified boy. ③

Earl G. Ingersoll, in "City of Endings: Ian McEwan's *Amsterdam*", focuses on Ian McEwan's novel *Amsterdam*. The novel begins dramatically with an ending, the cremation of character Molly Lane's remains. Although her husband George has deliberately chosen not to mourn her passing with a memorial service, Molly's friends and former lovers have come together to mark the end of her pain-tormented latter days. Molly's ending brings a heightened awareness of their own possible ends

---

① Shou-Nan Hsu. "Truth, Care, and Action: An Ethics of Peaceful Coexistence in Ian McEwan's *Solar*". Papers on Language & Literature, 2016, 52(4): 326-349.

② Lewis H. "Ghost in the Machine". The New Statesman, 2019, 148(5467): 36-41.

③ Levy E P. "Postlapsarian Will and the Problem of Time in Ian Mcewan's *Enduring Love*". Renascence, 2009, 61(3): 169-192.

to at least two of her mourners, Clive Linley and Vernon Halliday, and precipitates a complex structure of endings, or deaths, ranging from physical demise through the trajectory of sexuality to issues of narrative closure. In the end, that construction of endings is represented by *Amsterdam*, McEwan's symbolic city of endings. McEwan ends his story with two deaths, both the logical outcomes of the death having taken place before this novel begins. ①

6. New Historicism

Jacob Aron, in "It Is the 1980s, Al Is Rising and Alan Turing Is Alive...", discusses Ian McEwan's novel *Machines Like Me*, which is set in alternative version of the 1980s in which mathematician Alan Turin is still alive and artificial intelligence(AI) is being developed. ②

Earl G. Ingersoll, in "The Moment of History and the History of the Moment: Ian McEwan's *On Chesil Beach*", presents literary criticism of the book *On Chesil Beach* by Ian McEwan. It examines the novel's representation of romance, marriage, and sexual relations in Great Britain before the sexual liberation movement of the 1960s and the use of the birth control pill. The sexual behavior of characters Edward and Florence is discussed. Other topics include historical fiction, sexual abuse, and sexual consummation in marriage. The author compares the book to works by writer Virginia Woolf. ③

---

① Ingersoll E G. "City of Endings: Ian McEwan's *Amsterdam*". Midwest Quarterly, 2005, 46(2): 123-138.

② Aron J. "It Is the 1980s, Al Is Rising and Alan Turing Is Alive...". New Scientist, 2019, 242(3226):42-43.

③ Ingersoll E G. "The Moment of History and the History of the Moment: Ian McEwan's *On Chesil Beach*". Midwest Quarterly, 2011, 52(2): 131-147.

7. Comparative Study

Ziauddin Sardar, in "Welcome to Planet Blitcon", examines the writings of three of Great Britain's best known writers, Martin Amis, Ian McEwan and Salman Rushdie, and states that they seem to believe that civilization is under threat from Islam. This paper examines the influence of the writer Saul Bellow on these men. The author of this paper calls this trio of men "blitcons", which means "British literary neoconservatives". ①

8. Ethical Study

Elizabeth Weston, in "Resisting Loss: Guilt and Consolation in Ian McEwan's *Atonement*", argues that Ian McEwan's *Atonement* retraces the development of twentieth-century fiction from modernist amorality to postmodern relativism, incorporating their shared acknowledgements of the subjectivity of narrative. However, the novel both draws upon and moves beyond these modes of subjectivity as part of an ethically committed exploration of memory and history. On the one hand, McEwan's writer-figure, Briony, fails to grapple ethically with historical memory, preferring consolation to the real historical record. McEwan's novel itself, in containing Briony's work within a measure of critical distance, does not offer consolation. Rather, it creates an experience in which readers must move beyond Briony's shortcomings and toward a more nuanced acceptance of history's traumas, of the damages of war, and sexual violence, which is a way to truly do justice to historical memory. ②

---

① Sardar Z. "Welcome to Planet Blitcon". The New Statesman, 2006, 135(4822): 52-54.
② Weston E. "Resisting Loss: Guilt and Consolation in Ian McEwan's *Atonement*". Journal of Modern Literature, 2019, 42(3): 1-18.

Janine Utell, in "*On Chesil Beach* and Fordian Technique: Intertextuality, Intimacy, Ethical Reading", argues that Ian McEwan's use of Fordian elements and techniques in his novella *On Chesil Beach*—specifically allusions to *The Good Soldier*; impressionism as an epistemological and narrative strategy; and elements of narrative discourse such as perspective, time, and order—direct our attention to the plot of intimacy, what is sayable and unsayable in the representation of intimacy, and to what kinds of knowledge narrative provides access. These moves teach us a form of ethical reading generated by the thinking of Emmanuel Levinas: how to navigate McEwan's representation of desire, intimacy, and alterity in order to recognize the epistemological and ethical commitments and problems engendered by narrative. [1]

9. Cultural Study

Jessica Griggs, in "Funny Thing, Climate", discusses an interview with novelist Ian McEwan whose written works are noted for their scientific themes. Topics include his novel *Solar* and its contents that deal with development of a carbon-neutral electric generation technology; aspects of human nature that are reflected in his novels; and McEwan's opinion on the use and applicability of humor in fiction writing. [2]

10. Biographical Study

Suzanne Gray, in "Locating the 'Usefully Problematic' in a Novel and a Memoir by Ian McEwan", looks at aspects of a novel and a memoir, written over the

---

[1] Utell J. "*On Chesil Beach* and Fordian Technique: Intertextuality, Intimacy, Ethical Reading". Journal of Modern Literature, 2016, 39(2): 89-104.

[2] Griggs J. "Funny Thing, Climate". New Scientist, 2010, 206(2754): 24-25.

same period in 2001, by author Ian McEwan. In *Mother Tongue*, his memoir, McEwan reflects on his insular upbringing on various military bases abroad. His father, a soldier, is a periodic presence whose volatile moods interrupt the home-life. He is strongly attached to his mother. Meanwhile McEwan's novel, *Atonement*, employs the perspective of an adolescent girl, antagonistic to the link forming in her sister's mind towards someone else. In the novel, this situation leads to a denial of oedipal hierarchy, and ultimately to what Chasseguet-Smirgel terms "pseudo-creative" solutions. *Atonement*, however, lays stress on the integrating effect of the creative process itself. The author of this paper explores this from the Kleinian viewpoint of the here and now, and contrasts this with that of Chasseguet-Smirgel, and with the more recursive temporality found within the French tradition.[①]

11. Theological Study

Bruno M. Shah, in "The Sin of Ian McEwan's Fictive Atonement: Reading His Later Novels", argues that Ian McEwan is arguably the best living British novelist. His most successful novel, *Atonement*, was made into an internationally successful film. And indeed, through analysis of his novels, it is clear that Ian McEwan believes literature—precisely as fictive—might very well bear the task of atonement for postmodernity. His novels, though, are patently hopeless. Because McEwan doesn't accept or see the causes of sin as such—formally understood as rebellion against the Creator—his diagnostic aesthetic of our postmodern malaise is incomplete and ineffectual. The literary or fictive atonement that he would achieve through his novels does not satisfy. This article aims to reveal the philosophical-literary characteristics of Ian McEwan's later novels. The ultimate goal of this

---

① Gray S. "Locating the 'Usefully Problematic' in a Novel and a Memoir by Ian McEwan". British Journal of Psychotherapy, 2018, 34(1): 147-158.

critical reading, though—tending toward an "evangelical lection"—is to transfigure McEwan's imaginative and creative virtuosity for otherwise disappointed Christian readers, precisely by envisioning his novels in the dark light of their redemptive deficit. [1]

Vaughan S. Roberts, in "Implicit Sacraments in *Atonement*: The Movie", argues that the movie version of Ian McEwan's novel *Atonement*, directed by Joe Wright, raises interesting questions about implicit religion in films. This paper explores how the film of *Atonement* develops and introduces Christian themes into the storyline, and the way in which this might reflect more widely upon the place of Christianity in a secular world. [2]

---

[1] Shah B M. "The Sin of Ian McEwan's Fictive Atonement: Reading His Later Novels". New Blackfriars, 2009, 90(1025): 38-49.

[2] Roberts V S. "Implicit Sacraments in *Atonement*: The Movie". Implicit Religion, 2008, 11(3): 297-308.

Chapter 20

Julian Barnes

Julian Barnes(1946-)

Julian Barnes is the author of several books of stories, essays, a translation of Alphonse Daudet's *In the Land of Pain*, and numerous novels, including the 2011 Man Booker Prize winning novel *The Sense of an Ending* and the stunning *The Only Story*. His other recent publications include *Keeping an Eye Open: Essays on Art* and *The Man in the Red Coat*.[①]

[①] http://www.julianbarnes.com/bio/index.html.

Critical Perspectives

1. Narrative Study

Yili Tang, in "Character Narration and Fictionality in Julian Barnes's *Flaubert's Parrot*", argues that Julian Barnes's *Flaubert's Parrot* is a hybrid book resisting any attempt at genre classification. It also serves as the embodiment of Barnes's concern and experiment with the interplay of life and fiction. Enlightened by James Phelan's rhetorical theory of character narration and his rhetorical approach to fictionality, this article examines the form and function of fictionality in *Flaubert's Parrot*, to investigate how Barnes fashions a novel that resonates with greater truth than the factual material. It argues that an important aspect of the function of fictionality in *Flaubert's Parrot* is that it invites and, indeed encourages, intense readerly involvement and vicarious experience by the use of character narration. Barnes's pursuit of greater truth in fiction lies in the readers' search for the emotional authenticity and ethical situation in writing one's or their own lives during the process of reading, which makes the act of reading rewarding in itself. [1]

Frederick M. Holmes, in "Divided Narratives, Unreliable Narrators, and *The Sense of an Ending*: Julian Barnes, Frank Kermode, and Ford Madox Ford", presents literary criticism of the book *The Sense of an Ending* by Julian Barnes. Particular focus is given to Barnes' allusions to the nonfiction book of the same title by literary critic Frank Kermode and to the novel *The Good Soldier* by writer Ford

---

[1] Tang Yili. "Character Narration and Fictionality in Julian Barnes's *Flaubert's Parrot*". Word & Text: A Journal of Literary Studies & Linguistics, 2019(9): 176-189.

Madox Ford. Details on the roles of narrative and memory in Barnes' novel and in Kermode's literary theories are presented. Unreliable narrators and intertextuality are also discussed. ①

2. Philosophical Study

Samuel Piccolo, in "Petites Histoires, Meta-perspective: Meaning and Narrative in Julian Barnes", analyzes the depiction of meaning and narrative in the book *Levels of Life* by Julian Barnes. Topics discussed include the book's portrayal of the sin of height through the mistaken conviction about the permanence of an interpretation of the world, suggestion of Barnes about avoiding a predilection to commit the sin of height, and the belief of the author that love is secondary to the need of people to tell stories about their lives and stories about their loves. ②

3. Psychological Study

Carola M. Kaplan, in "The Go-Between: The Psychoanalyst as Love Mediator", argues that one of the most intransigent problems in the psychoanalytic practice is the apparently unhealable heartbreak experienced by a patient who has been dumped by a romantic partner. As Freud pointed out, the loss of the loved object is devastating because it is experienced as a loss of the most vital part of the self. The author's experience with jilted patients has made it clear that the most important response to these seemingly endless litanies of grief is patience. An

---

① Holmes F M. "Divided Narratives, Unreliable Narrators, and *The Sense of an Ending*: Julian Barnes, Frank Kermode, and Ford Madox Ford". Papers on Language & Literature, 2015, 51(1): 27-50.

② Piccolo S. "Petites Histoires, Meta-perspective: Meaning and Narrative in Julian Barnes". Papers on Language & Literature, 2021, 57(3): 275-301.

important resource that the author enlists in maintaining patience is imaginative literature, which helps us to find a pattern in therapy sessions, particularly when a patient is dealing with the exigencies of losing romantic love. The author notes that, "Recently, I have been working with a patient I call Gloria, whose live-in lover left her for another woman. Ordinarily feisty and independent, Gloria responded to this loss with an almost complete collapse. In reaction, I found myself overcome by a feeling of helplessness, which puzzled me until I realized that the collapse of this independent woman reminded me of my mother's descent into incapacitating depression when I was a child. What helped me to regain perspective was Julian Barnes' (2011) novel *The Sense of an Ending*, which brilliantly illustrates the perplexing blindness in romantic love of an otherwise intelligent and self-reflective man. Barnes' novel helped me to understand my patient's difficulties in exchanging her idealized portrait of her ex-lover for a more realistic picture of a fallible human being. Buttressed by the insights into romantic love offered by this and other literary works, I was able to remain steady and patient as Gloria worked through her grief and achieved a greater sense of purpose and selfhood in the process". ①

4. Thematic Study

Catrinel Popa, in "Lost and Found Relics, Forgeries and Mystifications in 20th Century Historiographic Metafiction", attempts to highlight the significant subversive potential of postmodern literature, its scepticism regarding the positive sciences' claim to anchor the discourse in stable representational grounds. In this paper, the primary textual focus is on three historiographic metafictions: Silviu Angelescu's *Calpuzanii* (*The Forgers*), Julian Barnes's *Flaubert's Parrot*, and Milorad Pavić's lexicon-novel *Dictionary of the Khazars*. ②

---

① Kaplan C M. "The Go-Between: The Psychoanalyst as Love Mediator". Psychoanalytic Inquiry, 2019(39): 367-373.

② Popa C. "Lost and Found Relics, Forgeries and Mystifications in 20th Century Historiographic Metafiction". Transylvanian Journal of Multidisciplinary Research in Humanities, 2021, 26(2): 169-176.

5. New Historicism

Brian Finney, in "A Worm's Eye View of History: Julian Barnes's *A History of the World in $10^{1/2}$ Chapters*", analyzes the way in which Julian Barnes presents a brief information on world history in his book *A History of the World in $10^{1/2}$ Chapters*. Topics discussed include comparison of the work of Barnes with *The History of the World*, by Walter Raleigh; theme of the second half of the title of Barnes's book; and approaches of Barnes to history as expressed in the book.①

Laurent Milesi, in "Zo(o)graphies: Darwinian 'Evolutions' of a Fictional Bestiary", puts to the test Darwinian evolutionist theories, especially the key concepts of adaptation, natural selection and survival of the fittest, in the reading of several plots and fictions (some of them are Ark-related animal fictions) concerned with evolution, trauma, adaptability, mimicry/mimesis and survival: Julian Barnes's *Flaubert's Parrot* and *A History of the World in $10^{1/2}$ Chapters*, Timothy Findley's *Not Wanted on the Voyage*, Robert Kroetsch's *The Studhorse Man* and John Fowles's *The French Lieutenant's Woman*. Weaving its critical argument with reference to several of Derrida's reflections, "zo(o)graphies" is structured in a series of interlinked tableaux, bestiaries as well as insets. Following from the opening evocation of Peter Greenaway's Vermeer-themed film *A Zed & Two Noughts*, this study eventually attempts to recast the problematic of the evolution of literature and literary forms as involution and regression.②

---

① Finney B. "A Worm's Eye View of History: Julian Barnes's *A History of the World in $10^{1/2}$ Chapters*". Papers on Language & Literature, 2003, 39(1): 49-70.

② Milesi L. "Zo(o)graphies: Darwinian 'Evolutions' of a Fictional Bestiary". Word & Text: A Journal of Literary Studies & Linguistics, 2021(11): 15-41.

6. Post-colonial Study

E. Dodson, in "The Partial Postcoloniality of Julian Barnes's *Arthur & George*", argues that Julian Barnes's 2005 novel *Arthur & George*, unlike the rest of his oeuvre, has been read as a "subtly postcolonial narrative". His fictionalized historical portrait of the English-Indian lawyer George Edalji contributes to the postcolonial project of making empire visible within Britain. Barnes's postcolonialism, however, is only partial. The Edaljis are isolated in Barnes's otherwise completely white Edwardian England. Furthermore, Barnes's depiction of Arthur Conan Doyle risks perpetuating heroic accounts of this imperial figure and the nation he embodies. The partial postcoloniality of *Arthur & George* has wider implications for conceptions of Julian Barnes and of the contemporary English novel. [1]

7. Ethical Study

Maja Medan, in "The Ethical Aspect of Constituting History in Julian Barnes's *A History of the World in $10^{1/2}$ Chapters*", deals with the ethical aspect of the process of constituting history that is problematized in Julian Barnes's *A History of the World in $10^{1/2}$ Chapters*. The reduction mechanism of interpreting in the sole act of history/truth and fiction as labeling systems of a certain culture questions the nature of history/truth as the object of our knowledge. The ethical character of this reduction is connected to the question of the relation of power and knowledge that

---

[1] Dodson E. "The Partial Postcoloniality of Julian Barnes's *Arthur & George*". Journal of Modern Literature, 2018, 41(2): 112-128.

Barnes particularly provokes in his book.①

8. Socialism Study

Aura Sibişan, in "Julian Barnes—A Cosmopolitan Author", presents aspects of the work of Julian Barnes from a contemporary cultural perspective, and discusses the British writer's response to the dissolution of meaning in contemporary society. Cosmopolitanism and a critical view towards simulacra are two attitudes that may define a meaningful life, in Barnes's view. In the novel *England, England*, we find challenges to conventions of the novel as a genre, and a discussion of the human costs of the "society as spectacle". Therefore, the insidious processes of transformation of meaning are exposed by the British writer in *England, England*.②

Christine Berberich, in "England? Whose England? (Re) Constructing English Identities in Julian Barnes and W. G. Sebald", explores the notions of identity construction. Focusing on "Englishness", it examines theories of identity formation, memory creation and nation-building alongside travel writing and notions of the picturesque. The focus of the debate throughout is on two novels of the 1990s: Julian Barnes' dystopian *England, England* of 1998 and W. G. Sebald's *The Rings of Saturn* of 1995 (English translation, 1998). Both novels play with traditional ideas of national identities and stereotypes by presenting their readers with the literal "construction" of alternative versions of England and the English.③

---

① Medan M. "The Ethical Aspect of Constituting History in Julian Barnes's *A History of the World in $10^{1/2}$ Chapters*". Europa: Magazine about Science & Art during the Transition, 2013, 6(11): 61-64.

② Sibişan A. "Julian Barnes—A Cosmopolitan Author". Bulletin of the Transilvania University of Brasov, Series IV: Philology & Cultural Studies, 2015, 8(2): 95-106.

③ Berberich C. "England? Whose England? (Re) Constructing English Identities in Julian Barnes and W. G. Sebald". National Identities, 2008, 10(2): 167-184.

L. E. Delgado, in "The Sound and the Red Fury: The Sticking Points of Spanish Nationalism", cites the British author Julian Barnes' novel *England, England*, which offers a satiric and dystopic vision of the process of national identity formation. The goal of this essay is to distill the essence of Englishness itself, preserving it in a delimited space. [1]

9. Linguistic Study

N. Vladimirova and Y. Nagornaya, in "The Semiotics of a Ship and Its Modelling Features in the Novels of William Golding, Julian Barnes, and Gregory Norminton", study the semiotics of the ship as an image of the world in cases of the novels *To the End of the Earth* by William Golding, *A History of the World in $10^{1/2}$ Chapters* by J. Barnes, and *The Ship of Fools* by G. Norminton. The ship is considered as a new version of the Biblical Noah's Ark—a miniature society. The authors believe that the text integrates the new "generative model" creating at the same time new forms of fictional conditionality and types of literary generalization. [2]

---

[1] Delgado L E. "The Sound and the Red Fury: The Sticking Points of Spanish Nationalism". Journal of Spanish Cultural Studies, 2010, 11(3/4): 263-276.

[2] Vladimirova N, Nagornaya Y. "The Semiotics of a Ship and Its Modelling Features in the Novels of William Golding, Julian Barnes, and Gregory Norminton". Vestnik IKBFU, 2013(8): 146-150.

Chapter 21

V. S. Naipaul

V. S. Naipaul(1932-2018)

Born in Trinidad into a Brahmin family, Naipaul was educated at Queens Royal College, Port of Spain, and went on a scholarship to University College, Oxford. After marrying an English woman, he settled in London, became a literary journalist, and turned eventually to writing *The Mystic Masseur*. Set in the Caribbean and based on his own early years in Trinidad, *A House for Mr. Biswas* established Naipaul's reputation as a novelist. His Booker Prize-winning novel *In a Free State* began a trend in his fiction and his reportage toward the uncompromising and pessimistic portrayal of postcolonial culture and politics. Notable for exploring such issues are the novels *Guerrillas* and *A Bend in the River* and personal narratives such as *India: A Wounded Civilization*, *A Congo Diary*, *The Return of Eva Perón*, and *Among the Believers*.[1]

---

[1] Richetti J, Bender J, David D, et al. The Columbia History of the British Novel. New York: Columbia University Press, 1994.

Critical Perspectives

1. Narrative Study

Robert Boyers, in "The Devil's Tail: Reading from the Lives of Authors", presents a personal narrative which explores the author's experience of spending a day interviewing V. S. Naipaul, who is teaching undergraduates at Wesleyen University in Connecticut. [1]

2. Philosophical Study

Venkanna Nukapangu, in "Speculating Socio-Political Scenario of India in V. S. Naipaul's *An Area of Darkness*", argues that diaspora novels have brought a new sensation on the literary horizon, painting the works of arts with multicultural colors. Naipaul wrote three Indian travelogues on India. The major theme of the novel *An Area of Darkness* is alienation and isolation. It records the failure of his attempt to settle in India. In this novel, Naipaul began a painful confrontation with the civilization that nurtured him in his earliest years, and which marked him as a kind of resident alien in the west. *An Area of Darkness* was frankly personal. The novel embellishes the writer's precarious relationship as an outsider and an insider, resulting aggressive comments on Indian Society's socio-political existence. [2]

---

[1] Boyers R. "The Devil's Tail: Reading from the Lives of Authors". The Virginia Quarterly Review, 2010, 86(4): 199-206.

[2] Nukapangu V. "Speculating Socio-Political Scenario of India in V. S. Naipaul's *An Area of Darkness*". Utopia y Praxis Latinoamericana, 2020, 12(25): 425-431.

3. Psychological Study

Irina Strout, in "'Who Are the Mimic Men?' Or the Crisis of Identity in V. S. Naipaul's Fiction", presents a literary criticism on the 20th century fictional books *The Mystic Masseur* and *The Mimic Men*, by Trinidadian author V. S. Naipaul. Particular focus is given to the depiction of identity, identity crisis and mimicry within the aforementioned novels, including in regard to the relationship between colonialism and mimicry. ①

4. Biographical Study

Jeffrey Folks, in "The Art of Redemption: V. S. Naipaul's *The Enigma of Arrival*", describes Naipaul's attempt to create a character that resembles his background in the novel *The Enigma of Arrival*. It also analyzes the authobiographical novel's thematic concern of man's determination to pursue the truth and restore justice. ②

William H. Pritchard, in "Naipaul Unveiled", presents an overview of various depictions and treatments of biography of the British writer V. S. Naipaul. Topics discussed include details that cited from several works, biographical commentaries by others, as well as various interviews and self-representations of Naipaul himself. The author of this paper also discusses the relationship of his writing style and personality to his sexual life. ③

---

① Strout I. "'Who Are the Mimic Men?' Or the Crisis of Identity in V. S. Naipaul's Fiction". Atenea, 2012, 32(1/2): 85-96.

② Folks J. "The Art of Redemption: V. S. Naipaul's *The Enigma of Arrival*". Modern Age, 2018, 60(4): 23-30.

③ Pritchard W H. "Naipaul Unveiled". The Hudson Review, 2009, 61(4): 431-440.

Laura Shapiro, Shehnaz Suterwalla and Ray Sawhill, in "A Tale of Two Giant Egos", focus on the friendship of between Paul Theroux and V. S. Naipaul. Topics discussed include how they met in Uganda in 1966; how their friendship disintegrated; and Theroux's book *Sir Vidia's Shadow*. ①

5. New Historicism

Thomas F. Bertonneau, in "V. S. Naipaul & the Dream of Blood: Atavisms in Universal Civilization", focuses on author V. S. Naipaul and compares his works to those of author Joseph Conrad. Particular attention is given to Naipaul's thoughts on the concept of the "universal civilization" and on the effects of abolishing history, including in Islam fundamentalism. The author discusses the characters and literary themes of Naipaul and Conrad, including colonialism destructive ideologies in modernity, as well as how Naipaul is influenced by Conrad. Third World radicalism and race politics are also discussed. ②

Paul Lay, in "All of History Is There", discusses the history of West Indies. The author also talks about the book *The Middle Passage* by Trinidadian-born Nobel Laureate V. S. Naipaul. ③

Jeffrey Folks, in "Naipaul's Way", focuses on the literature of V. S. Naipaul, novelist and winner of the Nobel Prize for Literature in 2001. The author discusses Naipaul's literary techniques in various works including *A Way in the World*. Naipaul's fictional themes are real but not historical, including exile, liberation, and return. ④

---

① Shapiro L, Suterwalla S, Sawhill R. "A Tale of Two Giant Egos". Newsweek, 1998, 132(6): 64.

② Bertonneau T F. "V. S. Naipaul & the Dream of Blood: Atavisms in Universal Civilization". Modern Age, 2009, 51(3/4): 238-249.

③ Lay P. "All of History Is There". History Today, 2020, 70(10):3.

④ Folks J. "Naipaul's Way". Modern Age, 2007, 49(2): 171-177.

6. Canonization

Jason Cowley, in "The End of the Make-believe", focuses on V. S. Naipaul's writing in *The New York Review of Books*, which questioned whether the novel has a future. Topics discussed include Naipaul's view on when the most important works of fiction have been written; information on the novels of Martin Amis; and Naipaul's experiences as a writer.①

7. Post-colonial Study

William Ghosh, in "Caribbean Travel and the 'Realistic Shock': Lamming, Naipaul, Condé", claims that African cultural forms survived in Caribbean societies, and this was interrogated when Caribbean writers traveled to West Africa. A common trope, "realistic shock", is found in many travelogues and memoirs that describe this journey. In this trope, an encounter with the "real" Africa dispels earlier "romantic" notions of the continent as source-culture or homeland for Caribbean people. During the years of decolonization and independence, George Lamming and V. S. Naipaul used this trope to express skepticism toward claims for African-Caribbean connection. But Maryse Condé used the trope differently, to articulate a new understanding of the relationship between the Caribbean and Africa.②

Jeffrey Folks, in "Naipaul and the Barbarians", examines Naipaul's characterization of the protagonist Willie Chandran as well as other characters. The

---

① Cowley J. "The End of the Make-believe". The New Statesman, 1999, 128(4422): 50.
② Ghosh W. "Caribbean Travel and the 'Realistic Shock': Lamming, Naipaul, Condé". Research in African Literatures, 2019, 50(2): 177-197.

themes of self-liberation, civilization and colonial society, and modern culture are discussed.①

Baidik Bhattacharya, in "Naipaul's New World: Postcolonial Modernity and the Enigma of Belated Space", explores the political issues found in the works of V. S. Naipaul. The author presents the problem of the commonly viewed dichotomy between Naipual's negative political biases expressed in his literature and the benefits of his criticism on imperialism in the Caribbean. It is suggested that rather than filtering through his views, a critical analysis of Naipaul's attitudes in themselves as an effect of the system is warranted.②

David M. Traboulay, in "V. S. Naipual on Tradition and Modernity in the Third World", examines the works of Trinidadian writer V. S. Naipaul on the nature of the post-colonial world. Topics discussed include commendation of the values of Western civilization against the barbarism of the Third World; reflection of views on the inhumane ways of modernization in the Third World in Naipaul's works; and rejection of a synthesis between modernity and religion.③

Arnold Rampersad, in "V. S. Naipaul: Turning in the South", focuses on the book *A Turn in the South*, by V. S. Naipaul. Topics discussed include Naipaul's knowledge of the Southern United States; search for the meaning of Southern history as the book's main theme; Naipaul's journalism; and Naipaul's ability to see the South as part of the problem of the Third World.④

Thomas F. Halloran, in "Postcolonial Mimic or Postmodern Portrait? Politics and Identity in V. S. Naipaul's Third World", presents a literary criticism of the novel *The Mimic Men*, by V. S. Naipaul, analyzing his depiction of the political

---

① Folks J. "Naipaul and the Barbarians". Modern Age, 2009, 51(3/4): 251-261.
② Bhattacharya B. "Naipaul's New World: Postcolonial Modernity and the Enigma of Belated Space". Novel: A Forum on Fiction, 2006, 39(2): 245-268.
③ Traboulay D M. "V. S. Naipual on Tradition and Modernity in the Third World". Community Review, 1998(16): 66-74.
④ Rampersad A. "V. S. Naipaul: Turning in the South". Raritan, 1990, 10(1): 24-47.

and social elements of cultural identity within the Third World. Naipaul's aggressive views against polemic distinctions between the First and Third World are cited along with the balance of personal psychology and group politics manifested through the characters of the story.①

Divya Sood, in "Empire, Power, and Language: The Creation of an Identity in V. S. Naipaul's *The Mystic Masseur*", presents a literary criticism of the novel *The Mystic Masseur*, by V. S. Naipaul, and discusses its depiction of the themes of imperialism and the formation of social and national identity in Trinidad. The main character Ganesh's search for self-identity is analyzed in relation to that of the identity formation of a postcolonial society.②

Petal Samuel, in "The Sound of Luxury: Antiblackness, Silence, and the Private Island Resort", offers insights on the link between silence and the luxury quality and experience at private island resorts. Topics discussed include the impact of this resort exclusivity and seclusion on local communities, particularly minorities that live in the area, the luxury resort experiences published by *Fortune* magazine editor Leigh Gallagher and writer V. S. Naipaul, and the depiction of black people in the promotional materials of various Caribbean luxury resorts.③

8. Comparative Study

Gregory McNamee, in "V. S. Naipaul vs. Jane Austen", features novelist V. S. Naipaul. Particular focus is given to Naipaul's opinion about his writing ability. He points out the susceptibility of women to sentimentality, as well as

---

① Halloran T F. "Postcolonial Mimic or Postmodern Portrait? Politics and Identity in V. S. Naipaul's Third World". Atenea, 2007, 27(1): 121-134.

② Sood D. "Empire, Power, and Language: The Creation of an Identity in V. S. Naipaul's *The Mystic Masseur*". Atenea, 2007, 27(1): 93-101.

③ Samuel P. "The Sound of Luxury: Antiblackness, Silence, and the Private Island Resort". The Black Scholar, 2021, 51(1): 30-42.

women's view of the world. It cites Zadie Smith and Phyllis Dorothy James as some of the women writers who can compete with Naipaul's work. Also included are information on the resolved feud between Naipaul and fellow writer Paul Theroux. ①

9. Cultural Study

Elizabeth Powers, in "Among the Barbarians: V. S. Naipaul and His Critics", focuses on writer V. S. Naipaul and his work which include novel *A House for Mr. Biswas* and two nonfiction *The Middle Passage* and *The Loss of El Dorado*. It mentions that the successes and failures of native traditions and values have no grounding in the Western pattern. It also mentions writing style of Naipaul with effect of the realism. ②

Akeel Bilgrami, in "Cry, the Beloved Subcontinent", features the book *India: A Million Mutinies Now*, by V. S. Naipaul. Topics discussed include Naipaul's method for the study of culture; movement toward unification in India found in religious communities, most particularly among the Hindus; existence of communal tension between Hindus and Muslims; ancient origins of the Brahmanical ascendancy; idea of a monolithic and majoritarian Hinduism as a mythical creation; and views of the author that the idea of an Indian nation needs a redefinition of the process by which unity can be retained. ③

John Leonard, in "Who Has the Best Tunes?", argues that as much as Islam, Salman Rushdie blasphemes Thatcherism. He's unkind, too, to V. S. Naipaul. Pitting levity against gravity, altogether impious, *The Satanic Verses*, is one of those

---

① McNamee G. "V. S. Naipaul vs. Jane Austen". Kirkus Reviews, 2011, 79(15):1280.
② Powers E. "Among the Barbarians: V. S. Naipaul and His Critics". The Hudson Review, 2019, 72(2): 193-214.
③ Bilgrami A. "Cry, the Beloved Subcontinent". The New Republic, 1991, 204(23): 30-34.

go-for-broke "metafictions"—a grand narrative and a Monty Python sendup of history, religion and popular culture. Postcolonial identity crisis and modernist pastiche are also discussed. ①

10. Social Study

Graham Huggan, in "V. S. Naipaul and the Political Correctness Debate", discusses the oppositionality in V. S. Naipaul's writings which attack the educational system of his native Trinidad. Topics discussed include role of education in the production of the colonial subject, and compromise of the specificity of postcolonial literatures/cultures in the political correctness debate. ②

Shegufta Yasmin, in "*A House for Mr. Biswas* and *Kuberer Bishoy Ashoy*: Similarities between V. S. Naipaul and Shyamol Gangopaddhay", argues that V. S. Naipaul's *A House for Mr. Biswas* and Shyamol Gangopaddhay's *Kuberer Bishoy Ashoy* are written in different background, but they have tremendous similarities in characters' portrayal, plot and philosophy. In this paper, these common features and similarities between two novels are shown. Both Mr. Biswas and Kuber want an individual house for themselves to find their own identity. For both of them, an "individual house" is turned into their dream, goal, target and life. ③

11. Biographical Study

Isaac Chotiner, in "V. S. Naipaul Is Who He Is", asks about Naipaul's

---

① Leonard J. "Who Has the Best Tunes?". The Nation, 1989, 248(10): 346-349.
② Huggan G. "V. S. Naipaul and the Political Correctness Debate". College Literature, 1994, 21(3): 200-206.
③ Yasmin S. "*A House for Mr. Biswas* and *Kuberer Bishoy Ashoy*: Similarities between V. S. Naipaul and Shyamol Gangopaddhay". ASA University Review, 2013, 7(2): 257-260.

views. He says he does not regard the places he visits in terms of possible social reforms from which they would benefit. He cites authors he is reading, including Thomas de Quincey and Thomas Mann. He says many of the most famous British authors do not appeal to him, including Charles Dickens and Jane Austen. ①

Mohamed Bakari, in "V. S. Naipaul: From Gadfly to Obsessive", reports on V. S. Naipaul, the 2001 Nobel laureate for literature. Of Indian ancestry, Naipaul is a grandchild of Hindu Brahmins who found their way to the Caribbean island of Trinidad as indentured labourers to escape the grinding poverty of Utterpradesh. Naipaul's was just one of a stream of families that were encouraged to migrate to the West Indies from the former British colonies of India. ②

Patrick French, in "Leaving the Ghetto", discusses the early life in London of the Trinidadian writer V. S. Naipaul. The author also examines Naipaul's conscious attempt to remake himself as a British citizen and writer. ③

12. Theological Study

Hossein Nazari, in "The Mad Muslim Mob: De/Mythologising Shi'i Iran in V. S. Naipaul's 'Islamic' Travelogues", argues that the advent of the 1979 Islamic Revolution made Iran and Islam dominant representational motifs in western media and literature. The preponderance of such representations revolved around the Iranian nation's identification as a Shi'i Muslim-majority polity. As such, the Revolution's trajectory and its landmark events—such as the 1979 hostage crisis— were often construed in light of this fact. Prominent among literary representations of post-revolutionary Iran in western literature are V. S. Naipaul's "Islamic"

---

① Chotiner I. "V. S. Naipaul Is Who He Is". The New Republic, 2012, 243(19): 14-18.
② Bakari M. "V. S. Naipaul: From Gadfly to Obsessive". Alternatives: Turkish Journal of International Relations, 2003, 2(3/4): 243-259.
③ French P. "Leaving the Ghetto". The New Statesman, 2008, 137(4891): 54-55.

travelogues, *Among the Believers* (1981) and *Beyond Belief* (1998). This paper presents Naipaul's representations of Iran and Shi'i Islam in the two travel narratives, highlighting some of the most popular instances of myth and disinformation that the texts propagate. Thematic critique of the narratives is intended to shed light on the author's Orientalist approach and his engagement in a historical historicism, which—coupled with a conspicuous ignorance of Iran, Islam and Shi'ism—has resulted in two of the most notorious literary tirades on Islam and the Muslim World. ①

Amin Malak, in "Naipaul's Travelogues and the 'Clash of Civilizations' Complex", offers theological perspectives on the travelogues of writer V. S. Naipaul and a literary analysis of his diatribes against Islam in Samuel Huntington's essay, *The Clash of Civilizations*. A comparison between Naipaul's and Huntington's generalizations about non-Western cultures and Islamic imperialism is discussed. ②

Peter Watson, in "Lost in the Swamp of Modernity", focuses on the main ideas that shaped the 20th century. Topics discussed include non-western achievements; Islamic countries visited by V. S. Naipaul; and burden of religious fundamentalism. ③

---

① Nazari H. "The Mad Muslim Mob: De/Mythologising Shi'i Iran in V. S. Naipaul's 'Islamic' Travelogues". Journal of Shi'a Islamic Studies, 2016, 9(3): 273-300.

② Malak A. "Naipaul's Travelogues and the 'Clash of Civilizations' Complex". Cross Currents, 2006, 56(2): 261-268.

③ Watson P. "Lost in the Swamp of Modernity". The New Statesman, 2001, 130(4561): 30-31.

Chapter 22

Salman Rushdie

Salman Rushdie(1947-)

Born in Bombay, Rushdie attended school in Bombay, in England, and eventually at King's College, Cambridge. After working as an actor in experimental theater and as a copywriter, he published his first novel, *Grimus*. A five-month trip to Pakistan and India prepared him to write the Booker Prize-winning *Midnight's Children*. His novel *The Satanic Verses* created an intercultural controversy when Ayatollah Khomeini deemed the novel sacrilegious and called for the death penalty against Rushdie. He is also the author of *Shame*, *The Jaguar Smile*, *Haroun and the Sea of Stories*, and *Imaginary Homelands: Essays and Criticism 1981-1991*. [1]

---

[1] Richetti J, Bender J, David D, et al. The Columbia History of the British Novel. New York: Columbia University Press, 1994.

Critical Perspectives

1. Narrative Study

Neil Ten Kortenaar, in "Salman Rushdie's Magic Realism and the Return of Inescapable Romance", focuses on the incompatible framework of magic realism in the novel *Midnight's Children*, by Salman Rushdie. Topics discussed include origin of the pattern of the narrative on tales of Rushdie; narrative resolutions available to the bildungsroman in the three endings of the novel; and social construction of identity represented by a baby switch. ①

2. Philosophical Study

Jennifer Bardi, in "Such a Voice Is Needed: The Humanist Interview with Salman Rushdie", presents an interview with author Salman Rushdie, who has been named as the 2019 Humanist of the Year by the American Humanist Association. Topics discussed include information on his fourteenth novel, *Quichotte*, which is compared as a modern remake of *Don Quixote*, how religion poses a grave threat to civil liberties and freedom of the individual, and writing characters from marginalized groups. ②

---

① Kortenaar N T. "Salman Rushdie's Magic Realism and the Return of Inescapable Romance". University of Toronto Quarterly, 2002, 71(3): 765-785.

② Bardi J. "Such a Voice Is Needed: The Humanist Interview with Salman Rushdie". The Humanist, 2019, 79(6): 12-16.

Joel Kuortti, in "Dreams, Intercultural Identification and *The Satanic Verses*", examines the ways in which Salman Rushdie's fictional novel *The Satanic Verses* has worked as a point. Topics discussed include discussion on the level of dreams in the novel; issues on the undefined usage of the word "fundamentalism"; and conclusion. [1]

3. Biographical Study

R. Davis, in "Salman Rushdie's East, West: Palimpsests of Fiction and Reality", focuses on the literary and critical endeavors of Salman Rushdie based on postcolonial and diasporic condition. Topics discussed include comments on the identity of immigrant writers; topics of emphasis of the immigrant writers; and proposal of alternative discourses. [2]

4. New Historicism

Bruce Robbins, in "Too Much Information", discusses the role of information in novels. It suggests that critic James Wood's criterion for the proper novelistic way is feeling and that Salman Rushdie's descriptions of the Amritsar massacre in *Midnight's Children* also make readers feel. The author concludes that the feeling or emotion in commodity origin scenes comes from an anticipation of a character's death and that avoiding atrocity is politically necessary. [3]

---

[1] Kuortti J. "Dreams, Intercultural Identification and *The Satanic Verses*". Contemporary South Asia, 1997, 6(2): 191-200.

[2] Davis R. "Salman Rushdie's East, West: Palimpsests of Fiction and Reality". Passages: A Journal of Transnational & Transcultural Studies, 2000, 2(1): 81-92.

[3] Robbins B. "Too Much Information". Novel: A Forum on Fiction, 2010, 43(1): 78-82.

5. Post-colonial Study

Sara Upstone, in "Domesticity in Magical-Realist Postcolonial Fiction", argues that the depiction of domestic space in the postcolonial novel *Midnight's Children* by Salman Rushdie shows the relationship between domesticity and colonialism. Citing the view of the home as an embodiment of the values of colonialism, the author examines the reclaimed status of the home as a space free of colonial metaphor and the subversion of colonial processes through this depiction in postcolonial novels, which the author claims has implications for both colonial discourse and postcolonial gender politics. The author discusses magic realism, gendered domestic space, and the portrayal of domestic space, colonial resistance, and women in *Midnight's Children*.①

Ali A. Mazrui, in "*The Satanic Verses* or a Satanic Novel? Moral Dilemmas of the Rushdie Affair", presents a discussion about the decision of the Muslim world to ban the book *The Satanic Verses*, by Salman Rushdie. Topics discussed include difference between the Western interpretation of the concept of treason with that of the Muslim world; example of the clash of cultures in the question of comparative defamation; discussion of the concept of censorship in different countries; and debate over language and religion brought about by the book.②

6. Comparative Study

Fouad Ajami, in "The Fire This Time", discusses the Islamic uproar over the

---

① Upstone S. "Domesticity in Magical-Realist Postcolonial Fiction". Frontiers: A Journal of Women Studies, 2007, 28(1/2): 260-284.

② Mazrui A A. "*The Satanic Verses* or a Satanic Novel? Moral Dilemmas of the Rushdie Affair". Alternatives: Global, Local, Political, 1990, 15(1): 97-121.

anti-Islamic cartoons being circulated throughout the Arab world. The author compares the situation to the response to Salman Rushdie's *The Satanic Verses* and Ayatollah Khomeini's death sentence against Rushdie. ①

7. Cultural Study

Rufus Cook, in "Place and Displacement in Salman Rushdie's Work", evaluates Salman Rushdie's writings and his arguments on cultural displacements. Topics discussed include cultural displacement as a way of seeking freedom; exploration on the relationship between reality and fiction in *Shame*; and purpose of Rushdie's "off-centering" narrative technique. ②

John Leonard, in "Rushdie as Orpheus, on Guitar", presents information about the book *The Ground beneath Her Feet*, by Salman Rushdie. *The Ground beneath Her Feet* is Rushdie's goodbye to Bombay novel. Rushdie likes the book too, and there's a lot more Bombay, India in *The Ground beneath Her Feet*. ③

8. Linguistic Study

Dana Bădulescu, in "Rushdie's Sorcery with Language", looks into how postcolonial writer Salman Rushdie does a work of "magic" with languages in order to find his own voice to tell his unrooted and hybrid stories. Hybridity and unrootedness are essential aspects of his writing. This study traces Rushdie's experiments with languages from *Midnight's Children*, the novel where he felt he found a voice of his own, and through to *The Enchantress of Florence*, a novel of

---

① Ajami F. "The Fire This Time". U. S. News & World Report, 2006, 140(6): 30.
② Cook R. "Place and Displacement in Salman Rushdie's Work". World Literature Today, 1994, 68(1): 23-28.
③ Leonard J. "Rushdie as Orpheus, on Guitar". The Nation, 1999, 268(17): 25-32.

linguistic and artistic refinement. From one novel to the next, Rushdie found new inflections of his voice in his narrators and characters, who "chutnified" English, "translated" their languages into their idioms, aestheticized and palimpsested their world, "disoriented" it, turned it into a "hypertext", or seduced the readers with their stories. ①

9. Theological Study

F. Miller, in "Open Letter to Salman Rushdie", presents an open letter by the author to Salman Rushdie on the third anniversary of the Iranian spiritual leader Ayatollah Khomeini's decree ordering the murder of Rushdie because of "blasphemy" in his novel *The Satanic Verses*. The author of this essay says that a few years ago, he worked as a part-time guidance counselor in a small parochial elementary school in East Harlem, New York. More than sixty applied for the jobs, putting the staff in an awkward bind. All the applicants had attended the school at one time or another. The author tells this true story with his personal experiences which he wants to be remembered by all. ②

Peter Jones, in "Rushdie, Race and Religion", discusses the issues raised by Salman Rushdie's *The Satanic Verses* and the nature of Muslims' complaints against this book. Topics discussed include response of the so-called Liberal Inquisition; theology of blasphemy and apostasy; political dimensions of the Rushdie affair both in Great Britain and internationally; legal limits of freedom of expression; worldwide battles between western secularism and Islam; "fatwa" issued by Iranian leader Ayatollah Khomeini against Rushdie; moral understanding; identity argument; people's beliefs and their identity; public cultures of multi-faith societies; law of

---

① Bădulescu D. "Rushdie's Sorcery with Language". Philologica Jassyensia, 2012, 8(2): 129-142.
② Miller F. "Open Letter to Salman Rushdie". The Nation, 1992, 254(9): 304-306.

blasphemy; and cultural diversity. ①

Bernard Lewis, in "Behind the Rushdie Affair", considers the implications of the "fatwa" issued by the Ayatollah Khomeini against the life of author Salman Rushdie. Topics discussed include the literary form of *The Satanic Verses*, and the lack of novels in Muslim culture; discussion of the outcry against the book after its publication in America; the issue of Muslims in a non-Muslim land; Islamic requirement to "enjoin good and forbid evil"; law concerning punishment for insulting the Prophet; and discussion of the extent of jurisdiction for Islamic law. ②

10. Reader-response Study

Amitava Kumar, in "Salman Rushdie and Me", reflects on his admiration for the author Salman Rushdie. He comments on his experience reading aloud transcripts from Rushdie's book *The Satanic Verses*, along with fellow writer Hari Kunzru, at the Jaipur Literature Festival in India despite the fact that the book is banned in the country. Religious issues which resulted in the banning of the book are discussed, including a fatwa established by Iran's Ayatollah Khomeini for Rushdie's death. The author also comments on the impact of the microblogging website Twitter on the ways in which individuals communicate and chronicles his evolving relationship with the literary works of Rushdie. ③

---

① Jones P. "Rushdie, Race and Religion". Political Studies, 1990, 38(4): 687-694.
② Lewis B. "Behind the Rushdie Affair". American Scholar, 1991, 60(2): 185-196.
③ Kumar A. "Salman Rushdie and Me". Chronicle of Higher Education, 2012, 58(25): 9-11.

Chapter 23

Kazuo Ishiguro

Kazuo Ishiguro (1954-)

Kazuo Ishiguro is a British author who was born in Nagasaki, Japan. The setting of his first two novels was in Japan, but he bears no resemblance to the Japanese style of writing fiction. Some of his novels include *The Unconsoled*, *When We Were Orphans*, and *Never Let Me Go*. His novels *The Remains of the Day* and *Never Let Me Go* were adapted into films in 1993 and 2010 respectively. His short story collection *Nocturnes: Five Stories of Music and Nightfall* was published in 2009. It also got a nomination for the James Tait Black Memorial Prize. Ishiguro has also written screenplays for *A Profile of Arthur J. Mason* which aired in 1984 and *The Gourmet* in 1986. He has received immense appreciation with his work being translated in over thirty languages and has been given many awards. He was ranked on number 32 on "The 50 Greatest British Writers Since 1945" by *The Times*.

Ishiguro married Lorna MacDougal in 1986. They currently live in London. In 2017, he won the Nobel Prize for Literature for his works that "uncovered the abyss beneath our illusory sense of connection with the world". [1]

---

[1] https://www.famousauthors.org/kazuo-ishiguro.

Critical Perspectives

1. Narrative Study

Elif Toprak Sakiz, in "Implications of Narrative Unreliability in Kazuo Ishiguro's *The Remains of the Day*", analyzes the predominating narrative unreliability in Kazuo Ishiguro's *The Remains of the Day* (1989) within the framework of rhetorical narratology with a specific focus upon the notion of subjectivity. The homodiegetic narrator, the ageing butler Stevens, is far from fitting unproblematically into the definition of unreliable narrator. The exploration of the employment of narrative unreliability in the novel must, therefore, be aligned with central themes like the national identity and Englishness precisely because it is through Stevens's narration that these grand narratives can be revealed as fiction. What is at issue in the novel is also the very act of narration itself, which is problematized as evasive, nonauthoritative, repressed, and obfuscating. Stevens's narration is profoundly retrospective, looking backwards not only to retrieve the past memories of "great" days in the service of Lord Darlington, but also to base his own subjectivity upon this "greatness". In this respect, by dealing with various functions of the use of an unreliable narrator in *The Remains of the Day*, it is possible to come up with certain implications of Stevens's unreliability that is rendered manifest by means of evasion or repression of narration, fallibility of memory, and disintegration of subjectivity and national identity. [①]

[①] Sakiz E T. "Implications of Narrative Unreliability in Kazuo Ishiguro's *The Remains of the Day*". Gaziantep University Journal of Social Sciences, 2019, 18(3): 1050-1057.

Ben Howard, in "A Civil Tongue: The Voice of Kazuo Ishiguro", studies the style involved in the use of the first-person narrative voice by author Kazuo Ishiguro. Topics discussed include elements of the monologue of a character in the book *A Pale View of Hills*, which contemplates the physical fact of death; defensiveness involved in the narrative voice of the main character in the book *An Artist of the Floating World*; and inclusion of the element of irony in the book *The Remains of the Day*.[①]

Jeff Nunokawa, in "Afterword: Now They Are Orphans", discusses the novel *Never Let Me Go*, written by author Kazuo Ishiguro. The novel features a first-person narrator who was bred to become an organ donor. Rather than being angry with the situation, she treats life with a quiet grief.[②]

2. Philosophical Study

Will Kanyusik, in "Eugenic Nostalgia: Self-Narration and Internalized Ableism in Kazuo Ishiguro's *Never Let Me Go*", presents that Rosemarie Garland-Thomson has argued that Ishiguro's novel *Never Let Me Go* deconstructs ableism's binary structure by postulating the existence of clone characters who occupy an abject position in a eugenic dystopia precisely because their genetically engineered, idealized able bodies exist to be used to "cure" the disabilities of others. The article builds on Garland-Thomson's work, discussing the role of science fiction in Ishiguro's book as a means to explore how ableist narratives contribute to cultural norms that enable an overt disciplining of disabled bodies that still occurs, despite it

---

① Howard B. "A Civil Tongue: The Voice of Kazuo Ishiguro". The Sewanee Review, 2001, 109(3): 389-417.

② Nunokawa J. "Afterword: Now They Are Orphans". Novel: A Forum on Fiction, 2007, 40(3): 303-304.

no longer being socially acceptable, and posits protagonist Kathy's story as a narrative of disability identity that exposes the contradictory nature of a belief in the able body and its opposition to disability. Putatively able-bodied, Kathy narrates her experience of the world from a subject position that undermines a stable construction of the body within an ableist framework, ultimately showing these distinctions to be untenable. By discussing the role of first-person perspective in Ishiguro's novel as a means to interrogate internalized cultural narratives that perpetuate ableist practices, the article examines how cultural notions of ability and disability function as terms that define through exclusion the citizen-subject in liberal democratic societies.[①]

Rachel Carroll, in "Imitations of Life: Cloning, Heterosexuality and the Human in Kazuo Ishiguro's *Never Let Me Go*", explores the representation of human cloning in Kazuo Ishiguro's speculative fiction, *Never Let Me Go*, published in 2005. It investigates the possibility that Ishiguro's exploration of the contingency of human identity has a significant, if oblique, relationship to heteronormative constructions of heterosexuality and the human. In order to trace how a fiction of human cloning might give rise to questions of heteronormativity, the author of this article focuses on issues of reproduction and their relationship to normative constructions of heterosexuality. The controversies prompted by the potential prospect of reproductive human cloning can be attributed in part to the ways in which it challenges the heterosexual prerogative to reproduction. The author aims to situate human cloning within the context of other technologies of assisted reproduction and to theorise its challenge to the heterosexual prerogative to

---

① Kanyusik W. "Eugenic Nostalgia: Self-Narration and Internalized Ableism in Kazuo Ishiguro's *Never Let Me Go*". Journal of Literary & Cultural Disability Studies, 2020, 14(4): 437-452.

reproduction within feminist and queer frameworks. ①

Mehmet Ali Çelikel, in "*The Unconsoled* and *A Family Supper*", argues that Kazuo Ishiguro's lengthy novel *The Unconsoled*, published in 1995, and his short story *A Family Supper* bear resemblances to each other as the protagonists in both works take a journey to their past. Ryder, the protagonist of *The Unconsoled*, travels to a nameless European city, while the unnamed protagonist of *A Family Supper* travels back home to visit his father after his mother's death. Ishiguro's narration in both of these works functions to depict the journey of a protagonist to his past as a spatial restriction. The purpose of this study is to analyze these two texts by Ishiguro in terms of the existence of their characters in relation to their spatial ontology and their past to point out the relationship between space and memory. ②

3. Psychological Study

Rosemary Rizq, in "Copying, Cloning and Creativity: Reading Kazuo Ishiguro's *Never Let Me Go*", argues that Kazuo Ishiguro's dystopian novel *Never Let Me Go* is set in Britain, in a boarding school called Hailsham. Through the adult voice of one of the children remembering her time growing up there, the reader gradually learns that Kathy and her friends have been raised as artificially-generated clones, manufactured to provide body parts for "normals" in the world. The narrative deploys flashback and hindsight in order to interrogate the essentialism of biological origins, raising complex questions concerning the relationship between

---

① Carroll R. "Imitations of Life: Cloning, Heterosexuality and the Human in Kazuo Ishiguro's *Never Let Me Go*". Journal of Gender Studies, 2010, 19(1): 59-71.

② Çelikel M A. "*The Unconsoled* and *A Family Supper*". Gaziantep University Journal of Social Sciences, 2014, 13(1): 59-67.

memory, copying, creativity and selfhood.①

Irina Toma, in "Contemporary Exile in Kazuo Ishiguro's Novel *When We Were Orphans*", aims at deciphering those types of contemporary exile materialized in the person of the cultural orphan bereaved of national and personal identity. The nostalgic mood of Ishiguro's previous works still persists, although it sometimes acquires tragic accents in a world dominated by chaos and alienation. Dealing, in his personal manner, with the complexity of the margin-center relation, Ishiguro offers us a challenging approach on the contemporary decentered and borderless post-imperial order. Nostalgia breeds revolt and Ishiguro's heroes cannot help resisting their rootlessness, although their struggle hardly ever brings about the long wished-for personal wholeness.②

Bruce Robbins, in "Cruelty Is Bad: Banality and Proximity in *Never Let Me Go*", discusses the motif of cruelty in the works of author Kazuo Ishiguro. The author examines Ishiguro's insight into the bleak truths of the human psyche, focusing on the novel *Never Let Me Go*, which details the life of a woman who cares for clones in a dystopian England of the 1990s.③

Liliana Hamzea, in "The Subaltern Voice and Professional Ethics", analyzes the relationship between professional ethics and the voiced manifestations of Kazuo Ishiguro's protagonist in the novel *The Remains of the Day*, and attempts to reveal issues of identity and self-knowledge. At the same time, the analysis focuses on the

---

① Rizq R. "Copying, Cloning and Creativity: Reading Kazuo Ishiguro's *Never Let Me Go*". British Journal of Psychotherapy, 2014, 30(4): 517-532.

② Toma I. "Contemporary Exile in Kazuo Ishiguro's Novel *When We Were Orphans*". Petroleum-Gas University of Ploiesti Bulletin, Philology Series, 2009, 61(2): 61-66.

③ Robbins B. "Cruelty Is Bad: Banality and Proximity in *Never Let Me Go*". Novel: A Forum on Fiction, 2007, 40(3): 289-302.

role of the narrative voice in connection with the self-assumed lack of assertiveness and agency of the protagonist narrator. [1]

4. Thematic Study

Lev Grossman, in "The Return of the King", discusses author Kazuo Ishiguro and his book *The Buried Giant*, focusing on Ishiguro's writing career and the success of his previous novel *Never Let Me Go* which was adapted into a motion picture. According to the article, Ishiguro won the Whitbread Award for his second novel entitled *An Artist of the Floating World*. It states that *The Buried Giant* features Saxons, Britons, and England following the rule of the late King Arthur. Samurai and swords in literature are examined. [2]

Lauren Jervis, in "Childhood in Action: A Study of Natality's Relationship to Societal Change in *Never Let Me Go*", discusses the implications of natality in the society, and depicts the world with the human clone children, and the relationship to the change in the society. It also reveals the importance of political recognition, relationality, and education in the actualization and development for the creative action. It also explores the limits and workings of natality in the book. [3]

Keiko Matsui Gibson, in "Re-examining Human Dignity in Literary Texts: In Seeking for a Continuous Dialogue between the Conceptual and the Empirical Approaches", deals with the treatment of human dignity in three novels: *The Ballad of Narayama* by Shichirō Fukasawa; *Never Let Me Go* by Kazuo Ishiguro; and

---

[1] Hamzea L. "The Subaltern Voice and Professional Ethics". Bulletin of the Transilvania University of Brasov, Series IV: Philology & Cultural Studies, 2010, 3(52): 299-306.

[2] Grossman L. "The Return of the King". Time, 2015, 185(8):50-52.

[3] Jervis L. "Childhood in Action: A Study of Natality's Relationship to Societal Change in *Never Let Me Go*". English Studies in Canada, 2012, 38(3/4): 189-205.

Still Alice by Lisa Genova. The article argues for a rich understanding of human dignity, an understanding that cannot be reduced to rigid principles. Cultural forms, imagination, and fantasy employed in literary fiction allow readers to see this richness.①

S. W. Lee, in "Of Dignity and Servility", focuses on the book *The Remains of the Day*, by Kazuo Ishiguro. This is Ishiguro's third novel. It incisively examines the heavy price of human servitude. Ishiguro's writing is subtle and controlled, skillfully pulling readers into perceptions of the world while allowing them to see those perceptions. Unlike many of his contemporaries, Ishiguro chose not to write an autobiographical account based on his experience as a Japanese in Britain; instead, he created a character whose personality and language are perfectly British; by contrast, Ishiguro's first two novels take place in Japan, where he has not been since childhood.②

5. Biographical Study

Keith McDonald, in "Days of Past Futures: Kazuo Ishiguro's *Never Let Me Go* as 'Speculative Memoir'", presents information on the literary work of a British novelist, Kazuo Ishiguro. He presented the autobiographical exchange in his 6th speculative science fiction memoir, *Never Let Me Go*. The novel is narrated by a thirty year old graduate of Hailsham boarding school, Kathy, and it has many techniques of autobiographical memoir. The novel has the heightened sense of drama

---

① Gibson K M. "Re-examining Human Dignity in Literary Texts: In Seeking for a Continuous Dialogue between the Conceptual and the Empirical Approaches". Dialog: A Journal of Theology, 2017, 56(1): 53-60.

② Lee S W. "Of Dignity and Servility". The Nation, 1989, 249(21): 761-763.

and emotion because it emphasizes the late twentieth century in England when children were cloned. ①

6. New Historicism

Chanda Williams, in "Abject Adaptations: Disability in Clone Culture and Adaptation of Kazuo Ishiguro's *Never Let Me Go*", explores the 2005 science fiction novel *Never Let Me Go*, by Kazuo Ishiguro. Topics discussed include the dystopian setting of the novel and the narrative of the protagonist named Kathy, its depiction of subjects such as human cloning and disabilities particularly in procreation, and a literary comparison between the novel and its 2010 film adaptation directed by Mark Romanek. ②

D. Serdaroğlu, in "A New Historicist Approach to Kazuo Ishiguro's *When We Were Orphans*", argues that New Historicism, flourishing in the 1980s as a new contemporary literary approach, proposes new viewpoints to the understanding of history and challenges the conventional understanding of history by pointing out the private histories. New Historicism deals with the representations of history rather than the history itself, since it believes that there is not one history but multiple histories. The purpose of this article is to analyze the representation of history in Kazuo Ishiguro's *When We Were Orphans* from the New Historicist viewpoint by focusing on the concepts of time, memory and narrative technique, hence to reveal how history is narrated in subjective multiple ways and how personal histories and public histories are intermingled. ③

---

① McDonald K. "Days of Past Futures: Kazuo Ishiguro's *Never Let Me Go* as 'Speculative Memoir'". Biography: An Interdisciplinary Quarterly, 2007, 30(1): 74-83.

② Williams C. "Abject Adaptations: Disability in Clone Culture and Adaptation of Kazuo Ishiguro's *Never Let Me Go*". Midwest Quarterly, 2020, 61(2): 274-288.

③ Serdaroğlu D. "A New Historicist Approach to Kazuo Ishiguro's *When We Were Orphans*". Gaziantep University Journal of Social Sciences, 2017, 16(3): 785-795.

7. Traumatic Study

Titus Levy, in "Human Rights Storytelling and Trauma Narrative in Kazuo Ishiguro's *Never Let Me Go*", examines Kazuo Ishiguro's novel Never *Let Me Go* as a type of bildungsroman that presents coded models of contemporary human rights issues. It shows how autobiographical storytelling functions within the novel as a form of rights claim that gives voice to the suffering of an oppressed social group. The article demonstrates how the text grapples with the effects of storytelling on individual psychologies, both as a constructive response to atrocity and as a potentially dubious method of overcoming traumatic experience. It also underscores Ishiguro's sensitivity to the ways that aestheticized forms of traumatic experience are consumed by the general public with a mixture of empathy, indifference, and perversion.[①]

8. Post-colonial Study

Linda Belau, and Ed Cameron, in "Writing in Translationese: Kazuo Ishiguro's *The Remains of the Day* and the Uncanny Dialect of the Diasporic Writer", argue that with his third novel, Kazuo Ishiguro crafts a postcolonial work that illustrates how the crisis of decolonization is linked inextricably to the crisis of subjectivity itself. Unlike the novels of Achebe, Rushdie, and other postcolonial writers who represent colonial and postcolonial conditions by focusing on the actual postcolonial contexts, Ishiguro accomplishes his postcolonial critique by focusing

---

① Levy T. "Human Rights Storytelling and Trauma Narrative in Kazuo Ishiguro's *Never Let Me Go*". Journal of Human Rights, 2011, 10(1): 1-16.

more on the issue of cultural difference within the developed world than on issues explicitly resulting from the decolonizing process in the colonized parts of the world. Furthermore, his focus on the issue of cultural difference in Britain is not articulated around issues of immigration and assimilation of the other but, rather, around the internal otherness of the British subject itself. Ishiguro's novel in effect argues that this internal otherness, always present to some degree, emerges most prominently during the breakdown of the Empire, when the traditional symbolic coordinates for British identity are weakened. Ishiguro expresses this perspective in his novel by ever so faintly re-inscribing a traditional narrative form to reflect its internal strangeness or foreignness, by providing an uncanny narrative documentation of the consciousness of a second-class British subject during the height of the decolonization period, and by constructing a narrative that sublimates his own unique diasporic position as a means of coming to grips with his somewhat unique and personal ethnic and cultural conflicts. [1]

Ryan Trimm, in "Telling Positions: Country, Countryside, and Narration in *The Remains of the Day*", presents literary criticism of the novel *The Remains of the Day* by Kazuo Ishiguro. Particular focus is given to definitions of post-colonial English identity based on country houses and the English countryside. Connections are drawn between the novel and the book *Howards End*, by E. M. Forster. An overview of the characters and of the plot is also offered. [2]

---

[1] Belau L, Cameron E. "Writing in Translationese: Kazuo Ishiguro's *The Remains of the Day* and the Uncanny Dialect of the Diasporic Writer". Diaspora: A Journal of Transnational Studies, 2007, 16 (1/2): 67-91.

[2] Trimm R. "Telling Positions: Country, Countryside, and Narration in *The Remains of the Day*". Papers on Language & Literature, 2009, 45(2): 180-211.

9. Ethical Study

Roxana Patraş, in "A Rhetorical Approach to Kazuo Ishiguro's *The Remains of the Day*", argues that Kazuo Ishiguro's *The Remains of the Day* does not stand on an ineffable love. Released in 1989, the novel tells the story of Stevens, who once worked as a butler at a stately home in England. Since the novel has transgressed literary inquiries and provided a case study for research on ethical conduct in public service, international relations, politics, social psychology, historiography and many other social domains, Stevens' situation, and particularly his "rhetorical situation" seem designed to invite further thinking. By departing from the novel fragments narrating the course of the 1923 Conference, from the butler's objective witnessing to various speeches delivered by Lord Darlington's guests and from a rhetorical theory of situatedness, this essay proposes a rhetorical approach to Ishiguro's novel.[①]

Max Watman, in "Ignorant Armies Clash by Night", focuses on the fiction book *Never Let Me Go*, by Kazuo Ishiguro. The book bluntly confronts the possibility that the technological abilities of human beings might outpace ethical abilities. This is, of course, immediately demonstrable in the real world, i.e., without the clones. Words are used in ways never heard before, so as to develop sympathy for the clones, and understand that they are, if not people, beings with feelings who love, want to be cool, and enjoy the company of their friends.[②]

---

① Patraş R. "A Rhetorical Approach to Kazuo Ishiguro's *The Remains of the Day*". Philologica Jassyensia, 2017, 13(2): 217-224.

② Watman M. "Ignorant Armies Clash by Night". The New Criterion, 2005, 23(9): 61-67.

10. Cultural Study

A. Ionescu, in "Architectural Projections in Kazuo Ishiguro's Early Prose and the Concept of Uchi", argues that the house, as a metaphor, has been used to symbolize an array of things; it has stood for family, stability, or safety, but in the texts of Kazuo Ishiguro, it gains new meaning. The symbolism of the house is central in all of his novels. However, in the first two, the setting makes the representations of the home have an echo of Japaneseness which the others lack. In *A Pale View of the Hills*, the house is viewed through the eyes of the narrator. In *An Artist of the Floating World*, the house is presented as an old-fashioned, but grand Japanese-style villa. The aim of this paper is to identify the instances in which the Japanese other is captured in the symbolism of the house through one of the key components of the Japanese culture, the concept of uchi-soto (within-without). [①]

Irina Toma, in "Postmodern Nostalgia in a Multicultural Context", focuses on some of the novels belonging to Kazuo Ishiguro. The paper aims at illustrating the multiple facets of nostalgia, as it functions in the postmodern world, at the crossroads of cultures and identities. The nostalgic mood of Ishiguro's works sometimes acquires tragic accents in a world dominated by chaos and alienation. Nostalgia becomes a means of survival and Ishiguro's heroes find in the nostalgic mood a way to regain their dignity and to achieve both catharsis and consolation. [②]

Alexander M. Bain, in "International Settlements: Ishiguro, Shanghai, Humanitarianism", discusses the globalization of literary studies by focusing on the

---

① Ionescu A. "Architectural Projections in Kazuo Ishiguro's Early Prose and the Concept of Uchi". Philologica Jassyensia, 2014(10): 247-255.

② Toma I. "Postmodern Nostalgia in a Multicultural Context". Petroleum-Gas University of Ploiesti Bulletin, Philology Series, 2010, 62(1): 147-152.

relationship between literary and cultural studies, humanitarianism, and human rights. The author examines the effects of globalization on the work of author Kazuo Ishiguro, particularly his novel *When We Were Orphans*. ①

Charlotte Innes, in "Dr. Faustus Faces the Music", appraises the book *The Unconsoled*, by Kazuo Ishiguro. Like other writers who switch styles, Ishiguro surely sparks passions of every hue. The author says that for him, this is the first Ishiguro novel to arouse not only admiration but also visceral excitement. If controversy is new for Ishiguro, who has long been admired for his easy narrative style, he certainly knows what it's like to be misunderstood. In *The Unconsoled*, it's almost as if Ishiguro took reviewers' misconceptions to heart and cast a fog of vagueness over characters, setting and action to avoid stereotyping. ②

Alison Marcotte, in "Kazuo Ishiguro: Celebrated Author on How Technology May Alter Our Humanity", presents an interview with Kazuo Ishiguro as author of *The Remains of the Day* (1989) and *Never Let Me Go* (2005). In the interview, they talk about the similarities between our world and Klara's, and focus on the role of libraries in our life. ③

11. Social Study

Lisa Fluet, in "Immaterial Labors: Ishiguro, Class, and Affect", discusses the character Mr. Stevens in Kazuo Ishiguro's novel *The Remains of the Day*. The author focuses on Stevens' attitudes towards his job as a butler, which he believes

---

① Bain A M. "International Settlements: Ishiguro, Shanghai, Humanitarianism". Novel: A Forum on Fiction, 2007, 40(3): 240-264.
② Innes C. "Dr. Faustus Faces the Music". The Nation, 1995, 261(15): 546-548.
③ Marcotte A. "Kazuo Ishiguro: Celebrated Author on How Technology May Alter Our Humanity". American Libraries, 2021, 52(3/4): 24.

is instrumental in determining the fate of society. The implications of class consciousness on generational identification are examined. [1]

12. Linguistic Study

Ji Eun Lee, in "Norfolk and the Sense of Loss: The Bildungsroman and Colonial Subjectivity in Kazuo Ishiguro's *Never Let Me Go*", argues that Kazuo Ishiguro's book *Never Let Me Go* reshapes colonial subjectivity through a sense of loss. Topics discussed include Ishiguro's borrowing of notion of mimicry, which characterizes colonial subjectivity as a state of ambivalence between assimilation and dissimilation. [2]

13. Theological Study

Arthur Bradley, in "Illusions of a Future: Ishiguro, Liberalism, Political Theology", explores the fate of political theology in Kazuo Ishiguro's speculative fiction *Never Let Me Go*, and by implication, in contemporary fiction more broadly. To pursue a reading of Christianity that extends from Hegel through Lacan to Žižek, the article argues that political theology's future may perversely lie in a materialism emptied of all transcendental guarantees. Political theology is the historically privileged master fantasy or illusion which reveals the fantastic or illusory status of our entire relation to the real in (neo-) liberal modernity. In conclusion, the article argues that Ishiguro's fiction may thus be read less as a melancholic dystopian study

---

[1] Fluet L. "Immaterial Labors: Ishiguro, Class, and Affect". Novel: A Forum on Fiction, 2007, 40(3): 265-288.

[2] Lee J E. "Norfolk and the Sense of Loss: The Bildungsroman and Colonial Subjectivity in Kazuo Ishiguro's *Never Let Me Go*". Texas Studies in Literature & Language, 2019, 61(3): 270-290.

in total ideological capture or surrender than as the representation of a state of immanent freedom beyond the power relations of (neo-) liberal subjectivity. ①

14. Translation Study

Rebecca L. Walkowitz, in "Unimaginable Largeness: Kazuo Ishiguro, Translation, and the New World Literature", suggests that the process of translation is leading to a cultural and political homogenization of fiction. This is because translation negates the need for readers to learn new languages and leads to less linguistically complex text, and because the world market requires stories that everyone can share and identify with. Author Kazuo Ishiguro is examined. ②

---

① Bradley A. "Illusions of a Future: Ishiguro, Liberalism, Political Theology". Political Theology, 2018, 19(7): 638-642.

② Walkowitz R L. "Unimaginable Largeness: Kazuo Ishiguro, Translation, and the New World Literature". Novel: A Forum on Fiction, 2007, 40(3): 216-239.